Crashing into Love

The Bradens

Love in Bloom Series

Melissa Foster

About the Love in Bloom Big-Family Romance Collection

The Bradens at Trusty is just one of the series in the Love in Bloom big-family romance collection. Characters from each series make appearances in future books, so you never miss an engagement, wedding, or birth. If this is your first Love in Bloom novel, you have many more loving, loyal heroes and sexy, sassy heroines waiting for you!

Download a free Love in Bloom series checklist here: www.melissafoster.com/SO

Get **free** first-in-series Love in Bloom ebooks and see my current sales here: www.MelissaFoster.com/LIBFree

Visit the Love in Bloom Reader Goodies page for downloadable checklists, family trees, and more! www.MelissaFoster.com/RG

For my readers

Thank you for inspiring me on a daily basis

Chapter One

IT WAS SUPPOSED to be a quick trip to her hometown of Trusty, Colorado. A few days of hanging out with her parents and catching up with old friends, and then she was off to Los Angeles to meet up with her best friend, Trish Ryder. At least that's what Fiona told anyone who asked—other than Trish, or Fiona's sister, Shea, of course.

Fiona tipped her margarita back and finished it off, thinking about how surreal it had been the night Trish had called her to say that she'd been cast as the lead female in the upcoming action film *Raiders of the Past*. Trish was going to be working with the most famous director in the country, Steven Hileberg. It was one of the biggest events in her acting career to date, aside from the nomination for the Academy Award last year, and she and Fiona had celebrated with a virtual party for two via Skype. That was four months ago, which to Fiona felt like forever, given how Trish's career opportunity had unlocked a door Fiona had spent years trying to figure out how to open. It had taken Trish exactly ten words to convince Fiona to take a leave of absence from her job as a geologist at the Bureau of Mines and Geology and become her personal assistant during filming.

Jake Braden is cast as the stuntman for Zane Walker.

Done.

"Sis, are you even paying attention to me?" Shea was four years younger than Fiona, and the youngest member of the Steele family. She was as fair as Fiona and her twin brother, Finn, were dark. Shea was also Trish's public-relations rep. Fiona and Trish had met in college, and by the time Trish needed a PR rep for her career, Shea had become well-known in the industry. Fiona had been thrilled with their instant connection.

"Of course." Fiona tossed her chin, sending her long brown hair over her shoulder, and held up her empty glass, indicating to the waiter that she needed a refill.

"Sure you were. Then, what do you think?" Shea blinked her baby blues expectantly.

Fiona winced. She hadn't meant to zone out, but she'd come to the Brewery, a local bar, hoping to see her ex-boyfriend Jake, who she knew was in town visiting his family, and he was nowhere in sight. Her stomach had been tied in knots for the past two hours she'd been watching the door, as if she could will him to walk into the bar. She was sure that when Jake finally came face-to-face with her, he wouldn't be able to resist her. Their connection had been too deep, their love too strong, and their passion had always left them both craving more.

"Just as I thought." Shea leaned across the table, her shiny golden locks curtaining her face. "He's. Not. Coming."

Fiona rolled her eyes. "That would be just my luck, wouldn't it?"

"Finn called me yesterday," Shea said.

"What's my evil twin up to?" Finn was anything but evil, but their family had always joked that one of them had to be more evil than the other. Fiona had dubbed Finn the evil twin. She didn't even know how to be evil—not that he was any better at it.

"Not much. He was visiting Reggie in New York, and when I told them that you were going to finally try to reconnect with Jake, Reggie got all big brotherish and said he was going to check him out. Whatever that means in the world of private investigators," Shea said with a laugh. Reggie was their eldest brother, and a private investigator.

Fiona rolled her eyes. "I'll be surprised if Reggie doesn't call Jesse and Brent, just to add a little torture to the next few weeks. As if I'm not nervous enough." Jesse and Brent were younger than Fiona, and they were also twins. Reggie, Jesse, and Brent could be overpoweringly protective. She was glad to have Shea to buffer her in this situation. But Finn had a softer touch, and she wasn't surprised he'd called Shea instead of her.

"Don't worry. I told him to call off the dogs. He knows you don't need hounding right now. I've got your back."

"Thanks, Shea. Do you think there will ever come a time when our brothers aren't looking out for us?" She was just waiting for Jesse and Brent, to get wind of her going to LA. She half expected them to hire a bodyguard for her.

"No way. I think when a brother is born, they come with protective genes, and we sisters are born with big tattoos on our heads that only brothers can see, which read, *Oh my. I'm a girl. Help me. Help me!*" Shea laughed.

The waiter brought Fiona's drink. She thanked him and gulped half of it down. Margaritas served two purposes: They alleviated the ability to focus and provided a false sense of courage. She didn't need alcohol to hinder her ability to focus. The mere thought of Jake took care of that. But she desperately needed the liquid courage.

"The one time I get up the guts to finally try to talk to my ex, he decides not to go out for a beer. Jake always goes out with his brothers when he's home." Fiona had been trying to figure out how to reach out to Jake for the last few years, but Trusty was so small, it was impossible not to realize he avoided her every time he was home. Fear of rejection had kept her at bay, but with the trip to his movie set in hand, she felt like it was now or never. She was finally taking the risk, despite the possibility of being rejected.

"Have you considered that maybe he heard you were going

to be here and decided to skip it? This *is* Trusty, Colorado, where gossip spreads faster than chicken pox." Shea finished her drink and sat back, eyeing the men in the bar. "You have a great life, Fiona. And I know you have your pick of men back in Fresno. Besides…" Shea eyed the guys at the bar. "There are plenty of good-looking guys here."

Fiona glared at her. From an outsider's perspective, her life probably did look pretty damn good, and in some ways it was. Taking a leave of absence to try to reconnect with Jake had been an easy decision when she'd made it, because she'd made it from her heart, completely ignoring her brilliant brain, which was waving red flags and urging her to remember why she worked so hard in her profession and what she was working toward. For a girl who loved geology more than shopping, Fiona's job was exciting as hell. And her social life…Well, her social life probably looked good, too, *from the outside*. Trish was a great best friend, and they got together as often as their schedules allowed. Shea split her time between Colorado, Los Angeles, and New York, so they also saw each other fairly often. And while Fiona was asked out a few times each month, she'd gone out on only the occasional date. And she couldn't really count the invitations, considering that for the last two years she'd turned down all but a few. She guessed that most girls would kill to be asked out by some of the scientists who had tried to woo her. They were well educated, well mannered, and, well, *stable*. *Boring*. Why was it so hard to find a *real* man? The kind who could make her go damp with one hot stare and had hands and a talented mouth that could finish the job. The kind of man who took what he wanted and liked a woman to do the same.

Shea held her hands up in surrender. "I know. I know. You're done sowing your oats and wasting time. There's only Jake Braden. *Jake, Jake, Jake.*"

Exactly. Jake Braden is the only man I want.

Shea lowered her voice. "Fi, it's been sixteen years since you dated him. Sixteen years. And rumor has it, he's not the guy he used to be. You broke him, and you broke him bad."

Like she didn't know that? Fiona and Jake had dated for two years in high school and had planned to attend the same college, and then they were going to get married. Her life had been planned in a nice, neat package. She'd had every girl's dream at her fingertips. Jake had been attentive and loving, and he wasn't the least bit afraid of commitment. The Bradens were a loyal and kind family, and Fiona knew her life with Jake would have been stable and adoring. Jake would have followed his dream of becoming a stuntman, and Fiona would become a geologist, and they'd have lived happily ever after.

That was the plan.

Reality wasn't quite as pretty.

On her mother's insistent advice, Fiona had ended things with Jake two weeks before they were set to leave for college. She'd taken off for Penn State the morning after breaking up with him, unwilling to stick around for two weeks for fear of giving in to his pleas of staying together—and to see what she was missing. While Jake was hundreds of miles away, she'd buried herself in a new life, which included working her ass off to maintain good grades, sowing her wild oats—which was a ridiculous notion, because she had none—and finally, securing her graduate degree. It wasn't until a few years later, after her career was settled and she slowed down long enough to breathe, that she realized the enormity of her mistake. She hadn't been missing a damn thing. Jake was all she really needed.

And now here she was on a Tuesday evening, back where she'd ended things with him so long ago, wishing she could go back in time.

"Well, Shea. Maybe it's time I put him back together."

ALL JAKE WANTED was a cold beer and to hang with his brothers. They were all in town for the wedding of their youngest brother, Luke. He and his wife, Daisy, had taken off for their honeymoon yesterday. Jake had another week before he was expected on set for his next movie production. He'd given in to family pressure and had agreed to stick around to help his brothers Wes and Ross fix the roof on Wes's shed instead of heading back to LA for what would have been a week of partying. Being back in Trusty made him anxious. He loved his family, but the town was about as big as his thumb, and he'd spent a decade and a half avoiding Fiona Steele. He knew from friends that Fiona was in town, and he didn't need to run into her tonight.

Tonight it was just the guys. Their sister, Emily, had brought her fiancé, Dae Bray, to Luke's wedding. She and their mother, along with their brothers' fiancées, were going to Ross and Elisabeth's house for a girls' night, freeing up Dae and Jake's brothers for a guys' night out. He didn't give a rat's ass where they went as long as they didn't run into *her*.

"Emily said she heard Fiona was going to Fingers in Allure, so we're cool." Wes grabbed Jake's arm and dragged him across the driveway toward their eldest brother Pierce's rental car, where Ross stood by the open door.

"Come on. It's not every day we get to have a beer together." Pierce lived in Reno with his fiancée, Rebecca. Ross, Wes, Emily, and Luke lived in Trusty, and Jake lived in Los Angeles. Nights out with his brothers were indeed a rare occasion.

"Fine, but I'll take my car. Come on, Dae. You can ride with me." Jake climbed into the driver's seat of his rental Lexus SUV. He wanted to hang out with Dae and get to know him a little better anyway, and as long as Fiona wasn't going to be at the bar, then he was cool with it. God knew he needed a drink—or six—after watching his siblings nuzzle up to their significant others all weekend. He loved them all, but he could take only so much of that lovey-dovey shit before he lost his mind. Give him a blonde under each arm and he was a happy dude.

A few minutes later Jake pushed through the front doors of the Brewery with one arm slung around Wes's neck as he ground his knuckle into the top of his brother's head. He pushed Wes away with a loud laugh. Wes smacked him on the back and pointed to the bar.

Music filled the air from the country band playing in the back. As the five men crossed the crowded floor to the bar, Jake spotted at least three hot babes he wouldn't mind taking home for an hour or two. That was, if he were back home on his estate in LA. Picking up women in Trusty posed issues. He'd have to go to their place, which was good for a quick escape, but it was Trusty, which meant he'd leave a buffet for the hungry rumor mill in his wake. And Jake had no interest in feeding that frenzy.

He wouldn't be going home with anyone but his brothers tonight.

Pierce ordered a round of beers and made a toast. "To Luke and Daisy."

They clinked bottles, and Jake sucked down half of his. A hot blonde with hungry eyes standing on the other side of Ross leaned forward and caught Jake's eye. He cracked his most effective panty-dropping smile and checked her out.

Even if he had no intention of hooking up with her, a little eye candy was never a bad thing. Not too skinny, nice rack, and…He leaned back and checked out the rear view. Nice ass.

Ross grabbed his arm and turned his back to the blonde. "She's been with half of the single guys in town."

"Do I care?" Jake arched a brow.

"You sure as hell should." Ross was the Trusty town veterinarian. He, like Jake and their other brothers, had never dated women from Trusty. It was easier to date women from neighboring towns and avoid the gossip.

Jake ran his hand through his thick dark hair and sucked down the rest of his beer, set the bottle on the bar with a loud *Ahh*, and motioned for another.

"Emily said you weren't exactly picky," Dae said. All of the Braden men were more than six feet tall, with dark hair and hallmark Braden dark eyes. Dae fit right into the tall, dark, and built-for-a-fight mold, although he wore his hair much longer than the close-cut styles Jake and his brothers sported.

"Life's short, man. Gotta share the love." Jake thanked the bartender for his drink and leaned his hip against the bar, allowing himself a better view of the tables and the dance floor in the back of the bar. "I don't remember there being this many good-looking women in Trusty."

Wes turned around and eyed the dance floor. "Your standards have gone to shit, bro."

"Ouch, man. That hurts." Jake laughed.

"Come on," Pierce said. "Let's get a booth in the back where we can talk." As the oldest, Pierce was used to directing. Their father had left before Luke was born, and Pierce had stepped in and watched over them all. Pierce owned resorts all over the world, and there had been a time when Pierce matched Jake woman for woman—a playboy without any interest in settling down. But meeting Rebecca Rivera had changed all of that. Jake was the last single Braden, and he intended to keep it that way.

"Sounds good to me. I forgot how meat-markety bars are. Haven't been in one for a while," Ross said as he followed Pierce away from the bar.

Jake watched them take a few steps. They were a good-looking bunch, no doubt, but something about the way his brothers carried themselves had changed since they'd each entered couplehood. The sharp edges they'd honed hadn't exactly turned soft—Braden men were alpha to the core—but Jake noticed less of a swagger and more of a confident, my-woman's-waiting-at-home hitch in their gait.

"I'm gonna grab another beer. Meet you there in a sec." Jake waved them off and eyed the blonde again. She was twisting her hair around her finger and eyeing him like he was a big old chocolate bar. *Oh yeah, baby. You can have a piece.*

She smiled and sauntered over. She arched her back and leaned in close, giving Jake a clear view down her sweetly low-cut blouse.

"Jake Braden, right?" she said in a heady voice.

"The one and only." He held her seductive gaze, but hell if in the back of his mind he didn't hear his brother's words. *Your standards have gone to shit, bro.*

Standards. Jake wasn't sure he had many of those left, and he liked his life that way. Uncomplicated. No ties to anyone other than himself and his family. He tossed back his beer and ordered another.

Blondie slipped her index finger into the waist of his low-slung jeans. Her eyes widened as she wiggled that finger against his skin, searching for drawers she wouldn't find. Jake grinned.

"You've got quite a rep around here." She glanced down at her finger, still hooked in the waist of his jeans. "Is it true that stuntmen do it rough?"

Jake leaned down and put his mouth beside her ear, inhaling the scent of her sweet perfume and letting her anticipation build before answering. He knew how to play the game. He was a master at it. Hell, most of the time he felt like he'd invented it. He did a quick sweep of the bar, readying to tell her just how good he could be—*rough and raw or gentle as a field of daisies*—when his eyes caught on Fiona Steele sitting at a booth near the back of the room and staring directly at him. His gut clenched tight.

Fuck.

Blondie tugged on his waistband, bringing him back to the current situation, where he was leaning over a twentysomething blonde who may or may not have slept with half of Trusty. His brain was stuck. He couldn't think clearly. Fiona was there, and she looked so damn good that he felt himself getting hard. If his dick were a guy, he'd knock the hell out of it. He'd done a damn good job of avoiding her for all these years—well, except last year, when in a moment of weakness he'd tried to find her the last time he'd been back in town. He never had found her, but he'd found a brunette from another town more than willing to take the edge off his pent-up frustrations.

He forced his eyes away from Fiona, grabbed his beer from the bar, and stalked toward the back of the bar without a word to Blondie.

"Hey!" Blondie called after him.

He kept his eyes trained on the back wall of the bar with one goal in mind, to find his brothers and drink himself into oblivion.

"Jake."

He hadn't heard her voice in years, and it still sent heat searing through him—and stopped him cold. *Walk. Keep moving.* His body betrayed him and turned to face Fiona Steele. His eyes swept over her flawless skin. Her sharp jawbone and high cheekbones gave her a regal look. Not in a pretentious way, but in the way of a woman so naturally beautiful that it set her apart from all others. His eyes paused on her almond-shaped eyes, as blue as the night sea. God, he'd always loved her eyes. Her face was just as beautiful as it had been when she was a teenager, maybe even more so. He shifted his gaze lower, to her sweet mouth, remembering the first night they'd made out. They were both fifteen, almost sixteen. She'd tasted like Colgate toothpaste and desire. They'd kissed slowly and tenuously. He'd urged her mouth open, and when their tongues touched for the first time, his entire body had electrified in a way he'd never matched with any other woman. Kissing Fiona had made his entire body prickle with need. He'd dreamed of her kisses, longed for them every hour they were apart. They'd made out between classes and after school, staying together late into the night. Her mouth was like kryptonite, stealing any willpower he'd ever possessed.

Until that summer afternoon, when that mouth he'd fallen in love with broke his heart for good.

"Jake," Fiona repeated.

He clenched his jaw and shifted his eyes over her shoulder—not seeing anything in particular as he tried to move past the memory of losing the only person he'd ever loved. He'd spent years forcing himself to forget how much he loved her and grow the hell up, and in doing so, he hadn't allowed himself to even say her name. And now he didn't want to hear it coming from his lungs. Instead he lifted his chin in response.

"You look great. How have you been?"

Maybe no one else would have picked up on the slight

tremor in her voice, or the way she was fidgeting with the edge of her shirt, but Jake remembered every goddamn mannerism and what it meant. Good. She should be nervous.

He knew he was being a prick, but years of repressed anger simmered inside him. The memory of the first time they'd made love slammed into his mind. He remembered the almost paralyzing fear and the thrill of it being her first time, and his. He'd worried that he wouldn't last or he'd do something wrong, but his biggest fear had been that he'd hurt her. He turned away, trying to force the thought away. Little did he know that two years later, she'd be the one doing the hurting.

"Great, thanks," he managed. It was no use. He couldn't resist meeting her gaze again, and the moment he did, he felt himself being sucked into her eyes, stirring up the memories he'd tried to forget. He couldn't look away. Not even when the memory of her dumping him all those years ago came back like hot coals burning him from the inside out. She'd stopped taking his calls, and though she'd returned his texts for the first day or two, after that it was like she'd vanished without caring that she'd ripped his guts out.

She shifted her eyes and he saw them lock on Wes. She smiled in his direction, then quickly looked away.

What the hell was that about? Jake pointed his thumb over his shoulder. "Gotta go meet my brothers."

"Oh." Fiona dropped her eyes, breaking their connection.

Jake's synapses finally fired and he turned away, catching

sight of Shea waving from a booth to his left. She'd been barely a teenager when he'd left for college, as starry-eyed and naive as the day was long. He lifted his chin in greeting and stalked back to his brothers' table.

"I'm outta here." He felt the heat of Fiona's stare on his back.

"What? You haven't even had a beer with us." Pierce smacked the seat beside him. "Sit your ass down, bro."

Jake blew out a frustrated breath. "She's here."

Wes and Ross exchanged a knowing glance that made his blood boil. He got the feeling that they'd known Fiona was going to be there. *What the hell is going on?*

Pierce grabbed Jake's arm and yanked his ass down beside him. "Sit down and have a beer with your family and Dae."

Normally Jake would tell Pierce to piss off when he was in a mood like this, but something strange was going on inside him. He was too angry and confused to bother. He couldn't get the image of Fiona's beautiful face out of his mind. *Goddamn it.* He picked up Pierce's beer, and when Pierce opened his mouth to complain, Jake shut him up with a fight-me-for-it glare and sucked it down. He should have grabbed the blonde chick and left the bar for a night of no-strings-attached sex. Now he was bound to be up all night, trying to forget the hopeful and pained look in Fiona's eyes—the same damn look she'd had when she'd kicked him to the curb.

"You didn't have to be a dick to her," Wes said. "You look

like a rattlesnake coiled to strike."

"That was an asshole move," Ross agreed. "You left her standing there looking stupid when she was just trying to say hello."

Jake looked away from them, breathing harder by the second.

"Jake." Dae's dark eyes turned serious. "Weren't you with her for two years or something? She's probably trying to mend fences or find closure."

"Yeah?" Jake rose to his feet and slammed the beer down on the table. "Well, I'm not that guy anymore, and I have no interest in mending a damn thing." He turned on his heel, stormed over to the bar, grabbed Blondie's hand, and dragged her outside, chased by the forlorn look in Fiona's eyes and the clawing ache of wishing it were her he was helping into his car.

Chapter Two

JAKE WATCHED THE sun rise over the mountains from a lounge chair on his mother's deck. It had been a long time since he'd watched a Colorado sunrise, and he bristled against the memories it stirred. He lifted his mug of black coffee to his lips as the glass doors opened and his mother, Catherine, came out to join him. She tightened the belt on her fluffy blue robe and smiled, squeezing his shoulder as she passed. He lifted the mug in her direction.

"Thanks, honey." She took a sip. "How long have you been out here?"

Jake shrugged and rubbed his unshaven jaw. "Couple hours." His voice was rough from lack of sleep.

"Have fun with your brothers and Dae?" Catherine had hair the color of Jake's, and it fell past her shoulders, still tangled from sleep. She smiled, despite the early hour. Jake had few memories of her not smiling. She'd raised Jake and his siblings on her own after their father left her for another woman when she was pregnant with Luke.

"Always do." His mother had taught Jake and his siblings to be responsible and loyal, and he couldn't help but wonder what she knew of his lifestyle over the past few years. He was pretty sure his siblings had tried to buffer her from the lascivious details of his raucous personal life, but he didn't want to know the answer.

She handed him the mug, and he took another sip before setting it down on the deck beside his chair. Catherine leaned on the railing, looking out over the mountains.

"It's pretty, isn't it? I'll never tire of watching the sun rise." She turned a warm gaze to Jake.

He leaned forward, resting his forearms on his knees, and sighed. "It is pretty."

"You okay? Need something for a hangover?"

He lifted his eyes. *I need something for a lifeover.* "Nah. I'm good. Thanks, Mom. Just tired, I guess. How was your night? Did you stay out late with Em and the girls?"

"Oh, goodness, no. I hung out for an hour, then let them have their fun. They don't need me hanging around, but it was nice of them to invite me." She took another sip of his coffee. "I don't think I've ever seen Emily so happy and settled. She's usually got an edginess to her, like she can't sit still."

Jake had no idea how to respond to that. Women looked at things completely differently from guys. He'd never thought of Emily as being unsettled. She was *Emily*. His little sister, someone he loved and protected, but he hadn't noticed if she was edgy. She had a ton of energy. Wasn't it that simple? Was that a bad thing? She seemed happy now, but she'd seemed happy before meeting Dae, too.

"I think Dae's good for her," his mother added.

"He's a nice guy." His cell vibrated. He pulled it from his jeans pocket and saw the name *Ready* flash above a phone number. He pressed Ignore and set his phone on the deck.

"Everything okay?" his mother asked.

"Yeah, fine." *Ready*. He had names like that for many of the women he hooked up with. Ready happened to be a buxom blonde with two similarly built friends he'd spent a few hours with. *Willing* and *Able*. Jake liked to work hard and play harder, to keep his mind off of the fact that he never played for keeps. But the sight of Ready's name on his phone after seeing Fiona only made him feel shittier. He needed to go for his morning run. Pounding out a few miles always cleared his mind. He'd had the same workout routine since he was fifteen and he never missed it, no matter what condition he was in from the night before. He glanced at his mother and decided to visit with her for just a few more minutes.

Being home brought a dichotomy of emotions that never failed to shake him up. He loved seeing his family, but he'd lost a big piece of himself after Fiona had broken up with him, and coming back home brought discomfort akin to walking around with sandpaper scraping against his skin.

Jake's phone vibrated again. His mother's eyes dropped to it. "Isn't it before dawn in LA?"

"Yup." He picked up the phone and saw Emily's name on the screen. *Damn.* He had no desire to deal with what he knew would be the third degree. He handed the phone to his mother and leaned back in his chair.

"Emily? What would she want this early?" Catherine answered the phone, and before she could say hello, Jake heard Emily's voice. "Is it true? Tell me it's not really true."

Jake scrubbed his hand down his face and held his hand out for the phone.

"Good luck." His mother handed it to him.

"Good morning, Em."

"Jake." She said his name like an accusation. "Is it true? Did you go home with Sarah Chelsum last night?"

Jake imagined Emily's brows drawn together as she paced her living room, arms crossed, a scowl on her pretty face. She was as protective of her brothers as they were of her, but what he was hearing wasn't protective at all. It was disgust.

"It's the ass crack of dawn. You got up to ask me that?"

"Jake!"

"Chill, sis. No. I didn't go home with her." He shifted his eyes away from his mother.

"You left with her. Apparently everyone in Trusty saw you."

"You mean Dae saw me leave the bar, and he told you."

She blew out a loud breath. "No. Dae and three friends who all texted me last night. I *waited* to call until now."

"Christ," he mumbled.

"Christ? Is that all you can say? You know everyone in town is going to be talking about this, and Fiona is home, so she'll find out."

Jake gritted his teeth. "Do you think I give a rat's ass about what anyone thinks of me, much less what *she* thinks?"

"Jake…"

"Emily…"

She huffed into the phone.

"I gotta go for my run. Good to talk to you, sis."

"Wait, Jake—"

He handed the phone to his mother. "I'm going for a run. Want to talk your daughter off the ledge?"

She took the phone and covered the mouthpiece with her hand. "Jake. Sarah Chelsum? She's ten years younger than you."

Jake rolled his eyes, then kissed his mother's cheek. "Have faith in me, Ma. You didn't raise an idiot." *Just an asshole.*

FIONA GAZED OUT at the overlook on the side of Old Hill Road. She was wearing a tank and running shorts and was thinking about how often she and Jake had run along that route. They'd run together nearly every morning before school and most weekends during the two years they'd dated. She'd calculated it once and knew it was more than one thousand hours of easy conversation and heated innuendos. More than one thousand hours of running side by side with the only guy who'd ever really understood her. And she'd spent thousands of hours since then thinking about meeting him here and hoping they could rekindle their relationship, because once she'd been with Jake Braden, nothing and no one else measured up. Not geology, not family, and sure as hell not any guy.

Fiona bounced from one foot to the other in anticipation of seeing him. She checked her watch, though she wasn't sure exactly what time he might go running. Especially since he'd left the Brewery with Sarah Chelsum last night. The thought made her sick to her stomach, but not sick enough to give up on him. He used to be as much a creature of habit as she was, and she knew from friends that he'd been running their trail in the mornings since he'd been home.

She looked out over Trusty, thinking about how many times she and Jake had kissed in that very spot and how many times over the years she'd come back and revisited the memories. Sometimes she wondered how she could have been so stupid to break things off before college—and other times she didn't have the strength to question it, accepting that it might have been the right choice.

Sow your oats her mother had told her that summer, right after her father had moved out. *Experience life.* The advice had helped her do well in school, because if she'd stayed with Jake, she would have been sidetracked by him. Once they'd broken up, she'd thrown herself into her schoolwork and into drowning her doubts. But it hadn't taken her long to realize that while her mother's advice had helped her academically, it wasn't good advice for her heart. She'd partied hard and dated a handful of guys, which was enough for her to know deep in her heart that Jake was the right guy for her. The *only* guy for her.

She kicked at the dirt and glanced down the road, wondering if she would have known he was the only man for her if they'd stayed together after high school. Or when they ran into rough spots, would either of them have had second thoughts? The day her father came home and announced that he was leaving because her mother didn't *get* him and he'd found someone who did had sparked a whole new set of worries. How many relationships actually lasted forever? Jake's own father had left his mother for someone else. No matter how all consuming their love had felt, would it have been enough to stand the test of time? Her mother's advice had come on the heels of her father's leaving, making it seem even more sound.

Strangely, she'd never worried Jake might cheat on her.

He'd been as loyal as a person could be, and he'd never once questioned her fidelity to him. But once her mother began urging her not to tie herself down so young, she'd become scared. She trusted her mother's judgment, and after her father left, her mother had shared stories of how much they'd loved each other when they were Fiona's and Jake's age. That had scared her even more. Could a person's feelings change so much over the years that their values changed?

Fiona had taken her mother's advice and dated in college and she'd slept with a few guys, but her heart was so full of Jake that it was a futile effort. It had taken Fiona years to get up the courage to approach Jake again, but she didn't care how long it had taken. Or that she'd spent years agonizing over her feelings for him. At least now she'd done it. It was a start, even if a rocky one. She was as sure of her love for Jake as she was that she'd needed that time after high school to figure it out.

Some mistakes *had* to be made. *Didn't they?*

She heard the even cadence of his footfalls coming up the road, and it sent a storm of worry whipping through her. He'd barely been able to look at her last night. Maybe this was a bad idea. She looked at the hill on the other side of the road and the bank at the ridge behind her. Short of hurling herself down the side of the mountain, there was no escape. She had no choice but to go through with her plan and hope for the best.

She took a few tentative steps toward the center of the road and drank him in. He was running in nothing but a pair of black running shorts, a sheen of sweat glistening off his insanely defined muscles. An armband was secured to his bulging biceps. A wire ran to a pair of earbuds. She'd thought he looked delicious last night in his low-slung jeans and tight T-shirt, but holy cow...Jake had always had an athletic build, but the man barreling up the hill was a bronze god. Pure, unadulterated power.

He lifted his eyes and met hers.

A very angry god.

Crap.

Jake's brows knitted together. His hands fisted, and the muscles in his arms flexed as he sped up and ran right past her. Fiona was momentarily stunned. She shook it off and sprinted up the hill after him.

"Hey." He probably couldn't even hear her with those damn earbuds in. She touched his elbow to get his attention. He stared straight ahead and kept up his pace as they rounded a bend at the top of the hill.

Really? This is how you're gonna play it?

Fiona knew just how stubborn Jake could be, although she had never been the target of his efforts. Oh wait. Yes, she had. The mere fact that he'd avoided her for more than a decade proved that. Her stomach was tied in knots, but she wasn't going to back down just because he was ignoring her. She sprinted ahead of him and turned around, running backward in front of him.

Jake tore his earbuds from his ears. "What are you doing?"

She noticed he had yet to say her name, and it annoyed her. "Running." They'd trained this way in high school. Jake had taught her that she used different muscles running backward, and it helped her hone her other senses. As Jake picked up his pace and circled around her, those other senses kicked in to gear, telling her that she might have stumbled across a hornet's nest.

She wasn't allergic to bees. *Bring it on.*

She spun around and caught up to him.

He shoved one of his earbuds back in his ear. When he went to do the same thing with the other, she grabbed his wrist and stopped him. Jake came to an abrupt stop, nearly sending her tumbling onto the pavement. She used his wrist as an anchor.

They were both breathing hard, standing inches apart. Fiona was thrown back to the million times they'd been in the same position and he'd pulled her against his sweaty body and sealed his mouth over hers.

"Why are you here, Fiona?" The venom in his eyes pierced her confidence.

"I…" She looked away, shocked by how disgusted he'd sounded when he'd said her name. She'd had no idea that she'd hurt him so deeply.

"What?" His eyes narrowed, and he ran a hand through

his hair.

Her stomach dipped. She loved when he did that.

"I thought we could talk." There. She'd said it.

"There's nothing to talk about." He shoved the earbud back in his ear and took off up the hill.

Fiona knew it would be hard, but they'd shared so much and cared so deeply for each other. She didn't think he'd really turned off all of those feelings.

Shea's words came screaming back to her. *You broke him, and you broke him bad.*

She turned away and took off in the opposite direction, blinking away tears and wondering if she'd been wrong.

Maybe some mistakes could never be fixed.

Chapter Three

IT WAS SIX o'clock by the time Ross and Wes showed up at Wes's house to help Jake with the roof of the shed. Wes ran a dude ranch just outside of Trusty, and he looked the part today in faded jeans and his cowboy boots. Ross was the town veterinarian, and Jake had to smile at his older brother, who must have come straight from work, as he was still wearing a pair of khaki pants and a Trusty Veterinary Clinic polo shirt. Jake knew how busy they were, which was why he'd agreed to help in the first place. Besides, Jake was still reeling from his run-in with Fiona, and physical labor was a great way to work out his frustrations. His career demanded a whole different level of physicality. There was no bigger thrill than jumping out of burning buildings or off a moving train. Jake lived for the rush of the risk, and he was one of the best damn stuntmen in the country—but he missed the manual kind of physical labor.

He wiped the sweat from his brow and gazed down at the

ground, where Wes and Ross were stripping off their T-shirts. They were both heavily muscled and well skilled with tools of any kind. When they were growing up, the boys had all taken care of their own cars and any repairs around their mother's house. Each one always trying to outdo the other.

"Don't even bother," Jake called down to them.

Wes stopped with his shirt halfway over his head. "Why not?"

"I'm done. This was a piece of cake." He climbed down the ladder and handed Wes his tool belt. "Replaced the plywood and reshingled it. You should be good for many years."

"Damn. Really?" Wes slapped Jake on the back, then wiped his sweaty hand on his jeans. He picked up Jake's T-shirt from the ground where Jake had tossed it, and Jake used it to wipe his face.

"Y'all bring me a beer?"

Ross reached into the paper bag he'd set on the ground and handed Jake a beer. "Elisabeth said Emily called you at the crack of dawn."

Jake nodded, wiped his brow again, then guzzled the beer. "Yup. She was all over me about that chick from the bar."

"I told you not to hook up with her." Ross rubbed the back of his neck. "Emily cares, Jake. She doesn't like people talking trash about any of us, and you gave the town a reason to."

"I'm a big boy, Ross. I can handle a few rumors." Jake finished his beer, rethinking his decision to stay in town. He didn't really want to deal with rumors, but moreover, running into Fiona had done strange and confusing things to him, and he didn't want to deal with that, either.

"You don't have to. You live a million miles away. She's in the thick of it day in and day out," Ross reminded him.

"Whatever." As if Jake didn't feel shitty enough after the way he'd blown off Fiona two times in a row. He was confused and angry about all of it, and the last thing he needed was to catch hell from his brother.

"Come on." Wes nodded toward the deck. "Take a load off. Callie and Lis should be here with pizza soon."

"So, what was that stuff you pulled last night?" Wes asked as they settled into the deck chairs.

Jake slid him a narrow-eyed stare. "You tell me."

Wes and Ross exchanged a glance, as they had last night, and Jake flexed his hands.

"You're the one who left with Sarah," Ross reminded him.

"You guys told me that she was going to Allure, remember?"

"She?" Wes asked.

Jake finished his beer.

"You still can't even say her name?" Ross asked.

"What the hell is going on? Why do you care if I say her name? And why did you take me there last night? There's no way you didn't know she'd be there." He wiped his face again. "Stop looking at each other and fess up."

Wes held his hands up in surrender. "Hey, as far as I knew, Fiona was going to Allure."

"That's what Em said." Ross's lips quirked up as he glanced at Wes again.

Jake shoved him and shook his head. "Jackass. If I find you're full of crap, heads are gonna roll."

Ross and Wes both laughed.

"What's the big deal?" Ross asked. "So you talked to Fiona. You guys ended it a long time ago. There's no need to be a dick to her, is there?"

Jake sighed. He didn't need to be reminded of his less-than-stellar behavior. He couldn't change the way he'd reacted to Fiona and the emotions she'd stirred in him. He could only survive it in the best way he knew how, and the best way he knew how was to keep his distance and pretend it never happened.

"Seriously, Jake. You're not a stupid kid. Would it hurt to talk to her?" Wes waved to Callie as she and Elisabeth pulled into the driveway.

"I talked to her this morning."

Wes's head snapped back to Jake. "You did?"

"I did." *And it totally screwed with my head.*

"And?"

"And...you should go help Callie." He pointed to Callie

carrying two big pizza boxes.

Wes got up and took the pizza boxes from Callie, then greeted her with a passionate kiss. Ross was right behind him, pulling Elisabeth into an embrace. Jake was glad for the distraction from talking about Fiona, but Ross and Elisabeth were all whispers and rubbing noses with about a hundred sickening little kisses. Jake turned away. He'd watched his siblings fall in love over the past few years, and each time another one of them took the monogamous plunge, it got a little tougher for him to remain as immune to the idea as he'd once been. Except there was only one woman's image that accompanied the thought, and he wasn't going down that path again.

He took the pizza boxes from Wes and set them on the table, flipped the top, and took out a slice.

"Jake, thank you for fixing the roof." Callie reached for a slice of pizza. She'd come from work and was still dressed as a prim librarian in her knee-length sheath with a strand of pearls around her slim neck.

"Happy to help. It's done, so you shouldn't have any more trouble."

"You finished? Already?" Callie's eyes widened. Her brown hair was pinned up in a tight little bun, which Wes was quick to take down by removing the pencil that she'd used to secure it in place. Callie shook her hair out and held the slice of pizza up for Wes to take a bite.

"You guys are too cute," Ross said.

"Hey, we're pretty darn cute, too." Elisabeth slid an arm around his waist and kissed his cheek.

"We're the epitome of cute." Ross kissed her softly.

"The epitome of sickening." Jake smiled to soften the tease, trying not to think about the fact that part of him envied his brothers' relationships. He finished his slice of pizza and grabbed another.

"I heard you saw Fiona today," Elisabeth said with a tentative smile. She tucked her blond hair behind her ear and shrugged at Jake's deadpan stare. "What? I had lunch at the Trusty Diner. Margie asked me about you guys." Margie Holmes had worked at the Trusty Diner as a waitress since Jake was a kid. She was the eyes and ears of the small town.

Jake wondered what she thought of Fiona's recent pursuit.

"I was there for coffee this morning," Callie added. "She was quick to fill me in on your night with Sarah, too." She wiped her mouth with a napkin and sat beside Wes. Wes reached for her hand.

"Nothing to fill you in on with Sarah, and yeah, I saw Fi—her when I was out running this morning. So what?" It was like Margie had video surveillance drones hovering over the town.

"Nothing." Callie sat up straighter and pressed her lips together. She was usually careful about saying and doing the right thing. Jake could tell by the worry in her eyes that she thought she'd crossed a line.

"Sorry, Callie. Really, there's nothing to tell. I drove Sarah to her house last night, but I never even went inside." Jake reached for another slice of pizza, then thought of seeing Fiona and lost his appetite. When he'd looked up from the pavement and seen her standing there in those curve-hugging spandex shorts and tight tank top, he'd nearly lost it. It was all he could do to keep moving.

"Wait," Ross said. "You didn't hook up with Sarah? So why'd you take her out of the bar with you?"

Jake shrugged. He'd asked himself that a hundred times between last night and this morning. "Habit, I guess. I'm not used to leaving places alone."

That was bullshit. He left plenty of places alone. He just didn't want to leave alone after his run-in with Fiona. He'd planned on taking his frustrations out in his normal way, with a night of banging-hot, meaningless sex, but then he'd left the bar and taken a few breaths to clear his head. Even clearheaded, his mind had been wrapped around Fiona and the look of shock on her face as he'd stormed out. Thoughts of Fiona and Sarah had collided, and something unfamiliar had happened. His conscience had kicked in. Sarah wasn't a kid, but she was young compared to Jake—a beautiful, willing young woman, but too young nonetheless.

And more important, she wasn't Fiona.

The thought had shocked him into reality. Jake had driven

Sarah home, and much to her dismay, he'd walked her to the doorstep like the gentleman the Braden men were known to be, and he'd bade her good night—sans a kiss or even a hug. Well, okay, *he* no longer had the rep of being a gentleman, but he sure as hell didn't need to leave a trail of one-night stands in his own hometown. It was an eye-opener that hit him like a brick in the face, and it pissed him off that he'd fallen so far from the Braden reputation.

Jake had driven home facing a new frustration. The realization that, after seeing Fiona, the urges he felt *couldn't* be tamped down by just anybody. The itch he'd felt was different from his usual need for release. It was a desire for something more. A deeper connection. A connection he thought he'd left behind long ago and no longer needed—and that had scared the hell out of him and pissed him off in equal measure.

Emily and Dae pulled into the driveway. Pierce and Rebecca stepped from the backseat.

"Great," Jake mumbled.

"Emily will be relieved to hear you didn't sleep with Sarah." Ross patted Jake on the back.

Dae opened Emily's door for her, and they crossed the yard hand in hand. Jake took a moment to really take stock of his sister. She walked easily beside Dae, and she gazed up at Dae like...like...*like Fiona used to look at me.*

Yeah, now he saw it. That extra bounce in Emily's step, the rosy glow of love on her cheeks. He glanced around the table. Wes was holding Callie's hand. Elisabeth sat on Ross's lap, one arm around his neck, a smile on her lips. Jake couldn't deny the longing buried deep in the pit of his stomach. He forced himself to bury it deeper and cleared his throat in an effort to clear his mind.

"Bro." Pierce patted Jake's back.

Jake nodded. "Hey, Pierce. Hey, Rebecca. How are you?"

She embraced Jake. "I'm good. How was your day?"

"Good, thanks. Fixed up Wes's roof, had a nice run." *Nice.* Right, that's not exactly how he'd classify his run when he'd nearly lost his mind over being faced with Fiona for the second time in less than twenty-four hours. "Are you guys still heading out tomorrow?"

"We postponed our meeting so we could stay for the annual County Fair." She looked up at Pierce and smiled.

The County Fair was a big deal in Trusty, and it had always been a family affair for the Bradens. After two run-ins with Fiona, Jake was even more rattled by the idea of going and possibly running into her again.

Pierce kissed her temple. "Family first."

"He also didn't want to meet with the guy we had the meeting with. The guy is a jerk, but he's a jerk that we're going to make hand over a sweet deal," Rebecca reminded him. Rebecca's mother had died a few months before she and Pierce met. She'd spent two years caring for her mother, and after her mother passed away, leaving a mountain of medical bills, Rebecca had been forced to live in her car for a brief period of time, until she'd found her footing again. She'd been too prideful to accept financial help, and in the year since, she'd finished her degree and moved out of waitressing and into the acquisitions department of Pierce's Reno resort.

"Only because you're such a keen negotiator." Pierce kissed her cheek. "It'll be great to see Danica and Blake. I haven't had a chance to meet their baby yet. Chessie's got to be a year old by now. Danica's sister Kaylie's band is playing at the fair this year." Their cousin Blake Carter and his wife, Danica, lived in the neighboring town of Allure. They'd met after Blake's friend died in a tragic accident, when he'd sought help from Danica, who had been a therapist. It was love at first sight, and although Danica'd had to give up her therapist's license in order to be with Blake, she'd never regretted it. And their cousin had never seemed happier. They were wildly in love with their baby girl, Francesca, who went by the nickname Chessie.

"Yeah, I'm not sure I'm going." Now that Jake knew Fiona was trying to reconnect with him, he wasn't exactly excited about hanging around in Trusty. That boat had sailed long ago. No need to try to hash it all out now. If she needed some type of cathartic closure, she could damn well find it on her own. He didn't need to relive the pain of losing the only woman he'd ever loved.

"What?" Pierce released Rebecca and pulled Jake away

from the others. "Dude, what the hell are you talking about? You don't back out of a family outing, not when they come so few and far between lately. You'll crush Mom."

Jake arched a brow. "You're pulling the Mom card? Really?"

Pierce laughed under his breath. "You're going to miss Kaylie sing? She's as famous as you are now."

Kaylie had received a big recording contract a few years back, and it was a big deal for someone so famous to return to the tiny town and sing at the fair. Not to mention that all of their cousins from Weston, Colorado, would be there, too.

"Okay, now your cards are getting lame." Jake looked over his shoulder at his brothers. He would like another evening with them, but the idea of running into Fiona again made his stomach burn.

"Fine. I'm pulling the big-brother card." Pierce's voice grew serious. "You're going."

"Pierce." Jake shifted his eyes away. "Man, I don't want to see her. Don't you get that?"

Pierce stepped into his line of vision with a sobering look in his eyes. "We all know that, Jake. We hear you loud and clear on that front, okay? I know you don't want to talk about this, but have you ever thought that maybe the reason you're such a player is because Fiona hurt you so badly?"

Jake gritted his teeth.

"Face it, dude. She hurt you bad. There's no shame in

that. It happens."

Jake grabbed Pierce's arm and dragged him toward the driveway, buying himself a few seconds to soothe his seething anger. "And why would I want to see a woman who kicked me to the curb?"

Pierce stared at Jake so long Jake fought the urge to grab him by the collar and shake him.

When Pierce finally spoke, his voice was dead calm. "Because you're not over her."

"*Pfft*. Bullshit."

"You can't even say her name, Jake."

"That's called hatred." Jake narrowed his eyes, every muscle in his body rigid and hot.

"That's called denial."

Chapter Four

"HE WASN'T EXACTLY receptive to you, sis. It's been two days and he hasn't reached out even once. Do you really think it's smart to put yourself on the line *again*? Maybe you should rethink this whole thing." Shea was lying on her side on the bed in Fiona's childhood bedroom. She was as graceful and sleek as Fiona was strong and lean, and she was as honest as the sky was blue.

After what Shea said, Fiona wondered if she *was* too confident for her own good where Jake was concerned. It had been a lifetime since they were together. Maybe he really had changed too much for them to ever reconnect. The way his face had gone from the intense face of determination to an angry mask of something too dark for her to acknowledge when he'd seen her on Old Hill Road had her second-guessing her whole idea. But her stubborn heart refused to listen to those concerns.

"Shea, I *know* him. I know the man he was." She

smoothed her black silky tank in the mirror and assessed her snug-fitting cutoffs.

"He was barely a man back then." Shea went to the closet and tossed Fiona her favorite pair of cowgirl boots. "I hate to remind you again, but you broke him, and guys don't bounce back from that stuff. They're like little girls inside, all weepy and uncomfortable when they've been dissed. If anything, he probably hates you for making him feel vulnerable."

Fiona glared at her sister as she shoved her feet into her boots. God, they felt good. Being a grown-up was totally overrated. She could live in cutoffs and boots.

"You're supposed to be on my side, Shea. Why are you trying to talk me out of this? You know how much I love him."

She pulled Shea up to her feet from where she was crouched by the closet.

"I just don't want you to get hurt."

"Well, I'm not giving up. Other than the nervous energy ripping through my body like a frigging tsunami, I feel like this is the right thing to do. I trust my instincts."

A supportive smile reached Shea's eyes. "I know you do, which is why I'm one hundred percent behind you. But...you taught me to be straight up, so that's what I'm doing. If he's a major douche bag to you again, I can't guarantee that I won't go off on him."

Fiona folded her into her arms. "I love you for that, but

even when you're mad, you're cute as a button."

"Fierce. I look fierce, like you." Shea pushed from her arms and gave Fiona a quick once-over. "You look so hot, Fi. If he turns you away this time, he's a fool."

"I have news for you, sis. We're all fools. Maybe it isn't smart to put myself on the line *again*. After he turned me down twice and threw Sarah Chelsum in my face?" She bit back the bile that came with that thought and draped her arm over Shea's shoulder. "Come on. Let's go make Mr. Tall, Dark, and Angry face his demons."

"Demon Slayer. That's what I'm going to call you from now on."

I hope I can live up to it.

FIONA STEPPED FROM the car and inhaled the smell of popcorn, fried foods, and the unmistakable smell of farm animals. Friday nights marked the end of a hard week of farm and ranch work for many, and the annual County Fair was a much-needed reprieve. It looked like the whole town had turned out for it. Acres of grass served as the fair parking lot and overflowed with farm trucks, cars, and motorcycles. The din of the fair brought a smile as she looped her arm through Shea's.

"I forget when I'm at work how nice it is to come back

home." She patted the lump of cash in her pocket. Life in Trusty was simple compared to her typical busy life, where she was in an office, chained to her geographic information system (GIS), analyzing data such as relationships of geochemistry of rocks to their magnetic response or where mineralization occurs relative to faults and folds. Or she was camping on a work site, up at first light and working until nightfall. While she loved her work, she always forgot how a simpler life could be just as enjoyable.

"You used to say Trusty was too simple for you. Remember when you left for college? You told me that you might never come back."

Had she said that? She couldn't remember, but if she had, she had probably been so upset over their parents' separation and breaking up with Jake that she thought she'd never want to come back. But she could never really stay away from Trusty. All of her memories of Jake were there, and Jake was never far from her mind. She felt closer to him just being back home—despite his gruffness. She still believed that beneath that unsettled facade, the warm and sensual man she loved was still there. She just needed to cut through the fortress he'd built around his heart and sneak inside.

They weaved through the busy lot toward the lights of the fair.

"You scared the heck out of me," Shea admitted.

"Aw, Shea, I'm sorry. I think when you're that age you

think the grass is always greener somewhere else."

"Is that why you really broke up with Jake?" Shea kept her eyes trained on the grass as they fell into step behind a crowd of people entering the fair.

Fiona sighed. "No, not really. I was scared. That was the summer Dad left, remember? And Mom got all...I don't know. I guess now I understand that she was just overwhelmed and probably feeling lost after Dad left. And bitter, of course."

"Run over by a tractor would probably be a more accurate description."

"Yeah, I guess. She was pushing for me to sow my wild oats. God, I hate that phrase, but it's exactly what she said to me." Fiona made her voice an octave higher. "*Fiona Faith, you think you know what love is, but trust me, you need to go out and sow your wild oats. I know you think you have none, but there's a whole world out there that's going to tempt you. Better to get the temptation over with now, so you're sure when you settle down.*"

"She said that to you?" Shea's eyes widened as they paid for their tickets at the old-fashioned ticket booth and passed through the roped-off entrance into the fair.

"Yeah." Fiona couldn't help but scan the crowd, hoping to see Jake, as they followed the hordes of people walking along the trampled grass. "Didn't I ever tell you that?"

"No, but then again, you never talk about that summer. I just can't believe you took her advice. But I guess it makes sense. You were so upset when Dad left."

Fiona had been heartbroken when their father had chosen

to leave. She'd felt stuck between her parents, wanting to be loyal to her mother, who *hadn't* cheated on their family, and wanting to keep her close relationship with her father. In the end, it was too difficult to do both, and she'd gone two years without much contact with her father. In the years since, they'd maintained a distant relationship, but she'd never confronted her father about his leaving.

"Mom really rattled me. I mean, if Mom said not to trust my feelings, who was I to think otherwise? She was Mom, you know?"

"Yeah, I know. Do you know what she said to me when I left for college?" Shea tugged her toward a roller coaster.

"Sow your wild oats?" Shea hadn't dated many guys in high school. She'd been popular but had chosen to hang out with groups of friends rather than getting tied down with a relationship. Lord knew, with her long blond hair and gorgeous figure, she was asked out all the time, but as far as Fiona knew, she still hadn't had a long-term boyfriend.

"No. Just the opposite. She told me that I should open myself up to someone and that she hoped I found the right guy to make me happy."

"What is with our family members doling out strange advice? Finn told me to practice abstinence and it would heal my heart." Fiona laughed.

"He's always been...earthy."

They both laughed at that while they waited for their turn

on the ride.

The line for the roller coaster moved quickly, and while Fiona processed the difference in their mother's advice to each of them, they moved to the front of the line. Ten minutes later they were buckled into their seats, waiting for the ride to start.

"You know what I think? Maybe Mom realized she made a mistake telling you to sow your oats." Shea laced her fingers with Fiona's as the roller coaster rolled up the tracks, giving them a birds'-eye view of the fair below.

At the top of the hill, Shea leaned across Fiona and pointed to the makeshift stage. "You can't miss those Bradens. Check that out."

The roller coaster crested the hill and zoomed down just as Fiona noticed the broad-shouldered, tall, dark Bradens gathered together like a sports team. She left her stomach somewhere near the top of the hill, but her heart was wrapped around one of the broadest of the men below. She'd recognize Jake anywhere. At six three he was hard to miss, with linebacker shoulders and the nicest ass she'd ever seen. Not that she could see it from the roller coaster, but the image of Jake's body was seared into her mind. She wanted to join Team Jake in the worst way, but she'd benched him once, and he clearly wasn't eager to hear her offer.

As the roller coaster climbed the next hill, she drew upon every inspirational saying her lacrosse and soccer coaches had ever said to her: *It's not whether you get knocked down; it's whether you get up. Only he who can see the invisible can do the impossible.* Crap. She needed more courage! Every rejection from Jake sliced a little deeper, and she wanted her skin to be too thick for the thickest of verbal slashings. The roller coaster rolled over the peak and plowed toward the ground at breakneck speed.

Make sure your worst enemy doesn't live between your own two ears.

Thank you, Laird Hamilton.

With her sister's hand in hers, she threw her arms up in the air and screamed a loud, indiscernible scream, releasing any lingering doubt.

I can do this.

As the roller coaster eased to a stop, Shea bumped shoulders with Fiona and laughed.

"Let's go, Demon Slayer."

"I know this is the right thing to do, Shea. I know it is, and I'm not giving up until he looks me in the eye and says he doesn't still love me. When he says those words..." She swallowed the lump that came with the thought. "I'll put my frigging tail between my legs and slink away. Until that stubborn and beautiful man tells me that, I'm still in the game."

JAKE WAS WOUND so tight he wanted to take off for a

five-mile sprint, jump from a burning building, or bang some nameless, faceless chick until he was too tired to move. Since he was with his brothers and a few of his cousins and there was no burning building in sight, the first and second of those options were off the table. And since the thought of banging any woman other than Fiona had made him ill ever since he'd run into her in the bar, even his go-to stress reliever was nothing more than a fallen fantasy.

He was screwed.

One hundred percent screwed.

He had no choice but to put on a friendly face, pretend he didn't get a funny feeling in his gut every time his brothers or cousins snuggled up to the women they loved, and act congenial. His eyes slid over the crowd, lingering on every chestnut-haired, slender woman around five foot five. His pulse ratcheted up, and conflicting emotions coursed through him with every sweep of their faces. He hadn't been able to stop thinking about Fiona.

Goddamn Fiona.

She'd sliced right through the concrete walls he'd erected. It was all he could do to remain impassive when confronted with her feminine curves and her sweet voice, which slid right through his chest.

Why the hell was he even pondering her at all? She had *crushed* him and walked away without ever looking back. Even as he thought it, he knew he was powerless to remain impassive. Fiona owned a piece of him that he knew no one else could ever touch.

I'm totally screwed.

He tried to focus on Kaylie's voice as she sang a country song, but it was no use. Even the beat of the music made him think of Fiona and the way she loved to dance.

"Come on, Jake." Rex Braden, Jake's cousin from Weston, Colorado, was six four with shoulders like a Mack truck and massive arms and legs born from years of working on the Braden ranch. He tipped his ever-present Stetson and pulled his fiancée, Jade, against his side. They both had jet-black hair, Jade's to her waist, Rex's over his collar. With her piercing blue eyes, Jade was as strikingly beautiful as Rex was handsome. "We're heading over to the dance."

Jake ran his eyes over Rex's brother Treat, carrying his new baby boy, Dylan, in one arm and holding his four-year-old daughter Adriana's hand. Adriana was named for their mother, who had passed away when they were very young. Treat's wife, Max, reached for Jake's arm.

"Come on, Jake. Treat's going to be busy dancing with Adriana. I'll need a dance partner."

"Dance?" He arched a brow toward his brothers, hoping they'd pick up on his sarcasm and save him from dancing.

Pierce gave him a shove toward the grassy area that had been cleared and lined with hay bales to be used as a dance floor. "Go on."

"A'righty, then," Jake relented. He supposed he might as well try to have a good time. He was a damn good dancer, but he'd have to watch his moves. Jake was used to dirty dancing with the ladies back in LA, not dancing with his cousin's wife.

Max was an easy dance partner. She was confident and kept up small talk, which to Jake's surprise, eased his tension. He'd been so damn focused on avoiding Fiona that he had lost track of how nice it was to catch up with everyone.

"What's it like coming back home?" Max asked as Kaylie belted out another song.

Jake thought about the question. He was surrounded by his brothers and their fiancées dancing and laughing. He'd missed his cousins. His uncle Hal had six children. Treat was the oldest, and then came Rex, Dane, Savannah, Josh, and Hugh. All but Dane, Rex, and Josh were happily married now, and those three were engaged. When they were younger, they'd spent a lot of time together, but over the last few years Jake had been wrapped up in his career, and they'd seen each other only a handful of times.

"It feels good to be home." The small town had its downfalls. One of them being that Fiona could show up at any time; the other being gossip that ran thicker than sludge, and of course Trusty was…Trusty. It was small and safe, not at all the way Jake liked to live his life. Although there had been a time when he'd been so comfortable there that he'd imagined him and Fiona getting married after college and living outside of LA, in a cabin in the woods, enjoying the same quiet life they'd grown up with in Trusty. He'd buried that pipe dream ages ago, and he had no room for anything quiet in his life now.

"I know Treat misses seeing you." The music slowed and Max pulled her dark hair back and secured it with an elastic band. She was a beautiful woman, slim and bright eyed. A natural beauty. "Can you spare a slow dance?"

Jake shrugged. "Sure, but would you rather I took care of Adriana and Dylan so you can dance with Treat?"

"Obviously you've never tried to get Adriana away from her daddy." She nodded at Adriana, who was wrapped in Treat's arms, her lithe arms around his neck, her cheek pressed to his. Treat was a formidable man at six foot six, the same height as his father, Hal. Adriana looked even smaller in his big arms.

"Where's Dylan?" Jake asked.

Max nodded toward Jade, who had the baby bundled in her arms, a loving look in her eyes. Rex was gazing over her shoulder, his dark eyes soft.

"She wants one," Max said. "Can you tell?"

"Oh, yeah. Looks like Rex is on board with that." He placed his hands on Max's lower back, and they fell into an easy, slow dance.

"I know it's kind of taboo to talk about this, or at least it seems that way, but what about you, Jake? Do you ever think about settling down?"

Something about Max's sincere gaze brought out a side of Jake he didn't often allow himself to acknowledge. Thinking of Fiona, he said, "There was a time when I was sure I would." He shrugged, as if to say 'nuf said.

Max didn't take the hint.

"But not anymore?" He could tell by the look in her eyes that she knew she was pushing his buttons.

"Let's just say that I'm not the settling-down type any-more."

"Why?"

He gave her a deadpan stare.

"Oh, come on, Jake. I know your rep, but look at Hugh." His cousin Hugh was a race-car driver who used to live as fast of a lifestyle as Jake, until he fell in love with Brianna Heart and her daughter, Layla. They were married weeks after they met. Tonight the newest addition to their family, ten-month old Christian, was bundled in a stroller. Hugh had one arm around Layla and the other around Brianna, who had a hand on the stroller. They took up a good amount of space on the dance floor. *One big, happy family.* Even Jake couldn't deny the tweaking he felt in his heart.

*If he can do it...*He didn't allow himself to finish the thought.

"He does look happy." He cleared his throat and turned away.

"People change, Jake."

He looked down at Max and shook his head. "Okay, Max. Who put you up to this?" He narrowed his eyes and looked at each of his brothers, though none of them were looking in his direction.

"Nobody." She fidgeted with the ends of her hair and shifted her eyes away.

"Mm-hm." He wasn't buying it. A tap on his shoulder pulled his attention.

"It was me, but Max would never tell you that." His mother came up from behind him and smiled at Max. "Thanks, Maxy. Would you mind if I cut in?"

"Of course not. Thanks for the dances, Jake, and if my opinion means anything, I think you're too great of a guy not to let yourself fall in love."

Jake rolled his eyes and settled into his mother's arms.

"You shouldn't use Max like that."

"I didn't use her." Catherine looked pretty. She usually wore her dark hair long with a side part, and tonight she had it pinned away from her face with a barrette, accentuating her high cheekbones.

"What would you call it?" He scanned the dance floor and wasn't quite as relieved as he thought he'd be that Fiona was still nowhere in sight. Maybe she wouldn't show up after all. He wasn't sure how he felt about that, either.

"Oh, Jake. I call it a mother's job. Isn't it hard to always be wound so tight? Isn't it exhausting?"

"Mom, I don't really want to have this conversation." He clenched his jaw, and she reached up and stroked it.

"I can see that."

He shifted his eyes away.

"I only want you to be happy," she said.

"Thanks, Mom. That's a nice thing to say." Despite the fact that she was pressuring him, he enjoyed this time with his mother when he wasn't otherwise occupied with harassing his brothers. "How are you doing, Ma?"

"Me? Good. You know me. Not much gets my goat."

"Dating?" He'd never actually seen his mother with a man, but he would like for her to be happy, and he assumed that she was reflecting her own desires on him.

She laughed. "Been there, done that."

He furrowed his brow. "I guess so. Then why are you pushing for me to go down that road?"

"Oh, honey. Parents want their children to be happy, and just because my love life turned out not quite as I'd hoped doesn't mean I don't believe in love." She looked over her shoulder at Wes and Callie, dancing cheek to cheek, and beyond them, Pierce and Rebecca, gazing into each other's eyes.

"Love is wonderful, Jake." She met his gaze. "Of course, you've been there, so you know that."

"I seem to remember love kicking the crap out of me."

His mother glanced over his shoulder. "It does that. Kicks your ass, then sucks you right back in and washes all that hurt so far away you barely remember it. But you have to let it in, Jake. You have to be open to it."

"I think I've had enough pushing for one night." Jake took a step back. "I love you, Ma, but there are some things I have no desire to relive."

"Jake." She put one hand on her hip and raised the other palm toward the sky like she was waiting for an explanation.

He waved her off and stalked off.

"Hey, Jake." Emily grabbed his arm as he passed. One look at his angry face and she let go like he'd burned her. "You okay?"

"Fine. Thanks, Em. I'll be back." *Maybe.*

He kept his eyes trained on the trampled grass as he headed as far away from the people he loved as he could. The farther from the band he walked, the softer the music became. After talking with his mother and Max, he felt raw, exposed, like a wound with the bandage ripped off. He slipped around to the back of the snack building and leaned against the concrete wall. His head relaxed back, connecting with the cool concrete blocks with a low *thunk.* He scrubbed his hand down his face and placed one booted foot flat against the wall. His eyes drifted closed, and he breathed deeply. What the hell was going on with him? He'd lived in an iron box since he was a young man. Survival of the strongest. Survival of the fittest.

Survival of those who could hide the best.

"Jake?"

Hell. Jake opened his eyes and leveled them at Fiona, who was looking too damn hot for his current frame of mind in her sweet-ass cutoffs with a silky top that outlined her luscious breasts.

Screwed. That's exactly what he was.

He sank his hands into the pockets of his jeans. "Hey, Fiona."

He didn't even have the energy to be angry. His mother was right; being angry was exhausting. Although, with Fiona closing the distance between them, rocking her cowgirl boots in a way that had always turned him on, he could sure use a second wind.

She smiled, the kind of smile that used to melt his moods like butter—and seemed to have a similar effect today.

"You're actually talking to me today?" She leaned against the wall beside him.

Every nerve came to life from her close proximity. He nailed his eyes to the grass and shrugged. "Guess so."

"Good." She sighed. "I was beginning to think you hated me."

He closed his eyes for a beat. He wanted to believe he hated her, but hearing it from her lips made him realize how far from hating her he really was.

"Yeah, sorry about that. I guess I was a bit of a prick."

"Shea says I shouldn't blame you."

"I always liked Shea." He felt himself smile and stole a glance at Fiona. *Aw, hell.* Bad move. Her easy smile and mischievous gaze drew him in, and it took all of his focus to tear his eyes away again.

Silence filled the space between them. Not that there was much space. Jake could practically feel her breaths as if they were his own.

"I'm sorry I bombarded you at the bar and on your run. I would say I didn't mean to, but it was pretty deliberate."

He heard the smile in her voice and couldn't stop himself from looking. Her smile used to set his world aflame.

Well, damn.

Apparently, it still made his stomach go funky.

He pushed from the wall, hands still in his pockets, and kicked at the grass. He had to do something with all the nervous energy that was coiling tight low in his gut and turning to something else altogether.

"Well, congrats. You've knocked me off-balance. Not many women can say that. In fact, I can't think of another who could." He met her gaze and paused. Had to, for the surge of heat that he'd been pretending never existed was burning a path between them.

"What do you want, Fi?" *Fi. Where the hell did that endearment come from?* He hadn't said it or allowed himself to think it in years.

She shrugged one shoulder and nibbled on her lower lip. "I'm not sure. I just…"

Just what? Wanted to fuck me up a little more?

He clenched his jaw to keep from allowing his mouth to get him in trouble.

She pushed from the wall and stepped right past his comfort zone, made his body cord tighter. And hotter. She pinched his T-shirt at his abs, the way she used to. By the look on her face, the old habit took her as much by surprise as it had taken him, but she didn't let go.

"Jake…" His name hung in the air between them, filled with unspoken wonder and pillowed by desire that was becoming thicker by the second. "I…What would you say if your ex realized she'd made a mistake? A big mistake. And wanted to try to get back together?"

He gripped her slim, feminine wrist. She held tightly to his shirt. She had a strong grip. Fiona was strong in so many ways, but he remembered her weaknesses. He stepped forward, and she stepped back. Her back met the concrete. Jake set his free hand against the wall, beside her head, and leaned in close. She smelled like sweet apples and warm cinnamon. Jake had the urge to touch her hair, the way he used to love to run his fingers through it. He pressed his palm flat against the wall to keep from doing just that. With his other hand, he removed her hand from his shirt and pressed her wrist against the wall. His body ached to press forward, to feel her hips against his again in a way it had never ached for any other woman. Because with Fiona, he knew the depths of pleasure making love to her would bring and the power she had to pull him under her spell. The noise of the fair fell away. There was only the two of them and the heat sizzling between them.

"It's too late, Fi. I'm not the same guy I was." His chest burned, like it did the day she'd broken up with him all those years ago. He couldn't fall back down into that dark abyss. He gritted his teeth against the want that was driving through him with the power of dynamite.

She blinked up at him through thick lashes and dragged her tongue over her teeth, sending lust straight to his groin. Her free hand touched his chest, and he lowered his eyes to it, wondering if she could feel the way his heart was thundering—and if hers was doing the same. By her heaving breasts and the darkening of her baby blues, he imagined it was.

"But maybe somewhere inside you still are," she said just above a whisper.

He closed his eyes again. This was dangerous territory. They were too damn close, and it felt too damn good. He dropped his hands, freeing her. Her hand fisted in his shirt, keeping him close.

"Fiona." He breathed her name and wanted to breathe it again and again and again. She was deliciously familiar—the closeness, the challenge of what he should do and what she knew he wanted to do, the revving of his fucking engine that had him hard as a rock. Damn his body. Damn him. *Damn her.* He didn't need to get tangled up with her again. He'd barely survived her the first time.

"I'm not that same guy." He gripped her wrist, tore her hand from his shirt, and forced himself to step back. "You don't know me anymore, and trust me, Fi. You wouldn't like me if you did." *I'm not sure I like me.* He scrubbed his hand down his face and turned away.

"I don't care that you were with Sarah Chelsum." Her words fell fast and desperate.

Jake turned to face her, softening when he saw her eyes had gone damp.

"Fiona…" *Why do I care what she thinks?*

In three steps she was upon him again, hands clutching his shirt, thighs pressing against his. Tears streaming down her cheeks.

"I don't care, Jake. It doesn't matter."

He forced himself to twist from her grip again. "You don't get it, Fiona."

"I do, Jake. That's just it. I get it. You use women as an escape. You could sleep with half the girls in town and that wouldn't matter, because I know that when you come back to me, you'll never stray."

Come back to you? He moved in close again. "I would never sleep with another woman from Trusty. You don't know me, Fiona. Don't try to act as though you do." She was the first and only woman he'd ever slept with from their hometown, and as much as he played it off like he regretted it, he never had.

"You took her home, Jake. Everyone's talking about how they saw you leave with her. Someone saw you walk her up to the door. People know, so you don't have to bullshit me."

"People around here don't know squat. I drove her home. No kiss good night. No quickie in the backseat. Nothing. Not that I care what anyone around here thinks."

"Maybe not." She lowered her voice again. "But you obviously still care what I think, or you wouldn't have corrected me."

Hell. He ran his hand through his hair and blew out a frustrated breath.

"Look, I don't know what you're thinking will happen between us, but in two days, I'm out of here. Back to LA. Back to my life."

She nodded.

"There's nothing there, Fi. It's done. Whatever we had…" He shrugged.

The sounds of the fair began filtering back into his ears. Jesus, how long had they been standing there? He'd completely fallen into her, oblivious to everything around him. When had he begun breathing hard? *He* was still hard. He forced his legs to carry him away from Fiona. He had no idea where he was going, didn't care, only knew he had to walk away before he gave in to the intense desires warring within him.

"Jake."

He heard desperation in her voice. His emotions warred within him.

Go back.

See where it goes.

Walk, you fool.

Walk away, fast and furious before what's left of your heart gets ripped to shreds.

Jake shoved his hands in his pockets before walking around the corner of the building, leaving Fiona, and his past, behind.

Chapter Five

THE NEXT MORNING Jake pushed his body hard, sprinting up a hill and around the bend toward Old Hill Road just as the sun peeked over the crest of the mountains. He loved this time of the morning, when the town had yet to rise and the shadow of night still lingered in the coolness of the air and the dewy grass. There was a peacefulness in those early hours that had always appealed to Jake. Before checking email or stressing over what he had to get done, he'd pound out a few miles and clear his mind. Only today, as he veered onto Old Hill, his mind was anything but clear. It was reeling with the anticipation of seeing Fiona again. He debated turning around and running another route, but he didn't know what the hell he wanted anymore. He had no clue if he wanted to avoid Fiona or sweep her into his arms, and he wasn't about to dissect it as he pushed his muscles hard and picked up his pace.

Seeing her at the fair had totally knocked him off-kilter.

And when she'd touched him—Lord, when she'd touched him—he'd gotten sucked right back into her again. For a few minutes, there had been only him and her and that crazy, magnificent electricity that had always been there connecting them. Never in a million years would he have thought he'd feel a damn thing when he was near her again.

And what was all that stuff about when he came back to her? *You could sleep with half the girls in town and that wouldn't matter, because I know that when you come back to me, you'll never stray.* Was she living in a fantasy world? *I would say I didn't mean to, but it was pretty deliberate.* He lifted his gaze and scanned the empty road. His stomach tanked. What the hell was up with that? Shouldn't he be happy that she wasn't there waiting for him? Wasn't that what he wanted? To be Fiona-free forever?

It sure as hell was, but last night...

The air cooled as he reached the overlook where Fiona had been standing yesterday morning. *Waiting for me.* He jogged to the edge of the road and looked out over the town, hands on hips, breathing hard. In less than forty-eight hours he'd be back in Los Angeles, back at his estate, back to his life. Fiona would be a lifetime away again. Out of sight, out of mind.

He rubbed an unfamiliar ache at the back of his neck.

A noise caught his attention, and he turned, hope swelling in his chest as he gazed down the road. He was earlier than yesterday; maybe she was just running late today. A deer burst through the trees, ran into the middle of the road and stopped, enormous black eyes meeting his. It turned and leaped back into the woods. He stared at the empty road, longing to see Fiona and wondering what in the hell he was thinking. Fiona was a bad idea, and if anyone knew bad ideas, it was Jake. He was the king of them. His entire social life was a bad idea. There was only one thing that could keep him from getting into trouble with Fiona, and that was a big metal bird that would carry him far, far away.

Chapter Six

MONDAY EVENING FIONA and Shea met Trish for dinner at a restaurant that was near the set where they were going to film *Raiders of the Past*. Fiona had lived in Fresno, California, for several years, but she'd never had the guts to visit Los Angeles. It might be a big city, but she hadn't wanted to take any chance of running into Jake, no matter how many times she'd sat in her car and debated it. She hadn't even been sure she could handle seeing him in Trusty. She'd known she was still in love with Jake for what seemed like forever, but she also knew how he'd gone to great lengths to avoid her, and she wasn't sure she could handle his rejection. She wasn't sure she could handle any of it, really—her desire for him or the risk of reaching out to him...until her boss had offered her a promotion that would mean heavy travel and no chance for settling down. Running two geological teams would become her life. It was a dream job, something she'd been working toward for years, and if the paper she'd recently submitted was published, it would give her even more credibility in the position.

She was at the peak of her career, but taking that dream job would mean letting go of an even more important dream. When Trish had offered her the chance to come to LA, no strings attached, to try to reconnect with Jake, the timing couldn't have been better. This was her chance to follow her heart, so she would finally know if she should let go of the man she loved once and for all.

"So?" Trish leaned across the table and whispered, "Give me all the dirt."

Shea reached for Fiona's hand. Fiona took it and gave it a grateful squeeze. Trish's hazel eyes were wide and expectant. She somehow managed to make a gray cotton tank top and jeans look hot. When Fiona didn't answer right away, she reached across the table, revealing the large, colorful butterfly tattoo just above her elbow.

Fiona released Shea's hand and shooed Trish's hand back to her side of the table. "I'm fine, you guys. Jeez. It's not like I expected him to forgive and forget overnight."

A blond waitress came and took their orders. Fiona waited for her to leave before filling Trish in on the harsh details she'd already shared with Shea.

"I saw him three times, and each time he was a little more receptive." At least that was how she was playing it in her mind, regardless of how cold he was toward her the morning she'd waited for him on Old Hill Road or at the bar.

"I'd say he was more than a little receptive at the fair." Shea leaned against the corner of the booth and raised her slim brows. "Don't you think?"

"Yes…and no."

"Why? Tell me. I'm good with figuring out guys," Trish urged. She was nothing like the typical actress stereotype. She loved geology as much as Fiona did. She'd even studied it in school because her parents had insisted that if she wanted to be an actress, she had to have a fallback career, *just in case*. The personalities of the geologists that Fiona worked with rarely veered into the excited range unless they were talking about earth processes like earthquakes and volcanic eruptions, investigating metals or minerals, or discovering new ways to extract natural gas, water, or oil. Trish's personality was what had first drawn Fiona to her, during a geology course their freshman year. Fiona had been impressed by her intelligence and her forthright demeanor. Trish went head-to-head with the professor the first day in class, and from that day forward they'd been best friends. It was wonderful to be friends with someone who had the same interests she did but was more fun than most people who understood her field of study.

"Well, you know how I told you that Jake and I had this *zing* between us?"

"Yeah, yeah. Zings are good." Trish smiled.

"*Very* good, if you know what I mean, and he definitely

felt it, too." Fiona felt her cheeks heat up as she thought about the impressive bulge in his low-slung jeans.

"He got hard," Shea said flatly.

"Shea!"

"What?" Shea took a sip of her water.

The waitress brought their food, and Fiona waited until they were alone again to respond.

"You don't have to tell the whole restaurant that he got aroused," Fiona whispered.

Trish rolled her eyes. "Fi, you're in LA. Nothing shocks people around here. Go on. This all sounds good, so what's the bad part?"

"That was it. I mean, there was this moment when everything else disappeared. The fair, the noise, the smells. God, did I ever tell you how good he smells?"

"Yes," they both said in unison.

"Sorry." Fiona pushed salad around on her plate, then speared a few pieces of lettuce with her fork. "We were so close, and it all came right back to me. The way it felt to be in his arms, to kiss his lips." She sighed dreamily, longing for what they'd had. "I was sure we were going to kiss, and then..." She shrugged. "He turned and left."

"He left?" Trish's shoulders slumped.

"Yup. Told me that I didn't know who he was anymore, and then he was gone." *And my heart broke a little more as I watched him walk away.* She turned her attention to Shea. "It was this amazing high, like when we rode that roller coaster, and then suddenly I was spiraling down toward the earth at a million miles an hour without any brakes."

"Oh, Fi." Trish's eyes filled with compassion.

Fiona spread her palms on the table. "It's okay. I'm good. Really. I'm not giving up. He softened toward me. It might have been only for a second, but I saw the old Jake in his eyes. I know he's in there, and I have a feeling he's not over me."

"No matter how much he claims to be," Shea pointed out.

Fiona glared at her.

"No, she's right, Fi," Trish said. "He probably *wants* to be over you—don't you think? Sounds like from what you've told me, you really hurt him."

"She was his first love, and she didn't just hurt him—she broke his heart. The whole town talked about it for, like, a year." Shea draped her arm around Fiona. "Oh my God, Fi. Is that why you said you didn't want to come back when you left for college?"

Fiona had tried to forget how bad it felt to be the talk of the town for hurting Jake. In truth, it had taken her a long time to *want* to go back home. She'd found a summer job in Pennsylvania and had remained there after that first year, and by the time she'd come back the following summer, the gossip had died down. She'd seen a few harsh stares, but they'd quickly stopped.

"It was part of the reason. But it was really hard to be in

the place where most of my recent good memories were of me and Jake." She shrugged again. "But eventually I sucked it up. I couldn't leave you alone, right?"

"I would have eventually dragged you back. When I could drive, of course." Shea laughed. "Now, my brave, confident, beautiful sister tossed aside the one and only Jake Braden. And she's going to get him back, because she's Fiona Faith Steele. Right, sis?"

"That's my hope." She knew she didn't sound very hopeful.

"What am I sensing here?" Trish asked.

"It's just...It hurt to see him so angry and to know I caused it. And he wasn't just angry. You were right, Shea. I really must have hurt him worse than I imagined for him to react the way he did, and that's a horrible feeling, knowing I hurt someone I love."

"You were a kid," Shea said. "You need to forgive yourself and harness that energy to win him back."

"We're here for six weeks. Take your time, figure out what you really want, and then go for it. I'm here for you, and if you decide you don't want to pursue him, then we'll just have fun and pretend he doesn't exist."

"You're the best friend ever, Trish."

"Hey." Shea stuck her lower lip out in a fake pout.

"You're the best *sister* ever."

Trish pointed her fork at Fiona. "You know what they say

about best friends."

Fiona arched a brow.

"A good friend backs up your story and posts bail for you. A great friend helps you hide the body, but the best friend…The *very* best friend knows how to *dispose* of the bodies." Trish flashed a conspiratorial grin. "I've got your back, girlfriend."

"Good to know, although I don't think we'll be needing that particular skill."

"Yeah, I know, but still. I'm here for you no matter what." Trish leaned back in her chair and looked around the restaurant. "How cool is it that we're ten minutes from the studio where I'll be filming *Raiders of the Past* with Zane Walker? Did you ever imagine when we were in college that I'd actually end up here?"

"Now, that's something I can finally answer." Fiona lifted her glass in a toast. "Yes, I did. I never had any doubt about you making it as an actress. And here's to Steven Hileberg, who found the sexiest, sassiest, smartest actress to play the part of the leading lady. Here's to having a hot and brilliant best friend." They clinked glasses. "And to a hot and brilliant sister who would definitely help me dispose of the body if I asked her to."

"You know it." Shea clinked glasses again.

"I hate that I'm nervous just because I'm working with Steve Hileberg. I rarely get nervous anymore," Trish admitted.

"I have all my lines memorized and everything, but the production assistant is super stressed. When I arrived yesterday, he was running around like there was a fire in his pants, and that makes it harder to remain calm, especially when Hileberg has a reputation for being a hothead perfectionist."

"Why is the production assistant so stressed?" Fiona knew it was probably a naive question, but she assumed the actors would be more nervous than the assistants. Of course, she had no idea what a production assistant really did.

"They pretty much have to be running at full speed all the time. The main PA gets all sorts of hell if anything goes wrong. Let me check my calendar and see what's on tap for this week to make sure we're on the same page." Shea pulled out a day planner and studied their upcoming schedule. "You have a preproduction cast dinner a week from Friday night."

"You must have that date wrong. Production starts tomorrow, so that wouldn't be *pre*production." Trish flagged the waitress over and asked for the check.

"I know. They should just call it the *cast dinner*. Apparently, Zane Walker wasn't free until then, and you know the world revolves around Zane." Shea reached for her wallet. "I'd like to revolve around Zane. He's totally yummy."

"You can have Zane. I only want Jake, and I have a feeling he might freak when he realizes I'm here." Fiona reached for her purse. "I've got it, sis."

Trish slapped her credit card on the table, stopping them

both. "My treat. You're my PR rep, and you're my personal assistant. This one's on me." She waved her credit card at the waitress.

"Thanks, Trish," Shea and Fiona said in unison.

"You also have a meeting with the set director tomorrow morning, and you need to be on set at least an hour early for your scene tomorrow afternoon in case they're ready early," Shea said to Trish. "But you know this already."

"Old hat to me. Get there early or they freak out." She rolled her eyes. "Fi's got all this in her calendar, and she's already given me hell about making all the meetings and scenes on time. Fi, even if you and Jake become an item, you'll still help me keep my schedule, right?" Trish tapped her finger nervously on the table, but Fiona knew Trish would do just fine without her. She'd been acting for years and didn't even need an assistant. She was just trying to give Fiona a sense of feeling needed, and she appreciated her efforts.

"Of course. You do know I might suck as an assistant, right? I'll do my best to nag you and make sure you don't miss anything. But if by some miracle Jake and I do end up together, all bets are off. I'll try to do a good job, but my brain may end up in the clouds."

"I'm sure it will. I'll send you texts, Fi, so you don't forget." Shea put her purse in her lap. "I won't be on the set, but, Trish, you don't even need us. I think we all know that."

"What? Yes, I do! I need you like I need chocolate. You

comfort me." She fluttered her eyelashes with the tease. "So, Fi. You didn't tell Jake you were coming?" Trish shifted her eyes to Shea in a way that translated to, *I'm not sure that was such a great idea.*

"It's not like we had a chance to catch up and talk about work. It was all I could do to remember to breathe when we were together." Fiona had been worried about the same thing ever since she'd seen Jake at the fair. "Besides, this was *your* idea."

Trish held her hands up. "Agreed. It was totally my idea for you to come and try to work things out with him. It's what you've wanted the whole time I've known you. But given that you saw him and didn't warn him you'd be here..." She scrunched her face and sucked in air between her teeth. "I just worry. I mean, what if he's got a girlfriend on set—or six, given his reputation?"

Trish's words hit too close to home. Fiona tried to ignore the pain ripping through her chest at the truth behind them. "That wouldn't change if he knew I was coming, so..."

"Fiona can handle it. Right, Fi?" Shea patted her on the back, then turned her attention to Trish. "And if not, then we're here to get her so drunk she won't remember why she was here in the first place, and I'll hire you a personal assistant, so Fiona can go out to the desert and dig up rocks until she feels better."

"God, I love you." Fiona hugged Shea. "I'll be fine. I know

all about his reputation. Although he claims he didn't sleep with Sarah Chelsum."

"The girl from the bar that you texted me about?" Trish asked.

"Uh-huh. He said he just took her home."

"That's true," Shea agreed. "After you told me what he said, I asked Jeanette, who asked Lisa, who asked Cara, who is Sarah's very best friend. She confirmed it. Not that Sarah didn't try to get all up in his junk, but he turned her down and left her at the front door, and apparently she tried to play it off like he didn't until I started nosing around."

Fiona couldn't repress the smile spreading across her lips. "So...I guess I did have an effect on *Mr. I'm Not the Same Guy I Was*, after all."

She tucked that little confidence booster away. She needed every bit of confidence she could muster after the way Jake had left her standing there behind the snack building at the fair.

IT FELT DAMN good to be home. Jake stretched out on the leather sofa in the expansive living room of his Mediterranean-style home, closed his eyes, and reveled in the comfort of being back in his world, where he was king and no one passed judgment on him. He'd arrived home and found a group of friends already celebrating his return. This was a common occurrence, as his friends knew that his backyard was there to be enjoyed, and when he was in LA, he often left his doors unlocked for his buddies to come and go as they pleased. It had driven Pierce mad the last time he'd visited, because the house was never quiet. Jake liked it that way. The less time spent alone and in his own head, the better. And since running into Fiona, he needed chaos to silence the echoes of her voice. His thoughts had taken all sorts of reverse sprints, revisiting their encounters and dredging up memories that sent him into a tailspin he had yet to recover from.

He felt the feathery touch of delicate fingers trail up his abs and grinned as the woman leaned in close. Even with his eyes closed, he knew it was Jerria. Her perfume gave her away.

"I've been wondering when you'd get back," she said in a throaty voice.

Jerria had acted in one of the flicks where Jake had been a stuntman a few months ago. He couldn't remember which one, and as she pressed her breasts against his chest, he wondered why he felt claustrophobic instead of hot and bothered in a good way. She kissed his neck and made a sweet little noise in her throat that should have turned him on, but it had the reverse effect. He pressed himself in to the couch and gently pushed her back.

"Hey, Jer." He pushed up to a seated position, trying to hide the annoyance in his voice. Why the hell did he go from being relaxed and happy to be surrounded by friends to wishing he were alone? He glanced out the back doors, remembering when Pierce had come to visit when he and Rebecca had first begun dating. His brother's voice came slamming back to him. *There's a hell of a lot more than tits and ass out there waiting for you.* Jake had laughed him off, thought he was being punked. But as his mind reverted back to Fiona's hopeful eyes, the feel of her close to him, the way his body reacted to her with something much more profound than merely a desire for sex, he realized his brother wasn't joking.

Jerria had blond hair down to her ass and wore a skimpy yellow bikini. Pert nipples gave away her aroused state. A week ago she'd have been the perfect welcome-home gift. A no-strings-attached romp all wrapped up in a teeny-weeny bikini. Now he was bothered by the assumption that he'd fall into bed with her—even if the assumption would have been true a week ago.

This was totally messed up.

"I've missed you." She ran her fingers through his hair.

Jake gripped her wrist and pulled it from his hair; then he slid her other hand off his thigh, where she'd taken purchase like a cat clawing its prey. He pushed to his feet and paced, leaving her to stare, jaw agape, from where she was kneeling beside the couch.

He was just as confused as she was.

"I'm too tired for this," he mumbled. Maybe that was it.

Like hell that was it. Fiona had gotten under his skin.

"Jake Braden too tired for sex?" She moved to his side, and he shrugged away from her pawing fingers. "I'm sure I can wake you up."

Everything felt wrong and grated on his nerves. The music was suddenly too loud. Jerria standing in his living room in a bikini with lust in her eyes made him feel dirty. The din of his friends out back felt like an intrusion. All combined, it riled him like fingernails scratching a blackboard.

He needed to escape. He snagged his keys and headed out the front door.

It was dark, and the cool night air woke him up. What was he doing? His eyes swept over the four-car garage, his Harley and Ducati sitting out front, and past that, the seven-acre estate. He debated climbing on one of his bikes and driving fast and far, but something told him that when he returned home, the demons would still be haunting him.

He headed back inside and did what he'd never done in all the years he'd lived in Los Angeles. Instead of opening his doors to stars and models, he kicked them out, reclaiming his house. He ushered his friends out the door with excuses of needing to prepare for his upcoming gig.

Unfortunately, that left him with silence.

Jake wasn't very good with silence.

He sank into the couch and palmed his cell phone. There were any number of people he could call and shoot the breeze with, but that would negate having the house to himself. He didn't want to shoot the shit. He wanted to understand what the hell was happening in his head. He leaned his elbows on his knees, then sat back with a frustrated sigh and stared up at the ceiling.

Jake clenched his jaw against the nagging realization that he'd been pushing so far away that he'd fooled himself into believing it didn't exist.

Fiona hadn't just gotten under his skin—in sixteen years, she'd never left.

Chapter Seven

TUESDAY MORNING WAS a blur of activity. Trish's meeting with the set director went on forever and turned into a meeting with several other "set" people. Working on the set of a movie was much more chaotic than Fiona had anticipated, and she was only Trish's assistant. It seemed everyone was always rushing, and tension simmered among the people in charge. Almost everyone had a radio or a headset, and messages were constantly coming through. Fiona made the mistake of asking someone if he needed to respond—she'd thought he hadn't heard the message squawk through. Then he'd shot her an arctic stare, shaken his head, and walked away without responding. Luckily, Zane Walker's personal assistant, Patch Carver, a brown-haired twentysomething guy with chiseled features and a sleeve of tattoos, had clued her in to the fact that no one answered radio calls unless they were meant for them, even though they were all relaying messages on the same channels.

Now it was midafternoon, and Fiona was watching Trish await her scene. Trish looked cute in a pair of khaki shorts and a white button-down top that was open to her naval and tied at the waist. She wore leather hiking boots and thick socks, and all Fiona could think about was how hot it was on the set with the bright lights and how hot Trish's feet must be. They were filming on a set that had been constructed to look like the inside of a cave. Fiona was trying to remain silent, having already seen too many glares from the director aimed at two men who must have made sounds that she hadn't heard.

Fiona knew Trish was nervous by the way her finger kept dragging against the edge of her shorts. That was her thing. She used to do it before exams. Fiona called Trish's nervous habit *fringe-seeking therapy*. She wished she could run over and tell Trish how great she was going to be and make her laugh so she would calm down. But she didn't dare move as Trish walked onto the cavernous set and recited her lines while Fiona silently cheered her on.

Fiona spotted Zane approaching Trish. He and Jake looked so much alike that she did a double take. Zane's dark hair was cropped short, and his square jaw sported about five days' worth of scruff. He was well built, though narrower through the chest and arms than Jake. While Jake walked with purpose, Zane walked with an air of knowing he was being watched. She hadn't seen Jake since she'd arrived in LA, but she knew from Trish's script that Zane had a scene where he climbed the side of the interior of the cave and then fell into a pool of what the script stated as *muck*. She was fairly certain that the man who kept checking his shoes for dirt wasn't about to get his hands dirty by climbing up the wall, much less fall into a pit of muck.

"Cut!" an authoritative voice boomed through the set.

There was a flourish of activity and urgent commands as people ran onto the set. Fiona watched, totally clueless as to what she was supposed to do. Should she see if Trish needed anything? Should she offer her water? One woman primped Trish's hair while another pressed a makeup pad to her cheeks and forehead.

"Relax. They're just getting ready for the stuntman to come on set." Patch stood beside Fiona with a clipboard in his hands and a headset connected to his ear.

She shouldn't feel like her heart stopped beating or her lungs collapsed at the thought of Jake showing up. He was the reason she was there, after all. But she had no control over her emotions when it came to Jake.

"Oh," was all she could manage. She heard Jake's voice before she saw him approaching out of her peripheral vision as he patted Patch on the back.

"Good to see you, Pat—"

Apparently, he had about the same reaction to Fiona as she did to him. Jake's brows sank into a confused slash. He stopped walking, which worried Fiona. He couldn't hold up the scene, and everyone was turning, watching. Waiting.

Oh God, this was a very bad idea.

She hadn't thought it through well enough. He was staring at her with an expression she couldn't decipher. He was either mad, confused, or something in between, but one thing was for sure. He wasn't smiling.

"Jake Braden, Fiona Steele. She's Trish's assistant." Patch motioned to Fiona.

"H-hi." At least she sounded starstruck instead of lovestruck. She looked self-consciously down at her shorts and *Geologists Dig It* T-shirt. Maybe she should have dressed sexier, but she'd never had to dress sexy to get Jake's attention, and when she'd gotten dressed that morning, she was confident that it wouldn't take the right clothes to win him over. That eventually he'd look at her and be unable to resist the electricity flaring between them.

Jake gave a curt, silent nod, then crossed the set to where the hustle and bustle was happening. The women who were primping Trish ran to Jake. He was dressed identical to Zane, and it took a minute for Fiona to realize that was on purpose. *Duh.* Her mind really wasn't working.

"He's just stressed, but he's a really good guy." Patch elbowed her, pulling her out of her Jake-induced stupor. "Don't take that personally."

She breathed deeply. She could do this. It was just like watching a movie. That's all. A movie with the man she adored who was about to fall fifty feet into a pool of muck.

Trish caught her eye, flashed a big smile, and waved. Fiona managed to give her a thumbs-up before they started filming again. If she didn't want to make a fool of herself, she was going to have to buck up and put on her own performance.

"Oh, no big deal. I actually know Jake. We...grew up together." There, see? She could act like a normal person, not a woman hoping to strip away her angry ex-boyfriend's suit of armor.

"Really? So you're from Colorado?" Patch asked.

"Yeah."

Someone yelled "Set!" which Fiona knew meant that they were ready to film. The procession of commands that came next, *roll sound, rolling, rolling camera, slate*, and finally, *action*, was also different from what Fiona had imagined. She'd always thought someone closed what she knew now were called the *clapper sticks* and then the director yelled, "Action!" If nothing else, she was gaining quite an education in filmmaking, and she could see why people were drawn to the industry. Every stressful second was as thrilling as it was painstaking. To see the hard work of all of these people come together in a blockbuster movie must be equivalent to geologists finding evidence of supervolcanoes in Utah.

Jake, looking very much like Zane, only stronger, manlier, and about a thousand times sexier, used his fingers and booted toes to climb the arched wall, hanging nearly parallel to the ground by the time he reached the peak of the cavern. Fiona held her breath. She had watched all of Jake's movies over and over, but she'd never seen him doing the stunts in person or thought about what it was really like for him to do them. And in reality, it had always looked like the actual actors were doing the stunts, so although she knew Jake was doing them, she never even considered the tremendous danger involved and the courage it took for Jake to carry them out. Then again, Jake had always been courageous. She'd never seen him cower from anything, and she knew he thrived on risk. He had spent his teenage years doing everything and anything that spelled danger, along with his brother Wes. They'd skydived, mountain climbed, bungee jumped, gone caving, and more by the time Jake was sixteen. He'd even introduced Fiona to riding ATVs and dirt bikes. She'd accompanied him on a few low-mountain treks, but she wasn't the daredevil Jake was by any stretch of the imagination. She'd always admired his courage, and she'd been as enamored by Jake's thrill of being a daredevil as she had been with every other part of him. Jake wouldn't be Jake without his love of all things risky—and she would never try to change that. Well, except where other women were concerned. Being risky in his professional life was one thing. But if she had her way, he'd never want to be risky with anyone but her again.

She turned away when he fell, his arms and legs flailing as he careened into the pool of muck, landing with a loud *thud* and sending sprays of brown gunk everywhere. Fiona secured her hand over her mouth to keep from gasping.

Please be okay. Please be okay.

Jake disappeared beneath the surface and out of view for a few seconds, then popped back up and sprang to his feet. It looked like the earth was moving beneath him. He was covered in muck, but his beaming smile shone through the dank mess as he raised his hands over his head and *whoop*ed.

"Cut!" the director's voice boomed again. "Jake, how many times do I have to tell you? No hollering until I say cut!"

"It was perfect, and you know it." Jake waved him off as a woman handed him a towel and another woman wiped the muck from his skin.

Fiona assessed his every step. She needed to see that confident stride to believe he hadn't been hurt. After only a few steps, she could see he was carrying himself with the same powerful presence as always, and relief washed through her. Only Jake would talk back to the director. She wondered if all the other women on set found that as much of a turn-on as she did. She loved his confidence—and remembered how much she'd liked it in bed.

"Intense, isn't it? He's the best." Patch crossed the set to Zane and handed him a bottle of water, which pulled Fiona from her naughty memories and set her in motion toward Trish to do the same.

Jake set a bead on her as she passed in front of him. She

wanted to congratulate him and tell him how riveting it was to watch him, but it was all she could do to hand Trish her bottle of water. Luckily, Jake was a good distance away, and she had time to get her brain functioning properly again.

"You okay?" Trish asked.

"I think I should be asking you that." She tore her eyes from Jake. "Everyone's so intense."

"It's cool, isn't it? I can't believe in all these years you've never visited me on set. I'm glad you're here." Trish glanced at Jake and lowered her voice. "Your man is hot."

"Wicked hot." She knew just how hot he was, and apparently her body remembered, too, because she felt her nipples harden beneath the heat of Jake's intense stare. How would she make it through six weeks of this? And if they found their way back together again, how would she make it through a lifetime with the man who made her feel like she'd swallowed a dose of pure lust for lunch?

Chapter Eight

BY THE TIME Jake had wrapped his scenes for the day, the sky was clouding over and the temperature had dipped with the sun, which meant they were in for an evening storm. He could use the cooler temperatures. He was dirty, hot, and so tightly wound he thought the wrong move might send him spinning like a top. He'd seen Fiona several times throughout the afternoon, though he wasn't sure she'd spotted him after she'd seen him on the first set. He'd watched her between takes, laughing with Trish, talking with Patch and Zane, and getting friendly with just about everyone who was working on the movie. He'd even seen the director talking with Fiona. What could she possibly have said to capture Steven Hileberg's attention? And why the hell was she working as Trish's personal assistant? She wasn't an assistant. She was a geologist.

Jake's assistant, Trace, was a bright college grad with a major in music, and her aspirations were grounded in the entertainment industry, so it made sense for her to work in the business. She played bass guitar and found inspiration in being around others in the entertainment field, whereas Jake knew Fiona's geological aspirations couldn't have changed that much. *What the hell is she doing?*

Jake headed to his trailer to shower.

"Jake!"

Jake turned at the sound of Jon Katon's voice. Jon was one of the production assistants. He was tall, with sandy-blond hair and striking blue eyes, and like so many other runners on set, Jon was an aspiring actor. "Hey, some chick was looking for you."

"Yeah? What else is new?" He laughed, but it was a facade. Part of him was hoping it was Fiona, while another part was tamping that hope down with an ineffective sledgehammer.

"Right, well, she was pretty persistent. Said she had something for you. I told her where your trailer was but that she should find Trace."

Jake glanced at his trailer. He'd once entered his trailer and found two naked actresses making out on the couch. He'd added extra locks to his trailer door, but errant fans came with the territory—even if those "fans" were other industry professionals. Luckily, stuntmen worked behind the scenes and were largely ignored in the public eye, but actresses he'd worked with and their assistants were another story altogether. That was the last thing he wanted to deal with on a day like today, when he'd been haunted by thoughts of Fiona all day.

"Don't worry. I saw her across the way a little while ago on another set. She's not waiting for you."

"Cool. Thanks, man." Relieved, he headed into his trailer.

Jake's trailer was more of a mobile estate, equipped with a sixty-inch plasma television, an upscale living room and dining set, a full bath, and a second story. At fifty-three feet long, it was on par with the A-list actors' trailers in size and accommodations. He stripped off his shirt and filled a glass with water. His schedule was on the table, thanks to Trace. He sat on the leather sofa and opened a folder she'd left him. Inside he found an envelope with his name handwritten across the front. He'd know that loopy script anywhere, even after all these years, and he realized that Fiona had been the one looking for him. He wasn't sure how he felt about that.

"Fi, what have you done?" His lips curved into an unexpected smile as he opened the envelope and withdrew a black-and-white photocopy of their high school yearbook's senior prom page. He hadn't seen it in more than a decade, but he remembered it as if it were yesterday. He'd worn a heather-gray tux, and Fiona had worn a strapless white dress with a crisscross bodice and a gold sparkly swatch that ran from her hip, up the center of the bodice, and over one shoulder. She looked stunning, and that night had been amazing. They'd been crowned prom king and queen and had spent the evening gazing into each other's eyes, dancing, and laughing with friends. Jake had never felt as happy as he had that night.

He'd seen a future with Fiona, and he'd imagined every night would be as incredible as that night was. When the parties ended, they'd gone to the lookout on Old Hill Road and watched the sun come up. Other couples had used the prom as a night to sneak away to neighboring towns and rent hotel rooms, but he and Fiona's relationship had been so much deeper than sex.

Making love with Fiona had been the most intense and passionate sex he'd ever experienced. He'd never experienced anything similar since—and until the past few days, he'd accepted that he never would. He knew that came with their intense emotional connection. But the hatred that he'd mustered toward her, he was realizing, wasn't hatred at all. It was his worst enemy, his most dreaded weaknesses—fear and hurt—all bundled together and misconstrued.

It was easier to be angry than to be hurt, though not less painful.

Not less painful at all.

He flipped the photograph over and read the handwritten note. *We were always hanging by a moment. I don't want to hang anymore. Fi.*

It was all he could do to keep from getting up and putting "Hanging by a Moment" by Lifehouse on the stereo. He stared at her note for a long while and finally set it all back into the folder and pushed it across the table.

By the time Jake finished showering, it was after seven, he

was starved, and it was pouring rain. It never rained in Los Angeles. Before walking out of his trailer, he snagged the envelope from Fiona, folded it, and shoved it in his pocket. He wasn't done mulling it over quite yet.

He climbed atop his Ducati motorcycle, wondering why, of all nights, the skies would open up tonight, when he had his bike instead of his car and his mind was drenched in thoughts of Fiona. The sidewalks were empty as he drove away from the gates, save for a woman holding a newspaper over her head and—*Fiona?*

Jake pulled over a few feet ahead of her, jumped from his bike, and snagged the extra helmet. Fiona was soaked, despite the newspaper soggily hanging over her head. He took off his helmet and handed her the other, silently teasing himself about this being some crazy setup put on by the rain gods.

"Jake."

"Come on," he hollered above the driving rain. "I'll drive you wherever you need to go." When she didn't take the helmet, he moved the newspaper and slid the helmet over her head, catching the faintest smile as it settled over her face. He lifted the face shield, and she blinked out at him, looking adorable and...surprised.

"Where to?" As he stood beside her in the driving rain, he realized that the eight-hundred-pound gorilla of anger he'd been carrying around wasn't there. Instead, all he felt was a desire to help her get where she needed to go.

"You don't have to…" She held his gaze.

"Fiona, where are you headed?"

She gave him the address of the apartment she'd rented.

"That's a long walk. Why didn't you take a cab?"

"I tried, but I didn't see any." She was dripping wet and shivering.

It felt natural for Jake to slip out of his jacket and help her put it on, the way he used to take care of her. The sleeves hung well past her hands, and she looked so vulnerable that he had the urge to take her in his arms and hold her. Another urge that knocked him off-balance.

"There's a service. I guess no one told you. Have you had dinner?"

She shook her head.

"Okay. My place is closer. Why don't we swing by there, have a bite, and we'll get my car and I'll take you home." He had no idea where *that* idea came from, but he was going with it. Maybe it was time to give his crappy attitude a rest and deal with whatever this was.

"Jake, you don't have to. I feel terrible taking up your night."

He arched a brow. "No, you don't."

That earned him a genuine smile. "Yeah, you're right, but—"

He took her hand and led her to the bike. The feel of her hand in his was as comforting and familiar as falling into his own bed after being away from home for way too long. He helped her onto the bike, then climbed on in front of her. She wrapped her arms around his waist, and he gently tugged her closer, bringing her chest flush to his back, her thighs against his. As the bike roared to life, she tightened her grip, making him grin even wider.

As much as he would have liked to drive slowly just to feel her sweet body pressed against him, he didn't want her out in the rain any longer than she needed to be. He zipped around the last bend and up the hill toward his house. He pulled up the long driveway, tipping off the sensors that turned on the outside lights, illuminating the two-story estate. The press of a button on his bike opened his garage door. He parked and climbed off the bike, then helped Fiona take her helmet off. He was glad to see she was smiling instead of looking surprised.

He tried not to stare, but her pert nipples pressed against her drenched shirt. The way her shorts fit like a second skin and his jacket hung several inches too long added a flare of innocence to her sexy ensemble. She looked hot as hell.

He watched her smile falter at the sight of his cars: a midnight-blue Aston Martin, black Jaguar, red Ferrari, and farthest from them, his Mercedes McLaren.

"Are all of these cars yours?"

"Yeah." He grabbed her hand again and took a few steps toward the door, then realized what he'd done and stopped.

He looked down at their hands, then up at Fiona, who was still smiling like she'd just won a prize. *Aw, hell.* He fricking loved her smile.

"Old habits and all that." He led her inside and stopped in the laundry room to grab fresh towels. He slipped his jacket from her slender shoulders and hung it on a hook beside the dryer; then he gently pressed the towel to her shoulders. She watched him with a warm gaze as he dried first one arm, then the other, slowly running the towel over her skin. They stood inches apart, and he realized she was staring at him in a way that made his body hot despite being soaking wet. And she was shivering. He wrapped a dry towel around her back and arms, and she curled her fingers around the towel to hold it up. Their fingers brushed for the briefest of seconds, and it brought his eyes to hers again.

He tore his eyes away to gain control of his conflicting emotions.

"I'm sorry. You must be freezing."

"I'm okay," she said softly.

He knelt to dry her legs, and the second he touched her calf, his body flashed hot. He rose to his feet and handed her the towel.

"You'd better…uh…"

"Of course. Sorry." She took the towel in a trembling hand and dried her legs.

It had been so many years since they'd been so close to

each other that by the time she finished drying herself off, Jake was fighting the desire to touch her again. He had never envisioned Fiona in his house, and here she was, more beautiful than any woman he'd ever seen and looking at him like she'd never left all those years ago. How easy would it be to kiss her? To lower his lips to hers and taste her again? To strip those wet clothes from her body and make sweet love to her?

Hell. What was he thinking? He drew in a long breath and took her hand again. *Goddamn it.* He hadn't meant to, but there it was, enveloped in his, feeling fucking perfect as he led her into the great room.

"Wow. You live here?" Her smile faded as she looked around.

"Most of the time," he said. "I travel for movies and own several houses, but this is my primary residence." He was usually proud of what he'd accomplished and of all he had, but now he felt like he sounded pompous.

"Jake, this is…" She walked through the great room, to the glass doors, and peered into the rain at the illuminated bar and pool in the backyard.

Watching Fiona assess his home brought pride and embarrassment. He'd hired the best decorators to outfit it with dark, masculine colors and the finest handmade furniture. The image he presented with his houses and cars was a far cry from the down-home guy he used to be, who hated pretentiousness.

As he watched Fiona take it all in, he wondered if this was really who he had become, or if, like his anger, it was a front meant to keep the world at bay. To keep anyone from seeing who he really was. To keep anyone from seeing the man Fiona had slayed.

"It's not what I expected, I guess." She stammered for a moment. "I didn't realize you had such fancy taste."

No, he guessed she wouldn't have. When they were together, he'd never needed material things. He had Fiona and his family, and he was perfectly content. Hell, he would have been content sleeping in a tent with Fiona. He ran his hand through his wet hair, forcing those memories aside for the moment, and led her upstairs. He walked past the guest rooms and pushed open the doors of the master bedroom. It wasn't until he was halfway to his closet that he realized he'd brought her directly into his bedroom. He'd never had any woman in his bedroom, and with Fiona it was automatic, like his body knew that Fiona would one day come back into his life and it knew just what to do when she did.

Jake tried not to dissect what that meant, even though it took him by surprise. He went into the walk-in closet to find her clothes to put on. He heard Fiona behind him. She leaned against the doorframe, looking wet and cute. His protective urges came rushing back. Fiona was strong and capable, but he knew she was also feminine and had a vulnerable side. Even when they'd first begun dating, he'd wanted to protect her from everything, from physical harm to disconcerting sights like animals that had been hit by cars and were left lying on the side of the road. And now he wanted to carry her into the bathroom, run a warm bath, and wash every inch of her until she felt safe and her body warmed. He forced himself to turn his attention to the task at hand—finding her something dry to put on.

"This closet is bigger than the apartment I rented."

"Yeah. It's pretty nice." He found a pair of smallish sweatpants and a T-shirt and handed them to Fiona. She'd probably fit in one leg of his sweats. "I'll run a bath for you, and then I'll toss your clothes into the dryer."

She followed him into the bathroom, and he sensed her trying not to look around.

"Fiona, I've got nothing to hide in here." He looked at the counter, where his colognes were lined up beside his toothbrush and toothpaste.

"I didn't think…"

"No, but you're trying not to look around." He smiled to let her know he wasn't irritated.

Her cheeks flushed. "Thanks for picking me up. I really didn't plan to run into you this time." She smiled and ran her finger along the edge of the counter as he ran the bath.

He nodded. "I'm sure you didn't."

He watched her as she touched the end of his toothbrush, then lifted his cologne bottles one by one, inspecting them. Maybe he should have been annoyed that she'd taken his words as a blanket statement to look through his things, but he wasn't. He was puzzled by how much he liked seeing her in his bathroom, touching everything. Her eyes lifted to his, and she smiled.

"Then again," he added, "you did wait for me at Old Hill Road, and you were somehow able to get this into my trailer." He reached into his pocket and withdrew the envelope she'd left for him.

"I tracked down your assistant, Trace. She's lovely, by the way." She leaned against the counter and fidgeted with the ends of her wet hair.

He set the envelope beside her, drawn to her honesty. She'd never been one to dance around the truth, and he appreciated that she didn't skirt around tracking down Trace. She was still the same Fiona she'd always been. Life hadn't jaded her as it had him, and it made him want to be closer to her, to share in that innocence again.

"Fi, what do you want from me?" He didn't recognize his easy, soft tone, and as he moved closer to her, nothing about him felt familiar. Not the nervous fluttering in his gut or the way his breathing seemed louder, felt heavier.

"I don't want anything *from* you, Jake. I…" She lowered her gaze and ran her finger along the edge of the counter again. "I just want another chance to see if…" She waved her hand in the air, as if he'd figure out the rest of her sentence. Worry, hurt, and something else passed through her blue eyes.

"It's okay, Fi. I'm not going to bite your head off." At the moment he was fighting a killer urge to fold her into his arms and kiss her, and it shocked the hell out of him. "I was a dick back in Trusty, and I'm sorry for that. It's…been a long time."

"You are? Sorry, I mean." Her eyes warmed again.

Her voice was tender and sweet and almost too much for him to take. *Almost.* He was still nursing pretty sharp wounds, regardless of how his mouth was spouting emotions without checking with his head first. He took a moment to think before answering this time.

"Yeah. I am sorry. There's no reason for me to be that way toward you."

She let out a relieved sigh and nodded.

"I just don't know what you want." He eyed the envelope. Did she really want to try to work things out after all these years? Why? Did he?

Along with being angry, Jake had become distrusting. He'd lived in the land of ladder climbers for so long that the first thing that came to mind was what did she want from him? But he knew Fiona wasn't interested in using him for her own personal gain. With that thought, he realized how jaded he'd become. If he and Fiona tried to work things out, he'd have to deal with that side of himself—and several others.

If…

When had that even become a possibility?

The mirrors steamed up as warm water filled the tub. They were standing inches apart. He could hear every breath she took and noticed that her breathing had become shallow again, as it had downstairs. The urge to reach out and touch her, stroke her cheek, to feel the curve of her hips in his palms, was overwhelming. He fisted his hands, and he swore her soft blue eyes darkened. He remembered that look in Fiona's eyes. It had been a very long time, but it was a look no man could ever forget.

"I think you do know." Her lips parted.

The air between them pulsed, alive with want and need and all things in between, and hell if he wasn't hard as steel. Fiona pushed from the sink and reached for him.

"Jake." Her eyes shifted away.

He was lost in desire as he settled his hands on her hips and nearly groaned at the feel of her sweet curves in his hands after all these years.

"Jake! The water."

The surprise in her eyes drew his to the tub, where water was trickling over the edge and wetting their bare feet. How'd he miss that? He shut off the water and yanked a towel from the rack, trying to clear the lust from every crevice of his being. This was not an easy task with Fiona crouching beside him on the floor, wiping up the water and bumping against his shoulder, her knees accidentally brushing his thighs. Were her knees *accidentally* brushing his thighs, or was she trying to give him a signal? *Hell.* What was he doing? His thoughts had gone to hell in a handbasket.

They rose to their feet at the same time, bumping chests.

"I should…" Her eyes dropped to the tub.

"Right." His heart thundered in his chest with what he thought she *should* do, and it had nothing to do with bathing unless he was naked in that tub with her. He reached down and opened the drain to the tub to keep from reaching for her.

"Let it drain a bit so it doesn't overflow." He thrust his thumb over his shoulder. "I'll be…I'll wait out here. Just, uh, toss your clothes out and I'll throw them in the dryer."

She swallowed hard and barely nodded as he forced himself to walk out of the bathroom and shut the door behind him. He leaned his back against the wall and closed his eyes, willing the eight hard inches in his pants to ease and knowing there wasn't a chance in hell of that happening.

The bathroom door cracked open and Fiona's arm reached out, holding her clothes. Jake took them, and for a brief second their fingers brushed again, sending a shock of anticipation through his veins. When the door closed again, he lowered his eyes to the black lacy thong tangled with a matching bra and her other wet clothing. He stared at the bathroom door. She was naked, probably sinking all those delicious parts into the warm water that very second. He couldn't resist her. He reached for the bathroom doorknob.

His cell phone vibrated in his pocket, which felt really sweet, considering his jeans were stretched tight from his erection, giving that vibrating ringtone a whole new benefit and pulling him from the insanely bad decision he'd almost made.

Chapter Nine

THE AIR IN the bathroom was thick with steam and Jake's masculine scent. His hungry gaze had bored right through Fiona, making her wet with desire. Her body hummed with the urge to satisfy her ache for Jake. She gazed at the door, and her pulse kicked up impossibly faster. She slid her fingers between her legs, feeling her slick, oversensitive sex. She closed her eyes, knowing she could take herself over the edge in two minutes; then maybe she could have dinner with Jake without wanting to rip his clothes off. Her fingers knew what to do, stroking the bundle of nerves as her mind conjured up the image of Jake standing so close she could practically taste him, his drenched T-shirt clinging to every muscle. She imagined her hand as his and sank deeper into the water.

I just don't know what you want.

Oh, but Jake, I could tell by the look in your eyes that you do. Oh, yes, you do.

Her limbs tingled with the promise of a mounting orgasm.

Her breaths came quicker, her legs tensed beneath the water. She bit down on her lower lip, craving the release.

"Fiona?"

Her hand stilled. "Um...Yeah?" *Crap. Crap. Crap.* She looked around the empty bathroom and crossed her arms over her chest, feeling exposed and embarrassed. She drained the tub and reached for a towel.

"Pasta okay for dinner?" Jake called through the door.

She'd rather have him for dinner, and now that she had what promised to be a magnificent orgasm trapped inside her, she wouldn't be able to think, much less eat.

"Sure," she managed.

She dried off at a frantic pace and pulled his T-shirt over her head. It hung nearly to her knees, and it dawned on her that she had no underwear to put on. She knotted the end of his shirt at her waist and looked at the sweatpants with dismay. Not exactly the right attire to try to woo an ex-boyfriend back into her arms, but what could she do? She pulled them on, then rolled down the waistband to just below her belly button. Jake was a thick, muscular guy. Fiona wasn't willowy, but she was going to have a hard time keeping these pants on for reasons other than the naughty thoughts racing through her mind.

She scanned the sink for a comb, then reached for a vanity drawer and hesitated. He could have anything in there. Another woman's stuff, condoms, sex toys. *Anything.* Her stomach tightened, and not in the luxurious way it had when she was busy getting dirty while she was supposed to be getting clean. She decided against the show-and-tell scenario and finger-combed her hair, fluffed it as best she could, and tried to pinch the flushed look from her cheeks. No luck there, of course. She reached for the doorknob and her nerves prickled.

The bedroom was empty. Fiona let out a relieved sigh and took a moment to see just how different grown-up Jake was from the young man she remembered. The furniture was masculine and substantial, made from dark, expensive-looking wood. The brown bedspread was several inches thick and looked soft as butter. She glanced at the door, tiptoed over to the bed, and ran her finger over the to-die-for softness of the comforter, just like the T-shirt he'd given her to wear, which felt like an old favorite. This was a whole new side of Jake she'd never experienced before. He was always so easygoing, never giving two hoots about material things beyond typical boy toys—dirt bikes, hunting rifles, and cars.

The dresser had not a speck of dust on it, which told her that he paid his cleaning people well, because as organized as Jake was—and he was mighty organized for a man—he'd never been one to settle down long enough to do a load of laundry, much less dust.

He's drying my clothes.

Well, that didn't exactly count. If she didn't have her own

clothes she'd have to wear his home, and she was sure he wouldn't want her leaving with them. She picked up a framed photograph of Jake and Pierce from the dresser. It must have been taken in the last few years, because all the innocence and softness of young men was gone. They looked like rugged men, both unfairly handsome, as was their entire family. But they'd never acted like it when they were younger. She remembered noticing something different in Jake at the Brewery, something beyond the conflicting emotions in his eyes. He'd been tense in a way that had shaken her a little. It wasn't until he'd stormed out with Sarah in tow that she'd realized what it was. She'd heard the rumors, seen pictures in the rag magazines. It wasn't usual for a stuntman to be photographed, but Jake wasn't just any stuntman. He traveled in circles of famous movie stars and dated some of the most glamorous models and actresses so often that the paparazzi had begun following him early on in his career. She knew he was a player of the worst kind, but to see it firsthand had shocked her. In all those magazines, she'd never once seen him look happy, and he hadn't looked happy that night.

She gazed down at the picture in her hands, and the smile on his full lips reached his eyes. He was happy when he was with his family. He should be—he had a great family. A family who loved him and supported one another. Her family was the same way, or at least it had been before her father had left. Sadness washed through her. At least she knew her father, which was more than Jake ever had. Her heart squeezed at that thought.

"That was taken at Ross's engagement dinner."

She startled as Jake came to her side. "I'm sorry. I didn't mean to snoop." She set the picture down on the dresser.

Jake smiled, looking more relaxed than she felt as he placed a hand on her upper back and leaned in close. "Yes, you did."

His husky voice sent a shiver down her spine. The fact that she heard a smile in his voice only made her feel more like a naughty girl who'd gotten caught with her hand in the candy jar.

He pressed his hand a little firmer to her back. "Come on. Let's go downstairs."

He sounded so relaxed that she wondered if she'd imagined the sexual vibrations between them. *Oh my God, that would be just perfect, wouldn't it?* He walked behind her down the stairs, making her self-conscious. Jake used to love to tease her about how cute her butt was, and it was all she could think about now. She hadn't spent much time worrying about how her body had changed since she was eighteen, and she wasn't really worried about it now, but thanks to the heat of his gaze—which she didn't have to see in order to sense—she was aware of her shape now more than ever and was glad she'd continued running all these years. Could Jake send any stronger conflicting messages? A minute ago she thought she'd imagined their connection, and now she could practically feel his eyes blazing against her back and her legs were turning to spaghetti again.

As they stepped into the living room, Fiona noticed that the whole house felt very masculine, and although Jake was masculine to his core, she wondered if he'd even had a hand in the decorating. She didn't *feel* him anywhere in the house, except maybe in the bedroom.

She followed him into the spacious kitchen, where he opened one of the darkest wood cabinets she'd ever seen and handed her two wineglasses.

"Sorry I don't have smaller clothes for you to wear."

"No, you're not." She smiled with the tease.

He grabbed a bottle of wine and invaded her personal space, sending her heart into a frenzy.

"No, I'm really not." His eyes darkened and locked on hers. "In fact, I kind of wish I was out of clothes altogether."

This was the teasing, flirty Jake she knew and loved, but she didn't trust that the angry Jake had left the scene that quickly. She followed him into a cozy, dimly lit alcove off of the living room, where he'd set a table for two. Even in the driving rain, the view of the city was amazing, all sparking lights blurred against the dark sky.

He pulled out a chair for her and scooted it in beneath her. She was surprised by how intimate his gestures were becoming and a little skeptical about what it all meant.

"So, you're done being mad at me?" she asked while he filled their glasses. Dinner smelled delicious, and it looked even better. She hadn't even known he could cook, but the meal before her was a visionary delight of different-shaped pastas, colorful vegetables, and a creamy sauce that made her salivate almost as much as Jake in his tight T-shirt did.

"I wouldn't jump to that conclusion." He sipped his wine and narrowed his eyes into a seductive gaze. "But you're here, and we have history."

"So…what? You feel obligated to be nice to me?" *Why did I have to ask that?*

He leaned back and picked up his fork. "I don't know what I feel, but it's dinner and conversation. We're not jumping in the sack together."

Okay, then. Cleared that right up.

She lowered her eyes and speared a piece of pasta, alarmingly annoyed. Why would she think they were going to jump in the sack? And with his reputation, why didn't he want to? That should probably tell her more than his acts of generosity ever could. The problem was, she had no idea if it was a good or a bad message.

She stole another look at him, and his smirk told her he was trying to get to her. Well, two could play at that game.

"This is really good. Thanks for making it. I didn't even know you could cook."

His lips quirked up in a cocky grin. "I'm a man of many talents."

Wow. "A man who can cook—that is a talent. But a man who cooks wearing nothing but an apron, now, that's a sight worth seeing."

Jake held his fork up with a piece of pasta on a tong and looked at it as he twirled it slowly. "Aprons don't hang low enough in the front to cover my junk, so I choose to go without."

Fiona's fork stilled halfway to her mouth, which went dry. She set her fork down and drank her wine in one gulp. Jake was quick to refill her glass.

"You were great on the set today." She had to change the subject because Jake could outplay her in the sexual innuendo game. She didn't even know why she'd thought she could compete.

His brows drew together. "All in a day's work. You and Patch got pretty close, huh?"

"He was really helpful. Everyone was, actually. Even Zane was easy to talk to and super helpful."

"Zane's a good guy. He's a close friend, actually." Jake clenched his jaw, and Fiona knew she'd struck a nerve. She decided to play it up.

"You know, he's even more handsome in person than on the big screen. He asked me if I was going to the cast dinner next Friday night."

"Next Friday night?" He finished his wine and refilled both of their glasses.

"Yeah, Trish and I are going." She sipped her wine, feeling more relaxed and bolder than she had before. Wine was her new best friend.

"Are you going to be there?"

"Yeah, I'll be there," he grumbled.

"Great. Then we'll probably see each other." She was glad he couldn't see under the table, where her feet were bouncing with nervous energy.

They finished eating *and* finished the bottle of wine. At some point Jake got up and fetched another bottle. When he returned, he sat beside her instead of across the table. They talked about Luke and Daisy's wedding and how strange it was for Fiona to see Trish and Jake making a film together, which reminded Fiona that she knew someone else in the business.

"Well, you remember Kaira Pepper, don't you?" she asked. Kaira's family had moved to Trusty for her last two years of high school, when her father had tried to make a go of farming. After a heart attack took his life, Kaira and her mother moved back to Illinois, to be closer to her mother's family.

"Everyone remembers Kaira. Hot little blond number, now a porn star." He guzzled his wine.

Fiona leaned forward, absentmindedly placing her hand on his thigh. "She's not a porn star. She's a model."

"Whatever. Same, same."

"Totally not the same." She finished her wine and suddenly became very aware of the feel of his muscles, hot and hard, beneath her hand.

"You're right. I don't even know why I said it. They're not the same thing, but she really did do porn." He took her hand in his and rose to his feet, pulling her up with him. She swayed, grabbing hold of his shirt for balance. His eyes went dark and sexy again, and it was all Fiona could do to keep from going up on her toes and kissing him. She fisted her hand in his shirt, telling herself not to do it, but her brain must have had a bad connection to her body, because she was lifting up on her toes with a bead on tasting those delicious lips of his.

No. No. No. Yes, please, yes.

Jake slipped an arm around her waist and shifted his eyes away. She felt his body go rigid right before he took a step to the side, bringing her with him.

"Come on. I'll show you a little of Kaira's work." His tone was gruffer than it had been a moment ago.

She felt her chest and neck flush as he guided her down a staircase and through a large room with a pool table and bar and into another, darker room with theater-style seating. *Wow.* The old Jake would have scoffed at theater-style seating, seen it as pretentious.

As he dug around in a cabinet, she realized what he'd said. Was he really going to put on porn? *Oh crap.* She wasn't ready to watch porn with Jake. With a remote control in one hand, he sat on the floor in front of the seats and patted the spot beside him. Her heart melted a little. There was definitely still some of the old Jake in him.

He pushed a button, and every nerve in Fiona's body strung tight as she waited to see what he was putting on. Kaira appeared front and center, wearing barely there lingerie and looking sexy enough for Fiona to consider changing teams.

"Wow. She's totally hot," she whispered. She heard Jake laugh under his breath. It was a welcome sound, which eased her embarrassment after almost kissing him—again.

"You're right. It's not porn, but she is nearly naked."

"I'm almost afraid to ask why you have this." She couldn't take her eyes off of Kaira, strutting her curvaceous figure down a runway in front of a roomful of people, along with six other incredibly hot models who looked ten feet tall.

"Because she gave it to me." He turned to face her, and she wondered if he was trying to get her jealous.

It was working.

"So…you dated her?" She hated the pitiful weakness in her voice.

"I don't date, Fiona." Angry Jake was back. Tension rolled off of him. "She wanted to get into acting and thought if I passed this along to my agent, he could help."

"Oh." *You don't date?* She hadn't really heard the rest.

"He couldn't help her, but it was worth a try." He turned off the video and faced her in the dark, leaning one arm on the couch behind her. "Why are you looking at me like that?"

"Like what?" *Gulp.* Her stomach had tanked when she'd thought of Jake dating Kaira, and she knew that despite his clearing up that he didn't date, her eyes probably still relayed disappointment. Not only that, but if he didn't date, then why did she think she could win him over? Maybe he could see the hope in her deflating, too.

His tone softened. "The way you looked at me that time we went to the 4H festival and I accidentally let go of the helium balloon I'd won for you."

She smiled, having forgotten about that. She probably was looking at him in the same way. "I wanted it for that little girl we'd seen in the wheelchair, remember?"

His hand dropped to her back, and she felt him fiddling with the ends of her hair like he used to, swamping her with warm and wonderful memories and filling her with hope.

"Yeah, I remember." His voice was low and husky. She didn't need to see him clearly to know he was feeling the same spark of heat she was. "You always had the biggest heart." His hand stilled between her shoulder blades, then moved away.

She wanted it back. He turned away, and the air in the room shifted, became cooler.

"Well, you had the biggest heart except where I was concerned."

Oh no. She'd worried over having this discussion for years, and now that it was upon her, she could barely think.

Everything she'd planned on saying was lost in the hurt that lingered in his tone.

"Jake."

"It's okay, Fiona. It was probably a good thing that we broke up."

"A good thing?" She couldn't tell if he was deflecting or serious.

"Sure. I mean, how many people who were together in high school stay together forever? I would have just hurt you, and it would've ended badly."

"That's not true, and you know it."

"Do I?"

He faced her again, and now that her eyes had adjusted to the darkness, she saw the anger lingering in his eyes, no matter how he'd softened his tone.

"You loved me, Jake. You could have cheated on me anytime in those two years. There were plenty of opportunities for both of us to stray."

"And you're sure I never did?" He arched a brow, and for a split second she doubted what she knew to be true.

She nodded, unable to find her voice.

His hand landed on her back again, and she stiffened against it to keep from relaxing into his touch.

"You're right. I never would have back then. But now..." He shrugged.

"I was messed up back then, Jake. When my dad left, it

totally messed with my head."

His hand caressed her back. "That was a rough time for your whole family. I remember Reggie storming back into town with an ax to grind."

Reggie had been interning in New York the summer their father had left. He had become superprotective of her and Shea after their father left.

"None of my brothers have forgiven our father. I think that's the reason Reggie became a private investigator. He was never going to be duped again—at least that's how it seemed." Brent and Jesse lived in Harborside, Massachusetts, and avoided their father at all costs. And then there was Finn, who was a smoke jumper and thrived on risk as much as Jake did. He had a heart of gold—except where their father was concerned.

"And how about you, Fi? Did you ever make peace with your old man?"

She nodded. "As best as I could, sure."

Jake looked away. "Good. I'm glad for that. I know you were close."

"Jake, I'm sorry you got ripped off in the father department."

He swung his chin back in her direction with a slight smile on his lips. "Yeah, such is life. People get ripped off in lots of departments."

Ouch.

He rubbed his neck and stretched it to the right, then the left, then rubbed it again.

"Here, let me rub it for you." She shifted so her body faced his.

"I'm fine."

"Oh, come on, Jake. I remember how your neck tenses up, and you took a hard fall today. It's the least I can do after you rescued me." She gently turned his body so she could reach his neck from behind. She used both hands to massage the sides of his neck, then pressed her thumbs into the tight muscles and stroked down under his shirt and away from his spine, trying not to think about the desire pooling low in her belly.

With one hand, Jake reached behind him and pulled his shirt over his head. Fiona's breath left her lungs in a rush. This might be too much. Her chest prickled with heat as her hands settled back onto his neck. He placed his hand over hers, pressing it firmly to his skin.

"I'd forgotten how good you were with your hands."

She closed her eyes, trying not to hold on to the innuendo in his voice. She was so filled with desire for him that she feared she was turning everything he did into what she wanted to see.

He squeezed her hand, then released it, and she felt him relax into her touch. She swallowed to keep from making any sounds of pleasure, because touching Jake again brought pleasure to every one of her senses, except taste, and, boy, did she ever want to taste him. She slid her hands over the crest of his shoulders, kneading the muscles that were corded tight.

"I never meant to hurt you," she said just above a whisper, a little surprised at the words. She hadn't been thinking about saying them; they'd just come out on their own.

He nodded silently.

She slid her hands down his biceps and scooted closer, pressing her thighs against his hips to stabilize herself so she could press harder as she kneaded the tension from his arms.

Jake sighed and leaned his head back against her chest. She blinked rapidly against the threat of tears. She felt his barriers coming down and knew she wasn't imagining it, and she reveled in everything about him, the smell of soap on his skin, the feel of him unwinding, accepting their friendship. After how he'd reacted at the bar, it was more than she'd thought possible.

"We always were hanging by a moment," he said. "But I never realized it back then. I always thought we were solid." He reached behind her and wrapped his arm around her waist, hugging her to his back. "But I guess you were like 'Drops of Jupiter.'"

"Train sings that," she whispered. She knew the song well. It was all about a girl who leaves her boyfriend to find herself, but only finds herself lonely in the end. They could have written that song about *her*.

"Did you find everything that you were looking for, Fi?"

He turned his upper body and gazed into her eyes. "*Is* heaven overrated?"

"Anything without you is overrated. That's what I found out."

He touched his forehead to hers and her hand slid down his chest. She felt his heart thumping to the same frantic beat as hers. Felt him press his hand more firmly on her back.

"Fi, I'll disappoint you," he whispered.

She shook her head, whispered, "I don't believe it."

His hand moved up her back to her neck, stealing her thoughts completely. His lips were so close, but even more overwhelming was knowing his heart was opening, even if cautiously. She felt it in his touch, saw it in the depths of emotion in his eyes.

"I don't want to hurt you," he said with a serious tone.

"I never meant to hurt you, and I'll spend my life being sorry. I'll never do it again, Jake. I've missed you too much."

"Did you hear me, Fi?" His brows drew together. "I'm not the same guy I was."

She ran her hand through his hair, and he made a noise in his throat that rattled through her. "You're not the guy you are now, either. You're somewhere in between, and I want to find out who that person is."

"You're my kryptonite," he said just above a whisper as he tugged her in closer, their lips brushing. "I never could resist you."

"Then don't."

He searched her eyes, and she hoped he saw how much she wanted this, how much she wanted *him*. In the next second, their lips met, and her body felt as though it had burst into flames. The kiss was soft and rough at once, tentative for only a second, maybe two, then aggressive and greedy. His tongue swept over hers. He tightened his grip on her and tugged her down to the floor with him, sweeping her beneath him, folding her into his embrace as he deepened the kiss. His lips were as soft as she remembered, but his scruff scratching her cheeks was new and tantalizing. The kiss was more intense, better, needier and more possessive. She never wanted the kiss to end, and when his hand slid beneath her T-shirt and he brushed the underside of her breast with his thumb, she moaned with pleasure.

Yes, please. Touch me. Make me yours. Become mine.

Jake pulled back, brows drawn together again. "Hear that?"

She couldn't hear past the rush of blood racing through her veins and her heavy breathing. She shook her head.

"Damn." He sat up, taking her with him, and gazed up at the ceiling.

"What is it?" She heard something faint but couldn't make it out.

"Sorry, Fi." He rose to his feet and helped her to hers. He dragged his eyes down her body. She felt exposed. Her nipples were hard, she was damp between her legs, and her insides quivered with need. "Christ, look at you."

She reached up and touched her hair. "I couldn't find a comb."

"No, you're..." He shook his head. "Way too hot for these assholes." He pulled her against him and inhaled a long breath. The kiss he pressed to the top of her head was reminiscent of years past and made her feel safe in his arms.

"Come on." He took her hand and led her upstairs. Voices and laughter filtered in from outside. It had stopped raining, and there were at least ten people milling about by the pool.

"I'm sorry. I didn't know you were expecting people." She crossed her arms over her chest. She wasn't even wearing a bra, much less underwear. "Where are my clothes?"

With an arm securely around her, he took her back to the laundry room and closed the door behind them. He took her clothes from the dryer.

"I wasn't *expecting* people. This is my life now, Fi." He searched her eyes, then cupped her cheeks and kissed her again, long and passionate, in a way that felt strangely like an apology.

She didn't know what to say and probably couldn't have spoken at the moment if she wanted to. She wanted another kiss—or a hundred more. She turned her back and pulled off his T-shirt, then put on her bra. Jake wrapped his arms around her from behind, kissing her neck. She stilled long enough to enjoy a full-body shudder from the swipe of his tongue up the length of her neck.

"This is your life." She drew her brows together. "What does that mean?" She put her shirt on, then turned to face him. He had a hungry look in his eyes, but while she was able to think, she wanted to understand what he meant.

"Jake?" It came out as a plea.

"I'm sorry." He shook his head as if to clear his mind. "People come over pretty often, without warning."

"Jake?" a female voice called down the hall.

Fiona felt her eyes widen. Jake ignored whoever was calling him and closed the gap between them, pulling Fiona's hips against his hard length. He kissed her again, a passionate kiss that made her knees go soft and left her wanting more.

"You'd better get dressed because that thong you're holding is reminding me that you're not wearing any underwear."

She could barely think after that searing-hot kiss and with him looking at her like he wanted to devour her. She was about as functional as a drunk.

"Jake?" The woman's voice sounded closer, startling Fiona's brain into functioning again.

"Maybe you should go see your friend while I finish changing." She didn't want him to go. She wanted him to stay and kiss her again and again, but that woman's voice was drawing out Fiona's claws of jealousy. If she was going to have a chance with Jake, this was the tip of the iceberg of things she'd have to be strong enough to deal with.

JAKE KNEW HE needed to deal with the woman in the hall, but he didn't want to leave Fiona. The kisses they'd shared stirred memories and emotions that he thought he'd long ago lost the ability to feel, and he wanted to feel them over and over again—with Fiona. He'd forgotten how a kiss could transport him someplace warm and erotic, wonderful and illicit, instead of just being a vessel for releasing pent-up anger. He'd forgotten how a kiss from Fiona could do those things for him, and now that he remembered, he didn't want to take a chance that one of those goddamn actors out there would find her just as appealing and come with far less baggage than he was carrying around.

"Jake?" The woman's voice was getting farther away.

He breathed a sigh of relief.

Fiona turned around and slid Jake's sweatpants slowly down her hips. Holy hell. There was no way he'd be able to keep his hands off of her. He shoved his hands into the pockets of his jeans and turned away to keep from pulling her close again.

"God, Jake. People just come and go? I feel like I'm in high school, hiding out at a party."

"If we were in high school, hiding out at a party, I don't

think you'd be pulling *up* those cute little shorts."

He turned back as she zipped her fly and watched at him with a coy smile. He reached for her hand, trying to ignore the voice in the back of his mind reminding him that while she could take him where no other woman could, she had the power to crush him. She had left him once, when he was good and kind. A completely different person than he was now. When he was a better person. What hope did he have that she'd stick around this time with that hanging like a noose around his neck?

"I can call a cab so you can hang with your friends."

Friends. The term made him cringe inside. Sure, he had a handful of friends he could call if he was in a pinch, but he wasn't fooling himself. They were all part of the act that had become part of him. They came over for the parties or the prestige of being at Jake Braden's house. They kept him from spending time in his own head, picking apart all the emotions behind the floodgates that Fiona opened in the blink of an eye.

He pushed the uncomfortable thoughts away and pulled her against him.

"Not a chance." This felt right, having her with him, holding her. God, he actually *wanted* to hold her, not just sleep with her. It had been years since he'd felt that desire—and a rude awakening to how far he'd fallen.

"Jake, it's okay. I don't mind."

He heard in her voice that it wasn't really okay, even if she wanted him to believe it was. Maybe she even wanted to think it was, but it didn't take a rocket scientist to see the hope in her eyes.

He also knew what the people beyond the laundry room door represented: the man he'd become. He was so conflicted that his gut ached. He felt as though he were playing a game of tug-of-war. On one end was Fiona, beckoning him back to the safety of who he'd been, who *they'd* been, and offering him love that he knew was all encompassing. But he couldn't forget that it had also been disposable, at least to her. Nor could he forget that there was a world between who he had been and who he was now. On the other side of the rope were all those people on the other side of the door, and a whole hell of a lot more, representing the life he'd created, the reputation he'd built. How was he supposed to navigate the two?

He folded Fiona in his arms again and searched her eyes. She couldn't know how to fix all the things crawling out of the dark places in his mind, and even though she'd hurt him once, she nurtured parts of him that opened his eyes to what he'd become. And if he really was the person he portrayed... Hell, he had a lot to figure out, but one thing was for sure. Fiona deserved honesty.

"Fi, I can't make you any promises. Not about us, or about what we did downstairs. And I definitely can't make you any promises about myself. Most of the time, beyond being a stuntman, I'm not even sure I know who I am anymore."

She swallowed hard, and he could tell by the watery look in her baby blues that she was trying hard to hold back tears.

"What I can tell you is this. I've never felt anything like what I felt when we kissed. You do something to me that no other woman ever has, and frankly, I don't want any other woman to try."

"But?" The hope in her eyes dimmed with his admission.

"But there's a lifetime between who I was and who I am now. I don't know how a person goes backward, or if it's even possible. I'm destined to mess up, and maybe in a big way. I don't know."

She rested her forehead on his chest and gripped his shirt in her hands. "I know."

He placed his hands on her cheeks and tilted her head up so he could see her eyes. He needed her to hear what he had to say, and he had to know that she understood the weight of his words—the ones he said and the ones yet to come.

"I hurt you, Jake, so it would only be fair."

"What are we, six? There is nothing fair about hurting someone who means something to you. If anyone knows that, it's us, right? Our fathers taught us the hell out of that lesson." He paused long enough for those words to settle into his *own* mind.

"I have no clue how I'll act in ten minutes, much less a week or a month." Jake reminded himself that honesty was important, because he wanted to promise Fiona he could do the right thing, and he knew it wasn't a promise he could make.

"It's not like I'm asking for a white picket fence and three point five children. I just want to try being us again. Day by day."

"Day by day?"

She shrugged, blinked away the dampness in her eyes. "Jake, I've got a lot of years out there, too. I'm not a saint, either. We both have stuff to work on. All I know is that I've been drawn back to you for years, and I've been too afraid to act on it. I was slightly intimidated by your success, but even more afraid you'd hate me for how I ended things...which I guess you kind of did, and I don't blame you. But as much as I tried to push away my feelings, I couldn't."

"Fi..." He didn't know what to say. He was still processing that she'd been drawn back to him for years but had been afraid to act on it. She was afraid because of the way he'd intentionally built a wall between them, and now he was kicking himself for it. She might say she wasn't a saint, but he knew Fiona wasn't a slut, either. She didn't have it in her to sleep with any guy who made a pass at her. The realization that he'd done just that with women nearly brought him to his knees. He wanted to thank her for taking the chance on him, but every way he tried to form the right words sounded weak in his mind, so he said the only thing he could manage.

"Okay. One day at a time. I think I can do that. I want to do that." It wasn't like he was used to committing for more than an hour at a time. This was a big step for him and it scared him, but he wanted to try. Damn, did he want to try. He held her again, silently hoping he wouldn't hurt her.

Jake walked out of the laundry room, his arm possessively draped over Fiona's shoulder, thinking about the previous night, when it had occurred to him how deep of a hole he'd dug for himself with this current lifestyle. He wasn't sure he could ever get out of it, much less whether he really wanted to. But as he walked into the living room and took stock of the people milling about, all he could think about was the woman he was holding and how he wanted to carry her upstairs and kiss her until they both forgot the years that had passed since they'd been together. That wasn't likely to happen, as Megan Flexx, an A-list, buxom brunette actress, wearing a skintight navy dress that barely covered her ass, was wrapping her arms around his neck and kissing his cheek despite Fiona's presence.

Jake gently extracted himself from Megan's grip. "Megan, this is Fiona. Fiona Steele, Megan Flexx."

"You were in the movie *Transformation*, right?" Fiona smiled at Megan, but Jake felt her shoulders stiffen.

Megan ran her fingers through her long hair and raked her green eyes down Fiona's body in a way that made Jake want to kick her out of his house. He tightened his grip on Fiona.

"Yes." Megan chewed a piece of gum like a cow, pausing

to blow a bubble. "Jake did the stunts in that film. That's how we met—right, Jake?" She ran her fingers down his chest.

Jake took a step back before she could get those nimble little fingers any lower.

"Uh, yeah." *Crap.* Fiona's feigned smile faded fast. "I want to introduce Fiona to a few people. We'll see you around." He guided Fiona toward the French doors leading to the back-yard. "I'm sorry about her."

"It's okay. You have a life, Jake. I get that. You weren't exactly expecting me."

You can say that again.

"Jake!" Kenny Clayton, an up-and-coming actor, waved from the bar by the pool, where he had a redhead draped on one side and a blonde on the other.

Jake felt like he was moving in slow motion as laughter and music filled his ears. Susie Clifton, a petite actress with big brown eyes, hollow cheeks, and slightly crooked teeth, handed Jake a drink.

"Thanks." Jake tightened his grip on Fiona.

Susie gave Fiona the same once-over, only slightly less noticeable than Megan's. Fiona was sexy as hell, and she was a natural beauty. She didn't wear much makeup, but she'd never needed it, and even with her hair tousled from the rain, she looked gorgeous. He was glad when Susie flashed a genuine smile and held a hand out in greeting.

"Hi. I'm Susie." Her Southern drawl was thick now,

which was how Jake knew she was sincere. She used her LA dialect when she was trying to impress, as she had when she'd first met him, and her hometown twang when she was just being a normal girl. It didn't happen very often.

"Hi. I'm Fiona."

Jake felt some of the tension ease from her shoulders.

"You are *so* lucky. Fiona is such a great name, unlike Susie. I mean, could I be any plainer?" Susie touched Jake's hand. "You keeping her all to yourself? She must be very special." Without waiting for a response, she took Fiona's hand and pulled her from Jake's grasp. "Come on. Let's get you a drink, too." She looked over her shoulder at Jake. "Go mingle. I'll take good care of Fiona."

Jake had the urge to follow them. He didn't want Fiona around the actors and up-and-comers. They were all players. Hell, nearly everyone in LA was a player—at least it seemed that way in his circles. He watched Kenny and the guys check out Fiona, and his chest constricted with jealousy, as it had years ago when they'd gone to the County Fair and a group of hotshot seniors from a neighboring town were checking out Fiona. He'd taken things into his own hands back then and warned them off. He hadn't felt that way toward any woman since. Until now.

"Dude, you okay?"

Jake turned and found Zane downing a drink.

"Yeah. I didn't know you were coming over."

Zane shrugged. "Figured if I could find a soft body to keep me warm tonight, it would be here." He patted Jake on the back and nodded toward Fiona. "Mm-mm-mm. She's a sweet one, isn't she?"

"Yeah. Real sweet." He gritted his teeth against the urge to warn Zane away from Fiona, but she wasn't his to claim. Not yet anyway. *Day by day.* What did that mean in terms of monogamy? He watched Kenny sling an arm over Fiona's shoulder and whisper something that made her laugh. He was shocked with the realization that he knew what he wanted *day by day* to mean. The idea of Fiona with another man made him crazy. It hadn't been easy to ignore the fact that she might be with other men when they were miles apart, but he'd managed it fairly well. Now that she was here with him and he'd tasted her sweetness again and held her...Now that he'd looked into her eyes and allowed her to touch the part of him that he'd buried away, it was impossible for him to ignore the cording of his muscles at the thought of her with another man.

"She's coming to the cast dinner. I might hit her up there." Zane sucked back the rest of his drink and lifted his chin in the direction of the bar. "I'm gonna fill up. Want one?"

Jake grabbed his arm much rougher than he intended to. "Cast dinner. Not a good idea, Zane."

Zane's brows knitted together. "Why not?"

"Because I've got something going on with her." Wow,

did he really just claim her? Jake took stock of the six-million-dollar smile spreading across Zane's face. Yeah, he'd claimed her, all right, and he had a feeling it was a smart move.

"Nice. That was fast." Zane glanced at Megan, who was making a beeline for Jake. "Want me to keep Fiona busy while you swing downstairs with Megan?"

Jake bit back the unfamiliar distaste at Zane's comment, and it took him by surprise. He and Zane had been each other's wingmen, and before he'd run into Fiona in Trusty, he'd probably have taken him up on the offer. But now he felt like that guy he'd been, the guy like Zane, was a world away from the man he'd like to be.

Jake shifted his gaze to Fiona, holding a glass between her hands, tension evident in the strength of her grip, eyes locked on the ground. Kenny's mouth was moving a mile a minute. There were two other guys with them who must have come with him, because Jake had no clue who they were. Susie was busy talking with another woman by the bar. She'd left Fiona alone. His protective instincts kicked into gear, spurring his legs into action as he blazed a path toward her.

"No, man. I'm good," he said to Zane before heading for Fiona. She must have sensed Jake's gaze on her as he closed the distance between them. She lifted her eyes as he slipped an arm around her waist, noting the relieved look in her eyes.

"Let's get out of here," he whispered as he turned back toward the house.

"But your friends?" She glanced over her shoulder. "I didn't get to say goodbye to Susie."

Zane lifted his glass as they walked by.

"Susie was really nice. I'd like to say goodbye to her, at least."

Jake was used to women wanting to leave parties with him, following his lead, not arguing about staying to say goodbye to someone they'd just met.

"She's fine. She won't care."

Fiona stopped walking and pressed her lips together. "Maybe not, but I do. It's rude, Jake. Just give me two minutes." She headed back toward Susie without giving him a chance to stop her.

Jake watched every determined step she took and noticed every longing gaze from the guys standing by the bar. Fiona walked directly to Susie without even a glance at the other men. She said something, to which Susie smiled, and then they embraced. It had been so long since Jake had cared about anyone that he'd almost forgotten what it felt like to take extra time to get to really know people. And there was Fiona, doing it naturally, at the risk of losing time they'd have had together. He respected the hell out of her for it and realized that he wanted her to see those qualities in him again, too.

When she joined him, she was much more relaxed. He laced his fingers with hers as they walked through the house.

"Thanks, Jake. She's so sweet. I really like her." She slowed their pace again. "Don't you want to at least go say something to your friends?"

"They're fine. They're not really friends in the sense that you think of friends, Fi." He guided her through the living room, snagged his keys from the table by the door, and headed toward the garage. "Most of them are takers, clingers. I never realized how superficially I knew most of them until just now." *And it bugs the shit out of me.*

The overhead lights turned on when he opened the garage door.

"I still can't believe these are all yours," she said, pointing at the cars.

Jake opened the door of his Mercedes McLaren for Fiona. "Far cry from who I am in Trusty, right?" He had a feeling that these luxuries would be another turnoff for Fiona. She was getting a clear view of his world, and damn if he didn't get a sinking feeling in his gut.

"You could say that." She gave him the address of her apartment again and fidgeted with the ends of her hair.

Jake reached across the console and took her hand in his. "Two worlds colliding, huh?"

"You might say that." Her voice was so soft he barely heard her. She gazed out the window, giving him a chance to drink her in. She twisted the ends of her hair in that nervous, adorable way she had that made him want to scoop her into his lap and reassure her.

It was surprising how for sixteen years Jake had felt like he was trekking through quicksand, and now it was as if those years had barely existed. Fiona's brows furrowed, then eased, and then her eyes narrowed. He saw the maturity in her features now that he'd missed back in the Brewery. Her eyes were more intense, as if she'd seen things that had strengthened her. He wondered if she'd been hurt along the away, and the thought tweaked those protective urges again. He realized the magnitude of what she'd risked that night in the bar and how it had taken tremendous courage for her to approach him.

You were strong enough to do what I've been pretending I didn't want to for years.

FIONA COULDN'T FIGHT the feeling that she might have bitten off more than she could chew. She didn't belong in Jake's new world. She wasn't a partier, at least not on a daily basis, and when she'd seen Megan Flexx drape herself over Jake, she'd wanted to claw her eyes out.

Jake opened the car door for her in the parking lot of her apartment complex and pulled her into an embrace before lowering his lips to hers and taking her into another thrilling kiss that pushed all those worries away.

He held her close, his eyes shifting as they crossed the

parking lot. *Some things never change.* She smiled to herself, remembering when they were younger, how he was always aware of their surroundings. As if at any time someone might jump out of the darkness and he'd be there to protect her. She'd always felt safe with him, and when he'd set that dark, protective gaze on her by the pool in his backyard, she'd felt it surrounding her like a safety net. It felt so right to be with Jake again, but around those people at his house, even though he'd done all the right things, she was uncomfortable. She'd known that he was popular, and she'd even anticipated seeing women clamoring to get to him, but to see it taking place in his own house was a shock. And knowing that men and women showed up unannounced was even more concerning.

One day at a time.

The apartment she'd rented was the only one on the top floor. They were alone in the dimly lit hallway as she unlocked the door and pushed it open, revealing the cozy living room. Beige walls were accented with cheap-framed artwork of the LA coastline. A faux-leather couch sat against the far wall beside a wooden end table with a large lamp that arced overhead.

Jake leaned against the doorframe, his dark eyes moving over the simple interior.

"Want to come in?" She took a step inside. Jake placed a hand on her arm and stopped her. His eyes went dark and lustful. He drew her back into his arms, and when their bodies connected, hers warmed in all the right places.

"I can't come in," he said in a gravelly voice. He slid his hand to the dip at the top of her ass, bringing with it a shiver of memories of that hand brushing her breast.

Her body hummed with desire again, and she wondered if he could feel it, too.

"Right. You have friends waiting. I'm sorry."

"Not because I have friends over." He ran his knuckle down her cheek. "Because if I go in there, I'm going to carry you into the bedroom, remove these pesky clothes..." He fingered the collar of her T-shirt, making her pant like a puppy. "And bury myself so deep inside you that we'll both forget what it was ever like to be with anyone else."

Yes. Please.

He pressed on her lower back, bringing her hips against the steel rod in his pants. She felt herself go damp and flush from chest to cheeks.

"Mm. You like that dirty talk." He nuzzled against her neck and whispered, "See? I didn't forget everything."

His lips skimmed her neck as he pulled the collar of her T-shirt to the side and settled his mouth over the curve of her shoulder. She sucked in a breath. He remembered more than just the words she loved to hear.

Her head fell back with a rush of excitement she hadn't felt in years as he sucked and licked the very spot that brought her up on her toes, craving more. One hand pressed against her lower back, while his other hand—*oh, that wandering, talented hand*—slid to the edge of her shorts. She fisted her hands in his shirt and pressed her mouth shut to keep herself from pleading for more.

"I want to touch you so badly," he whispered.

"We should go inside," she said in one heated breath.

"If we do, I won't leave," he said gruffly, and slid his finger beneath the edge of her shorts, rubbing her through her panties. "Christ, you're so wet."

She widened her legs, and it was all the invitation he needed. He took her in a mind-blowing kiss as he slid a finger beneath the damp material. She didn't care that they were standing outside her apartment. She was too lost in pleasure to think as he deepened the kiss and stroked her into a clawing, panting frenzy of need and took her over the edge with skill that could come only from someone who had known her body intimately for a very long time.

Chapter Ten

WEDNESDAY MORNING FIONA planned on walking to work again, not because of how fate had stepped in the day before, but because she really needed to clear her head. Thoughts of Jake swarmed like bees to honey, attaching to every thought. She stared into the open refrigerator.

Breakfast? *Hm…Jake sounds yummy.*

She should text Trish…*I forgot to give Jake my number.*

Next Friday's the cast dinner. *I'll see Jake.*

She had it bad, and at the same time, she had a nagging doubt about whether she'd misjudged what she could handle. She wanted to believe that she could deal with Jake's lifestyle, but she'd never imagined how wild it actually was. It worried her on many levels. What if he'd had unprotected sex? Oh gosh. There she was heading straight down the sex road again. She'd been so pent up with need last night she'd come fast and hard, and her body had ached for more all night long.

Sex with Jake was pure, unadulterated bliss when they

were younger. She could only imagine how much better it would be now. There was some value in gaining experience.

Her blissful thoughts deflated with the thought of how he'd gained that experience.

Stopitstopitstopit.

She closed the refrigerator and went to answer her ringing cell phone. It was probably Trish calling. She had left two hours before Fiona last night to meet with her agent. It was weird to think that she was spending time in Trish and Jake's world. It all seemed so removed from her own life, and here she was in LA after all these years. Then again, all sorts of strange things were happening at the moment.

Her mind circled back to Jake making her come apart in the hall last night.

Good Lord. What was I thinking?

That I wanted him.

Was it her fault he was sex personified? How was she supposed to resist him?

She was grinning like a schoolgirl as she lifted the phone to her ear, curious about who the unfamiliar number belonged to.

"Hello?"

"Care to open your door?" Jake's sensual voice brought a full-body shudder.

She turned and stared at the door, as if it might open itself. He was there? *You're here!* She looked down at her white miniskirt, peach tank top, and cute strappy sandals, then crouched down to check her reflection in the door of the microwave oven. *Oh my God. You're here. You're really here.*

"You're here?" She wanted to sprint to the door, throw it open, and steal another one of those magnificent kisses. This was the last thing she'd expected. She was sure he'd wake up this morning and all that anger would return, or at least he'd be as conflicted as she was.

"I'm here, Fi."

She heard the smile in his voice, and it sent her heart aflutter.

She opened the door. Jake reached for her as if it were the most natural thing in the world and pulled her into a deliciously intense kiss.

"I thought about you all night." His eyes took a slow, appreciative stroll down her body. "Maybe you should wear overalls."

"Jealousy looks better on you than Mr. Angry did." Inside she was doing a happy dance.

"I'm a fickle guy." He shrugged, but his eyes betrayed him with a serious gaze.

"You're one of the most decisive men I've ever known. Or at least you used to be. Come on in while I grab my keys."

He shifted his weight and leaned his hip against the doorframe. "I think I'd better wait here." His eyes bored into her, kicking her pulse into overdrive.

She grabbed her keys from the kitchen counter, thankful

for the space between them so she could try to gain control of her freaking hormones. Jeez, she felt like she was a teenager again, dating Jake for the first time, when every glance sent a shiver of anticipation through her.

His eyes locked on her as she crossed the room, making her self-conscious. She'd forgotten how intense his looks could be, how they made her feel exposed, vulnerable, and sexy all at once.

As she locked the door, he slid his hands around her waist.

"You know it's not like if you come inside my apartment you'll turn into a sex maniac."

He rubbed the scruff of his cheek against her face and she heard a sigh escape her lips. He knew every trick in the book to heighten her anticipation—and she loved it.

"Your apartment isn't what I want to come inside, Fi."

She blinked several times, trying to force herself not to melt right there in front of him. How were her legs supposed to work after that earth-shattering revelation? He turned her in his arms and placed his calloused hands on her cheeks, tilted her head up, and gazed into her eyes.

"Make no mistake about how much I want you. All of you. I could barely wait until dawn to see you, and I ran at least eight miles before coming to get you."

"Okay," she whispered, trying to mask her elation.

"This whole thing scares me, Fi. I'm going to fuck up. You know I am, and when I do, I'll be right back where I was sixteen years ago. Only it'll be my own undoing. I'll know why I'm there."

I'm going to fuck up. His surety righted her brain again. "Maybe you won't." *Please reassure me.*

"I told you, I'm not the same guy I was."

"You seemed like you were last night." Hadn't he? She was sure she'd recognized the Jake she'd known so well, even with evidence of his new lifestyle staring her in the face at every turn and dangling doubts in front of her eyes.

He took her hand in his and kissed her knuckles. "Being close with you comes naturally. The rest is buried so deeply that I'm not sure how to get it back, or if I even should. I live in a different world than you do. A whole different world."

She gulped down that ugly dose of reality as they walked downstairs and headed for his car.

He held her hand as he drove to the studio, and she didn't know what to think or how to calm her feelings.

"Apparently you made a friend last night. Susie really liked you."

"Really?" Well, that was good news. She liked Susie, and it gave her hope that perhaps everyone in Tinseltown wasn't superficial after all. Susie wasn't pretentious, and she didn't glom on to Jake or eye him when she thought Fiona wasn't watching, like some of the other women who were at Jake's house last night.

"Yes, and I asked her to spread the word to the others

about not showing up unannounced. She's got a line to just about everyone I know, so I'm sure that within hours she'll have told everyone to back off." He stopped at a light, and when he looked at her, his eyes were serious, assessing.

"You make my head spin, Fiona." He handed her his wallet from where it was sitting on the console. "Open that up, would you, please?"

She nervously opened his wallet, feeling like she was doing something far too intimate. She didn't know what she thought she'd find, but it wasn't a frayed and creased picture of the two of them pressed inside a plastic sheathing. She looked up at Jake, knowing he was the same man he'd been, at least somewhere inside.

"I've always carried it." Jake kept his eyes trained on the road. His strong jaw was relaxed, which surprised Fiona. She'd expected him to be grinding his teeth over something so personal.

She ran her finger over the photo. Jake's hair was longer, tousled by the wind. His face was peppered with a youthful sheen of whiskers, not as thick and dark as he now sported. He was looking at her in the same way he had right before he'd kissed her for the first time last night. She remembered the afternoon the picture was taken. It was a month before they'd broken up, and they'd spent the afternoon at the lake with Shea and Jake's brother Luke and his sister, Emily.

"Why?" She regretted that the word had slipped out.

His eyes never left the road, but a smile lifted the corners of his mouth. "I never really knew, but I've probably gone through fifty wallets and never could get rid of it."

"But you must have seen it every time you opened your wallet." She couldn't imagine him *wanting* to see it.

"Tell me about it." He slid his eyes to her. They weren't smiling.

Uh-oh.

"Why would you torture yourself? It's not like you even liked me for all that time. I mean, you pretty much hated me. If I were a guy, you would have decked me in the Brewery the other night."

Now his jaw clenched. "You're probably right."

"So…?"

He shrugged. "No clue." He turned on to the road that led to the studio. "Next Friday night, will you be my date for the cast dinner?"

Her heart skipped a beat. *Smooth subject change.* "Your date? Yes. Yes, of course, but are you sure? Zane said that it's a big deal, with all of the studio staff and the media."

This time when he looked at her, his smile reached his eyes. "Yes, I'm sure, and just so we're on the same page, does day by day imply monogamy? Because before I tell you to please steer clear of Zane Walker, I need to know I have the right to do so."

She laughed. "Zane Walker? Please. He'll have his pick of

women." *Oh my God, you're worried about Zane Walker and me?*

"Yeah, he will, but his scope was set on you last night, Fi."

Now she understood his need to sweep her out of there last night. Maybe it was more than just seeing that she had been feeling uncomfortable. He'd been jealous. The realization made her stomach flutter like a schoolgirl's.

As they neared the studio lot, Fiona noticed a crowd of people around the entrance and wondered what was going on. When Jake pulled onto the lot of the set, his car was immediately besieged by paparazzi. Cameras flashed and hordes of photographers shouted at the car. Even through the tinted windows, Fiona could see the cameras pressed against the glass. Bodies brushed against the side of the car as the mob moved in closer to get a better look.

"This is crazy. Do you deal with this every time you drive onto the lot?"

"Not really." He honked his horn and sped up just enough to force the crowd away from the car. He drove toward his trailer with a throng of cameramen jogging after him.

"What will they think when I get out of your car?"

He grinned as he parked the car. "They'll think we're together. They'll throw a million questions at you as soon as you get out. Just smile and ignore them."

"Ignore them?" It might be easier to ignore a herd of elephants.

"Yes. Ignore them." Jake reached casually into the center console, as if there weren't a bunch of people who looked like they were ready to climb on top of his car or break the windows, and handed her a flash drive.

"I made this a few years ago. I never realized why these songs appealed to me until last night. Now it kind of makes sense. It's the soundtrack of my life, or something like that. Regardless of what happens between us, I think you should have it." He looked over his shoulder at the paparazzi closing in on them.

Regardless of what happens between us. He kept doing this to her, sending conflicting messages. Reminding her that he might screw up as an aside, tossing it in with something that could possibly be sweetly nostalgic—or tragically angry—like every time he mentioned it didn't send her mind into a tizzy. She shoved the flash drive into her purse as someone banged on his window.

Jake spun around. The tension in his jaw relaxed when he saw Trace's face nearly pressed against the glass.

"Stay put. I'll open your door." He pushed the door open and stepped out.

"Someone must have…" was all Fiona caught Trace saying before Jake closed the door. Then he was at her door, and the media was upon them. He draped an arm around her and held her close as he walked toward his trailer amid the cameras and shouts.

"Smile like they're not even here," he said while smiling.

Fiona felt trapped, like the people shouting questions and thrusting microphones and cameras in their faces were vultures that might swoop in and peck them to smithereens. She pressed herself against Jake's side, amazed at his ability to ignore the mayhem and walk directly to his trailer, where Trace was now standing with her hand on the door, waiting to usher them inside.

They were both masters at this. It was like a finely tuned dance of the rich and famous. Fiona was so *not* made for this world. By the time they stepped into Jake's trailer, she was shaking all over. Her skin felt clammy, and her stomach knotted into a fiery ball.

Trace locked the door behind them and ensured all of the curtains were drawn. She crossed her arms and arched a pierced brow. "What the hell was that?"

"Media needs to eat, too," Jake said. "They take pics when I'm out on the town with my friends anyway, because I hang out with actors all the time, so now they have a few nice photos to keep them busy for a while." He led Fiona to a leather couch, sat down beside her, and took her hands in his. "You're shaking."

"I'm not used to that. How can you be so calm?"

He shrugged. "I'm the one who let the word out."

Fiona couldn't believe what she was hearing, and the pleased look on Jake's face only made her angrier.

"Tell me you're messing with me here." Trace's stick-straight, black hair was blunt cut at the shoulders. She was skinny as a beanpole and looked about eighteen years old with her dark eyeliner, skinny jeans, and plain white V-neck T-shirt. She had an earpiece hooked in place and a radio attached to her studded belt—and an angry look in her eyes.

He set a serious gaze on Fiona and cupped her cheek. "I'm making changes, and I wanted there to be no question as to who I'm with. The paparazzi are always taking pictures when I'm out with actresses. This will keep those actresses off my back."

Fiona opened her mouth to say something but didn't know if she should be honored or upset that he hadn't alerted her to the attack.

"Well, as sweet as that is, Jake, I'm your assistant." Trace crossed her arms and thrust her hip out. "It's my job to be apprised of these sorts of things, and I hardly think it's fair to ambush Fiona, no matter how good your intentions were."

"Thank you," Fiona said, surprised at how she and Trace had been thinking the same thing.

Jake's eyes filled with concern. "I didn't mean to ambush you, Fi. I didn't want to freak you out by telling you what I'd done."

"So it's better to let her fall prey to those animals completely unprepared?" Trace rolled her eyes and waved her hand in the air, black nail polish on all four fingers, blue on her thumb.

"Jesus, Trace. Don't you have something to do?"

Fiona could tell by the arch of his brow that he wasn't angry at Trace, and the way Trace shook her head with a playfully annoyed smile also told her that they'd had this type of discussion before. She remembered the director hollering at him for *whoop*ing before he'd yelled *cut*. This was her Jake, through and through.

"Yeah, like shooing out the dogs that you've left trails of food for. Sorry, Fiona. I'll try to keep them off your back today." Trace glared at Jake. "Next time take three seconds to text me, okay? Even if you're the one leaking the info, I should know so I can run interference."

"You're right," Jake conceded. "Sorry, Trace. Now please get out of here." He smiled and motioned with his hands for her to leave.

"Thank you, Trace." Fiona watched her leave and turned her attention back to Jake, who began explaining before she could say a word.

"Before you get mad, hear me out. I'm sorry, but I know how uncomfortable you were last night when Megan was all over me, and I know how uncomfortable I was with all the guys checking you out. If we have a chance in hell of having any kind of sane relationship, I had to do something. I'm sorry, Fi. I probably should have told you, but I wasn't thinking clearly. I still feel like I'm all wound up with no idea if I'm coming or going."

She rested her head back on the couch and sighed, already exhausted and the day had barely begun. "Is that a good thing or a bad thing, Jake? I'm so out of my element. Honestly, I appreciate what you've done." She met his gaze and paused, trying to figure out how to tell him what she was really thinking.

"But?"

"But it was awful watching that girl paw at you last night."

He opened his mouth to say something, and she pressed her finger over his lips.

"I know this is my issue. I know that this grand gesture that you made will probably change things, and I appreciate that. I said I could handle it, and I want to be able to. It's just proving to be more difficult than I imagined." She'd wanted to be with Jake for so long, and here she was throwing a monkey wrench into his efforts. She was confused and wanted to stop talking, but she couldn't. Something inside her needed him to know how she was feeling. They'd always been honest with each other, and she didn't want to start hiding things now, when they were on the cusp of what felt like something real.

"It's only been a day." He scrubbed his hand down his face. "And what you saw was nothing, Fi." He rose and paced. "When I go to a restaurant, fans are all over me. That's one reason I did this. Those media hounds will get our pic in every rag magazine by tomorrow morning. In fact, I'd be surprised if it's not already hitting the online gossip columns. That will at least pause the stampede."

He knelt beside her and placed his hands on her knees. "I did this for us. So we can have room to breathe."

"I know. I get it, Jake." She did understand it on a cognitive level, but that didn't make situations like Megan Flexx practically scaling Jake any easier to deal with. "I'm just being honest."

"Honesty is good. I want honesty, and you deserve it." He held her gaze, and a slow smile spread across his face. "One day at a time, right? Please tell me that I didn't mess up so badly that we'll never have more than those few hours together."

"Jake...I can't believe you want this as much as I do." She couldn't believe she'd let those words come out of her mouth.

"Neither can I."

"One day at a time."

MORNING MOVED INTO afternoon seamlessly as Jake went from one set to the next, nailing every stunt. Trace did her job well, and by the time Jake had a break, security was tightened and there was no sight of the paparazzi. He headed over to the set where Trish was filming to try to catch Fiona, and stopped when he caught sight of her talking with Zane and Patch. The jealousy tearing through him was ridiculous. He'd had women at his fingertips for the past decade, and he'd never once become jealous over any of them. Fiona walked back into his life and suddenly he went green with envy. His brothers would have a field day with this.

Zane saw him coming and excused himself from Patch and Fiona, intercepting Jake before he could reach her. He grabbed Jake's arm and dragged him farther away.

Jake had worked as Zane's stunt double for most of Zane's films since his career had taken off. They looked alike enough even without makeup that they could have been brothers, though at six three, Jake had a good two inches on Zane.

"Dude, what was with that PR stunt this morning?" Zane crossed his arms and glanced over at Fiona, who was looking at them with a curious gaze.

Jake held up one finger in her direction. "I'm giving it a go with Fiona and needed a little breathing space."

"Giving it a go?" Zane crossed his arms and looked down his angular nose at Jake. "What does that mean? Giving it a go?" He laughed. "You realize those pics will be plastered all over the Internet and gossip rags, essentially taking you off the market and putting you into the hot seat. The media will be tailing you everywhere."

"I threw them a bone with the agreement that they get these pics but they stay off our asses. We'll see if they listen, but I needed to do something."

"Why? I mean, she's hot, but, dude, *giving it a go*? As in not sleeping with other women?"

Jake wanted to explain himself to Zane about as much as he wanted to be trailed by the media, but Zane was as much Jake's cohort in womanizing as anyone could be, and they were friends. If he was really going to give this relationship a shot, he had to lay it on the line no matter how much shit he'd have to take.

Relationship.

That word was so foreign to him that even thinking it made him bristle—until he caught sight of Fiona again, smiling in his direction, and the word *relationship* had never sounded so good.

"Yeah, that's exactly what I mean." He'd watched his brothers fall like flies for their significant others, and he'd vehemently denied he would ever follow the same path. Then again, he'd never entertained the idea of trying to make things work with Fiona again.

"What's so special about this one? Why on earth would you agree to a monogamous relationship?" Zane pulled him farther away from Fiona. "Jake, wake up, man. You're at the top of your game. You've got a good thing going."

Jake didn't hear anything after Zane referring to Fiona as *this one*. He narrowed his eyes and stepped in close. "We've got a good friendship going, Zane. I respect you, so respect my decision. And if you refer to her as *this one* again, I'll have to teach you the meaning of respect. Got it?"

"Whoa. Back off, man. What has she done to you? You've known her what? A week?"

"A fucking lifetime." He glared at Zane.

"Wait." Zane's eyes darted between Fiona and Jake as understanding dawned on him. One night when they'd first met, they'd been drinking at a cast party and Zane had spouted off about broken hearts being a bullshit crutch. Jake had been too drunk to stop his story from spilling from his lips. He'd never mentioned Fiona's name, but he could tell by the widening of Zane's eyes that he'd figured it out. That had been the one and only time Jake had mentioned that part of his past to anyone in LA.

"Shit. She's the one who broke your heart? Damn, man." Zane coughed to mask a laugh. "And you're giving up everything for her? What the hell are you thinking?"

"I think now's a good time for you to shut up and for me to walk away before you say something that really pisses me off."

Zane held his hands up in surrender. "Sorry, man. Just sayin'." He patted Jake's arm. "Listen, if this is what you want, I'm all for it. For you, that is. Not for myself, of course. I've got no interest in giving anything more than a night of no-strings-attached sex a try. But hey, if this is where you're heading, I'm there for you. Really. She seems sweet, and she's sharp as a tack. You know she's a geologist? Of course you do."

Jake took a step away. "Yeah, she's damn smart, all right. And sweet, and between you and me, she fucking blows me away."

"Just one question. What does she think about all the ass you've been getting? That stuff's gotta come back to haunt you at some point. Do you really think this is possible? Small-town girl, big-time celebrity?"

"Hell if I know, and it seems weird hearing *you* of all people putting the pieces together. But I'm going to try." He already felt like he was playing with a team where he was a step behind. He didn't need anyone else doubting him.

Jake crossed the lot to Fiona and slid an arm around her waist, pressing a kiss to her cheek while eyeing Patch. Patch was a good guy. But he was also a damn handsome man, and just one of many men without the baggage of a string of women hanging around his neck, as Zane had so kindly reminded him.

"Hey, babe. Hey, Patch. How's it going?"

"Looks like it's going great for you two." Patch patted Fiona's arm. "I'll give you some privacy. Catch you guys later."

"Okay, see you around." Fiona waved to Trish, who was sitting in a chair having her makeup done.

"How's your day going?" Jake asked.

"Crazy, but good. Yours?"

He brushed her hair from her shoulder. "Better now. Did anyone bother you about this morning?"

"No, but Trish said it's all over the Internet, and Shea called me saying we should have spoken to her before doing that. I can't imagine what I must look like in those pictures. I felt shell-shocked." She lowered her eyes.

He lifted her chin and smiled at her. He remembered how strange it was the first time he'd seen himself online and in the magazines. It was like an out-of-body experience; he was laid bare for the whole world to see.

Aw, shit. Fuck-up number one.

He hadn't thought about how it might feel for Fiona. She wasn't in the limelight by choice.

"Hey, you'll look beautiful. Listen, I'm really sorry. I'm so used to all this stuff that I didn't take your feelings into consideration. I messed up, and I'm really sorry."

"Don't worry about it. I came here wanting to be part of your life." She paused and looked around the busy set. Worry passed over her baby blues, making his stomach take a nosedive.

"And this is your life."

"Talk to me, Fi."

She shook her head. "Did you do this for publicity, or did you really do it to try to ward off being approached by women when you were with me?"

159

"What? Why would you even ask me that?"

"Because Shea said sometimes—"

"I know she's your sister, but she doesn't know anything about me, Fi." He paced, realizing only too late, by the dejected look on Fiona's face, how harshly he'd spoken.

"I don't mean any offense toward Shea. I'm sure she's very good at what she does, but I did what I thought was the right thing for us. That's all I was worried about." He reached for her hand. "I'm sure Shea was just worried about the public-relations mess I've created for my PR rep, Luce. I'll deal with that." He'd already ignored several calls from Luce, and at some point he'd have to deal with her. Right now the only thing he cared about was making things right with Fiona.

"I thought this was the right thing to do for us, Fiona. The thought of you having to deal with what went on last night makes me sick to my stomach, and I know it's my own fault. I created it, and I can make it stop."

"Jake, whatever happens between us will have to stand the test of time, which I have a feeling will include all sorts of challenges where your career and lifestyle are concerned. I'm glad you did what you did." She went up on her toes and kissed him. "I really am. It was thoughtful, even if I felt ambushed."

"Really?" Thank the heavens above she hadn't turned into an unreasonable woman.

"Really. But..."

"Give it to me straight." He noticed that Trish was out of the makeup chair, which meant they'd soon be interrupted.

"Next time, can you just slow down and talk to me?"

He folded her into his arms. "Yes, of course. And don't worry. You'll look like a million bucks in those pictures, and if anyone says otherwise I'll take them out."

Trish headed in their direction.

"I have to get to work," Fiona said, eyeing Trish.

"What exactly do you do as her assistant? All the normal stuff?" He loved the way her eyes sparkled in the afternoon light, and he wanted her to keep talking so he could see them longer. He wasn't ready for their brief reprieve together to end.

"Don't tell anyone, but she's not paying me to do this, so she can't fire me. I couldn't take money from my best friend, and I'm not very good at this, so…I try to keep her organized and make sure she's got her lines memorized and she's where she's supposed to be. All the things that any good assistant would do. I kinda suck at it, though, and she doesn't need me *at all*. She's a professional. I know she's just playing it up so I feel useful. But the truth is, I've been a little sidetracked." She flashed a coy smile. "I took the job to be near you. I was offered a promotion at work, and I'm on a six-week leave of absence while I decide if I should take it. It worked out perfectly."

He touched his forehead to hers. "So you're more of a

groupie stalker than an assistant?"

"Yeah, you might say that."

"And you're taking a six-week leave of absence from work? You risked your job for me?" Everything she did blew him away, and it made him wonder if he could ever be that selfless. She was peeling back layers of Jake that he hadn't even realized existed and was forcing him to face sides of himself that he wasn't sure he liked.

Chapter Eleven

FIONA FLOPPED ONTO the couch in Trish's trailer with a loud sigh. Her trailer was about half the size of Jake's, but it was comfortable and clean. It was six o'clock, and Trish had just wrapped her final scene for the day.

"Can you believe I had to do that scene five times?" Trish sank onto the other side of the couch and put her feet on Fiona's lap.

"So what?" Fiona eyed Trish's feet. "You need to pay extra for foot rubs," she teased. "Oh, wait. I'm working for free." She kicked her feet onto the couch beside Trish. "Get to work, woman. My feet are tired from chasing you around from set to set, fetching scripts and bottles of water for the princess."

"I have a feeling this will be my first and only film with Steve Hileberg." Trish covered her eyes with her forearm and groaned. "I was so embarrassed. Five times, Fi. *Five.*"

"I would think they're used to that, and besides, when you finally got it right, it was amazing." She massaged Trish's feet as she watched her friend's lips curve up.

"Do you think so? You can be honest with me. If it totally sucked, I'd rather hear it from you than the critics. They're out for blood when they review movies." Trish lowered her hand and tugged at the bottom of the khaki shorts she'd had on in the last scene. "It's not like I can woo them with my body. I have to wear these boy shorts in almost every scene."

"Your scenes take place in the desert and in caves. It's not like you can wear evening gowns. Besides, you look hot in that outfit. I saw a bunch of the extras checking you out." She patted Trish's calf. "And you know you're an amazing actress. You were nominated for an Academy Award last year. You said yourself that you're just nervous because this is your very first movie filming with Steve Hileberg...and Zane Walker. *Zane Walker!* The whole thing is insane. I should bow at your feet."

Trish sighed. "Yeah. It is some crazy life, isn't it?" She pulled her feet from Fiona's lap and leaned in close. "It's also insane the way Jake looked at Patch like he wanted to throttle him."

"What are you talking about?" She didn't remember seeing anything like that.

"When Jake came to the set this afternoon to see you. He looked pissed at Zane after their little powwow, but he was also eyeing Patch. Sizing him up." She narrowed her eyes. "If you ask me, that whole thing he did this morning had less to do with getting women to stop coming onto him as it did to keep guys from coming onto you."

"*Pfft!* You're nuts." Was she? Jake had mentioned Zane looking at her. "I'm nobody, and he's...well, he's somebody."

"You can minimize it if you want, but for a guy who wouldn't even talk to you a week ago, it seems like he's publicly claimed you. And you're hot and brilliant and sweet. He *should* be jealous."

"He should? I think it's the other way around, and I'm already growing green with envy. Jealousy is not a good thing, and this whole situation is much more difficult than I had imagined it would be." Fiona rested her head back on the couch. "I think he did that thing this morning as much for his own head as he did for any other reason. He's doing all the right things, you know?" She turned her head and met Trish's comforting gaze. "When we kissed the other night, it was so much better than when we were younger, more intense, but it was also like all those years that we were apart never happened."

Trish reached for her hand. "But they did, Fi."

"Yeah. They did, and I think he's having a hard time figuring out if he's even capable of being faithful or something. He keeps telling me that he's going to screw up. Like he's preparing me for it."

"Or preparing himself?" Trish leaned back beside Fiona. "Guys are hardheaded; you know that. Maybe he's trying to keep himself from falling for you, just in case."

"That's not very reassuring." Fiona closed her eyes. "I was hoping you'd tell me that I'm being paranoid."

"I'm a realist, and guys are…guys. They try real hard sometimes, but then something happens and their brains deflate, or scramble, or God knows what. And they mess up. He probably knows himself well." Trish sighed. "As much as I love you, I have to admit that I would never be able to do what you're doing. I want things to work out for the two of you because you obviously love him more than life itself, and if today was any indication, I'd say that he also has strong feelings for you. What man would make such a public statement if he didn't? But I could never deal with women climbing my man like a mountain."

"A mountain?" Fiona laughed, but inside her heart was heavy with the reality of what Trish was saying and elated by her deeming Jake *Fiona's* man. When they'd lived in Trusty, Jake's exposure to women was limited to the small town. Now she'd seen firsthand what things would be like if she and Jake were together. As much as she hated to admit it, she'd also noticed how it had taken Jake's full concentration to try to ward his past away from their present.

Chapter Twelve

FIONA WAITED FOR Jake inside his trailer Wednesday evening while he met with the producers. It was more like a mobile luxury home than a trailer. She wondered how often Jake had to sleep in it. Was this trailer where he lived when he was on location? Or did he stay in hotel rooms? Or rent apartments? She tried to imagine what it would be like if she and Jake stayed together. Would she go on location with him? Would she want to? It was way too soon to think about any of that, but she couldn't help it. They might have only just found each other again, but she'd known Jake her whole life. Even though he'd changed in many ways, he still felt like *her* Jake. At least she'd seen parts of *her* Jake reappear over the last few days, and she had a feeling that more of that guy was inside him somewhere.

She was reading through the latest online edition of *Geology* magazine when her cell vibrated. She picked up her phone, hoping it was Jake, but her hope deflated when she saw Shea's name.

"Hey, Shea."

"Hi. Sorry it took me so long to call you, but I've been swamped. I just saw the pics from this morning. Have you seen them?"

"No. I don't want to. I know I'll look horrible." She pushed her computer across the table. "You know Reggie, Brent, and Jesse all texted me already, wanting to know what the *real* scoop was with me and Jake."

"Finn called me. He said he didn't want to hear you get all sappy over any guy, so I filled him in. They love you, Fi. They care. That's what brothers are supposed to do," Shea said.

"Yeah, but you know Reggie. He said he was going to run checks on Jake, so the private investigator in him probably ran a hundred different types of checks." Fiona laughed. Reggie was a little overprotective of her and Shea.

"Well, you have to admit, it's better than having brothers who don't care," Shea insisted.

"True. And they all like the Bradens, so it's not like they were upset or anything." Now that she'd had a little time to breathe, she was actually glad they'd even noticed. She knew how busy they were.

"Well, now that everyone's seen the pictures...take a look," Shea urged.

"No. I don't want to see them." She pushed the laptop farther away. She was dying to see the pictures and had been fighting the urge to take a peek at them for the past hour.

"Fi, you have to see them. Trust me. I promise you won't be upset. Please?"

Fiona eyed the laptop. "No, Shea."

"Fiona, trust me. Please? I know how much Jake means to you, and I know how hard that must have been for you this morning. But you have got to see the pictures. Everyone is talking about them."

Fiona rolled her eyes. "I know. I've been dodging remarks all day. Apparently, Perez Hilton picked them up, and they were streamed to the Huffington Post and *People* magazine's website."

"All the more reason for you to see them."

"*Ugh.* Fine. I guess if people are gawking at me, I should know how bad I look." She pulled her computer back toward her and typed *People.com.* She navigated to their photos under the heading *Stuntman Jake Braden's Off the Market!*

"Holy crap. Did you see the headlines on *People?*"

Shea laughed. "Yes. It's funny how quickly they pull these things together. But focus, Fi. Look at those pictures. You're gorgeous, right? Tell me what you see."

Fiona groaned. "Me, scared shitless."

"Look again."

Her eyes settled on Jake's sincere smile and traveled to his intense gaze, so full of emotion that she lost her voice in a rush of air. "He looks like he—" She'd dreamed of seeing that look in his eyes for so many years that she could barely think.

"Exactly, Fi. That's what the world saw, too," Shea said. "Jake's looking at you exactly like he used to. I was only a kid when you guys were dating, but as soon as I saw these pictures, I remembered. Fi, you know what this means?"

"Uh-uh." She couldn't take her eyes off the photo. Jake had one arm around her shoulder, and he was leaning in close. He looked happy. Truly happy. Not like the feigned smile she'd seen in magazines over recent years.

"It means you were right to take a chance, Fi. I think he still loves you, even if he doesn't know it yet."

The trailer door opened and Jake walked in. His eyes swept to the left, then moved in her direction. When they came to rest on her, the smile she saw in the pictures appeared on his handsome face. Fiona reached out and closed the laptop.

"I gotta go, Shea. Love you." She ended the call without waiting for Shea to respond. She was riveted by Jake as he walked toward her in his tight T-shirt and jeans that hugged his massive thighs and left little to the imagination. She rose to greet him, and he pulled her into his arms and took her in a greedy kiss.

She loved being in his arms again, and she didn't care if he'd ambushed her with the press or had lived a thousand lives while they were apart. She loved him now—this second—and his feelings for her were as palpable as his strong embrace.

When their lips parted, she missed the feel of them, and she reached up to touch her upper lip, where his scruff had scratched her. She wanted to feel it again—everywhere.

"That was too many hours to go in between kissing you."

"Yeah," was all she could manage as she clung to his arms, aching to kiss him again.

"I thought about you every minute of the day. Screwed up two stunts because I kept thinking about holding you." He lowered his lips to hers. "Kissing you." His hands roamed up her back, pressing their chests together.

"Should I be sorry?"

He smiled and sealed his lips over hers again, kissing her like he never wanted to let her go, which seemed like a perfect plan to her.

"Never be sorry. I had something really fun planned for tonight." He kissed the corner of her mouth, then ran his tongue along her lower lip.

"Fun?" she whispered, having no idea how she managed the word when her entire body was on fire.

"A date." He nipped at her jaw, causing her breathing to quicken. "Like a real couple."

His hands slid up her sides and she arched against him, wanting those big hands to wander all over her body. Now. Somewhere among the need coursing through her body she realized he'd referred to them as a real couple, and her heart soared. But her pulse was racing, and she wasn't sure she could form a coherent sentence to respond. Actions spoke louder than words, so she threaded her hands in his hair and held on tight as he lifted her into his arms. Her legs circled his waist and their mouths crashed together. She ran her hands through his hair, grasping for purchase as their tongues collided, pulling her into a frenzied state of breathless need. He pressed his arousal against her center, and a moan of desire escaped her lips before she could stop it. His hands slid beneath her ass, holding her tightly against him, grinding his hips, creating luscious friction and making her so damn wet her body ached for relief.

"Bedroom." The word came off her lips like a demand.

Jake pulled back and searched her eyes. "Fi?"

Her voice was tamped down by need she couldn't contain. Her heart slammed against her ribs in anticipation. She took his prickly cheeks in her hands and sealed her mouth over his again with a kiss that left no room for misinterpretation. Jake carried her to the bedroom, hands searching, tongue stroking, as they tumbled down to the bed. Fiona hadn't felt this much raw desire since she and Jake were together in high school, and she wasn't about to slow down. She tugged at his jeans, craving his impressive manhood. Wanting all of him. He tore her shirt from her body and tossed it aside. He took off his shirt as he knelt between her legs, then made quick work of getting her naked save for her bra and came down again, kissing her as his hands explored every inch of her skin.

"Off," he said as he unhooked her bra and tossed it aside.

His eyes went nearly black as he filled his palms with her breasts and brought his mouth to hers again, his tongue sliding over hers in rhythm to the slow torture his fingers were playing out with her nipples. Teasing her until she thought she might climb out of her skin. Her hips rose off the bed, pressing against his as she reached for his jeans again.

"Off," she pleaded.

Jake's lips quirked up in a devilish grin as he rolled to the side and swiftly divested himself of his remaining clothes. *Good Lord.* She'd forgotten just how *big* he was, how thick, and he seemed impossibly larger than she'd remembered. She licked her lips, wanting to taste him and knowing full well she shouldn't because of how many women he'd been with. Hell, she couldn't help herself. She wanted to bring him as much pleasure as she knew he'd bring her, and she reached between his legs. He gripped her wrist and pinned her to the mattress with a heated stare.

"No, Fi."

Her heart sank. She hadn't wanted to face the reality of the overzealous sex life she'd heard about, and here it was, literally staring her in the face.

"I haven't had unprotected sex, but I want to get tested before…" He lay beside her and cupped her cheek. His eyes pooled with emotion. "I don't want to take any chances, and if you'd rather not go any further, we can stop."

"And if I want to?" She could wait to taste him, but she wanted to be close to him, to feel him inside her. To be *his*.

"I have protection."

She nodded, and he reached into the nightstand and threw a handful of condoms on the bed with another coy grin.

"Confident, aren't we?" she teased, but inside she felt a pang of worry about his condom supply. In the next breath she shoved it away. This wasn't new information, and she wasn't going to allow it to ruin their intimacy.

"You and I have been down this road before. You tell me."

She yanked him back down on top of her, and this time when their lips met, it was in a slow, sensual kiss. Their naked bodies intertwined, his arousal pressed against her belly, her legs wrapped around his muscular thighs. Their skin heated as they explored each other's bodies. His calloused hands sent shivers to her core. She reached between his legs and stroked him, pulling a throaty groan from his lungs.

"Fi," he said urgently.

She stroked faster, and he gripped her wrist again.

"I've wanted you since I saw you in the bar. Do you really think that's a good idea?"

"I think touching you is the best idea I've ever had," she shot back, and arched up to lick his chest. He tasted salty and hot, and so manly her body pulsed with need. It had been too long since she'd been with a real man. A man made of muscles and vigor. A man who knew how to love a woman.

Jake Braden knew how to love a woman, and he was about to prove just that, as he slithered down her body, his hands caressing, his mouth loving, kissing, teasing a path down the center of her body.

He touched his forehead to her stomach and wrapped his arms around her waist, hugging her to him. Fiona felt herself tearing up. This was the Jake she knew. The sensual, tender man whose heart hungered to be loved. When he whispered, "God, I've missed you," she felt a tear break free.

He lay there for a long while, and Fiona soaked him in. She could hardly believe this was finally happening. They were finally together, and his walls were coming down. The feel of being in his arms again was better than she'd remembered, better than she'd hoped, but when he lifted his gaze and met hers, the love in his eyes sent her heart out of her mouth.

"Love me, Jake."

He reached for her hand and brought it to his lips before moving lower. He gripped her thighs, spreading them farther apart, all the while holding her gaze. Then his mouth was upon her. Her head fell back with the first luxurious stroke of his tongue. She dug her fingers into his hand as he teased her. Her nerves felt exposed and electrified. She tried to remember how to breathe—and when he slid his fingers into her, she lost all sense of the here and now. Lost in pleasure, she writhed against his talented mouth, feeling the swell of an orgasm low in her belly.

"Come for me, baby."

His lustful voice vibrated through her and sent her spiraling over the edge, stroking her into the longest, most intense orgasm she'd ever had.

IN ALL THE years since Jake and Fiona had been together, he had never forgotten how sweet she tasted or the sexy sounds she made when she came apart. He rested his cheek on her inner thigh, taking a moment to try to regain control of his desires. Being intimate with her again brought a rush of emotions, and he'd nearly come from the intensity of it all. Jake had never needed safety in his life, but regardless of what he needed, when he was with Fiona, he felt safe, and it blew him away. She was anything but safe. She'd left him once. She should make him wary, if anything, but when he'd entered the trailer tonight, the love in her eyes wiped that slate clean.

He kissed his way up her body, inhaling her scent and tasting her heated flesh. She was as new to him as she was familiar. Her curves were feminine and sexy as hell. Her breasts filled his hands, and as he brought his tongue to her taut nipple, she sucked in a breath and tightened her hold on his back. He loved the way she clawed at him, the way her body and heart responded to him on all levels. She was strong and tough, sensitive and caring. She was still all the things she was years ago, only more intense and wiser, and it endeared her to him even more. He looked into her love-filled eyes, and in that moment he knew he didn't want to just protect her; he wanted to love her again.

Wanted to.

He was already there. Even if clouded by memories of their past and what his life had become, beneath it all, his love for her had remained steady and true.

He folded her into his arms and held her tight. Too tight, he was sure, but he didn't want to let her go. Not again. Not ever. He felt her heart beating against his, and when he drew back, she touched his cheek.

"You feel it, too." It wasn't a question.

Oh yeah, he felt it.

"Fi…" He wanted to warn her again that he'd fuck up. He'd become too selfish to make this work, hadn't he? He'd become the type of man he'd loathed when he'd first come to Los Angeles. The type of guy who was only out for his own pleasure and didn't know how to feel.

She stroked his cheek again, smiled up at him with trusting eyes.

But he *was* feeling. She was helping him feel, making him realize he wasn't too broken to ever feel again.

"You look sad," she whispered.

"No, babe. I'm happy." He kissed her softly. "I haven't felt this much in forever."

"That was my fault." She shifted her eyes away.

"I've decided to blame it on your life instead. You couldn't weed through your family's upheaval back then. This is better." He kissed her again, then kissed each of her cheeks and her forehead, his feelings growing with every passing second. "Now we both know what's out there. We both know what we want, and we're learning who we really are. It'll take time to figure it all out, but I think maybe all that hurt had to happen."

She wrinkled her brow. "Hurt never needs to happen. I'm sorry, Jake."

"Babe, we're adults now. We know what we want, and even if it took me a while to get here, I know I want you."

She wrapped her delicate hand around his neck and pulled his mouth to hers. Their tongues slid over each other's with fresh desire and urgency that sent her hips off the mattress. He was throbbing with need, and before he could reach for a condom, she did. When she handed it to him, their eyes connected—and held—with a hundred different emotions.

Jake tore the wrapper open with his teeth, and she helped him roll it on. He hadn't allowed any other women to do that for him, and without any thought, he allowed Fiona to—and loved it. She lay back on the bed, and Jake could hardly believe he was lying with Fiona again. His Fiona. God, how had he ever let her go? As he lowered his body to hers and they joined together, he knew he'd fight till the death to keep her with him forever. He held her gaze as he filled her completely and wrapped his arms around her again, keeping her close. This was what he'd missed most, this closeness. This intimacy that he'd only ever found with Fiona.

The desire to love and be loved.

Their bodies fell into a natural rhythm. Jake laced his fingers with hers and held them beside her head, so he could look into her eyes as he loved her. She met his efforts with her own, lifting off the mattress, angling her hips to take him in deeper, her inner muscles tightening around him. *Christ.* He'd forgotten how good she was at this and how good they were together.

He pressed his cheek to hers. "I'm not going to last, Fi. Not this first time with you. It's been too long."

Her lips curved up in a knowing smile. "I'm not worried." She shifted her eyes at the pile of condoms spread over the blanket beside them.

He planted another hungry kiss on her receptive mouth, thrusting his tongue as he pumped his hips. She pressed on his lower back, urging him impossibly deeper, grinding her hips against his as their tongues danced to their own insistent rhythm. Her fingernails clutched at his skin as her head fell back again, her body racked with passionate spasms, pulsing around his potent rod. He heard his name sail off her lips as waves of ecstasy flooded him. Her cheeks were flushed, her breathing shallow. He wanted more of her. Always more. She was his weakness and his strength, at once. She had the power to ruin him and she was his driving force to be better, to be the man she deserved. She was worth the risk. She grabbed his ass, pressing their slick bodies together, taking in every inch of him. He gritted his teeth and buried his face in the crook of her neck, muffling his grunts, as thrust after powerful thrust drew out his powerful release.

They lay there for a long while, breathing hard, their bodies braided together. He listened to her breathing ease back to normal, felt her body melt into the mattress. Only then did he withdraw from between her legs. He squeezed her hand, then rolled to the side and disposed of the condom so he could hold her close again.

"Fi." Her name sounded like liquid emotion.

"Yeah?"

"I'm glad you didn't give up on me."

"I tried."

He blanketed her body with his, wrapping one arm around her waist, and tried to give her the most serious face he could muster after such an earth-shattering orgasm.

"You tried?" he asked.

She nodded. "No matter how I tried to escape you, you were always there. I saw your eyes in every man, heard your voice in my head. You haunted me from the moment I left for college until the very second you pressed your lips to mine in your house. And every second since."

He couldn't stifle his smile. "You fueled my anger, Fi. Drove me half insane, and you were a million miles away. I thought I'd explode in rage if I spoke to you again, much less kissed you. What I realized after you roped me in was—"

"Roped you in?" She raised her brows, her eyes alit with mischief as she ran her finger down his chest. "Yee-haw, cowboy."

He squeezed her ribs and she squealed. "Careful, or I'll ride you like you've never been ridden before, girlie."

She rolled her eyes. "Promises, promises."

He sealed his lips over hers again and kissed her silent.

"After you *roped me in*, I realized that what I was afraid of wasn't exploding with rage. It was feeling again. Allowing myself to get sucked back into the love we had. You opened that door and slipped right in, Fi. You broke me again, in a different way. A better way."

"Broke you of your philandering ways?" Her voice was teasing, but he could tell by the serious look in her eyes that she felt it, too.

"Yes. You wanted to slay the beast. Now you have me." *Just don't throw me away again.*

Chapter Thirteen

JAKE CAREENED OVER the top of a Jeep Friday afternoon and landed on the ground with a loud *thud*. He feigned a struggle to his feet and carried out his last fight scene for the day. Every punch he threw packed twice its normal power, every kick carried the weight of missing Fiona, whom he hadn't seen for any significant amount of time since they'd come together Wednesday night. She'd had plans with Trish and Shea Thursday night. He hadn't even been able to pick her up in the mornings because he'd had to meet with the executive producers of an upcoming film early yesterday morning and again this morning. They'd had a few quick chats between Trish's scenes, but he hadn't been able to hold her in his arms—and he craved the closeness. At least he'd made time before his scene to call his doctor and arrange for a quick blood test to be taken in his trailer under the strictest of confidences. That was one thing off his plate. While the blood had drained from his arm, he'd seen it as a chance for a new beginning. He was sure he'd been too careful for the test to be positive, but he didn't want to take a chance with Fiona's health.

He'd barely been able to think of anything but her since he'd seen her back home, and now that they'd come together, she was always there, lingering in his mind. It had taken him a few hours to figure out that the reason he'd been so jumpy and edgy over the last day and a half was because he was allowing himself to enjoy thoughts of Fiona after pushing her away for so long. Once he figured that out, it had taken another few hours for him to accept the unfamiliar feelings. Since then, he welcomed the gut-wrenching nervous feeling.

He was feeling again. That had to be a good thing.

One last uppercut, and the other stuntman crumpled to the ground in a perfectly orchestrated death.

"Cut!" the director yelled. "Nice ass-kicking."

Jake waved and took his battered body off the set to where Trace was waiting with a giant thermos full of ice water.

"You're the best, Trace. Thanks." Jake eyed her black miniskirt and T-shirt. Trace rarely wore skirts, and based on her smile, he had a feeling her partner was back in town.

"Thanks. Would you mind if I left to meet Carla?" Trace and Carla, a model, had been dating on and off for three years.

"She's back in town?" Jake was happy for her, although he had no idea how she put up with Carla's air of pretentiousness. Jake had known Carla before she began dating Trace.

She ran in some of the same circles he did, and he'd always felt she was anything but down to earth, while Trace was as real as they came.

"For the weekend, and I figured since you weren't shooting, I'd take advantage." She raised her brows.

"Yeah, sure." He guzzled the water.

"Awesome. Oh, and she's coming to the cast dinner with me next Friday. You said that was fine, right?" She reached for his empty thermos.

"Of course. Whoever you want to bring is cool with me."

"I arranged for your driver, so you're all set."

"Thanks, Trace. Listen, I know Carla will probably take care of a car for the two of you, but feel free to arrange for it on my account, okay?"

Trace arched her pierced brow, which sported a silver barbell rather than her typical silver hoop.

"Jake, you've gone soft on me." Her blue eyes had gone soft, too.

"*Pfft.* I offer that stuff to you all the time. You just never take me up on it."

"Yeah, but you don't usually do it until the very last second. Usually when your driver picks you up, I get a text that says, *Hey, you need a ride?*" She laughed and walked away.

"Trace," Jake yelled.

Trace turned. "I almost forgot. Fiona's off at six. She said she'd meet you at your trailer."

"How'd you know I was going to ask about Fi?"

"You had that sickeningly mushy look in your eyes. Soft, Jake. Soft, soft, soft."

"That's not what she says." He winked, and Trace waved, shaking her head as she walked away.

Back at his trailer, Jake showered and texted Fiona. *I'm at the trailer. Have a surprise for you.*

His phone vibrated a few minutes later. *A yee-haw cowboy surprise? Should I bring my spurs?*

He'd forgotten how quick-witted Fiona could be. What he had in mind hadn't been sexual, but as his mind traveled back to making love with Fiona, he felt a rise in his pants. It had been forever since just thinking about a woman had brought that reaction. He liked this whole *feeling* thing. How the hell had he gone so long without it?

He was still thinking up a response when someone knocked at the trailer door. Jake pulled it open, anticipating Fiona. His smile fell flat at the sight of Megan Flexx.

She climbed the steps and leaned in for a kiss.

Jake leaned back. "Megan. What are you doing here?"

"I'm filming across the lot." She narrowed her eyes and twirled her long dark hair around her finger. She blew a bubble with her gum, popped it loudly, then sucked the pink stickiness into her mouth in one fast inhalation. "Heard you were still here and thought we could...replay a few scenes from last month."

Jake's eyes darted around the lot, looking for Fiona—or

the press. The last thing he needed was a shot of Megan wearing a black dress short enough to qualify as lingerie entering his trailer.

"I've got plans, Me—"

She pushed past him and walked into the trailer. Jake followed her toward the bedroom.

"Megan. I don't have time for this." He put his hands on his hips, and Megan turned in to him and pressed her body to his.

"We'll be quick." She hooked her finger in his belt hoop, and he gripped her wrist.

"No." It was a first for him, turning down a quickie from Megan, and it felt like a first—strange and uncomfortable. Then again, he was turning down the hottest actress in the business.

She furrowed her brow and stuck her lower lip out in a crazy, sexy pout that would bring most men to their knees. It pissed Jake off. Not so much that it was coming from Megan, but that he'd created a take-me-as-you-want-me situation with not just Megan, but plenty of women, and now he had to clean up his own damn mess.

He abhorred messes.

She wrapped her free hand around his neck. "Oh, you want to play rough tonight? I'm all in."

"Jake?"

Jake felt the blood drain from his face. He turned as Fiona

stepped into the trailer. Her beautiful smile fell like lead as her eyes swept over them and filled with pain. She turned and hurried out of the trailer.

"Fi." *Fuck.* Jake dragged Megan to the door. "Out. Now."

"What the…?" She stumbled down the stairs.

"Sorry, Megan." He pulled the trailer door shut and scanned the lot. Fiona was nowhere in sight. *Damn it.*

"She's gone, Jake." Megan set her jaw in an angry frown. "What the hell was that all about?"

"I'm trying to be a good boyfriend, and I'm sorry that I don't have time to explain. It's not you. It's me, and all that appropriate shit. I'm no longer available." He pulled out his cell as he ran in the direction of the parking lot.

"I thought that was a PR stunt," she yelled after him.

"Not if I can help it," he mumbled as he spotted Fiona hurrying across the blacktop.

FIONA FOUGHT HARD against the tears that burned her eyes. Her chest ached. *I'm an idiot. Was that his little surprise? A threesome with Megan Flexx?* Her phone rang as she stormed across the lot with one thing in mind—getting the hell out of there as fast as she possibly could.

"Fiona!" Jake's frustrated voice chased her.

She fisted her hands and gritted her teeth. *I was stupid to come here and think this would work.*

A heavy hand landed on her shoulder. She stumbled, and Jake caught her in his damned strong arms.

"Fiona." Every muscle in his face was pinched tight.

She twisted, trying to free herself from his grip, but he was holding her too tight. "Jake, let go."

"Fiona, it's not what it looks like."

She froze at that stupid cliché. "Is that directly from a movie, because I've only heard it about a million times before. And it sounds just as lame coming from you as it does on the big screen." A tear slipped down her cheek and she looked away.

"Fi." His tone softened. "I promise you on all that is good in this world that I was not doing what you think I was doing. I might be a lot of things, but I'm not a cheat."

She wanted to argue that point, to push at his chest, yell at him, and let the crazy that was brewing inside her out, but Jake was right. In the years they'd dated, he'd never once cheated on her, and he'd had ample opportunity. She knew what he was like now. He didn't try to hide that from her. But in her heart, she trusted him. She still believed that Jake Braden's word was good as gold, even if she'd lost sight of everything he'd done to make her feel comfortable and jumped to conclusions. If he said it wasn't what it looked like, she knew he was telling her the truth.

He wiped her tears with his thumb and wrapped an arm

around her waist.

"I'm sorry, Fi. I know how it must have looked. Megan came to the door, and I thought it was you. She walked inside before I had time to think. I turned her down, and I'd do it a million more times. I don't want her." He crouched a little so he was looking up at her downcast eyes with emotion so fervent it weakened her resolve. When he whispered her name—"Fi"—and brushed his thumb over her lower lip, her anger wilted even further.

"You're holding me really tight," was all she could manage.

"I'm not letting go." He smiled, and it made her cheeks flush with embarrassment for overreacting.

She brought both fists to his chest and banged them lightly against his muscles.

"This is hard."

"Well, I work out every day," he teased.

She touched her forehead to his chest. "You kept telling me you were going to screw up, and when I saw you with her, I thought…"

"I don't blame you."

She met his gaze. "Yeah, but there's a part of me that thinks I'm being stupid for believing you, because you keep telling me that you're not the same guy you were before. How do I know *what* to believe? Maybe you made a mistake and you're trying to cover it up, or—"

"Or maybe I didn't and I don't want to be blamed for

something I *didn't* do." He searched her eyes and his gaze hardened. "I'm not the one who left you, Fiona. I'm not the one who chased you down and made me fall for you again, either."

"I know, but—"

"But nothing." He released her, and she wished he'd scoop her back into the safety of his arms. "I get that this sucks and that it looks like I fell right back into who I've been for all these years." He ran his hand through his hair and turned away.

A lump lodged in Fiona's throat, and when he turned back, the anger in his eyes had twisted to pain, and it slayed her, rooting her to the ground. He closed the distance between them and reached for her hand.

"Fiona, I don't know how you thought all this would go, but none of this is going to be easy. People have expectations, and granted they're expectations that I've created, but that doesn't go away in a day, or a week, or…"

She held her hand up and shook her head. "Stop. I get it, okay? I feel stupid for storming out, and I feel stupid for feeling stupid!" She banged her head on his chest three times, trying to figure out what to do. She trusted Jake through and through, but she'd let jealousy consume her. She took one deep breath, then another, trying to bring her rational mind to the forefront.

"Fi." He lifted her chin and smiled. "If I had walked in on

you and some guy, I'd have gone ballistic. You didn't do anything wrong, so you shouldn't be upset for storming out. And I can promise you that I'd never humiliate you by cheating on you. I don't think I knew if I could really say that to you before now, but now I'm sure. That's not where I'll mess up. I don't even know how I might mess up, but it's been a long time since I've had a girlfriend. Just know that I'll never hurt you in that way."

"Okay." The honesty in his eyes did her in. He may have changed in a lot of ways, but in her heart she didn't really believe he would cheat.

"I'm the one who alerted the media to our relationship, remember? Would I have done that—or gotten tested for every sexually transmitted disease known to man—if my plan was to hurt you?"

"You got tested?" He'd said he would, but she didn't expect him to run out and have it done so quickly. This floored her—and spoke volumes about Jake's integrity and his feelings for her. Now she felt even more stupid for assuming the worst.

"Yes, I got tested. Fiona, I do what I say I'm going to do. That hasn't changed, and neither has my ability to be faithful, which, believe me, surprises me as much as it probably surprises you." He laughed. "I don't mean that how it sounds."

"Yeah, you do." She felt the tension rolling away. "I shouldn't have assumed the worst."

"No, you probably should have, but now we both know that you don't have to. When I said I'd screw up, I didn't mean by fooling around with someone else behind your back. I'm not sure what I meant, but now I'm sure it wasn't that."

"So, you *want* a monogamous relationship?" She hadn't thought to question it before this. In her mind they were already there, but she hadn't realized until just now that clarifying that it was what Jake wanted was probably a good idea, despite the fact that he'd gotten tested.

"Here I was thinking we were already on the same page. Isn't that what you want? What all this was about?"

"Yes. Definitely yes, but we never said it, so…" *Now I feel even more stupid.*

He folded her into his arms again and kissed her forehead. "We've never had to say things with words, Fi. We just need to figure out how to navigate the rest of the world, and we'll either sink or swim. I'm a really good swimmer. The question is, how long can you hold your breath?"

I've held it for the last few years. I'm pretty sure I can hold on a while longer.

Twenty minutes later they walked hand in hand into one of the buildings. Fiona convinced herself not to feel stupid for assuming the worst about Jake, and she could tell by his easy steps and the smile on his lips that he wasn't upset with her about how she'd reacted. She only hoped that Megan Flexx wouldn't say something that made her feel foolish.

"Where are we going?" Fiona asked. The building felt like

a warehouse, with high, exposed-truss ceilings and hallways that echoed as they walked. They passed a doorway, and Jake draped an arm over her shoulder.

"It's a surprise. You know, actors and actresses come to the sets and they rarely get to see much more than the places they run their scenes. They give tours to strangers who will never work a day on a set, and they see more than the people who are sweating their scenes out day after day. And then there's you."

He stopped in front of a closed door and turned to face her. He rested his forearms on her shoulders and fiddled with her hair, making her heart do all sort of leaps and flips.

"You're here every day, helping your friend without being paid, because you wanted to get my attention. You put your own job on hold, your own life on hold, for that matter, and all you wanted in return was a chance at us being together again."

She crinkled her nose. "I sound like a loser, don't I?"

"No. You sound like my lucky charm." He pressed his lips to hers in a sweet kiss. "You deserve to have some fun other than pure enjoyment of my incredibly awesome body."

She rolled her eyes and choked back, *It's that cocky side of you that makes me want to play with your body right now.*

"So…" He pushed open the door, revealing an enormous room with rack after rack of clothing and costumes. He took her hand and led her inside, closing the door behind them.

"Are we allowed to be in here?" She'd never seen anything like it. Beyond the endless clothing racks, the wall to her right held shelves of footwear from floor to ceiling. Accessories of all shapes and sizes hung on the back wall along with weapons—swords, guns, whips, and more.

"It's all ours, and you can try on anything you'd like." He released her hand and waved toward the clothes. "Usually Trace grabs the clothes I need, so I haven't spent much time in here, but I thought you'd get a kick out of it."

Fiona walked down one of the wide aisles, trailing her fingers along the sleeves of hundreds of costumes. Her fingers ran over lush velvets, slippery silks, soft cotton, lots of spiky embellishments. The room smelled like dye, warm fabric, and strangely...plastic. Jake reached into a rack and withdrew a fluffy blue taffeta dress that was longer than she was tall.

"Princess?" He arched one thick, dark brow.

Fiona crinkled her nose and shook her head. She fingered through the rack and pulled out a hanger marked *Conan*, complete with sword and other gold accouterments; then she withdrew another one marked *Xena*. She held them at chin height and smiled.

"I'm game if you are." She held out the Conan costume, practically salivating at the idea of Jake wearing the little fur and leather crotch pocket like the one that Arnold Schwarzenegger wore in the movie.

"Babe, I'll dress up as the Easter bunny to see you in that

hot little number." He took the Conan costume and began undressing.

"Hey, you go over there." She pointed to the other side of the clothing racks.

"Fi, I think I've seen everything there is to see."

He stepped closer to her, and she pressed her hand to his chest and shook her head.

"Go." She pointed again.

She felt like a giddy teenager as she hid behind the clothing rack and put on the costume. The gold-plated bra fit almost perfectly, but the arm guards, which covered her shoulders and biceps, were a challenge to put on. She felt sexy as she slithered into the black miniskirt with gold panel flaps that hung from the front and rear. But it was the red leather gloves that made her feel like a total vamp. They stretched to two inches above her elbow, with black leather fingers and gold shields covering her wrist to elbow. She piled her hair into the long black wig and slipped the coiled whip into a holder on her hip. The sword was heavier than she'd imagined it would be, and when she slid the belt low on her hips, hooked the sheath to it, and slid the heavy sword into the dark leather, she felt seductive and naughty. She eyed the wall of footwear and found a pair of leather boots with gold embellishments. They weren't exactly what Xena wore, but they laced up to her knees. She smiled to herself, anticipating Jake's reaction.

"Hot damn." Jake's voice startled her.

She spun around and her jaw dropped open. She gawked embarrassingly at him with no hope of closing her mouth, as her brain was stuck in *holy-shit* mode. Every inch of Jake's tanned, muscular flesh was on display, save for a gold-plated leather pouch in the front that held his very large package. Beneath the leather belt was a swatch of what was supposed to be animal skin and fur. Fiona had no idea what it was, but she wanted to rip it off. A leather sheath hung from his right hip, complete with a gold-handled sword. Her eyes slipped lower, taking in the sinewy lines of his powerful legs, and then traveled up again, hovering around that sexy leather pouch. How could leather make a man look even more enticing?

She licked her lips as her eyes took another stroll up to his broad chest and shoulders. His arms arced out from his sides, all bulging muscles and thick wrists wrapped in leather. Around his neck was a leather strap with fake ivory tusks and a gold medallion in the center. The crowning glory was a leather headband adorned with jewels.

Jewels. She smiled, dropping her eyes again.

"Hey."

She was startled again, feeling her cheeks flush.

"Eyes up here, woman." He pointed to his face.

"I'm...trying." She forced her mouth to close and shifted her gaze up. The hunger in his eyes made her flush all over again and did something altogether sinful between her legs.

She was suddenly very nervous, afraid she'd go to great lengths to rip that leather from his body and then get in trouble for ruining a costume. In an effort to distract herself—and him, given his lustful stare—she unsheathed her sword and held it up in his direction.

"Stay back, you horny thing," she teased.

His lips lifted in a crooked smile. "My sword is way bigger than yours."

She waved her sword. "It's not the size that matters."

"You know how to do a lot of things well, Fiona Steele." He took a step forward, and she took a step back. "But I still wield my sword more skillfully than you." He narrowed his eyes as he moved in on her, hands at his sides.

"No argument there." She walked backward around the clothing rack. "But I know how to slay it."

He grabbed the sharp blade of her sword with one hand and tugged, slamming her into his bare chest. And, oh, did he feel good! She let her hands explore his hard muscles as he backed her against the wall.

"That you do," he said in a husky voice, before taking her in a kiss so lascivious she relinquished her sword, and he must have, too, because it clanked to the ground and his big, hot hands were all over her. Fiona was lost in the feel of his mouth, his hands, and his body. God, his body. He was so hard and hot, and…Her eyes flew open. Her arms and legs were wrapped around Jake. She was trying to climb him like scaffolding in the costume room!

She forced herself to tear her lips away, breathless. It was a good thing he kept ahold of her, because her spaghetti legs needed a minute to remember how to work. They gazed into each other's eyes for a long, silent moment. Fiona, weighing the idea of throwing caution to the wind and making love right there on the floor, and Jake looking like he was doing the same—only leaning more heavily toward the whole throwing caution side, while she feared getting caught.

She pushed at his chest halfheartedly. "We should look at more costumes."

"It's your night. Whatever you want, you shall have."

"That's full of delicious innuendo."

He pressed his stubbly cheek to hers. "It was meant to be."

He was wrong. He had a greater power to slay her than she did him. She wanted him more than she wanted anything else in the world, but being caught in a costume room having sex with Jake Braden seemed like something rag magazines headlines were made of, and after fending off a few paparazzi on the way into work that morning, she didn't trust that they weren't everywhere, no matter how paranoid that might seem.

She took a step away and snagged another costume without looking at what it was.

"Little Bo Peep?" Jake flashed a coy smile and picked up her sword from the ground.

"Why, Jake," she said with her best Southern drawl. "I bet

there's a wrangler outfit in here somewhere." She batted her eyelashes and disappeared around the side of the rack.

"So now you have a thing for my brothers?" His voice was filled with jealousy over his rancher brothers, Wes and Luke.

She went up on her tiptoes and looked at him over the clothing rack. "Hardly. I have a thing for Jake Braden in a pair of assless chaps."

"Careful. Good things come to those who wish." He searched through a rack of Western outfits.

They spent the next hour trying on everything from assless chaps to genie costumes and *Planet of the Apes* outfits. They laughed and kissed and chased each other around the room like teenagers, reminiscent of how they used to be. She loved this playful side of Jake, which conflicted with his überalpha side. His devilish grin made her want to be even coyer.

Fiona peered around the edge of one of the racks, hiding her body from Jake.

"Do you have a fan?" she asked.

"A whole entourage," he teased.

"*Ugh.* Remember, I knew you when you were a sixth grader who threw a fit when your brother stole your BB gun."

He leveled her with a dark stare. "And then I kicked the shit out of him."

"Gee, I don't remember that," she said with a teasing smile. "Fan," she reminded him.

He disappeared into a closet and pulled out a large metal

fan and flicked it on.

"Your fan, madam."

She sauntered into the center of the room wearing a Marilyn Monroe–style white halter dress and pulling a chair behind her. The skirt of her dress flapped in the wind of the fan. Jake stood up taller in his Jack Sparrow costume and raked his eyes down her body so slowly it felt like he took the dress off with the heat of it.

"Damn, Fi." He stepped closer and ran his hand up the back of her leg as she climbed onto the chair and turned her back to the fan.

Her dress rose up with the current from the fan. Fiona pressed her hands to her knees, pursed her lips, and flashed her best *come-hither* look, which she was pretty sure made her look like she was in pain, because she sucked at making sexy faces. Jake ran his hands up her thighs, and he shifted her to the side, bringing him face-to-face with her steamy lady parts.

"That seductive look is going to get you in trouble." He licked his lips before pressing them to the inside of her thigh. When she felt the slick glide of his tongue, she nearly toppled off the chair. Jake caught her in his arms and kissed her.

"I should bring you here every night." He set her feet back down on the floor and led her over to the closet where he'd retrieved the fan.

She couldn't remember the last time she'd laughed so hard or felt so uninhibited.

"Thank you for tonight, Jake. This has been really fun."

Jake held up one finger, disappeared into the closet, and when he came back out, he was holding up a dress identical to the blue dress Rose wore in the scene from *Titanic* where she stood at the bow of the ship with the wind blowing her hair.

"Jake." She felt her eyes widen as she touched the velvety material. "You remembered." *Titanic* had been their favorite movie. They'd watched it at least a dozen times over the two years they'd dated, and both knew most of the lines by heart.

"How could I forget?" He handed her the long blue gown. "Go ahead. Try it on." This time she didn't send him away. She was so touched by his thoughtfulness that she turned and swept her hair over one shoulder, allowing him to untie the top of her dress and help her into the other. He secured the wide satin tie around her waist and ribs and then draped the gold scarf over her arms.

He stepped back and drank her in. "Fiona, you are more beautiful than Kate Winslet could ever hope to be."

"Thank you, Jake. For everything."

He went back into the closet and retrieved a black jacket, dark pants, and white shirt that matched the ones Jack wore when he wrapped his arms around Rose from behind to keep her from jumping off the ship.

She helped him off with his Jack Sparrow costume, pausing when he was stripped down to his skivvies to admire his body for the hundredth time that evening. He stepped into the slacks, which fit snugly across his hips, and slipped his arms into the white shirt. Fiona stepped closer when he began buttoning the shirt and silently moved his hands away and buttoned it herself. The room was quiet, save for their shallow breathing and the wind of the fan. Fiona picked up the jacket and held it up for Jake to put it on. It was tight across his broad back, and the material strained against his biceps.

Fiona smiled up at him. "You should take it off so you don't split the seams."

"After." He wrapped his arms around her waist from behind, then turned them toward the fan. He gathered her hair over one shoulder, which was probably whipping him across the face from the breeze, and kissed the back of her neck.

"I swear, Fiona. Just being close to you again like this…It reminds me of everything we were together."

She leaned her back against him, feeling his heart hammering through his chest and his eager arousal against her butt. She held her hands out to her sides like Rose did in the movie.

"Let's do this." His voice fluttered in the wind of the fan.

She closed her eyes against the wind, remembering another time when she'd had to close her eyes against a big wind. Jake hadn't been with her then, but she'd felt like he was. She clutched his forearms and shared the memory with him.

"You, well, this, pulled me through a rough time when we were exploring for gold by drilling geophysical targets. We were flown to the drill rig by helicopter. On the flight out, I thought to myself, *Jake jumps out of these*, and it blew me away. I was so frightened, and I remember wondering how you were able to push past the fear and jump."

She turned and faced him, her hair blowing against her back, the ends of the scarf flapping beneath her arms. She pressed her hands to his chest, still getting used to being with him. Really *with* him.

"When the helicopter landed and I stepped out of the chopper, the wind was so strong I worried that I'd be swept into the water. It blew me back a few feet, and then I thought of you, standing behind me like this, and I stopped moving backward. It was like you were there with me. I felt your presence, and you stayed with me every minute of every day while I was on that rig. Every time fear got the better of me, I drew upon your voice, and I swear, Jake, I could actually hear you whispering, *I've got you, Fi.*"

He pressed his cheek to hers and whispered, "I've got you now, Fi." He touched his forehead to hers. "I wish I'd been there with you. We've missed out on a lot of years."

She heard sadness in his voice and hated that she'd been the cause of it.

"What I've realized over these last few days is that we can't go backward. We're either moving forward or we're wasting time. I can tell by the look in your eyes that you feel guilty about those missed years, but as I told you before, we probably needed that space and time to grow. And I don't want to go back. This is better. We're better. Even if we stumble along the way, we can still be better than we were."

"We were pretty great." She knew they would be better than before, because even this, here, now, was better.

"And we'll be awesome now. Back then we had no idea what we were capable of or what life had in store for us. We were dreamers, and we were full of indestructible teenage rebellion."

"You were filled with rebellion, and you still believe you're indestructible."

"Yeah, yeah. I know." He laughed. "Don't fool yourself, Fi. I think breaking up with me was rebellion, even if you don't see it that way. It was your way of fighting back against your father for tearing apart your family, and that's okay, because back then we didn't know anything beyond what we felt. Now we're armed with experience. So no more worrying about what might have been or what we didn't get a chance to have. We're lucky to have history to draw upon, but let's not dwell on it. Let's just see if we can blaze a new path to the future."

"You're really serious about us." It wasn't a question, and she didn't need confirmation. It was a realization, an acceptance.

"Yes, I'm serious. Being with you again..." He shook his head and looked away, as if he were watching a memory unfold before him. "I had buried everything good. You know how close my family is, and you've made me realize that I've created distance even with them. They have no idea what to make of me anymore."

"Yeah, they do." Fiona clamped her mouth shut. She shouldn't have said anything. Wes had done her a favor, and she didn't want to breach his confidence.

"What do you mean?"

"Just that they know who you are and they love you."

"Fi? You have that *cat ate the canary* look in your eyes."

She tried to distract him, even though she knew he wouldn't relent until she told him the truth. "Hey, look." She pointed to a random outfit on the racks. "Let's try those on."

He took her by the shoulders, and his eyes turned serious. There was no way she could lie to him. She bit the insides of her cheeks in an effort to keep from spilling the truth.

"Fiona Steele, what did you do?" His lips rose in a half smile, half you'd-better-fess-up and half playful threat that would probably lead to his hands that had traveled to her ribs giving them a squeeze.

"Jake, please." She trapped her lower lip in her teeth and closed her eyes tight.

"You think that's going to save you?" He folded her into his arms and kissed her, slipping his tongue between her teeth and making her laugh. He lifted her a few inches off the ground, kissed her again, and then set her back down.

"Okay, okay. Just don't tickle me." She drew in a breath.

"Just please don't be mad at Wes. He was only trying to help, and actually, it was Callie who came up with the idea, so you can't really blame your brother anyway."

"Callie." His eyes went serious again.

"Uh-huh. Well, and your mom." She fiddled with the edge of her scarf.

"Great." He shook his head.

"When I first got back to town, I stopped at Elisabeth's to get a pie to bring to my mom, and your mom and Callie were there."

He crossed his arms and lowered his chin, giving her a deadpan stare. "Go on."

"Well, you know your mom and I have always gotten along." There was no way for her to tell him without getting everyone in trouble. She reached for his hand, hardly able to believe she was going to tell him the truth and narc on his family.

"Can you please sit down? This is a lot to take in."

"Christ." He sat down, arms crossed, jaw muscles bunching, and set that stare on her again.

Fiona paced, deciding just to let it flow as fast as she possibly could, and once she began, she couldn't stop.

"I *might* have mentioned to your mom how I felt about you, and she *might* have mentioned that she thought you never got over us, and Callie suggested that I talk to you, so we all decided that doing it in public—at the bar—was the best idea in case you got really mad."

He leaned back and scrubbed his hand down his face. "Define *we*."

"I'd rather not," she said quietly.

"Fi."

Her heart thundered like a freight train. She knelt beside him and placed her hands on his very tense thighs. He didn't budge.

"I don't know how it happened, but somehow everyone thought it was a good idea to try again, and I was so scared, but I saw something in your eyes, Jake. I felt it when you first looked at me, even through your anger. And I think your family must have seen it there, too."

His silence was killing her.

"Talk to me, Jake. Please tell me that I didn't just ruin any chance we had."

He shifted his eyes away.

No, no, no!

"I don't blame you for being mad, but—"

"Damn it, Fiona."

She rose on shaky legs, and he tugged her down to his lap.

"You drive me fucking crazy," he said with a rough tone. "And as for my family…"

"Please don't be mad at them. All they really did was get you to the bar and the fair. That was it." She was so nervous she could barely think. The last thing she wanted was to be the cause of Jake getting mad at his family.

"I'm not mad." He let out a loud breath. "I might have to kick some Braden ass, but I'm not mad."

She let out a relieved sigh. "Then what are you?"

He sealed his lips over hers. She resisted at first, shocked and worried about what she'd revealed, but the kiss wasn't rough or angry. It was intense and somehow soothing at once. When they drew apart, the anger in Jake's eyes had softened.

"I have no idea what I am. It's hard to accept that my family saw right through me when I didn't even know this part of me was trapped inside. But I'm damn glad they did." He hugged her close. "Stay with me tonight, Fi. Please?"

Chapter Fourteen

FIONA WAS QUIET on the way to her apartment. She fidgeted with her hair and the edge of her seat, and she remained quiet when they stopped at her apartment to pick up her things for the next day before going to Jake's house.

"Are you okay, babe?"

"Yeah. Fine."

He doubted that, but it was obvious that she didn't want to talk as she gazed out the window. Jake used the silence to try to process what she'd told him. He remembered how hard Pierce had pushed him to stay in Trusty and go to the fair and how his brothers had given him shit for being a prick to Fiona. Now it all made sense—except Jake wanted to know why they could see feelings he hadn't known he still had.

At his house, he grabbed Fiona's bag from the trunk and slung it over his shoulder, then draped an arm around her, feeling tension in her movements.

"I'm really not mad," he assured her.

"It's not that." She fidgeted with the ends of her hair as he opened the door. She hesitated at the entrance.

"Come on, babe." He took her hand and led her inside, still trying to get a read on what was troubling her. Her steps were slow and reluctant. He set her bag down by the foyer and pulled her into his arms. Her eyes darted around the room, settling on the glass doors that led to the backyard.

"Don't worry. Susie's spread the word. We shouldn't be bothered, okay?" He tucked her hair behind her ear and kissed her forehead.

She shrugged. "It feels funny this time."

"More so than last time?" He wished women came with a handbook.

"A little. Jake, this is going to sound really stupid, but being here makes me think about all the other women you've been with." She lowered her eyes.

He lifted her chin and pressed a soft kiss to her lips. "I understand, and I'm sorry it's hurtful. I can't change the past, but I can tell you that I've never had another woman in my bedroom."

She rolled her eyes and scoffed. "I thought we were trying to be a couple, which means honesty, Jake. I'm a big girl, not a fool."

Jake took her hand and led her through the living room, down a narrow hallway, and stopped before a closed door. "You'll probably judge me by this, too, but I never wanted anyone in my room."

"I'm not judging you, just being honest about how I feel. You used to take me to your bedroom all the time, and that was in your mother's house. Do you really expect me to believe that you haven't taken women into your bedroom in your own house?"

"Jesus, Fi. I never understood why I didn't want a woman in my room." He stepped closer and held her hands. "It was because of you. I didn't realize it until just now, but when I brought you here, I brought you straight up to my room. You're the only woman who's ever been in there besides my cleaning lady."

He pushed open the door to the guest room, revealing a very plain king-sized bed and a dresser. The walls were white and unadorned. A black comforter matched the dark curtains. He watched Fiona's eyes slide over the furniture. She tilted her head to one side, opened her mouth to say something, then closed it. She released his hand and stepped into the room, turning slowly. Whatever she was thinking had her brows knitted together. She drew in a deep breath, then walked out of the room, pulled him away from the door, and closed it.

"Okay." She nodded and headed for the stairs.

"Okay?" He hurried after her as she walked upstairs and into his bedroom like she owned the place—and he loved it.

She spun around and smiled, closing in on him. She grabbed his shirt and tugged his face down to hers.

"I feel like you were telling me the truth, and I may be stupid, or maybe I felt what I wanted to feel, but I felt nothing but coldness in that room down there, and up here…It's hot, baby. Hot. Hot. Hot."

He wrapped an arm around her waist and ground his hips against her, tangling his other hand in her hair as he took her in a thought-stealing kiss. A wanton sound hitched in her throat, vibrating through their mouths and pulling him under. She was hot and sweet and kissed him greedily. Her hands grasped his hair, his back, his ass. Damn, he loved it when she grabbed his ass. He tugged her head back, and their lips parted with a rush of air. Her lips were plump and wet, her skin pink from his unshaven cheeks. Her lids were heavy, her eyes dark and sensuous as he took her lower lip between his teeth and sucked it into his mouth. She gripped his arms, her nails digging into his biceps as he swept his tongue over hers, then went for her neck, kissing, grazing his teeth over her skin. Her body began to tremble, her breathing became shallow. She clawed at his arm like she wanted to climb beneath his skin and fisted her other hand in his hair, pressing his teeth tighter to her flesh. His arousal throbbed beneath his zipper, aching for release.

She yanked his hair, tearing his lips from her neck. Her eyes were past seductive, past lust-filled. They'd gone straight to *fuck-me-hard*. He tightened his grip as she dragged her tongue along the edge of his jaw, taking him with her to that darker place where only they existed. He lifted her in his arms, burying his tongue in her mouth as he walked the few steps to his bed and set her down beneath him. He kneed her legs open wide. Her skirt hitched up to her hips as he rocked his arousal against her center and lifted her knees so he could press in tighter to her precious curves. She clawed at his back. He ripped his shirt off and pulled her mouth to his nipple, holding her there as she sucked and kissed him into near bursting. He couldn't take it much longer—he had to have her. He groaned with need, and her head fell back, giving him space to tear off her shirt and bra, leaving her bare from the waist up.

"Perfect. You're fucking perfect." He took her nipple, and much of her breast, into his mouth. She arched in to him, holding his head in place.

"God, Jake." She ground her hips against his hard length. "Please, now, Jake. Please."

He circled her nipple with his tongue, then moved to her other breast, giving it just as much attention as the first as he slid his hand between her legs and nearly lost his mind at the feel of her hot, wet panties. He had to taste her again. Once was never enough with Fiona. A hundred times wouldn't be enough. He tore the rest of her clothes from her body and lowered his mouth between her legs, groaning against her wetness as he loved her body in all the ways he'd missed for so very long. Fiona gasped for breath, fisting her hands in the sheets. Her hips thrust off the mattress and he pressed them back down, knowing how she loved his strength, his control, as he brought his mouth to her again, feeling the orgasm rip through her body.

"Oh…God…" she moaned.

He slowed his efforts, prolonging her pleasure, and slipped his fingers inside her, seeking the sensitive spot that would bring her over the edge again.

"Jake." She panted.

"Again, baby. Come for me again." He lowered his mouth to her again and felt her inner muscles clamp down as she gave in to the momentum of another orgasm and cried out his name.

"Jake. Please." She writhed beneath his grasp. "I have to feel you inside me."

He stood long enough to shed his clothing, then moved up her body and buried his tongue in her mouth, pressing his erection against her wet center as he reached for a condom. Jesus, she felt amazing. What he wouldn't give to plunge into her and feel her wetness swallow him whole.

"Hurry," she pleaded as he rose to roll the condom on.

He eased her legs farther apart with his knees and laced his fingers with hers, pressing her hands to the mattress. His body pulsed with need, and he was powerless to slow his urgency.

"I don't want to be gentle, Fi," he said quickly and probably too harshly.

"Then don't."

Her hips rose up to meet him, and he thrust into her, hard. They both gasped a breath at their joining, but he couldn't tame his ache for her. He thrust balls-deep over and over again, each time earning a gasp of pleasure from Fiona.

He sealed his lips over hers and kissed her hard, his whole body thrumming with desire. When she wrapped her legs around his waist, he nearly came undone. He tore his lips away, wanting to see the need in her eyes. The rapture on her face made his heart fill with love. She was his. Open and loving. She knew just what he needed, and the realization revved him up even more. He ground his hips to hers. They were as close as two people could be as he kissed her neck, stroking the sensitive skin beneath her ear as her legs fell open, and her body began to pulsate around him.

"Fi, I'm gonna…"

Her teeth were clenched, eyes closed, lost in her own release. The sight did him in. Two powerful thrusts sent him over the edge, teeth gritted, grunting with every magnificent pulse of his orgasm.

He folded her into his arms and nuzzled against her neck, unable to quiet his thoughts no matter how vulnerable they made him.

"Don't leave me again, Fi. Please."

He felt her melt beneath him.

"Never," she whispered.

He closed his eyes, still buried inside her, and for the first time in as long as he could remember, he thanked the heavens above. He'd lost faith for so long that he'd worried he might never believe or trust again.

He had been so wrong.

So very wrong.

Chapter Fifteen

THE NEXT WEEK passed with the comfort and thrill of getting acquainted with new sides of a favorite lover. Finn had finally called Fiona. She was beginning to worry about why he hadn't, despite his reaching out to Shea. He'd told her that he didn't want to get in the way of what she was doing. He'd known that she was still in love with Jake forever, but he'd always been careful not to tell her what to do about it. He'd said he was happy for her, and of course, he'd said that if she ever needed him, he would drop everything to be there for her. And she knew he would.

Fiona had spent every night at Jake's house since the previous weekend. They'd spent hour upon hour in each other's arms, making love, then dozing, and making love again, before getting up each morning to face the day together. They'd fallen into an easy pattern of going on early-morning runs, and in that sense it was just like old times. They teased each other, egged each other on to push themselves harder, and knocked teeth when they tried to kiss as they ran.

Jake enjoyed running the hilly trails, but Fiona's favorite run was along the beach. The crisp morning air and the salty breeze filled her with a feeling of newness and hope, while the hilly runs reminded her of home. After their run, while Jake worked out in his home gym, Fiona caught up on emails from her real job. They showered together—being sure to leave extra time for lovemaking and teasing beneath the warm spray. They had coffee, pretending they weren't ogling each other, before finally driving in to work together.

Some days Jake had meetings that took him off set and Fiona was on a dead run keeping up with Trish.

Fiona became closer to Patch and Trace, and Zane had taken to teasing her about Jake. *Where's loverboy? Where's Casanova?* It was all in fun, and she no longer felt uncomfortable around Zane or the other A-list actors. She'd even seen Megan Flexx crossing one of the sets, and Megan had lifted her hand in a tentative wave that Fiona had read as a peace offering.

Friday afternoon Jake surprised Fiona with a romantic picnic in the park. Well, not really a park, because they didn't have time to go off set, but he'd arranged to use the park setting of another movie. They'd finished their sandwiches and were stretched out on a blanket beneath a tree, holding hands while lying on their backs.

"Heard back from my doc." Jake pushed up onto his elbow with a serious look in his eyes.

Fiona's pulse raced. "And?"

His grin told her the results were negative. He lowered his lips to hers, and his tongue worked its magic, stealing her thoughts and making her body heat with desire. Jake's kisses held promises of gratifying sex and so much more. She wanted to climb inside them and bed down for the night. His big, strong hands moved slowly up her torso and gripped her ribs. When he tore his lips away, she moaned and tried to pull him back for more.

He brushed his thumb over her nipple, looking at her like he could devour her right there and then.

"You sure you want to get ready for the cast dinner at Trish's tonight and not with me?"

No. I want to go to your trailer and fuck your brains out.

"I..." She swallowed, trying to regain control and think rationally. His question took her by surprise. The cast dinner was the last thing on her mind. It took her a minute to remember that they were lying on an open movie set where anyone could see them. She had work to do, and so did he. Spending an hour devouring each other wasn't a viable option. She forced the thoughts from her mind and focused on his question. *Dinner. Getting ready with Trish.*

"If you don't mind. Shea sent over dresses and has a makeup artist and hairstylist coming to help us get ready."

"But Shea's not sending this over." He pressed his rigid length against her thigh.

"So unfair," she whispered and pulled him down for another delicious kiss.

"God, Jake." She tried to right her breathing and refocus *again*. She'd missed his virility and potency in the way he kissed her, the way he touched her. The way he freaking breathed. She was a goner. Gone. Gone. Gone.

"It'll be fun. You can pick me up at her place like a real date."

Jake nodded, but his eyes grew serious. "Okay, but you have no idea what these things are like. You might want to work off some nervous energy first." He ground his hips against her again.

Fiona closed her eyes, fighting the urge to rip his clothes off or give in and get ready for dinner at his place so they could have an hour to devour each other first. She'd promised Trish they'd get ready together, and she was so nervous, she needed Trish to assure her she'd be okay. She couldn't back out. She tried to make light of it to ease her own nerves and bring her head back into rational territory instead of the land of Jake Braden's manhood.

"How bad can it be? It's dinner at a restaurant." She'd asked Trace what to expect, and Trace had told her that it would be kind of crazy. That the stars who were in demand—Jake, Zane, and a number of others, as well as Trish as the up-and-comer—would be the center of attention. Fiona had expected that, and she felt secure enough to handle it.

"Everyone's there. The press, directors, producers, every

cast member. It's going to be loud, and half the people will be hyping the movie, while the other half will talk about what happens if it bombs." Worry lines streaked his forehead.

"That doesn't sound so bad."

He looked away, and Fiona's stomach sank. She wondered if he was trying to prepare her for another Megan Flexx encounter. He'd received a few sexy texts from women over the past few days, and he'd been honest about who they were. He'd even texted them back explaining that he was off the market. It had seemed a strange way to reference himself. Then again, social circles that revolved around single men and women were often linked to the term *meat market*.

And Jake was damn meaty.

"And…" Jake smiled as he sat up. "You'll be there looking hotter than hell and men will be ogling you."

Fiona climbed into his lap and wrapped her arms around his neck, relieved that jealousy was his issue and not something more ominous. She didn't even want to imagine what else it could have been.

"I have noticed, and it's not like you have anything to worry about."

Jake's phone vibrated, and she felt his body tense beneath her.

She slid off his lap. "Go ahead and get it. I need to head back in a sec anyway."

"It's okay." He reached for her again.

"Jake, we've made it through several sexy texts from women already. I think we'll be fine."

He shook his head and rubbed his eyes with his thumb and forefinger. "I really hate who I was, Fi."

"I don't. Well, I kind of do, but who you were helped you become who you are. Besides, out of all the beautiful women out there, you chose me. I feel special." His phone vibrated again. "So answer your phone."

He sighed and pulled his cell from his pocket. She saw relief in his eyes. "Hey, Em." He mouthed *Emily* to Fiona.

"Really? When are they coming?" Jake pulled Fiona closer as he listened to Emily. "We'll still be filming, but we could Skype with you."

Fiona loved hearing him say *we*.

"Me and Fiona." He held the phone away from his head.

Fiona heard Emily squeal. Jake cringed; Fiona laughed. She heard Emily talking a mile a minute.

Jake handed her the phone. "Chick stuff."

She pressed the phone to her ear. "Hi, Emily. It's Fiona. Your brother relinquished the phone. How are you?"

"Oh my God. Fiona. You guys are really together!" She spoke so fast that Fiona couldn't help but laugh. "I knew he wasn't over you. I knew you were meant for each other. I knew it. I'm so happy."

"So are we, Emily. Thank you."

Jake lay back on the blanket and rested his forearm over his eyes, keeping one hand on Fiona's thigh.

"I called to tell Jake our cousins Shannon and Sam are

coming into town. We were hoping he could come home to see them. We haven't seen them in years. But he said he's still going to be filming, but you could Skype with us."

"Sure. Just let us know when and we'll make sure we're around." Speaking of themselves as a couple felt really good. As if he was thinking the same thing, Jake squeezed her leg.

"Okay. Hey, I have to run. Dae and I are meeting Ross and Elisabeth at the movies." Emily gasped. "Oh my gosh! I just realized that when Jake does visit again, maybe you'll be with him and we can double date."

Fiona loved that idea so much she couldn't stop grinning after they ended the call.

Jake slid his arm away from his eyes and smiled up at her. "You realize all of Trusty will know about us in about seven minutes, right?"

"The Trusty grapevine is pretty rabid." Not that she minded at all.

Jake grinned. "The Trusty grapevine has nothing on Emily."

"Is that why you brought me into the conversation? I see. First you alert the paparazzi; now you alert Emily, Trusty's equivalent of the paparazzi. If I didn't know better, I'd think you were trying to send some kind of message."

He swept her beneath him. "I am. Loud and clear. Fiona Steele is now off the market."

Boy, do I like the sound of that.

Chapter Sixteen

LATER THAT EVENING, Fiona stood in Trish's hotel room in a designer black strapless cocktail dress, astounded at her reflection in the mirror, while the makeup artist Shea had arranged for them added the finishing touches to Trish's makeup.

"You're hot, Fi," Trish said. "Isn't she hot, Javier?"

Javier, the makeup artist, turned with an eyeliner pencil in his hand, pursed his thin lips, which matched his pencil-thin, skinny-jeans-clad body, and ran scrutinizing eyes over Fiona. Her stomach quivered under his assessing gaze.

"Honey, Jake Braden isn't going to know what hit him. With those smoky eyes and crimson lips that look like they were made for kissing? Mm-mm-mm. The man will be in heaven." Javier turned his attention back to Trish. "And you're going to have all those other men lining up for your attention, sugar."

"Thanks, Javier, but I'm not on the hunt for a man. I just

want to make it through this production without anyone hating me." Trish waved Fiona over to her. "Can you FaceTime Shea? I promised she'd get to see us."

"Yeah, of course. I forgot she flew back to New York last night. I'll use your laptop because it has a bigger screen." Fiona connected FaceTime on the laptop and called Shea. The side of Shea's head filled the screen.

"Hold on." Shea must have set the phone down, because her camera was pointing at the ceiling. "I'm just finishing up a draft contract. Hold on one sec." A minute later Shea picked up the phone. Her eyes widened as Fiona twirled in her dress. "Fi! Oh my God! Look at you! You look like you belong on the red carpet."

"I don't know about that, but Javier worked wonders, didn't he?"

Shea smiled. "You really do look amazing. You'll be the prettiest one there tonight."

"Ahem," Trish said loudly.

"Oh, let me turn the laptop. You have to see Trish. She's wearing an emerald-green dress that she had to paint on, and Javier did something awesome to her eyes that really brings out the green."

"I love your technical terms." Javier finished with Trish's makeup and touched his spiky black hair. "Awesomeness abounds, Shea. How are you, love?"

"I'm excited for them," Shea answered. "Thank you for

everything, Javier. Is Mikaela still there?" Mikaela was the hairdresser Shea had sent over.

"Mikaela had to leave," Fiona answered. "But she was also amazing. Look what she did to my hair. It's never been this shiny or this full." Fiona turned slowly so Shea could see the fullness and curl at the ends of her long dark hair.

"Gorgeous. Listen, Fi, I know I'm not your PR person, but I want to give you some advice." Shea's tone was so serious that Fiona's smile faltered.

"Okay."

"I know you're not used to any of this, but you need to act like you are, at least in front of the cameras. For Jake's sake, and for yours. Smile, keep your head up high, and no matter what happens, don't let anything but a smile show on your face."

"No pressure or anything, right?" Fiona couldn't imagine that she wouldn't be smiling all night, even if she was nervous.

"What I mean is, there will be people all over and eyes on you every second of the night. So, you know, if you scratch your nose, that's the moment they'll snap the pictures, so just be aware."

Fiona sighed. "That's a lot of pressure."

"You'll be fine. Just keep these in mind." Shea turned her phone toward her computer screen, where she had the photos from the paparazzi ambush of Jake and Fiona as her screensaver.

"Aw, Fi. I love the way he's looking at you. I'll never get enough of those pictures. We should print them and blow them up really big." Trish touched her shoulder.

"That man, he has it bad," Javier said as he gathered his things. "I'd give anything for Jake Braden to look at *me* like that." He winked, and they laughed. "Okay, ladies. Remember, no touching your hair or faces. No wiping your eyes, so no crying tears of joy, either." He leaned in between Trish and Fiona and whispered, "And only air kisses until you're far away from photographers."

They thanked Javier and listened to a litany of directions from Shea about holding their shoulders back, sucking in their nonexistent stomachs—*because the camera adds ten pounds*—and other things that made Fiona ten times more nervous than she had been before talking to her.

After they ended the call, Trish opened her mini-fridge and handed Fiona a bottle of Scotch and opened one herself.

"We need a drink. You're so nervous you've gone green."

"Green?"

"Kidding. Drink up."

They clinked bottles and downed the liquor.

Fiona cringed at the burning liquid sliding down her throat. "How do people drink that? It's nasty."

"Liquid courage, my dear. You'll feel better in a few minutes." She tossed the empty bottles in the trash and turned to answer the knock at the door.

"It's him." Fiona's stomach flipped.

"Of course it's him. I don't have a date, remember?" Trish opened the door and stepped to the side with a dramatic sweep of her arm. "Mr. Braden, won't you come in?"

Fiona's heart was beating triple time as Jake stepped into the room in a dark suit that looked as if it were made for him. She'd seen him dressed up in magazines, but it had been years since she'd seen him all gussied up in person for their high school prom. He'd been handsome then, but *wow!* Back then she couldn't imagine anyone looking more handsome. Now she realized how very wrong she'd been. Jake had filled out in all the right places, and although she'd already tasted, touched, and savored his delicious, naked body, there was something about seeing him in a suit that made her blood boil. She couldn't tear her eyes away.

"You look beautiful, Trish."

"Thank you." Trish closed the door behind him.

Jake's eyes locked on Fiona as he crossed the room and placed his hand on her lower back, kissing her cheek.

"You look ravishing," he whispered. "Can't I just take you home instead of going to dinner?"

Her whole body heated up.

"Okay, whatever you just said made the poor girl blush all over." Trish laughed.

Jake lifted Fiona's chin and kissed her softly on the lips. "Well?"

Fiona shook her head and smiled. "You can't miss your big night." She reached for Trish's hand. "And I don't want to miss your big night or Trish's big night."

"You'll have plenty of fooling-around time afterward." Trish rolled her eyes. "Are you filming this weekend?"

"They may need to do one scene, but as of right now, no." Jake's eyes ran between the two women. "Trish, do you want to ride with us? I'm sorry. I should have offered before now. That wasn't very thoughtful of me."

Fiona felt her heart squeeze. He might not have thought of it earlier, but the fact that he was thinking of it now meant the world to her.

"No, thank you. I promised myself that I'd show up alone. I'm making a statement."

"You are?" Fiona asked.

"Yes, in all the years I've been acting, I've never gone to an event alone, and I think the world looks at actresses as always *needing* a man on their arm." Trish smoothed her dress, stood up straighter, and drew her shoulders back. "I'm smart and secure and I want to arrive alone and smile so everyone knows it."

"I never knew you were such a feminist." Fiona laced her fingers with Jake's.

"I'm impressed," Jake said. "I don't know many actresses who would show up alone to an event."

"Thank you." Trish reached for Fiona's free hand. "Help

me with my hair?"

Fiona wrinkled her brow. *Your hair?*

"Mm-hmm." Trish grabbed her hand. "Jake, we'll be right back." She dragged Fiona into the bathroom and closed the door behind them, leaning against it and breathing hard.

"I don't want to go alone. I'm never nervous going to events when I have a date, and tonight I feel like I'm red-carpet-for-the-first-time nervous," Trish admitted.

"Wow, you are? You just blew me away out there." Fiona shook her head.

"I was acting. I'm good, right?" Trish managed a partial smile.

"You're spectacular, and you're coming with us." Fiona embraced her.

"I can't do that. This is your date. I think I can handle it alone. Just tell me I'll be fine. Tell me that acting is easy and that's what I need to do tonight. It's stupid that I'm nervous. I've gone to a bazillion events."

"No way. Who cares how many events you've gone to? Come with us. Jake won't mind, and we can lean on each other. I'm nervous, too."

"You sure?" Trish asked with a furrowed brow.

"Of course."

"You don't think I'm lame? I'm always the one who's strong."

"Well, tonight I'll be strong and you can be the beautiful

actress who is secure enough to show up without a date and with a best friend and her boyfriend in tow."

A smile spread across Trish's lips. "Boyfriend." She clutched Fiona's hands.

"I know!"

They wiggled their shoulders and hips and grinned like silly kids doing a happy dance, then both inhaled a loud breath and blew it out. They drew their shoulders back and put their game faces—or rather, adult faces—on.

"Ready?" Fiona asked.

"Let's do this."

JAKE AND FIONA sat across from Trish in the back of the limousine. Jake held Fiona's hand while she fidgeted with the edge of her fancy black dress. Her legs looked a mile long in a pair of black spiky heels, and no matter how much Jake tried to distract himself, he couldn't help but envision her legs wrapped around his waist, spiky heels and all.

He tried to push away the dirty thoughts, knowing they'd be barraged by cameras in mere minutes, not to mention that Trish was sitting across from them looking like she was about to go to war. He touched Fiona's cheek, bringing her eyes to his. The dark eye shadow she had on made her look even more alluring. He wanted to see her beautifully coiffed hair spread across his pillow as he loved her senseless. He didn't give a damn about the cast dinner, but Luce, his public-relations rep, had given him hell about the paparazzi stunt he'd pulled last week and made him promise to behave tonight.

He knew the rules of the celebrity lifestyle, and although he sometimes liked to break them, he knew that being with Fiona tonight would bring her further into his world. And he wanted that in a bad way. He wanted her to be comfortable in his world and to be seen with him wherever he went. He knew Fiona was nervous tonight, and he focused on making her feel at ease.

"You two look gorgeous," he said sincerely.

Trish looked up at him through thick lashes. "Thank you. It's crazy that I was nervous to go alone, wasn't it?"

"The first time I went to a cast dinner, I was alone, and I felt like I was going to be sick. Then I realized that everyone there was just a normal person. Like me and you." Jake draped an arm over Fiona's shoulder and hoped that she was hearing everything he was saying. He knew that Trish could handle herself, but he didn't want to direct all of his advice to Fiona, for fear of making her even more nervous. "Everyone will be two sheets to the wind by the time we arrive, and they'll carry on about the movie like it's going to be the best one yet. And it might. But they're no different from the people Fiona works with. They just think they are."

Trish shifted her eyes to Fiona, as if she was hoping Fiona

was listening, too. "Somehow I don't think they're just like Clark or Joe."

"Clark and Joe are two of the scientists I work with. They're pretty...scientisty. You know, quiet, serious," Fiona explained.

"Don't knock nerds," Jake said. "You know I have an engineering degree." Jake's mother had insisted that he get a college degree as a backup plan to his stuntman career, and he remembered Fiona once telling him that his intelligence was the second thing that had attracted her to him. The first being the way he'd looked at her when she was a teenager—like no one else existed.

"You are the sexiest nerd I've ever met." Fiona leaned over and kissed him, then glanced at Trish. "Well, the sexiest male nerd. Trish is the sexiest female nerd. In fact, you guys should make a new *Revenge of the Nerds* movie and show them how unnerdy nerds can be."

They rode in silence for a beat, and then Fiona said, "Nice try, but I'm still nervous."

He smiled in a way he hoped was reassuring. "I'll be right there with you. Think of it as having dinner with a bunch of really loud friends. Celebrities are regular people; they just have more exposure than other people."

Fiona shook her head. "Sorry, but Steven Hileberg is *not* a regular person. Zane Walker is *not* a regular person. *You're* not a regular person." She fidgeted with her dress. "Before I came here, I kept telling myself that you were just a regular guy. The same guy you were in Trusty, but, Jake, you're anything but that guy. You're a star."

Jake grinned. "That's just my job. What does that have to do with anything?"

The limousine parked in front of the restaurant.

"I don't want to take anything away from that." She looked at Trish. "And *you're* not a regular person either. You guys are both superstars. I should be nervous. I'm just me. Rock girl."

The driver opened the door for Jake, but he didn't move. He held Fiona's hand and her gaze.

"Rock girl. The hottest damn rock girl around." A smile spread across his lips. "I called you that the first time I asked you out."

"I remember." She smiled, and he wondered if she was remembering when he'd given her the nickname, too. Fiona had been in the science lab looking at pieces of rock through a microscope, and Jake had tried to get her attention by asking a million questions. Fiona hadn't lifted her eyes from the microscope until he'd said, *So tell me, rock girl. What do you like to do on Friday nights?* He later told her that he'd thought she didn't like him, and only then did she admit that she had been afraid that if she looked at him she'd lose her nerve to speak.

Cameras flashed through the tinted glass, drawing all of

their attention back to the moment.

"Trish, do you want to walk in with us?" Jake offered.

"No, thanks. I'll be fine," Trish said. "Come on, rock girl. We need to get this over with before you chicken out."

Camera flashes blinded Jake as he helped Trish and Fiona from the car. He slipped his arm around Fiona's waist and held her close.

"Jake, who's your mystery date?" a tall man yelled.

Jake wondered if he'd been hiding beneath a rock, since their pictures had been plastered all over the Internet for days. He gazed into Fiona's eyes as he answered.

"No mystery. The one and only Fiona Steele," Jake said with pride as they smiled for the cameras and walked into the restaurant, trailed by camera flashes and unanswered questions.

"Fiona, over here!" a man yelled.

She turned as if she'd walked the runway her whole life and flashed an easy smile. Appreciation and pride swelled in Jake's chest. He knew being the center of attention was nerve-racking for her, and yet there she was, carrying herself with poise and smiling as if she'd been walking the red carpet her whole life. He kissed her temple. Every step they took was met with dozens of camera flashes. Jake kept a tight grip on Fiona, and as they walked into the restaurant, he heard the paparazzi turning their attention to Trish.

"Trish Ryder!" a woman yelled, and cameras flashed behind them.

Spice, the upscale restaurant where the dinner was being hosted, was dimly lit and smelled like rich foods, expensive perfume, and money. Dark woods and plush seating occupied by men in Armani suits and women in designer dresses were regular sights at the upscale restaurant. The hostess had the rail-thin body of a runway model and moved gracefully through the restaurant in her long black skirt as she led them toward the private room in the back of the restaurant.

"You okay?" Jake whispered to Fiona.

"The one and only?" She raised her brows.

"You are, Fi. It just took me a long time to figure it out." Jake felt a hand on his arm and turned to find two blond women who looked familiar rising from where they'd been sitting with a group of people.

"Jake," one of them purred as she moved to kiss his cheek.

"Remember us?" the tall blonde said, eyeing Fiona. "We heard you were back in town."

Jake tightened his grip around Fiona's waist and felt her stiffen against his side. He noticed two actors rising from their seats, waving him over, a welcome distraction from the two women who were invading his personal space. He turned and spotted Trish and Zane heading in their direction. The space between tables was quickly filling with fans and other people in the industry. Jake pulled from the women's grasp and took a step away.

"Ladies," he said. "Nice to see you again."

He guided Fiona away, mumbling an apology to her, as Brenda Marlow, another actress, rose from her seat and embraced Jake, tearing him from Fiona.

"So good to see you again." She swooned.

Christ. He saw a sad look in Fiona's eyes as Brad Parlor, an A-list actor, grabbed him by the shoulder and pulled him away from Brenda and into a manly embrace. *Thank God.*

"Jake. Congrats, man." Along with doing Brad's stunts for his last five movies, Jake had done a fair amount of partying with Brad. "I hear your newest flick is going to be insane."

"That's the hope. They have a great cast." Jake eyed the tables ahead of them, noting several celebrities he recognized and anticipating an onslaught of greetings. He had one goal in mind, to get back to Fiona and get her through this quickly. "Excuse us, Brad."

When he turned, he was eye to eye with two actors from his last film. He greeted them, and a crowd quickly gathered. He shook hands and slapped the men's backs congenially, laughing at their jokes. One of the men drew his date up to her feet, and she wrapped her arms around Jake's neck in greeting. He didn't even catch her name as he was spun in another direction and into the arms of another actress who pawed at him like he was there for her taking. He hoped Fiona wasn't watching as he tried to fend her off, which proved far more difficult than he'd anticipated. She wrapped her fingers around the nape of his neck and whispered something about meeting her later.

People at neighboring tables stood to take photos, and being the practiced actor that he was, Jake smiled as if he were on a photo shoot, then used more force than he would have liked to pry himself from the hungry actress's hands. Zane and Trish, trailed by more camera flashes, joined him a few minutes later, and as he turned again to try to locate Fiona, his stomach sank. She was nowhere in sight.

At six foot three, he could see over most of the other people who were milling about. They'd moved farther into the restaurant and were in the midst of the cast and crew, making their way into the private, and crowded, dining room.

Where are you, Fi? He grabbed Zane. "You see Fiona?"

Zane looked around. "No."

"Goddamn it." He heard Trish laughing and turned, hoping to see Fiona, but Trish was talking with Trace and Carla. He pushed through the crowd and finally spotted Fiona, bent over, holding on to the back of a chair and fiddling with her shoe.

He helped her right her high heel, then wrapped her in his arms.

"I'm sorry, Fi. Are you okay?"

"Someone jostled me and I lost my shoe. I'm fine." She didn't look at him.

"Who knocked into you?" Annoyance simmered in his

gut, and suddenly he hated the damn function.

She shook her head, eyes serious. "How would I know?"

"Come on. Let's get you to a seat." He led her into the private room, which was just as crowded as the restaurant. Two weeks ago, Jake would have eaten up the mayhem and media attention. Now he wanted to wrap Fiona in his arms and whisk her away from the chaos.

One of the producers grabbed him and pulled him into a conversation with two other cast members. He felt Fiona's fingers slip from his hand, and as he reached for her, Zane slipped an arm over her shoulder with a curt *I've got her* nod. Jake's gut clenched. He knew Zane was being protective of her for him, but it didn't lessen the impact of knowing Zane was doing what he should have been doing.

"I want to talk to you about doing Zane's next movie in Sweetwater. In Upstate New York," the producer said.

Jake shifted his attention back to him. "Great. Sounds good."

"It's at Sugar Lake. Small-town romantic suspense," the producer said. "It's gonna kick ass."

Jake glanced back in the direction where Fiona and Zane had been, and he didn't see them anywhere. He'd lost track of her again.

"Great. Sounds good. We'll talk." He excused himself from the group, feeling as though smoke were coming out his ears from sheer frustration. He went in search of Fiona again.

"Jake, so nice to see you." Carla air-kissed his cheeks.

"Hi, Carla." Carla wore a white minidress and stood nearly a foot taller than Trace, who was stunning in a black designer dress. Jake narrowed his eyes at Trace.

"Have you seen Fi?"

Trace went up on her toes, which Jake knew wouldn't help. She was five three in heels, and as she strained to see around the massive shoulders in front of her, he knew she couldn't find Fiona any quicker than he could.

Jake touched her arm and smiled. "It's okay. I'll find her."

He moved through the crowd, looking over the heads of the others, and spotted Zane standing beside a tall, thin woman he didn't recognize. He caught his attention and held his palm up in the air.

Zane shrugged and shook his head.

Damn it. Why had he thought he could count on Zane to really take care of Fiona? He never should have left her side. Jake scanned the room and found her sitting at the table. He pushed his way past a group of people who were laughing too loud and knelt beside Fiona.

"Fi, I'm so sorry. This is crazy." He placed his hands on hers, and when she didn't meet his gaze, his stomach lurched. "I'm sorry I lost track of you. I won't let it happen again."

"It's okay. This is your job. I get it." Her tone was clipped.

"I got snagged by one of the producers. They want me to do Zane's next film."

He rubbed an ache in the back of his neck as he settled into a chair beside her. He could tell by the way she was looking around the room, at the floor, anywhere other than at him, that she was annoyed.

"I'm really sorry, Fi. I got pulled in a hundred directions."

"It's okay." She turned as Patch sat down beside her, and the two of them began talking.

Jake's heart ached as he watched how easily she talked with Patch, with a friendly tone and a genuine smile. When one of the producers asked her about a geological study that had been done near one of their sets, she exuded impeccable manners talking about her work with confidence. He knew she was being careful about using layman's terms, which was another thing Jake loved about her. Unlike most of the celebrities he was used to, who spoke of their work as if it were the most important work on the planet, Fiona was modest.

"Jake." A heavy hand landed on his shoulder.

Jake rose to greet Steven Hileberg. Fiona smiled graciously, and although Jake noticed that it didn't reach her eyes, he was fairly certain no one else would.

"Steven, you know my girlfriend, Fiona Steele." *Girlfriend.* The word felt foreign, but it also felt right, though he had a feeling he hadn't been a great boyfriend tonight by losing sight of her—even if it had been just a short period of time.

Steven was in his early sixties, with thick gray hair, wire-rimmed glasses, and piercing blue eyes. He took Fiona's hand

and kissed the back of it.

"Yes, of course. You made quite an impression on the cover of all the gossip magazines last week."

Fiona blushed. "I guess that's what happens when you date Jake Braden."

"Or maybe," Steven said with a warm tone, "it's what happens when Jake Braden dates *Fiona Steele.*"

He paused, as if he were allowing the words to sink in, and Jake wasn't sure who they were meant for. Him or Fiona. Or perhaps both.

"Jake, I wanted to let you know that we're not shooting that scene tomorrow." Steven patted him on the back. "So you two kids can enjoy a little time off."

When Jake was filming, he typically craved the hectic schedule. He worked hard and played hard, filming all day and partying well into the night. That seemed like a world away from what he wanted now. He was thrilled to have a day off to spend with Fiona. He glanced at her. She was fidgeting with her napkin in her lap. He wanted more than anything to be alone with her so he could take away the disappointment in her eyes.

FIONA FOLLOWED TRISH into an enormous ladies' room tiled floor to ceiling with marble, accented by bright lights and large mirrors and a sitting room furnished with luxurious couches and chairs. She felt like she'd walked into someone's home instead of a bathroom. She sank down onto the sofa and sighed loudly.

"Please shoot me, Trish." Fiona watched Trish eyeing her with concern.

"You mean because of the cold shoulder you're giving the most handsome man out there?" Trish sat down beside her.

"Yes. I don't know what's wrong with me. He got caught up in all those people when we got here, and he didn't even notice when I got pushed to the side. He didn't even look for me. He just…went and did his thing."

"Fi." Concern had left the building. Trish had an *are-you-serious* look in her eyes.

"No, you don't have to tell me. He's in demand. I get it. I *know* that, which is why I'm asking you to just…" Fiona mocked a gun with her finger and thumb, aimed it at her temple, and pretended to pull the trigger.

Trish laughed. "If I shoot you, who will make sure I get to my meetings and have lunch and make the right set times?"

"Oh, please. You don't need me, but I appreciate the way you are trying to make me feel like you do."

"Nice subject change." Trish leaned back and sighed. "Honey, what's got you all tied in knots?"

Fiona got up and paced. "It's me. I'm totally overreacting to Jake doing what he should be doing—playing it up for his adoring fans. I just can't seem to snap out of it."

"That means it's more than that. I know you, Fi. You're not a jealous girl who needs to be catered to, so spill it."

Fiona turned away, trying to figure out what was really going on in her head.

"I wish I knew what *it* was."

"Are you worried that Jake will forget about you, or he'll be with someone else?" Trish asked.

"No. I don't think that's it. I trust him. I know how he feels about me. No one could fake what's between us."

"Then what is it?"

She fidgeted with the arm of the sofa. "Do you think this is what life would be like with Jake? I mean, if we stay together, do you think it would always be parties and fending off women? God…How do celebrities *ever* have normal lives?"

"Okay, see? That makes sense. No gun necessary to solve this one." Trish rose to her feet and went to Fiona's side. "Do you want heartbreaking honesty or best-friend bullshit?"

Fiona groaned. "Heartbreaking honesty."

"Okay, pull up your big-girl panties, because I think it will be really, really hard, but doable. From what I've seen, I think it will take a concerted effort by Jake and a lot of compromise on your side."

Fiona wanted desperately to believe it was possible, but tonight was an eye-opener, and it scared her. "I was standing out there tonight watching the craziness, and at first it was exciting, but it became really fake really fast. And that's my own issue. I get that. But how do I manage it within the confines of our relationship?"

"How do you manage to put up with assholes when you're out on assignments? How do you put up with the jerks who treat you like you're a secondhand citizen because you're on *their* dig site?" Trish's tone softened. "Fiona, this is just a different crowd. They're not the enemy. They're just beautiful people who are full of themselves instead of nerds arguing over geological sites."

Fiona felt a rush of relief. Trish had always been good at taking apart situations and putting them back in working order.

"Thanks, Trish." She took Trish's hand and led her over to the mirror. "You know what I see? Two beautiful women. A beautiful actress and a beautiful nerd."

"I don't think anyone out there thinks of you as a nerd. Did you see the way the second and third producers were eyeing you on your way to the bathroom?" Trish fluffed her hair and settled a hand on her hip.

"You're crazy, but the point is, I think you're right. With my work, I have perspective, and here..." She assessed herself in the mirror. She saw a strong, capable woman who had a stable career and a man she adored. Those women out there had nothing on her. They might be taller, thinner, and richer, but she had a full heart, and she wasn't about to let insecurities ruin that for her.

"Here, I've put myself into a lesser category, and obviously that got the better of me. I think I'd better go apologize to my man."

"That's my girl," Trish said as she gave her a friendly shove toward the door.

Fiona stepped out of the bathroom and was surprised to find Jake waiting for her.

"Sorry. I just wanted to catch you before you went back into the dining room. Trish, I made arrangements for the driver to take you home whenever you're ready, but Fiona and I will be taking a separate car." Jake reached for Fiona's hand.

"Okay, thanks." Trish hugged Fiona and whispered, "You can do this."

Fiona smiled and watched her friend walk away.

"I'm sorry for cornering you," Jake said.

"I'm glad you did." She pressed her palms to his lapels. "I am so sorry for being a bitch tonight."

"You weren't a bitch." He drew her in close.

"I was, and I'm sorry. This was harder than I thought it was going to be," she admitted.

"Fi, it was my fault. I should have paid more attention to you."

"No, Jake. You were doing exactly what you were supposed to do. This is your world. Fans expect certain things, and I understand that. I just lost track of *myself* for a little while." She pressed a kiss to his lips.

"I'm proud of you, Jake, and I want to support your career and how hard you've worked. I know your job is in the limelight, and I think you're incredible at what you do. So do your fans, and that's important. I just needed to get my thoughts in line."

"Thank you, but it's a two-way street. My life is in the spotlight, but I want this to be *our* world, not just my world. I want you in it, Fi, and the only way that will work is if I make changes, too. Lots of them."

She could tell by the seriousness in his eyes that he was talking about far more than just losing track of her in the restaurant. He was already making a lot of changes, which made Fiona realize she should be even more patient with him and had to learn to make more concessions for him.

"For starters, I'm taking you away from this bullshit." He took her hand and led her toward the entrance of the restaurant.

Fiona looked over her shoulder as they whipped through the restaurant. Several people reached out to stop Jake, and he smiled and waved but kept moving, never relinquishing his grip on her.

"What about the cast and crew? Shouldn't you tell them we're leaving?"

"Already taken care of." He tucked her beneath his arm and held on tight as they left the restaurant and were barraged by paparazzi. Jake opened the door of his waiting Ferrari, and after Fiona was safely inside the car, he climbed into the driver's side.

"How did you get your car?"

"There's very little I can't do when I put my mind to it."

The engine roared to life, and Jake reached for Fiona's hand. "I love my job, Fiona, but I fucked up in there."

"No, Jake. It was my issue, not yours."

He leaned across the console and kissed her as photographers swarmed the car and cameras flashed through the tinted windows. "We've always made a great team. We'll figure this out."

As he drove away from the restaurant, she knew they would.

Chapter Seventeen

JAKE PULLED DOWN the long tree-lined driveway to his cabin in the mountains. Moonlight streaked through the trees, and as he pulled up in front of the A-frame log home on fifty acres, which he'd bought shortly after moving to Los Angeles, he felt the stress of his life fall away. There weren't many times that Jake wanted to escape his fast-paced life in Los Angeles, but there had been occasions when he needed a quiet reprieve. Usually those times came on the heels of visits to his hometown, where he'd faced memories of Fiona, and while he typically buried those feelings in booze and women, it didn't always work. Sometimes he needed to lock himself away just to regain his ability to pretend he didn't care and to be able to face his smoke screen of a life.

They'd been driving for almost two hours, and Fiona had dozed off about twenty minutes ago. He cut the engine and Fiona stirred. Jake leaned across the console and stroked her cheek. Her eyes fluttered open, and a sweet smile spread across her lips.

"Sorry," she whispered.

"Don't be. I've kept you up pretty late the last few nights." He kissed her softly.

"Mm." She wrapped her fingers around the back of his neck and pulled him into another kiss.

"I love late nights with you." She looked out the window and squinted into the darkness. "Where are we?"

"Away from everyone else." He came around and helped her from the car, then grabbed the bag he'd had the driver pack for them from the trunk. Putting an arm around Fiona's waist, they ascended the porch steps and he unlocked the door. "Fifty acres of wooded privacy." He pushed the door open and followed her inside the rustic cabin.

Fiona's eyes trailed over the bar to their left, which separated the cozy kitchen from the great room.

"This is really nice," she said as she walked through the great room, trailing her fingers over the arm of the couch and along the leather recliner. She touched the stone that surrounded the fireplace and picked up one of the framed photographs from the mantel. Her lips curved into a smile, and she tucked her hair behind her ear as she looked at the photo of Jake and his mother, taken about ten years earlier on his mother's deck.

"This is sweet," she said as she set it back down and picked up a picture of Jake, Luke, and Wes wearing cargo shorts and no shirts, holding up fishing lines full of fish.

Jake set the bag by the stairs. "Do you want something to drink?"

"Sure."

She looked at the other pictures of his family while he poured the wine.

He took off his jacket and tie and laid it across the counter. He didn't have a table in the cabin, only a bar with barstools. He'd never taken anyone there before, and he'd never minded the sparse accommodations. Now he wished he'd paid a little more attention, although the wish lasted only a brief moment. He knew that Fiona wasn't into material things, and she probably loved the rustic cabin just as it was.

"Do you come here often?" she asked, taking a glass from him.

"Sounds like a pickup line."

Fiona laughed as he settled onto the couch. "A bad one at that." She sipped her wine, then set it on the coffee table and kicked off her heels; then she stooped to remove his dress shoes.

"I bought this place shortly after I moved to LA. In a way, I bought it because of you." He watched her kneel between his legs and felt a tightening in his groin.

"Because of me? Because I was all-powerful even when you hated me?" She placed her hands on his knees, and a coy smile played across her lips.

You have no idea how powerful you are when I allow you into my head.

She slid both hands up his thighs, spreading them far enough for her body to fit between his knees, and she began unbuttoning his shirt, stopping after each button to press a kiss to his bare chest. Jake's breathing hitched when he tried to answer. He drank his wine in one gulp and set the glass down, so damn turned on he tried to lift her onto his lap. She fought against his efforts and pressed his hands back down to the couch, pinning him with a seductive stare.

"Feisty, aren't we?" She went back to work on the buttons of his shirt. "Relax. You always want control. This time it's my turn." She licked her lips, and he felt himself get harder. She dropped her gaze to his crotch, and he knew she felt it, too.

With the last button undone and the dark room lit only by streams of moonlight spilling through the windows, she pushed his shirt open and lowered her lips to his stomach. Her mouth was hot, her tongue wet, as she trailed openmouthed kisses along the waist of his slacks, sending a bolt of heat through his core. His stomach muscles tightened as her tongue glided along his hips, and she nipped at his taut skin.

"Jesus, Fi."

"You like?" She slipped her fingers beneath the waist of his slacks and unbuttoned them.

"Hell yeah, I like."

She slithered up his body, eyes dark and sinful, pressed her hips to his, and took him in a tongue-plunging kiss that nearly blew his mind. Just as he readied to pull her closer, she returned to the promising perch between his legs. She unzipped his pants and shimmied them down his hips, freeing his erection as she tossed them aside. She wrapped her slender fingers around his hard length. It was too much, watching her lower her mouth to him, in that sexy dress, with a wicked look in her eyes. He gripped the edge of the couch.

She licked the tip of his arousal, and his whole body shuddered.

"Congratulations on passing your blood test," she whispered.

"Jesus," he hissed.

He grabbed her forearms for no reason other than needing to hold on to her. She grinned as she opened her mouth and lowered it down upon him, taking all of him into her mouth until he felt the back of her throat. He sucked in air between gritted teeth, and his head fell back from the intense pleasure washing through him as she stroked the tip with her tongue and worked his shaft with her hand. He tangled his hands in her hair, fighting the urge to guide her but needing the contact. She moaned in pleasure, and the vibration made every muscle flex.

She pulled her mouth away slowly. "Mm, you like that."

"Fi." He was breathing hard, doing everything he could do not to turn her around and take her from behind.

"Jake," she whispered as she sank back on her heels and

licked his sensitive sac.

He felt his balls tighten and didn't even try to stifle the greedy groan that sent his head back and his hips bucking as she swallowed him again. Her mouth was a tornado of talent. He pulled her from him, sending his arousal to his belly with a muted slap.

"Fi, I'm gonna come."

She narrowed her eyes and licked him from base to tip, earning herself another groan. "We don't want that yet, now, do we?" She rose to her feet and lifted the skirt of her dress, revealing a black lace thong. Then she hooked her thumbs in the string and drew it down in a hip-swinging striptease that made *his* hips lift in anticipation.

She stepped from the thong and held it up between her finger and thumb, raising her brows seductively before tossing it behind her. She was the picture of seduction as she straddled his lap, never uttering a sound. Her eyes sent all the sinful messages he needed. She was more confident in her sensuality than she'd been in high school. The way she took control and the sexy way she moved above him reminded him of a tigress, powerful and graceful at once.

"Condom," he growled, fighting the desire to drive his erection into her wet center.

"I'm on the pill and you've been tested."

He narrowed his eyes, not wanting to ask the obvious.

"I've never not used condoms. The pill was for my own

peace of mind."

That was all he needed to hear—and he wasn't sure if he'd have been able to wait for a condom if she'd said anything different. He grasped her hips and lowered her onto his thick, throbbing shaft.

"Jesus…Don't move." The feel of her velvety insides made his entire body pulse with the need to undulate inside her, but he wanted more. He needed more of her. He reached around her with trembling hands and unzipped her dress, lifting it carefully over her head, then tossed it onto the coffee table.

She lowered her mouth to his neck and sucked, stealing his last ounce of restraint. He fisted his hand in her hair and tugged her mouth from his skin, crashing his mouth to hers as he ground his hips harder, thrust faster into her hot, wet center. She gyrated against him, creating friction like liquid fire. Buried deep, he shifted her beneath him so he could thrust harder. He ran his hands down her delicious curves and grasped her hips, holding them firm. She tore her mouth away, sucking in quick, sharp inhalations as she clutched at his arms.

She was gorgeous, lying beneath him, trusting and open. His heart swelled with love for her. He had no idea how he got from don't-fucking-talk-to-me to I-can't-imagine-a-day-without-you, but fuck it. He was there and was too far gone to ever want to turn back.

"Jake…" She panted.

Hearing the plea in her voice made him want to pleasure her more, but he knew that once she came, he was going to be right behind her. He sped up his efforts, taking her harder, angling her hips so he could penetrate deeper. He felt her thighs flex. She dug her nails into his flesh and closed her eyes as she cried out his name. The feel of her inner muscles convulsing around him, the sight of her in the throes of passion, the feel of her hips rocking against his as she came apart, knowing he'd taken her there, had him on the verge of coming. He wrapped her in his arms, tucked his face into the crook of her neck, getting as close as possible as the orgasm roared through him, and he filled her with everything he had to give. Emotionally and physically.

Chapter Eighteen

JAKE AWOKE SATURDAY to the smell of coffee and the sunlight streaking through the glass doors. He craned his neck and caught sight of Fiona standing barefoot on the deck, wearing his button-down shirt, her gorgeous legs bare to her toes. His lips spread in a slow smile with the memory of the evening before and the three times they'd made love. He felt himself getting hard. It seemed like he was in a constant state of arousal when he was with Fiona—or just thinking of her.

He didn't even try to fight it as he pushed to his feet and walked naked into the kitchen, still thinking about last night. After making love, they'd taken a warm bath together. Taking care of Fiona and washing her body had been even more erotic than making love to her. Every protective urge he'd ever felt had taken possession of him last night, and now, as he filled his coffee cup and went upstairs to put on a clean pair of boxer briefs, he knew that more than protective urges had claimed him.

His heart felt full. He felt complete and content like he hadn't since the last time they were together.

The loft was sparsely furnished, with a king-sized bed and a single dresser. The bedspread was hanging half off the bed from their tryst after their bath. He smiled to himself as he thought about making love in the bathtub. The memory of the dark look in Fiona's eyes when they dried off and tumbled to the bed, unable to satiate their need for each other, made him even harder. *Damn.* They'd rinsed off again and wandered back downstairs. They'd talked while lying together in the hazy moonlight and must have dozed off.

He gazed over the railing at the living room below. Hardwood floors and the cathedral ceiling gave the cabin an airy feel, but there was no denying the log cabin was rustic. Seeing Fiona's dress draped over the armchair and her heels beside the couch made him realize that the cabin was also very masculine. As much as her things seemed out of place in the otherwise dark and masculine room, they also looked very *right.*

He grabbed a pair of boxer briefs from the dresser and put them on, then went to the window and gazed down at Fiona leaning against the railing. She was staring off into the distance, with her hair tousled and one knee bent so only her toes were touching the deck. He could look at her all day. Watching her while she was unaware touched something inside him. He'd been awfully mean to her before they'd finally connected, and he wanted to make up for that. He'd spend a lifetime making up for it.

He went into the bathroom, washed his face and brushed his teeth, then went back downstairs and joined her on the deck.

"Hi," he said as he folded her into his arms from behind and kissed her neck.

"It is so beautiful here. It feels like a world away from LA."

"Two hours—not quite a world away, but just as good."

She turned and leaned against his chest. "I like it here."

"I like having you here." He kissed her lips. "In more ways than one."

"I think you accomplished that last night. On the couch, in the tub, on your bed." She played with the hair on his chest.

"You started it on the couch, Little Miss Innocent." He pulled her against him, and his hand met her bare ass. "Well, what do we have here?"

"I only had my thong," she whispered.

"Are you afraid the deer might hear you?" He kissed her then, long and slow. "Do you really think I'd whisk you away unprepared? With just a thong and a cocktail dress?"

"Yes?" She arched a brow.

He laughed. "Yeah, I probably would, but I didn't. I had the guy who brought my car to the restaurant pack a bag. I wasn't too thrilled about him rifling through the clothes you left at my house this week, but it was the best I could do on short notice."

"You're so thoughtful." She kissed his chin and pressed her hips to his.

"I thought you were pretty thoughtful—and *giving*—last night." He said it to make her blush, which she did so adorably well. He kissed her again, sliding his hands further onto her butt and letting his fingers graze the warmth between her legs.

"Jake," she whispered. "You're addicting."

"Some addictions are better than others."

He tugged her in close and sealed his lips over hers as he slid his hand between her legs. She was wet and ready and felt so damn good. She pushed at his briefs and freed his arousal, then pulled the shirt she was wearing over her head and tossed it onto the deck.

"God, Fi," he whispered as he lifted her easily into his arms. "You own me."

She wrapped her legs around his waist, circling his neck with her arms as she sank onto his hard length.

"Oh, Jake," she said in a throaty voice.

She felt incredible. Her thighs were soft and warm, her ass—Jesus, he loved her ass—spread wide as their heated flesh came together. He brought one hand to the back of her hair and tugged gently, tilting her face to slant his lips over hers in a kiss as he pumped her body to nail-digging pleasure.

She yanked her lips away and gasped for air.

"Jake…Oh…God, Jake."

He was lost in her and unable to speak as pressure burned down his spine and gathered between his legs.

"Come on, baby," he urged, thrusting faster.

She crashed her mouth to his, and he captured her cries as she came apart in sync with his own mind-numbing release.

He held her against him, feeling the urgent beating of her heart, the pleasurable spasms of her body around his. He wanted to stay like that forever, in each other's arms, united as one. He shuddered with the last of his release. Her body slowly melted against him, and he loved the weight of her in his arms. He loved everything about her, and he knew deep in his soul that he always had.

"Fi," he whispered urgently.

She leaned back and searched his eyes with a concerned gaze. "Am I too heavy?"

"No, babe. Never." He kissed her hard and fast to stifle the three words hovering on the tip of his tongue. The words had the power to change his whole life.

Just as you did.

He held her close again and swallowed his admission. This wasn't what he wanted her to remember—being naked in his arms—when he handed her his heart.

He set her down on the deck and handed her the shirt she'd had on earlier. Suppressing the urge to tell her how he really felt was like swallowing nails, and Fiona was looking at him like she knew he had a secret. He had to say something.

"Do you still like to ride dirt bikes?" He had no idea where *that* came from.

"That's what you wanted to ask me?" She buttoned the shirt as they walked inside. "I haven't ridden since we were kids."

No, it's not what I wanted to say, but it will have to do. When he finally did tell Fiona he loved her, he wanted to do it in a way she'd always remember. In a way that she'd always dreamed of. This, he didn't want to mess up.

"All the more reason we should. C'mon. Let's shower. We'll ride into town and get something to eat, then go for a ride."

"There's a town around here?"

He laughed. "A country store of sorts. It'll remind you of home."

Fiona wrapped her arms around his waist. "After spending time in your life and seeing your house in LA, I thought I might have been wrong about my old Jake being inside you somewhere."

"You can take the boy out of Trusty, but you can never take Trusty out of the boy." He swatted her butt as he followed her upstairs to shower.

Chapter Nineteen

"I DIDN'T REALIZE the driveway continued past the house." Fiona loved the woodsy view as they drove over rutted tire paths in the dirt, heading farther into the woods.

"I need someplace to keep my truck." He slid his eyes to her with a grin. When he was a teenager, Jake had wanted nothing to do with nice cars or fancy houses. Back then he was all about being rugged and real. She wondered if he had a souped-up monster truck hidden back there somewhere to go along with his new LA lifestyle.

A large barn came into view. Jake got out and unlocked the heavy metal chain hanging from the doors, then tossed the chain to the side. He pushed the doors open, revealing the beat-up old Ford truck from their youth. It stopped her cold. She stared at it for a minute or two, unable to move, rocked by memories and the disbelief that he'd kept it, before noticing what else was in the barn—two dirt bikes, an old motorcycle, and a black trailer she assumed was used for towing the bikes.

"I've never brought anyone else here."

"So, I'm your first. I'm honored." She smiled up at him as if it were no big deal, but inside she felt the thrill of their connection, and knowing he trusted her with this private oasis only solidified what she'd thought she'd seen in his eyes earlier that morning. She'd felt like his heart had opened up and swallowed her whole.

"It's fitting, don't you think? You were my first for other significant things." His lips quirked up in a crooked smile.

She felt her cheeks heat up, thinking about the first time they'd made love. She'd just turned sixteen and had been dating for a few months, and it seemed like they could never get enough of each other. They were always kissing, touching, groping—just like they did now. They'd driven up the mountain to a place where Jake used to ride his dirt bikes. She remembered how nervous they'd both been and how Jake had brought blankets, candles, and a bottle of wine that he'd snagged from his mother's wine rack, even though they didn't drink it, because he didn't want to drink and drive. He must have told her he loved her a million times, and she remembered not being embarrassed or feeling anything toward her body other than wanting him inside of her. When she'd seen him naked for the first time, she wasn't afraid of the things her girlfriends had been afraid of, like him not fitting inside her. She knew bodies were made to accommodate for that. What she feared most was how much she loved him. She worried that once they'd made love, everyone would see it on her face and somehow know what they'd done. But that chilly September night, as their bodies joined together for the first time and Jake held her like he never wanted to let her go, she knew that what they were doing was special and private. It wasn't something she'd brag about or wear on her sleeve. It was bigger than that, bigger than them.

She looked at him now, standing tall and broad, with that same look of love in his eyes, and she knew that no matter how immense their love had felt before, it had already grown into something impossibly larger over the last few days.

He held the keys out to her.

"Would you mind pulling the car in when I drive the truck out?"

She nodded, unable to find her voice. She ran her hand along the side of the old gray truck, still reveling in the memories. She pulled open the driver's side door and ran her hand over the worn leather bench seat. She smiled with the memories of sitting beside Jake, her head resting on his shoulder. Even back then he'd smelled like hard work and rugged strength.

Jake leaned an arm on the open door. "Same old Midnight."

She smiled at the nickname he'd given the truck after they'd made love that first night. She'd almost forgotten about it.

"You kept her all these years. I never would have imagined..." She walked around to the back of the truck and touched the silver handle on the tailgate. They'd made love in the bed of this truck many times, parked in the mountains around Trusty.

Jake came to her side. "A lot of good memories in this truck."

"Yeah," she said just above a whisper. "I still can't get over that you kept it. I would have thought that you'd want to get rid of the memories."

"I did want to." His eyes shot to the bed of the truck and then looked at Fiona and shrugged. "But every time I went to sell her, I couldn't do it."

She stepped closer, placing her fingers in the front pockets of his low-slung jeans. "I get a pain in my stomach every time I think of how I hurt you, and I know it must be hard for you to trust me again. I won't leave you again, Jake. Thank you for trusting me enough to give me another chance."

He cupped her cheeks in his palms, and his eyes became serious. "Babe, look at who you're talking to. I think we both have reasons not to trust each other if we want to go down that road. If there's one thing I've come to realize, it's that stewing over what we've done in our lives isn't going to help us build the foundation we want. I trust you, Fi." He kissed her forehead. "And I hope you know that you can trust me."

She nodded, afraid she'd cry if she tried to speak.

"If relationships were easy, they'd never grow." He nodded toward the car. "Let's move the car and get out of here."

Twenty minutes later they climbed a wide front porch to an old farmhouse with a distressed wooden sign above the door that read THE GENERAL STORE.

"Jake. Hey, man. How's it goin'?" a white-haired man said as he came out from behind the counter and embraced Jake.

"Stu, nice to see you. This is my girlfriend, Fiona." Jake reached for her hand.

Stu's kind dark eyes bounced between the two of them with a surprised look. He wiped his hands on his jeans and held a hand out to Fiona in greeting.

"*Girlfriend.* Is that right?" He raised his brows as though he liked the sound of it as much as Fiona did. "Nice to meet you, Fiona."

"Nice to meet you, too." His hand matched his voice, warm and soft.

The store reminded Fiona of the type of old-fashioned general stores they had in Harborside, Massachusetts, where her brothers Jesse and Brett lived. Behind the counter, medications were locked inside a glass cabinet. There were metal signs hanging on wood-paneled walls and rows of low shelves lining the center of the store. Fiona noticed that while there was a newspaper rack, there were no gossip magazines, and she was surprised when she felt relieved. They really were away from it all. She stole a glance at Jake as he talked with

Stu, and she wondered if he realized how much more relaxed he seemed away from the city.

"How's Kathy?" Jake asked.

Stu smiled. "Keeping me in line, like she's been doing for thirty years." He laughed as he went back around the counter and held up a ledger book.

"Thirty years. That's wonderful. Tell her I said hello." Jake led Fiona down the first aisle. "Do you want to eat out or cook at home?"

Home. The way he'd said it felt warm and inclusive for some reason. She must really be in love, because she was reading way too much into everything.

"It might be nice just to grill and relax, unless you'd rather go out to eat."

He pulled her against his side and whispered, "I'd rather eat out at home, if you know what I mean."

She playfully swatted him. "You're so bad."

"What can I say? You bring out the good, the bad, and the horny in me." He kissed her forehead and went about filling a handbasket with enough food to feed an army, as if he hadn't just made her stomach do triple flips.

Jake set the basket on the counter, and Stu worked an old-fashioned cash register while he rang up the groceries and packed them into a paper bag.

"How long are you on the mountain for?" Stu asked.

"We'll head back home tomorrow sometime." Jake took

out his wallet.

Fiona stopped leafing through the newspaper she was holding at Jake's references to *we* and *home*. She told herself to stop reading into things.

Still, she watched him with interest as he pulled cash from his wallet. His thumb rubbed over their photograph, as if it were an old, comfortable habit. She looped her arm through his, and without hesitation, he brought his lips to the top of her head. A little thrill rushed through her, and she wondered how she could know him for so long and still get so excited every time his lips touched her.

"Ready, babe?"

Oh, so ready.

After taking the groceries back to the cabin and eating a quick breakfast, they walked over to the garage. Beneath the cover of the trees the air was crisp, but Fiona wasn't chilly. How could she be when she was walking pressed against Jake's hard body?

"You sure you remember how to ride?" he asked as he pulled out the dirt bikes.

"I remember how, but that doesn't mean I'll do it well." Nerves fluttered in her stomach. "We're not doing something crazy like riding over ramps or anything, right?"

Jake's laugh was music to her ears. "I wouldn't do that to you. Would you rather not ride? We can just take a walk."

"No," she said quickly. "I'm nervous, but excited. I want

to do this. We used to have so much fun riding. I'm sure I'll be fine."

"Alrighty, then." Jake walked into the barn and grabbed helmets off a rack.

She could watch his ass in those jeans all day long.

"I feel your eyes on me."

Her eyes bloomed wide. He'd always known when she was watching him. It was like he had eyes everywhere.

He was grinning when he came back with the helmets. "It's okay. I can't stop staring at your ass, either." He pushed a helmet onto her head before she could respond. "We'll go slow, and if you need to stop, just stop. I'll be right there with you. I don't want you to do anything you're uncomfortable with."

"I'll be okay." She looked around at the thick woods, feeling cocooned from the rest of the world and wanting to stay that way.

Their eyes met and held. The air heated with something more than desire, although there was no denying the ever-present current of want that ran between them. Jake's eyes darkened, and his jaw dropped open as if he was going to say something. The way he stepped in close and searched her eyes caused her pulse to speed up in anticipation. She touched his arm, needing the connection to balance the weight of his silence. He exhaled a long, nearly silent breath, then closed his luscious lips and swallowed whatever had hung on them.

He placed his hand on her hip and nodded toward the bike. "Go ahead. Start her up."

She was already revved up. She moved on shaky legs to the bike. It had been so many years that she'd forgotten how different a dirt bike was from a motorcycle. It was less substantial, narrower, and although this was a nice bike, she knew it would also be a much rougher ride than Jake's motorcycle had been. She watched him mounting his own bike and wished she'd been sitting behind him as she had on the motorcycle, pressed against his hot bod while the vibration of the bike worked its magic on both of them.

Down, girl.

She started up the dirt bike and wrapped her hands around the handlebars, a rush of excitement soaring through her as she remembered the power of the bike. Oh, yeah, she remembered how to ride. Her body vibrated from the engine as she traveled over ruts and bumps, following Jake on a rough trail through the woods. The high-pitched growl of the bikes filled the air. Wind whipped against her skin, and she delighted in the feeling of freedom it brought. As untethered as Jake had become, she realized now that she'd become equally as hemmed in. Her idea of a wild night was dancing with Trish or Shea.

This was so much better.

Adrenaline coursed through her, driving a visceral hunger for more. More freedom. More power. More fun. She watched

Jake's powerful biceps flex as he powered through the path ahead, and she knew she'd experience all of those things with him, in a safe way. He turned back to check on her every few minutes, sometimes doling out a quick nod before turning back around. He'd always taken care of her, and she knew in her heart that he always would, despite losing track of her at dinner the other night. Having a girlfriend was as new for him as LA, his current lifestyle, and their relationship was for her. Certain things would take time to adjust to, but she counted herself lucky once again that they'd been able to overcome the breakup that had cut them both so deeply.

Half an hour later the woods thinned and the sun beamed across a grassy meadow. Fiona followed Jake through to the crest of a hill, where they parked their bikes. Her body continued to vibrate long after she'd cut the engine.

She pulled her helmet off and hung it on the handlebar while she took in the mountains and the town in the distance.

"This is beautiful," she said as he came to her side.

"So are you." He held his hand out and helped her off the bike.

"Flattery will get you everywhere." She went up on tiptoes and kissed him. He smelled like he'd been baking in the sun, which on Jake was heavenly.

"I'm counting on it." Hand in hand, he led her near the edge of the mountain and sank down to the grass, taking her with him. He slung an arm over her shoulder and sighed. "I like being with you again, Fi."

"Me too."

"Well, you always get to be with yourself, but for me it's a treat." He smiled at her and pulled her into a quick kiss. "You looked sexy as hell on that bike. Did it feel all right?"

"It felt amazing. Wild. I had forgotten how much fun it was to ride. I hadn't realized how boring my life had become. You know, I go to work for eight to ten hours a day, sometimes in the office, other times on a work site. Usually camping out, and that's fun, but it's still work. I miss this. I miss just picking up and enjoying the afternoon." She shaded her eyes from the sun and looked at him. Really looked at him. His cheeks were unshaven and his hair was mussed from wearing the helmet. His biceps were plump from harnessing the power of the bike, and he looked hotter than any guy she'd ever seen, but beyond his good looks, Jake radiated a different energy than he had a week ago. He was warm and thoughtful, and the hint of a smile that played on his lips seemed to have seated itself in his eyes, too.

"I knew I wanted to be with you, but I had forgotten how incredible it *felt* to spend time with you."

He raised his brows in quick succession.

"Not like that. Well, like that, too, but I meant *being* with you. You're so alive. I haven't met anyone who can make me feel as energized as you do, and it's more than just the dirt bikes or being here. We could have stayed in your cabin all day and I know I'd still feel the same way." She touched his cheek. "It's you, Jake. I've really missed you."

He pressed his lips to hers. "If you're surprised by how it feels to be with me, imagine how surprised I am at coming back together with you. At least you let yourself think about me. I can't believe I fought the memories for so many years. There were times when fighting them nearly brought me to my knees, the ache was so bad, but I'd convinced myself that letting those memories in would be a thousand times worse than the ache of pushing them away." He shook his head and looked out over the mountains. "I was so damn wrong, and it kills me. I hate to be wrong."

He tilted his face toward her and smiled. "Well, that and the fact that maybe if I hadn't fought so hard, we could have been together sooner."

Jake pointed to a hawk sailing across the sky, wings spread wide. "How great would it be to be a hawk? Nothing to do but hunt and fly. No peers to impress, no schedule to adhere to." He let out a loud breath, as if he were readying himself for something. "My life is crazy, Fi. You've seen what it's become. Days like this are few and far between."

"I know." She looked down, feeling as though he were giving her a hint not to get too attached to spending time with him.

"But a good part of that is within my control."

She lifted her eyes and met his steady gaze, hoping he

couldn't tell that her heart felt like it might crash through her chest.

"I don't want to make promises I can't keep—you know that about me."

She nodded, choking back the painful reminder that she was the one who'd promised him forever and then broke up with him, not the other way around.

"I'm not asking you for anything, Jake. I have never stopped loving you. I wanted a chance for us again, and I feel like you've given us that, but I don't expect you to promise me anything more."

He reached an arm around her as he looked away with a slight nod and pulled her closer to him. A few minutes later he rose to his feet and helped her up to hers. Without a word he took her hand and began walking toward a thicket of trees.

"What do you want, Fi?" he asked as they weaved through the thick branches.

The woods smelled like pine and grass with a hint of musk. Fiona thought she smelled fear in the air, then realized it was coming from her. How should she answer? Total honesty? *You, Jake. I want you. Forever.* She hesitated, worried that perhaps after their incredibly romantic time together he'd rethought what he really wanted. Maybe he was regretting spreading the word about his house not being open for parties, or for telling the girls who texted him that he was off the market.

Her stomach sank.

"I guess I don't know how to answer that." At least that was honest, and she'd put the ball back in his court. She wanted to ask him what he wanted, but when she opened her mouth to ask, fear stopped her.

He nodded, and they continued walking in silence. Eventually they came to another grassy clearing.

"You can ask me for things," he said as they sat on a fallen tree. He picked a weed from beside the stump and twisted it in his fingers.

"I know I can." She set her hand on his thigh, and he smiled. She knew he was telling her that whatever she wanted, he was willing to try to give, but *things* weren't what she wanted. She wanted Jake. All of him.

"Do you want to know what I want?" He dropped the weed and rested his forearms on his knees.

"You tell me. Do I?" *Please say yes. Please, please tell me I do.*

She felt his finger on her chin as he brought her eyes into focus and searched them for an uncomfortably long time, making her even more nervous.

"Fiona Steele," he said just above a whisper. It sounded intimate and important. "Is that fear I see in your eyes?"

"Maybe." The word crept off her tongue.

His brows knitted together. "Why, Fi?"

She pressed her lips together to keep from crying. *Because I love you. Because I don't want to hear if this isn't as real to you as it was last night.*

Why was she so worried? As she met his gaze, she realized that her love for him had deepened, and the fear of losing him now was sending her over the edge. She had to tell him. There were no two ways about it. Not telling him would just make her worry and feel even more insecure, and she really didn't want to be that person.

"Because, Jake. Because I love you, and I've loved you forever." *Why am I talking so loud?* She couldn't stop the truth from flowing like a river. "Because when I woke up in your arms, I let myself dream of doing it every day for the rest of my life." She pushed to her feet and paced. "Because I don't want to hear you tell me that you've changed your mind and that this whole thing was a mistake. That you need a different woman every night, or...or..."

Jake stood, and she turned away, horrifically embarrassed. She closed her eyes and held her breath, wishing she could sprout wings and fly away like the hawk. She felt his hands on her waist.

"Are you done?"

"I think so, but I don't trust myself." She clenched her eyes tighter.

"Hm."

Even with her eyes closed she felt him moving closer to her, felt his warm breath whisper across her cheek.

"If you don't open your eyes, my hands might start to

wander."

She laughed and opened her eyes. *Yup.* His broad chest was right in front of her, covered with a thin black tank top that she wanted to tear off so she could feel his bare chest, touch it, kiss it, and revel in it. She touched her forehead to the center of his chest and breathed him in.

"When has that ever stopped you before?" She tilted her face up and met his serious gaze.

"It wouldn't stop me now, but I knew it would make you laugh." He hooked his fingers in her belt loops and tugged her hips against his. The rough contact sent a shiver through her. No man had ever made her body react like Jake did. She was so screwed if he turned her away. He'd already ruined her for any other man.

"It's not often that I see this side of you."

She rolled her eyes. "Please. I'm an open book to you."

"In some ways, maybe. But this feels new." He pressed his arousal against her. "Well, *that* doesn't feel new, but seeing you embarrassed and flustered does. I kind of like it."

She halfheartedly pressed her fists to his chest, hoping he'd say more.

"You're adorable when you're flustered." He kissed her forehead.

"You're not helping." He was making her feel better, but he was also skirting the real issue, which made butterflies start flapping around in her stomach.

"Okay. You're right. Let me address the real issue. You love me." He smiled.

She waited for him to say more, but apparently the frustratingly handsome stuntman she loved was playing a different type of stunt, because he just grinned like he'd discovered gold and should be bowed to.

"Okay, yes," she relented. His reveling was driving her batty. "I love you."

"Good. Now that we've that cleared up…"

He turned to walk away, and she yanked him back by the tail of his shirt.

"What? Get back here. You can't just leave me hanging like that, you big oaf."

He laughed and folded her into his arms, then sealed his lips over hers while still laughing.

"What do you want me to clear up? How much I love to kiss you? Or haven't you noticed already?" He kissed her again, eagerly and thoroughly sinfully. "Or maybe how much I love to bury myself inside you? I could show you that here, too."

"No!" She laughed. "Wait. Yes!"

He kissed her again, muffling her laugh.

"Or maybe you need to hear how you have totally captivated my heart, my mind, and, well, you know you *own* my body."

She felt a tear slip down her cheek as he lowered his forehead to hers.

"Oh, Jake."

"From the moment I met you, I never stood a chance of not falling in love with you. I never stopped loving you, so there was no need to fall *back* in love with you. I just had to let myself *feel* again. And only you could make that happen. I love you, Fiona." His tone softened. "I wanted to find a romantic way to tell you, but I can't sit by and watch you worry." He took her hand in his and gazed lovingly into her eyes. "I don't want a different woman every night, and I don't think this has been any kind of mistake. This has been an awakening, Fi. The best damn awakening I could ever hope for."

He leaned in close, brushing her lips lightly as he whispered, "I'm so thankful that you didn't give up on me. You knew what I needed, and what I needed was you. I love you, Fiona, with every ounce of my being."

Their lips met in a long, loving kiss that magnified every word he'd said.

Chapter Twenty

SUNDAY MORNING JAKE was awake before the sun, as he was most mornings, in preparation for their morning run. Today, with Fiona's sweet softness draped over his body, running was the last thing on his mind. Ever since they'd reconnected, he'd felt himself changing. And since he'd told Fiona how he really felt, he'd felt himself opening up to her even more and becoming even more like the man he used to be. The knots in his stomach eased, and the feeling of needing to be doing something every minute of the day had lessened. Before Fiona walked back into his life, he hadn't fully realized why he was on such a fast path to oblivion.

Fiona's thigh was resting on his, her arm stretched across his chest. Her breath moved his chest hair just enough to tickle. He ran his hand down the curve of her hip, and she sighed in her sleep. He had a clear view of her slightly parted lips, which brought back memories of the night before. They'd grilled out on the deck. Then, after dinner, they'd gone for a walk and shared a bottle of wine. They'd shared a lounge chair on the deck and stargazed long into the night. *Stargazed.* How had he changed so much so quickly? He hadn't stargazed since they were teenagers.

He turned his head and looked out the window. Dawn was just beginning to break, and as Fiona turned over, giving him a lovely view of her derriere, the sun crept higher. As did the sheets above his erection. He slid his thigh over the back of hers and his arm across her shoulder, then rested his head on the back of her arm, nearly completely blanketing her slim figure. Beneath the fragrance of soap from the bath they'd shared the evening before was Fiona's unique, womanly scent, which he adored. She breathed deeply, and he pressed a kiss to her warm skin. He had missed this type of intimacy. Now that she was with him, he never wanted to wake up without her again. He finally understood how his siblings had fallen in love so fast. He'd been so adamant about never going down the monogamous road again—and with Fiona, once he kissed her again, it was all he ever wanted. It surprised—and pleased— the hell out of him.

How had everyone close to him known what he needed, and how had he missed it? He tightened his arms around Fiona, wondering why some other guy hadn't swept her off her feet before now. He kissed her shoulder and somehow innately knew that even if another man had tried, she wouldn't have been interested. Her love for him was palpable in everything she did and said, and it was bigger than both of them, as, he was realizing, was his love for her.

She turned over and smiled up at him, blinking away the haze of sleep.

"Ready for our run?" she asked groggily.

He kissed her cheek, and in that moment Jake realized he hadn't really changed that much at all. Fiona had cracked the armor that had weighed him down and peeled back his layers to who he really was, revealing the skin he was happiest wearing. He felt freer than he'd ever felt in his life.

"How about we skip our run?" He ran his thumb along her jaw, then trailed kisses along the same path.

"But…" She closed her eyes as he kissed his way down to her breast and dragged his tongue over her nipple. "Oh, God."

"Is that a yes to skipping our run?" He spread her thighs with his knees as he positioned his hips over hers.

Her hands pressed firmly on his lower back. "I think this is a much better way to get our exercise."

He lowered his lips to hers as their bodies came together. Her luscious curves, her wet, warm center, her delicious mouth, everything felt familiar. Their bodies moved together in perfect harmony, and as he gazed into her eyes, he sensed that she felt as if she'd come home, too. He reached down, and before he could angle her hips, she made the adjustment, taking him deeper. Her eyes fluttered closed, and she lifted her hips higher.

He nuzzled against her neck. "You feel amazing."

"So do...you." She bit her lower lip, and he couldn't help but drag his tongue along it in a way that he knew would arouse her even more. "Harder," she whispered.

Her hips rose off the bed to meet his efforts. He reached down and grabbed her ass. He needed to intensify her pleasure as he took her harder. Her eyes closed and her head fell back.

"Jake." She panted.

"Come on, baby." He slid his hand beneath her knee and brought her leg up by his ribs. "Come on, Fi. Show me how much you want me."

Her eyelashes fluttered and her lips moved, but no words came. He knew she was on the cusp of coming apart, felt her body stiffen, her nails dig into him. With two hard thrusts, her body quaked and quivered around him.

"Again," he urged, as he lifted her other leg, widening them, allowing him better penetration. Jake was throbbing, ready to burst, but watching Fiona come apart was one of his greatest pleasures. Her eyes opened wide, then slammed shut as she cried out an indiscernible cry that sent a tingling down his spine and sent him over the edge. He pumped and thrust through the very last pulse of his release, taking her in another mouthwatering kiss before rolling onto his back, slick and sated, beside her.

He reached for her hand and had no idea how long they lay there, but by the time they showered and dressed, the sun was up, and he wished they could start the weekend all over again.

Fiona cooked egg-white omelets and toast for breakfast, and they ate out on the deck. She crumbled a piece of toast on the deck railing.

"For the birds." She smiled as she sat beside him at the table. "Hear them chirping? That's so nice. I never hear that where I live."

"I can't tell you when the last time was that I listened for the birds, or even slowed down enough to hear them." He hadn't remembered her penchant for feeding wildlife until right then. "When we were kids, it seemed like I heard them all the time. But that might have had something to do with you always leaving out birdseed on my mom's deck and at your mom's house."

Fiona finished eating and smiled. "Do you remember that first summer we were together, when you tried to convince me that if I left food out for the birds you'd have to fight off a bear?"

"I had to do something so you'd believe I was the toughest guy out there." He patted his chest and flexed his muscles.

"There is no woman on earth who could look at you and think you were anything but a big, strong guy." She climbed into his lap and wrapped her arms around his neck. "Even when you're sensitive and loving, you're powerful. Your eyes burn right through me. Your touch sends me running for the bedroom." She pressed her lips to his and ground her bottom into his groin. "And that mammoth between your legs? We won't even go there. No wild animal has anything on you."

He gathered her hair in his hand and gave it a light tug, earning him a seductive gaze that nearly made him carry her back into the bedroom again. But he had other plans for today.

"See why I love you? You're very good for my ego."

"Why don't you carry me upstairs and prove to me just how manly you are."

So much for his plans…

BY THE TIME they left the cabin it was nearly noon. They'd spent only two nights there, but it felt like a lifetime. Driving around in Jake's truck had felt like old times, and Fiona had noticed how much happier Jake seemed at the cabin than he was in the city. After he'd told her that he loved her—she was still reveling in that particular admission—he seemed to fall back into some kind of comfort zone. He smiled more often, touched her every time he walked by, and when he loved her…Oh, the way he loved her! In his arms, she felt as though she were transported into another world and like she could finally be herself again. She hadn't slept with many men, but the few she had been with hadn't been the kind of guys to evoke the emotions and insatiable heat that she felt with Jake.

As they drove back toward what Jake had begun to call *the real world*, Fiona's mind drifted to her job and the life waiting for her back in Fresno. She hadn't allowed herself to think about the promotion or that her *real world* was so far away from Jake's. She'd decided before reconnecting with Jake that if they got together, she'd leave the promotion behind, and she knew she had to deal with that sooner rather than later. But not this very second.

She glanced at Jake's serious gaze and noticed how tightly he was gripping the steering wheel.

"You okay?" she asked.

"Yeah." His answer was curt, and even though he reached over and held her hand, he didn't make eye contact.

"You sure?" She wondered if he was thinking about work or worried about having missed something important. Their cell phones hadn't worked at the cabin, and he'd had to return a number of texts after they'd driven down the mountain. They'd become so close that she no longer worried about who the texts were from.

He glanced at her, then drew his eyes back to the road. "It's...nothing."

Uh-oh. "Jake, your *nothing* sounds like a whole lot of something."

"It is, but it's not a good something. It makes me an ass for thinking about it, much less wanting to ask you about it."

His hand clenched the wheel again.

"Now you're worrying me." *What could make you an ass?*

Jake remained silent.

"Jake, if you want to be with me, then we need to be able to communicate. It seems to me that we've handled some pretty touchy situations, so I can't imagine what's got your briefs in a bunch. Just spit it out."

He looked at her again out of the corner of his eyes, holding her hand tighter than he normally did. "Okay, but you have to promise not to hate me for it."

"Wait. I'm not sure I want to hear this. I feel like you just stabbed me in the stomach." She looked out the window, weighing the possibilities. He must have done something *really* awful to preface his admission with *that*.

"It's me who feels stabbed." His voice was husky and rough.

Fiona turned back toward him. "Just tell me, because now I feel like I'm going to be sick."

"It's just…Fi, I adore you. I mean, when I think of you, it's not just the sex that I think about, although you're like my fantasies come true. It's everything. But of course sex is a part of that, and when I think of you coming on to other guys in your past like you do to me…I can't take it." His fingers curled tighter over the steering wheel, and his knuckles turned white.

A laugh burst from Fiona's lips before she could stop it.

She smacked her hand over her lips.

"Wait." She tried to swallow her laughter, which was driven by relief and nerves, not because his jealousy was humorous. "Let me get this straight. My boyfriend, who has admitted to taking part in several threesomes and sleeping with just about any woman with legs, is jealous of me and my meager sexual history?"

"I told you it made me an asshole," he grumbled.

She laughed again, this time because his disgruntled voice was humorous.

"Jake, really? I told you I could count my sexual partners on one hand."

"It's not the number; it's the idea of you seducing them. Of you doing what you do to me, to someone else."

Now she couldn't help but tease him. "Aw, so you don't want to think about me doing this to someone else?" She unhooked her seat belt, leaned over the console, and rubbed him through his jeans, moaning in the most sensual way she could muster. His body instantly responded.

"Fi," he growled.

"Or this?" She unzipped his pants, setting his erection free, and lowered her mouth to him.

"Jesus, Fiona. I'm going to crash."

That only made her feel more empowered. She swallowed him from tip to base and loved feeling his entire body tense. She'd never been brave enough or had the desire to blow a guy in a car before, but with Jake she had a feeling there wasn't much she wouldn't want to do.

"Fi…o…na."

She felt his thighs flex and swirled her tongue over the tip while stroking him harder, knowing exactly how to take him over the edge.

"Fi, you're gonna…make me come."

"Then perhaps you should pull over." He did just that and threw the car into park. With one quick flick of a button, he reclined his seat.

"Jesus." He gripped her head as his hips bucked, and he filled her throat with his seed.

He breathed heavily as she tucked him back into his jeans and climbed over the console and up his body, taking him in the hottest kiss they'd ever shared. He devoured her mouth, despite the taste of himself on her tongue, and when they finally broke apart, his eyes bored right through her.

"You're the only man I've done that with," she admitted. "You're the only man I've ever felt comfortable showing initiative with the way I do with you."

Tension eased from his grip.

"But you're still an ass for having the guts to tell me that after all the things you've done with your little man down there." She pushed away, and he pulled her back and kissed her—hard.

"I never claimed to be anything but an ass, Fiona. I've

never been possessive or jealous with another goddamn woman, but I am with you. So, yeah, I am an ass, but I'm *your* ass, and you love me."

"You'll get no arguments from me." She kissed him again, and as she moved back into the passenger seat, she said, "You owe me one. And it better be damn good."

He grinned and shook his head as he buttoned his jeans and righted his seat. "If it's a payback, then I have to make it mind-blowing good, because you blew my fucking mind, Fiona."

"That's what you get." She was about to smirk; then she realized that she wasn't really one-upping him.

His smirk was far more appropriate.

She pointed at him. "I'll take that as a compliment, thank you very much."

"I do have a surprise for you." Jake squeezed her leg. "It's not a sexual surprise, but I promise you that I'll make that up to you three times over if you'd like."

"I'd like." She leaned over and kissed his cheek as he pulled back onto the road. "You've been surprising me in so many ways lately. I can't imagine what you have up your sleeve next."

"I could say the same for you." He let that hang between them, and Fiona was surprised she didn't feel herself blush.

Instead of driving back toward his house, he drove to the National History Museum. She'd been dying to visit the museum, but since she'd avoided LA, it was never an option.

"I'm sure you've been here, but I thought we could go together."

She was so touched that she decided to be honest with him about why she'd never gone. "I actually haven't been. I kind of avoided Los Angeles like the plague before getting up the guts to come out with Trish. I was afraid of seeing you, which I know is crazy given how big LA is, but I didn't want to chance seeing you with another woman."

He arched a brow. "See? I don't look like such a bad guy for being jealous anymore, do I?"

She rolled her eyes. "Anyway...The museum is closed for renovations."

"True." He parked the car and opened her door, pulling her against him. He did that a lot, and she loved it every single time.

"It is closed, unless you happen to know people in high places." Jake draped an arm over her shoulder as they walked across the empty parking lot toward a door marked DELIVER-IES.

"You know someone who runs it? We're really going inside?" Her pulse sped up at the prospect. The fact that Jake had arranged it made it that much more special.

He knocked on the door. "We're really going inside. And the Blue Moon Diamond exhibit is still here."

Fiona felt her eyes widen. "Are you kidding me? Oh my

God, Jake." She threw her arms around his neck and squealed with delight, kissing him several times.

"Wow, I'd have taken you sooner if I'd known it would make you that happy."

"The Blue Moon Diamond is twelve carats, one of the newest and rarest gems in the world because of its color. It's internally flawless, and, oh my God. Jake. This is so crazy!"

The door opened, and a short, dark-haired gentleman stepped outside and opened his arms to Jake.

"Jake, buddy." He embraced Jake and patted him on the back, then turned his attention to Fiona. "So this is Fiona." He held out a hand and Fiona shook it. "Nice to meet you. I'm Theo."

"Hi, Theo. Thank you so much for letting us visit the museum." She knew she was grinning like a fool, and she had no hope of stopping as he led them inside. She held tightly to Jake's hand as Theo brought them into the rotunda.

"Take your time and look around. I have to close up in about three hours." He talked with Jake for a few minutes about the exhibits and the areas they should avoid because of the renovations, then excused himself, leaving them to roam the museum by themselves.

There was so much to take in that Fiona felt like a kid in a candy store. She was overwhelmed at Jake's thoughtful surprise and couldn't stop smiling.

"Where do you want to start? Gems and minerals?" he

asked.

"Let's see the diamond so we don't miss it; then...you choose. I want to see as much as we can, but you know I'll love all the exhibits." She'd wanted to see the Blue Moon Diamond and had wrestled with venturing into LA for that reason alone, but the thought of seeing Jake with another woman had kept her from doing so. Now she could hardly believe that two of her dreams were coming true. Jake loved her. Loved her! And she was going to see the Blue Moon Diamond. It would be even more special seeing it with Jake.

They followed the map Theo had provided and found the diamond exhibit.

"How do you know Theo?" she asked.

"We filmed part of a movie here a few years back. He's a good guy."

"He must be. I still can't believe you did this for me. Thank you, Jake. This is beyond my wildest dreams."

"Then you're not dreaming big enough, babe. Remember when we were in school and we'd watch the geological documentaries on television? You know I'll always indulge your interests." He kissed her as they entered the room with the Blue Moon Diamond. "Sexual or otherwise."

"I'm counting on it," she teased. Only she wasn't teasing. She knew their love life would never get stale as well as she knew their life together could never get boring.

The diamond was magnificent. Brilliant blue with a shape

reminiscent of a full moon, and it was even more beautiful than it appeared in photographs.

"They found the diamond in the Cullinan mine in South Africa. It's one of the most significant discoveries in the world. Gosh, what I wouldn't give to have been the one to find it." She felt her eyes bloom wide and didn't even try to contain her excitement. "Can you imagine what that moment would have felt like?"

JAKE *COULD* IMAGINE what that moment would feel like, and he imagined it would be a lot like the way he'd felt the minute his lips had met Fiona's for the first time in more than a decade.

"I'd imagine it felt like the most thrilling moment of their lives."

Seeing the glimmer of excitement in her eyes warmed him all over. He knew he'd chosen the right place to take her. It dawned on him that he'd been so wrapped up in being with Fiona that they hadn't spent any time talking about her life. Her job. Her friends. They'd been too focused on making it through the mess of a life he'd created for himself.

The shocking realization momentarily consumed him. Had he really become that selfish of a man? They moved from the gems and minerals through the nature lab and the lab of mammals. All the while, Jake was wading through a pool of introspection, laden with uncomfortable truths.

He kept up with Fiona's conversation as well as he could as they discussed the exhibits, but he couldn't shake this harsh new realization. The fact that Fiona hadn't said something about it didn't surprise him.

She knows me.

On one hand, that was a very good thing. Fiona loved him regardless of his faults. But on the other, more uncomfortable hand, he didn't like that he had become so wrapped up in himself that he'd let such an important discussion go unsaid. Yet another reminder of how far he'd fallen from the man he used to be. It fueled his desire to do all the right things for Fiona from here on out.

The last exhibit they visited was the Aurora Butterfly of Peace, a world-famous collection of diamonds in varying colors arranged in the shape of a butterfly. Fiona looked intently at the gems.

"Do you know it took the men who put this together twelve years to collect the diamonds and assemble this? It has two hundred and forty pieces." She touched the glass case.

"No, I didn't. But it turns out there's a lot I don't know," Jake answered. *Like how to come out of my selfishness enough to be worthy of you.*

"Together, the diamonds total one hundred sixty-seven carats, and they come from all over the world: Russia, South Africa, Brazil, Australia. It's amazing, isn't it? That they could bring all of these rare finds together in one place?" Fiona snuggled against his side.

"*You're* amazing, Fi." She truly was, and he was going to do his damnedest to be the best man he could for her.

"Why are you looking at me like that?"

He folded her in his arms. "Because I think I've been a real jerk, and I'm only just realizing it."

"How can you say that? We just had the most incredible weekend, and look where we are." She waved her hand at the display.

"Yeah, but that's not what I'm talking about. Come on." He pulled out his cell phone and texted Theo to tell him that they were ready to leave. Theo met them in the rotunda and walked them to the back entrance.

"I can't thank you enough," Fiona gushed. "That was wonderful, and we really appreciate you taking time to let us in."

We. He loved hearing her say that with such confidence.

"No problem. Jake, we'll catch up and have a beer some-time." Theo patted him on the back.

Jake wanted to run out of there so he could talk with Fiona, but he calmed his jets long enough for a proper goodbye. "Sounds like a plan. Thanks again, Theo."

In the car, Fiona went on and on about the museum. Jake loved hearing her enthusiasm, but his mind was stuck on talking with her about her world, her life, her job. The job she'd left to seek him out.

They stopped and ate at a café on the way back to his house. Jake spent that time trying to figure out where else he'd gone wrong. His eyes were wide open now, and he swore he wasn't going to miss another damn thing.

Jake drove out to the beach. He knew it was one of Fiona's favorite spots. They left their shoes in the car and walked along the sand hand in hand. The sand was warm from the sun, and the beach was fairly crowded. Then again, wasn't it always? Crowds didn't bother Jake, but the more time he spent with Fiona, the more he craved alone time with her—even after having her all to himself for the past two days. Would he ever get enough of her? He doubted it.

"Why do I feel like you're mulling over something?" she asked.

"You always could read me." He sank down to the sand and patted the spot beside him.

"It's not hard when you go all reticent on me." She sat down beside him. "I could feel the tension in your hand." She leaned back on her palms and sighed. "But I'm not sure how you can be tense about anything after the perfect afternoon we've had."

"It was pretty perfect," he admitted. "I'm not really tense, just thinking. We've been all wrapped up in me and my life, my world, my job. I want to know about you, Fi."

She laughed. "That's what you're worried about? I think

you know me pretty intimately."

"You know what I mean. What's your life like in Fresno? What's your job like? Do you have many friends? Hobbies?" He looked her in the eye, giving her his full attention.

"Oh, you mean like my *life*, life." She drew three circles in a row in the sand, then pointed to the first one. "See this? This is Fresno." She pointed to the middle circle. "This is Los Angeles." Then she pointed to the last. "And this is Trusty. I have spent years doing this." She drew a line that began at Trusty and arced wide around Los Angeles, then met Fresno. "That's how I lived. I'd go home and visit, then get back to my real life trying to pretend you weren't just a short drive away. I'd do my job until the next time I went back home. I could have written a book called *Avoiding Jake Braden*."

"Jesus, Fi. Was I that bad?" He scrubbed his hand down his face.

"I don't know. It wasn't really you, Jake. It was me. I was afraid to see you again. I knew you avoided me back home in Colorado, and I didn't want to experience that here. But I thought about you every day, until one day Trish handed me a chance to try to make things right."

Now he felt even worse. He hated knowing she'd avoided him, even though he'd spent those years avoiding her. Nothing made any sense, and yet, somehow, they were able to overcome it all.

"But what's your life like? And what made you finally take

the chance? I've been so caught up in us that I haven't slowed down to think about your life without me." He read the suspicion in her eyes. "And I don't mean dating and all that other crap. You set me straight on that. I mean you, babe. Do you like your job? Is it intellectually stimulating? Do you hang out with friends a lot? Did you ever learn to paint?"

She blinked several times. "You remembered that?"

"Sure. You always wanted to learn. So I take it you never did?"

She shook her head, and it made him sad to think she hadn't fulfilled that dream. He wanted her to have everything she ever dreamed of.

"Why not?" He touched her hand.

She shrugged. "I got busy with work. You know how life is."

"Not really. I mean, I've been living in a fantasy world for years. My life isn't normal, and quite frankly, it's not the life I want."

"You have a great life."

"Sure, in some ways, but not in the ways that matter. When we were at the cabin, I didn't want to leave. I loved just being with you, having that time together without having to pretend for the media or worry about someone knocking on the door. I had forgotten how nice it was to enjoy the quiet. And then today I realized that I've gotten so used to focusing only on myself that I hadn't taken the time to get to know your world. I want to know everything about you, Fi. I want to know about where you live, what you do at work all day, what your hopes and dreams are."

"None of it is very exciting."

"Maybe not to you, but it's important to me. Do you live in an apartment? A house? Do you like it?" The more questions he asked, the more he wanted to get in the car and drive to Fresno so he could do more than talk about Fiona's world. He wanted to experience it.

"I live in a bungalow. It's simple, and at the end of a rural road, so it's very peaceful. And yes. I like it very much. It's very…me."

He nodded, picturing her in a bungalow. "Can we go there? Next weekend, maybe?"

She smiled but furrowed her brow. "You don't need to—"

"I want to, Fi. Tell me more. What about your job? You mentioned a promotion. Are you excited about it?" He realized as he waited for her to respond that her answer would be very telling. With their relationship moving so quickly, she might not tell him if she did love it for fear of not wanting to rock the boat.

"I like my job a lot." She looked out over the water.

"And?"

"And I was excited about the promotion. I've worked hard for it, but that was before coming here." She met his gaze, and there was so much emotion in her eyes that he wasn't sure if he was seeing what she felt or a reflection of his own feelings.

For a minute neither of them said anything. He didn't want to push her on that subject. He hadn't realized until that second exactly how much she'd put on the line by coming to LA.

"And hobbies?" A futile effort to change the subject and learn more about her.

She shrugged and looked down as she doodled in the sand. "I don't have much time for hobbies. I read a lot, and I hang out with friends, but work keeps me really busy. And as far as hopes and dreams go, I still want to make it to Greece one day. It would be really cool to discover something magnificent, but those aren't really things that I sit around and think about." She lifted her eyes to his again. "You are, Jake. My heart is so wrapped up in you that you're my hopes and dreams."

He wrapped his arms around her. "I love you, Fi."

"I love you, too."

"I want to see your world."

I want to be your world.

Chapter Twenty-One

AT JAKE'S INSISTENCE, they spent Sunday night at Fiona's apartment. Jake seemed to enjoy being around her belongings, even though it wasn't technically her apartment. She'd brought her own comforter and pillows from home, as well as a few photographs of her family that she set up on the bedside table. She'd made it as much hers as it could be for such a short period of time, but it still didn't quite feel like home. Although, now that Jake was there, it felt more like home than ever. After their run, they'd showered together, which she'd already gotten used to, and looked forward to, each morning.

"Fi, coffee's ready," Jake called from the kitchen.

She'd dreamed of mornings like this with Jake for so long, but while she'd hoped they'd come true, she never imagined it would really, truly happen. She was suddenly overwhelmed with emotion and sank down on the bed until the dampness in her eyes subsided.

"Babe?" Jake stood in the doorframe, shirtless, wearing a pair of faded jeans that hugged him tight in all the right places, his feet bare. His abs looked like a giant arrow pointing to the significant bulge in his pants.

She exhaled, giving in to the holiness that was his body. "You know how cats need to wear bells to warn their owners of their presence?"

He grinned. "Yeah."

"When it's this close to when I need to leave for work, you need to wear a shirt. And looser pants. And shoes. God, I even love your bare feet. This is so sick." She reached for the cup of coffee he was holding out, and he drew it out of her reach.

"Doesn't the coffee boy get a kiss?"

She rose from the bed, hooked her finger in the waist of his jeans, and banged her forehead on his bare chest. "Do you have to smell so good, too?"

"I'm waiting," he whispered.

She lifted her chin and accepted the kiss as if it were a big imposition, eye rolls and all.

"Oh, is that how it's gonna be?" Jake teased.

"What do you expect? You're standing there like a Hershey bar ready to be eaten, and I happen to be a chocoholic."

He licked his lips.

"God." She sank back down to the bed. "It's a good thing Trish isn't paying me, because there is no way my brain is going to function today."

They somehow made it out the door without falling back into bed, and several hours later, Fiona was still hot and bothered. She was talking with Patch away from the closed set while Zane, Trish, and Jake were filming a bedroom scene. A closed set meant that only critical staff were allowed to watch.

"Did you hear the rumor about Zane and Jake?" Patch asked.

"Which rumor would that be?" Fiona had no idea what he was talking about, but the set was ripe with rumors about everyone, so nothing would surprise her. She wasn't worried about hurtful rumors about him and other women. They'd come too far for that. She trusted him just as she had when they were teenagers. Even more so now that he'd made such immense changes in his lifestyle for her.

"They're being cast for the film at Sugar Lake. Well, Zane's being cast for the lead and Jake does all his stunts, so…Will you be there?" Patch shifted his chin, sending his dark hair off his forehead for a brief second; then it fell right back in place.

"Um…" *Will I?* She had no idea.

"Okay. I'll take that as an *undecided.* Sorry, Fiona. I thought you two were a sure thing. At least that's what Jake's told everyone." Patch nodded toward Jake and Trish, who were walking across the lot toward them. "I guess filming wrapped."

"Wait, Patch. Who is *everyone*?"

Jake waved and then touched Trish's arm. They stopped to talk, and Fiona wondered what he was saying to Trish if he'd told everyone that they were a sure thing. They were a sure thing, but she still wanted to know who *everyone* was.

Patch laughed. "Who is everyone? The guy alerted the media. Who do you think *everyone* is? I'd be surprised if anyone didn't think that."

"Oh, right. Sorry. I thought you meant he was telling individual people."

"It's Jake Braden. He says one word to the right person and the world knows. Honey, you were *his* the minute the paps took your picture." Patch glanced at Jake and Trish. "Secret meeting, I guess. I better go find Zane. He probably needs his water. If I ever make it big, remind me not to make my assistant get me water. It's so demeaning."

"See you later, Patch." Her cell phone vibrated. She withdrew it from her pocket and read the text from Shea. *They scheduled the postfilming dinner. Do you want me to get you a dress?* What would she do without Shea? She texted her back quickly as Jake and Trish approached. *Sure. When is it? Thanks!*

Her reply sounded far more excited than Fiona felt. She watched Jake approaching, his dark eyes locked on her like he couldn't wait to have her in his arms, and all she could think about was that when filming ended, their time together would also come to an end.

"Hey, babe." Jake put a hand on her lower back and kissed

her cheek.

"Hi. Hey, Trish."

Still dressed from her closed scene, Trish wore a silky robe tied at the waist. Fiona knew she was wearing lingerie beneath for the bedroom scene that was to be rudely interrupted by a fight scene. She looked beautiful in full makeup with her chestnut hair tousled. She didn't even look nervous anymore. She was a natural actress, and Fiona was glad to see that she'd gotten over her Steve Hileberg nervousness. Heck, Trish seemed to be a natural everything.

"Hey, Fi," Trish said. "We just heard about the postproduction actors' dinner. I'm going to ask Shea to get us dresses again."

"She just texted me and asked if I wanted a dress. So she's already heard, I guess." Fiona hooked her finger in the pocket of Jake's shorts. "Do I get to be your date?"

"Who else's date would you be?" Jake raised a brow. "Of course, babe. Trish? Do you want to come with us?"

"No, thanks. Actually, I have someone I want to ask." Trish tugged on the tie of her robe.

"You do?" Fiona felt her eyes widen. Trish hadn't said anything to her about having a crush on anyone.

"I just decided two minutes ago. I think I'm going to ask Clark."

Fiona and Jake exchanged a look. "Clark? As in Clark Kent? From my work?"

"Yeah. Why not? I mean, he and I always get along, and I think he'd really enjoy it." Trish must have caught the surprise in Jake's eyes. "What?"

"Clark Kent? You're bringing Superman?" He laughed.

"His name isn't really Clark Kent," Trish explained. "It's Clark Taver, but Fiona and I jokingly call him Clark Kent because he looks like him—dark hair, nicely built, with thick black glasses."

"I never even knew you liked him like that," Fiona added. "In fact, I didn't know you were in touch with him beyond when you came to visit me."

"I don't like him like *that*." Trish rolled her eyes. "We keep in touch via email and Facebook. We were chatting about the movie and he was asking all sorts of questions about the set and what it's like." She shrugged. "I thought it might be fun for him to go, and since I don't have a real date, why not? It's Clark. It's not like he'll try to get me to sleep with him or anything."

"Cool. I think that's really nice of you." It was just like Trish to do something like that. She was always thinking of others.

"I have to go to the little girls' room." Trish pointed to one of the buildings. "I'll catch up with you afterward."

"So, I guess Clark isn't a love match," Jake said as he settled a hand on her waist and kissed her neck, sending a shiver straight to her toes. "Not like us."

"He's a really nice guy, and they do get along really well, but I'd never put them together as a couple. He's not exactly my boss, but he is a superior. It's not like they could really have a relationship anyway. She's always jetting off for filming." As she said the words, she realized that Jake probably was, too. She really needed to think about how this relationship would work long-term, but she didn't want to think about that now. She was in a good mood, and she liked the happy wave they were riding.

"That's true, and from what she told me, her agent told her she's now an even hotter commodity." Jake furrowed his brow.

"Yeah, she told me that this morning, too." Fiona was happy for Trish, but thoughts of leaving Jake to go back to work weighed heavily on her mind, despite her efforts to push them away. She needed a distraction.

"Trish also said that you asked her if I could have Friday and the weekend off. She might have to film Saturday." She cocked her head and narrowed her eyes. "What do you have up your sleeve now?"

Trish came out of the building across the lot and headed toward them.

"I figured we'd go to Fresno and spend some time on your turf."

"But why Friday?"

"Because I want to see where you work, and I didn't think

we could do that Saturday. Trish said it was okay, unless you'd rather not."

"I'd rather. I'm just...surprised. My work isn't very interesting."

"Everything about you is interesting. For two years I listened to you dream about becoming a geologist, and I've never forgotten the look in your eyes. When we were at the museum I saw that look again. I want to see you in that world, Fi. You've been in my world for weeks. It's time for me to visit yours."

"Okay, but you may be highly disappointed."

"I doubt that. It's part of you, so how could I be anything but interested?" He kissed her again. "I've got to catch up with Zane, but let's meet at my trailer. Does six work?"

"Perfectly." She watched him walk away. "Mm-mm-mm. That man is yummy."

"You two fell hard." Trish grabbed Fiona's arm and dragged her toward her trailer. "Come on. I need to change. You're supposed to keep me on track, not ogle the hot stuntman."

"I can't help myself. So it looks like we're going to Fresno this weekend."

"So I heard. He loves you, Fi, so much." Trish closed the trailer door behind them.

"Yeah," she said just above a whisper as she lowered herself onto the cloth bench while Trish went into the bedroom to change.

"My agent thinks I'm going to get a bunch more leading roles in great films, and look at you and Jake. Can you believe how fast our lives are changing?" Trish hollered over her shoulder.

"No. It's crazy." *Crazy and wonderful and almost too good to be true.*

A few minutes later Trish came out of the bedroom in a pair of white shorts and a yellow tank top. She flopped on the bench next to Fiona.

"I just checked and Shea texted me, too. How does she find out about these things faster than we do?" Trish set her cell phone on the table.

"Maybe your agent called her because she wanted to make sure you got the press you deserved. It's a whole different world than mine is, isn't it?" Fiona fiddled with Trish's phone.

"Night and day. This is so far from journal articles, mineralization, and geochemistry that it must blow your mind." Trish rubbed her hand over her butterfly tattoo, which they'd been covering up with makeup on the set.

"I guess in some ways acting and geology are the same," Trish said. "In your job you're just looking at different types of relationships and models. In the entertainment business, we're working on emotional relationships and symbiotic couplings of characters. So they're different, but on some level they're still similar."

"Yeah, you keep telling yourself that." Fiona laughed. "What am I going to do, Trish?"

Trish kicked her feet up on the other side of the bench. "What do you mean? You're going to go back to Fresno and show off your hunky boyfriend, tell Clark I said hello, show Jake your adorable house, and then come back here and pretend to be my assistant for the next few weeks until we wrap. Then we'll go to a fabulous party."

"And then?" Fiona got up and paced.

"Then…" Trish watched Fiona, her eyes widening with understanding. "Oh. *Then.* Well, haven't you and Jake discussed anything about what happens after he's done filming?"

"He films longer than you do. I think he's set to be here for a few weeks after we leave, and no. We haven't really said anything other than what you already know."

"That the two of you are having wild, passionate sex and are too in love to spend a single night apart. I've got that part." She smiled at Fiona and rose to her feet. "Talk to him."

"Duh, but what about my promotion?"

"What about it? You knew about the promotion when you came here, and you said if you and Jake got back together you'd happily leave that behind and find something else in LA. Have you changed your mind?"

"No. Definitely not. But…I know it's early in our relationship and everything, but he hasn't said anything about me *not* going back to Fresno. Now he wants to go there, and it makes me wonder if he's thinking we'll have a long-distance relationship or something."

Trish pulled a soda from the fridge and handed it to Fiona, then cracked one open for herself. "Since when are you afraid to speak your mind? Ask him."

"It feels funny to do that. Like I'm rushing our relationship, or—"

"Rushing your relationship? You blew the guy on the side of the road." Trish sipped her drink. "That crossed a huge line for you. You're in uncharted territory, and I don't think you're rushing a darn thing. For you to do that, it's gotta be pretty serious, don't you think? Besides, you aren't exactly a *new* couple. You've got history. That counts for something. And the way he eyes you, you know he doesn't want you to be with anyone else. I think you should just ask him."

Ask him. It sounded so easy, so why did it feel so difficult?

Chapter Twenty-Two

AS JAKE DROVE into Fresno Friday afternoon, he felt the weight of Los Angeles fall away. There really was a different feeling that came over him when he left LA. Before he and Fiona got back together, he'd felt the opposite. Leaving LA had brought more stress than relief. Going home to Trusty had become a double-edged sword that he needed to recover from, rather than visiting home to recover from his chaotic life. And now, as they drove down the wide streets of Fresno and he reached for Fiona's hand, he relished in the freedom of leaving LA behind.

Fresno was nestled in the south Central Valley of California, not a far drive from LA, but a world away when it came to the environment. Fresno felt like any other busy town, while LA felt like a world in and of itself—bigger than life with expectations to match.

"Does it feel good to be back?" he asked Fiona.

She looked sexy in a short summer dress that stopped just

above her knees and a pair of strappy sandals, gazing out the window. "Feels weird, like I've been gone a lot longer than a month."

"Is this the first time you've gone away for so long?" He followed her directions toward her office and tried to imagine Fiona living there—without him. They'd spent so much time together that he was having a hard time imagining her anywhere else but by his side.

"I've been gone for a few weeks at a time for work, but this feels different. Maybe because you're coming back with me, or because there's a promotion waiting for me when I get back. I'm not sure."

He'd been thinking about her promotion a lot lately, and as much as he wanted to be with Fiona, she'd already given up so much in order to give them a shot at being together. The idea of asking her to give up even more seemed tremendously selfish, and he was trying to break the mold of *selfish Jake*.

He decided not to address the promotion just yet. He was looking forward to seeing Fiona in her element. He was proud of how much she'd accomplished, and he knew from talking with Trish how much her coworkers respected her.

"Turn left here. It's that glass building."

Jake parked in the lot beside the building and opened the car door for Fiona.

"Did you call and let them know we were coming?" He didn't know exactly why he wanted to see her in her office so badly, but Jake trusted his gut, and his gut told him that this was exactly where they needed to be today.

"Yeah, I left my boss a message."

The building felt clinical, with low-pile carpet and wide, silent hallways. The walls were white, with pictures of dig sites, rocks, and fossils. They took the stairs up to the second floor. He purposely gave her space to decide what was appropriate for public displays of affection in her office. He didn't reach for her hand or stand too close, and when she reached for his hand he was glad he'd let her make the choice.

"You're about to meet a bunch of scientists, so be ready for reserved personalities and serious discussions." She hesitated at the door, and he could tell she was nervous.

"If you're nervous, I don't have to go in. As much as I want to see you in action, I don't want to make you uncomfortable."

"You're not. I'm just…" She pressed her lips together and pressed one hand to his chest, inhaling deeply, then blowing it out slowly. "Jake, I'm a scientist. You're going to see me in scientist mode, and I haven't really thought about the difference until just now. The people in there know me as a scientist, not a dirt-bike-riding girl."

He ran his thumb over her lower lip and whispered, "Then I guess we shouldn't fill them in on all the dirty things you like to do."

She smiled, and he knew his effort to ease her tension was

working.

"I love you for your intelligence as much as the rest of you, Fi. I knew you were a brainiac when we were kids. How many teenage girls spent their lunch periods in a science lab? I'm an engineer, remember? We're made for each other. We can work hard, play hard, or, I'm realizing, thanks to you, we can just chill and enjoy each other. Have a little faith in me, babe."

"Sometimes I forget that you know the *real* me." She smoothed nonexistent wrinkles out of her dress, then pushed open the doors.

A blond receptionist with a pixie haircut and big blue eyes looked up from behind a computer and smiled. "Fiona. I didn't expect to see you for a couple weeks, but I'm glad you're here. Did Paul get ahold of you this morning?"

Fiona shook her head. "No. Deirdre, this is Jake Braden. Jake, this is Deirdre, our office manager."

"Nice to meet you, Deirdre."

"Hi, Jake." She turned her attention back to Fiona without as much as a second glance at Jake, which Jake wasn't used to. He was surprised to find that he was thankful for the lack of attention. Fiona was the star in here, and he loved seeing her as such. "Your article on the validity of fossil records was accepted to *Science Daily*. Paul's really excited."

Fiona's eyes widened in surprise. "It was accepted? Are you kidding me? Oh my God. This is huge."

"Definitely not kidding." Deirdre spoke in a calm, even

tone, as opposed to Fiona, who looked as though she might burst, with wide eyes and excitement coming off of her in waves.

"Congratulations, babe."

She threw her arms around his neck and laughed. So much for keeping a lid on public displays of affection.

"This is huge," she said as she led him through a set of double doors and into a large laboratory.

Jake had expected to see a bunch of nerdy people sitting around in lab coats looking through microscopes, which was ridiculous given that Fiona was anything but nerdy. Instead, the laboratory was filled with computer monitors, cumbersome equipment that looked like microscopes on steroids, elemental tables hanging on the walls, and shelves of resource materials.

They passed a large spectrometer, rounded a corner, and went through another set of doors. Three men turned as they walked in. A tall, dark-haired man's eyes locked on Fiona.

"Fiona. Did you hear?" He closed the distance between them, holding his hands out. Fiona took his hands in hers.

"Yes, Paul. I can hardly believe it." Her smile hadn't faltered since she heard the news.

"Believe it." Paul nodded. "As always, you hit your mark. I'm so proud of you."

"Thank you." Fiona looked over her shoulder at Jake. "Paul, this is Jake Braden. Jake, this is my supervisor, Paul

Marx."

Paul looked to be in his mid to late thirties, with a shock of dark hair and hazel eyes. He had the build of a runner, thick-legged and lean, and a firm handshake. This didn't look like a guy who dug up rocks for a living. He looked like a guy who dug up rocks and then carried them two miles.

"Jake. You grew up with Fiona, right?"

"Yes, sir." *And now I'm her boyfriend, so how about you let go of her hands?*

Paul pulled Fiona against his side. "You've got a great girl here. She's brilliant, and she's about to become a household name."

Fiona's cheeks flushed. "Among scientists maybe." She eased out of his arms and went to Jake's side. "Our studies showed that geological factors such as counts of fossil collections and geological formations are not independent measures of bias in the fossil record and that only the area of preserved rock drives biodiversity." She shrugged as if she hadn't spoken in a foreign language.

A blond-haired twentysomething guy came around a big desk where he'd been talking with another man who could only be Clark Kent, because his dark hair, black frames, and chiseled features had Jake doing a double take.

"Hi, I'm Joe." The blond man shook Jake's hand and nodded to the dark-haired man. "That's Clark. Fiona had suspected that the number of fossils wasn't dictated by the amount of accessible rock, but rather that the similar patterns displayed by rock and fossil records were due to external factors." He shook his head. "She was like a dinosaur with a bone. Well done, Fiona."

"When are you coming back?" Clark asked. "We wanted to discuss follow-up articles. Jackson and I have a few theories that feed off of what you've found."

"I'd love to hear them." Fiona turned to Jake. "Do you mind if I stay and talk for just a minute?"

"No. Take your time."

Fiona pointed to a wooden desk in the corner. "That's my desk if you want to sit down for a while, or I can show you where the coffee room is."

"I'll take him." Paul nodded to Jake. "It's just down the hall."

Jake followed Paul to the kitchen.

"Fiona's a hell of a scientist," Paul said as he filled a cup with coffee and handed it to Jake. "Cream and sugar's over there if you'd like it."

"Thanks, and yeah, she's successful in everything she does."

"I can see that." Paul leaned against the counter and eyed Jake over his mug as he took a sip of coffee.

Jake mulled over his strange response, unsure what to make of it.

"I'm sure she's told you about the promotion she's been

offered." Paul set his coffee down beside him.

"She's mentioned it." It was obvious that Paul thought the world of Fiona. Jake wondered how far beyond her job that went.

Paul nodded. "It's a hell of a position. She'd lead two teams of geologists."

Jake leaned against the counter beside him. "She's patient and she knows how to take control. I'm sure she'll be a great leader."

"Listen, Jake, we both know why Fiona took this leave of absence, and obviously the two of you have reconnected."

"She shared that with you?" The way Fiona had played up the *scientist* relationship, it surprised him to hear she'd shared her feelings with Paul, and the green-eyed monster clawed at him again.

"Not exactly." His thin lips curved up in a smile. "She said she was taking an unpaid leave of absence to work with her friend Trish on her movie. I wondered why a woman who was as dedicated to her work as Fiona is would take six weeks off, unpaid, when she was in the midst of some of this year's most important research." He shrugged and slid his hands into his pockets and crossed his legs at the ankle. "I did a little of my own research and came up with a theory."

"And your point is?" Jake assessed Paul's casual stance, the lack of threat in his tone, and his easy gaze and wondered what the hell he was getting at. This obviously wasn't a pissing match between two guys fighting over a woman. This had the feel of something altogether different, but equally as important.

"Fiona's a brilliant scientist. She's not a groupie who's leaving a job at a tanning salon behind." Paul's eyes grew serious again.

"I'm not sure I understand what you're implying. Not that it's any of your business, but Fiona isn't a fling, if that's what you're worried about."

Paul took another sip of his coffee, meeting Jake's stare. "I'm a scientist, Jake. Research is my thing. I'm fairly well versed in all things Jake Braden." He stood up tall and drew his shoulders back.

Jake rose to his full height, wondering where Paul was going with this.

"She's a good woman, Jake, as I'm sure you know. All I'm asking is that you're sure of her before you take her away from what is probably the biggest opportunity that will ever come her way."

Jake clenched his jaw, but really, how could he get angry? The harsh truth was that anyone who went online and typed in Jake's name would see that he hadn't been photographed with the same woman more than twice. Paul obviously respected Fiona as a scientist, and he wanted to protect her, but Jake couldn't help taking it one step further, just to be sure he wasn't misreading him.

"Just so we're on the same page here, Paul, are you interested in Fiona's career path or do you have other interests in her?"

Paul smiled again. "You're a sharp man. I guess I shouldn't have underestimated a man with an engineering degree. If I weren't gay, she'd be just the type of woman I'd go for. I can assure you, I care about her on a platonic level, not a sexual one. I'm very fond of her. She's a good person and an excellent scientist. I guess I'm a bit protective of her."

Jake tried not to show his surprise, or his relief. "Fair enough."

Paul withdrew his wallet and showed Jake a picture of a very handsome dark-haired man with a toddler on his lap. "My husband, Kane, and our son, Johnny."

"Two handsome guys." Jake withdrew his wallet and flashed the photograph of him and Fiona when they were teenagers.

"The love of my life, Fiona."

Chapter Twenty-Three

FIONA AND JAKE spent the afternoon walking through Fresno. After a nice dinner in a café, they went for a walk in the park and finally pulled into Fiona's driveway as the sun was going down. It felt good to be home. Fiona loved her 1950s bungalow. She loved the dark wood siding with the beige trim and the deep front porch with a center peaked eave. It was simple and small enough to feel cozy without feeling confining, and she got excited just thinking about Jake being there with her.

"Your house is really cute, Fi." He looked over the house before mounting the stairs to the porch.

"Thanks. I really like it."

"It was nice seeing your office today and meeting the guys you work with."

"I'm glad we went. I'd like to find a few hours to go over the ideas the guys want to explore."

"You could have stayed today. I would have come back

later. I'm a big boy, Fi. I can entertain myself."

"I don't mean now. I don't want to take time away from us. I just meant sometime soon. I'll figure it out." She was excited about their research, and even if she decided not to take the promotion, she still wanted to hear about it.

Jake touched one of the rocking chairs on the porch.

"I can see you sitting out here." He reached for her hand.

"I love it here." She gazed out at the grassy lawn and the woods that surrounded the house on three sides. "There's never any traffic since I'm so far from the main drag. Sometimes I even eat dinner on the porch."

He slid his hands around her waist and lowered his voice. "Don't you get lonely out here by yourself?"

She shook her head. "I like the quiet."

He pressed his lips to hers. She loved that he was there with her, standing on the front porch she loved, and that he'd wanted to be there. She remembered thinking, when she'd first seen the house with the Realtor, that Jake would like it, and she remembered the way she'd chided herself for thinking about him.

She unlocked the door, and Jake followed her into the wide center hall that ran the length of the house, ending at the stairs that led to the second floor.

"I love the hardwood," Jake said, peering into the living room. "Nice fireplace. I can see us sitting on your sofa with a fire blazing."

He went into the living room and looked over her pictures on her mantel. It reminded her of when she'd done the same thing at his cabin. It was a strange feeling to see people she knew as a teenager and then to see them all grown up. She'd seen his family through the years, but she no longer knew them as intimately as she once had. She wondered what Jake was thinking as he looked over a picture of her with her four brothers, Reggie, Finn, Jesse, and Brent. Standing behind Fiona was her twin brother, Finn. His hair had been longer then, brushing over his eyes and touching his collar. She was sitting on the grass in front of them all, smiling up at the camera like she was the happiest girl in the world.

Jake smiled. "I haven't seen Reggie or your brothers in years."

"I know. They're so busy. Reggie hardly ever comes back from New York, and Jesse and Brent are crazy busy at Harborside with the surf shop and restaurant. And you know Finn. We never know when we'll see him."

"We'll have to make a point of getting everyone together again." He took her hand and went through the foyer to the dining room. "This is really nice, Fi. It feels like you."

"Thanks." She watched him look over her antique hutch and the small dining room table. He was so tall and broad that the room felt smaller with him in it. Even so, it felt better. Fiona could picture him lounging on the couch watching football while she read beside him and sitting at the table sharing a meal.

"I really love your place, Fi. It's very *you*, and it feels like home."

Her heart squeezed at the way his eyes warmed when he said the word *home*.

As he lowered his lips to hers, his cell phone rang. He groaned.

"Go ahead and answer it." She walked into the kitchen. "Would you like some wine? We can sit out back on the deck." She glanced up as he took his phone from his pocket.

"Sounds great," he said to her before answering the call. "What's up, Trace?" He paused, listening, as Fiona handed him a glass of wine. "Goddamn it. Really?" He paused again. "I'm in Fresno." He looked at his watch and sighed. "I can be there in a couple hours. Is Trish filming?"

He narrowed his eyes as he listened. "Yeah. Don't worry about it. Okay. Thanks, Trace."

After he ended the call, his expression fell flat.

"What's wrong?"

"They're changing two scenes. They want to meet about it tonight, then shoot this weekend. I'm sorry, Fi. I wanted nothing more than to live in your world for a few days, but—"

"It's okay. Is Trish filming too?" She tried not to let her disappointment show.

"No, babe."

He reached for her, and it dawned on her how perfect the

timing was. She needed to have a serious talk with Paul about the promotion, and she wanted to go over Joe's and Clark's ideas.

"Why don't you go back, have your meeting, shoot your scenes, and I'll stick around and go over the research with the guys. I can have someone drive me back on Sunday afternoon."

"Sunday?" His voice was laden with disappointment.

"It's not like I want to be apart, but if I go back to LA, you'll be shooting and I'll be thinking about how I should be going over the research with Paul and the guys."

"I hate it when you make sense. But I don't want to put out your coworkers. I'll come get you Sunday."

"You're filming," she reminded him.

He scrubbed his hand down his face. "Then I'll send a driver to pick you up. You're my responsibility, Fi, not your coworkers'."

"Actually," she said just above a whisper as she dragged her index finger down the center of his chest. "I'm my own responsibility. You're my boyfriend, not my parent."

He touched his forehead to hers. "I don't mean it that way, babe. I love you, and I want to make sure you get back safe and sound. And it's going to suck spending two nights away from you."

"Just think of how much fun it will be when we're together again."

Chapter Twenty-Four

SATURDAY WAS TURNING out to be the longest goddamn day Jake had ever lived through. Every scene had to be reshot several times. He screwed up two stunts because he was too distracted thinking about what Paul had said to him, and to top it all off, he hadn't slept worth a darn without Fiona by his side. Waking up without her sucked. Going for a run without her was even worse—he didn't know how he had gone without her for so long. He checked his watch. It was nearing six o'clock, and they still had another scene to shoot. He flagged Trace over.

"Phone." He motioned with his hand for her to hurry up.

"You could say please." She slapped it in his palm. "What is wrong with you today? You're like a caged animal."

"Long day." He texted Fiona. *Miss you. Hope your research is going well. Xox.*

He handed the phone back to Trace, who was staring at him like he had six heads.

"This is not a long day, and you just had yesterday off. What's really wrong with you?" She crossed her arms and narrowed her heavily lined eyes. "It's Fiona." A smile crept across her lips as a scowl crept across his. "You're so in love you can't see straight. I never thought I'd see the day."

Jake narrowed his eyes. Yeah, he missed her, too damn much to think straight, but what was worse was that he'd seen the excitement in her eyes at the prospect of going over that research. Not that there was anything wrong with that. There wasn't. He was happy that she was doing something she enjoyed, but hell if it wasn't an eye-opener. He couldn't ask Fiona to give up *the biggest opportunity that will ever come her way*. That would be like her asking him to give up the next film. He wouldn't do that to her. Maybe the old Jake would, but now that he'd had his eyes opened to how selfish he'd become, there was no way he was going back down that road. That was the old Jake. The new and improved Jake—or maybe it would be more accurate to think of himself as the Jake who had reverted to the man he'd once been—would never ask Fiona to do that.

Fuck.

He was screwed.

He had finally allowed himself to feel again, to love, to admit all that he'd done wrong with his life, and for what? To realize that he couldn't have the one woman he really wanted unless they had a long-distance relationship or one of them traveled four hours to work each day? What about his filming schedule? He traveled more than half the year. There was no way he could be separated from her for that long. He'd lose his mind.

"Hey. Daydreamer." Trace tugged at his arm.

He must have zoned out, because he'd had no idea Trace was even talking to him.

She held out his phone, and he read Fiona's reply.

I miss you, too! I hope your stunts are safe and easy. This research is going to be a huge deal. We're going to work through dinner and probably late tonight. Can't wait to see you Sunday! Xox.

"You good? You got your Fiona fix, big boy?" Trace held her hand out for the phone again. "They're ready for you on set, and Hileberg just announced that he didn't like the last scene. They're reshooting. It's going to be a very long night."

BY THE TIME Fiona and the guys called it quits, it was after ten o'clock. Paul drove her home, and he agreed to pick her up in the morning to discuss the promotion. Trace had texted her earlier to say that Steven Hileberg was keeping everyone on set to film night scenes and that they'd called Trish in to shoot as well. Fiona felt horrible for not being there for her, even though she didn't feel as though she contributed much in the way of being an efficient assistant. At least she could have been there for moral support. She'd texted Trish, and of course Trish had said it was no big deal that she wasn't there.

She dug through her purse for her keys, and when she pulled them out, a flash drive came with them. The string had hooked to one of her keys. She stared at the little black drive for a few seconds before remembering that Jake had given it to her the first day he'd driven her to the set—the morning of the paparazzi ambush. His voice sailed into her mind. *I never realized why these songs appealed to me until last night. Now it kind of makes sense. It's like the soundtrack to my life, or something like that.*

The thrill of anticipation tickled her spine. She unlocked her door and took the stairs two at a time. She plugged the flash drive into her laptop, hardly able to believe she'd forgotten about it for so long. She was nervous and excited to hear the soundtrack of his life. She tossed her purse on the bed and undressed while she listened. The first song was "Hanging by a Moment" by Lifehouse. She moved to the easy and familiar rhythm as she brushed her teeth. The second song took her by surprise—and stung. "Go on...Miss Me" by Gloriana, which mentioned a person being unfaithful. She didn't like hearing that, especially since neither of them had been unfaithful, but the rest of the song sure rang true. She *had* missed him like crazy and wanted to get back together. He'd said this was the soundtrack to his life. Did that mean that somewhere deep in his heart he'd been hoping they'd get back together, too?

Fiona put on her sleeping shorts and a T-shirt and lay down on her bed, listening to the other songs on his list. "Here Without You" by 3 Doors Down, "Drops of Jupiter" by Train, "You and Me" by Lifehouse, and Alicia Keys's, "Fallen." She hated thinking about Jake listening to songs that marked how much she'd hurt him, but she forced herself to listen to the rest of the songs. The next two nearly did her in, "She's So Mean" by Matchbox 20 and "Please Forgive Me" by Bryan Adams.

It was no wonder he worked so hard to bury his feelings. If the songs were any indication, he'd thought about her even when he didn't realize it. It bolstered her confidence, and she bolted off the bed.

She knew exactly what she wanted to do, and she knew what she *had* to do.

First things first.

She pulled her laptop onto the bed and began putting together her own playlist. Darryl Worley's "I Miss My Friend" and "It's Not Over" by Daughtry were the first two she added, followed by "If You're Gone" by Matchbox Twenty, "State of Grace" by Taylor Swift, and "I Try" by Macy Gray. She added song after song. "I Choose You," by Sara Bareilles and "I Would've Loved You Anyway" by Trisha Yearwood were next.

Yeah, I would have.

She added songs that made her think of Jake, which was nearly every song under the sun, so she tried to choose songs that had specific meanings throughout their relationship.

When she added "3 AM" by Matchbox Twenty, she wiped a tear from her cheek. She'd missed him every minute of every day when they were apart. By the time she finished adding songs, it was nearly two o'clock in the morning.

She stood and pulled a box out from under the bed, then sat back on her heels and lifted the lid. Inside was the bear Jake had won her at the County Fair when she was seventeen. Its fur was matted from being tucked under her arm on lonely nights, and its black button eyes looked right through her. She picked it up and stroked it between its ears, then clutched it to her chest, thinking about the conversations she needed to have tomorrow, with Jake and with Paul.

Chapter Twenty-Five

IT WAS SIX o'clock by the time Jake arrived to pick up Fiona in Fresno. Hileberg had called for one last filming session, and when Steve Hileberg said he was filming, there were no negotiations. When she opened the door, Jake's chest swelled with love. Seeing her in an emerald-green tank top that clung to her breasts, skinny jeans hugging every delicious curve, and something shimmery around her eyes, Jake couldn't take his eyes off of her. He folded her into his arms, feeling as though they'd been apart for weeks instead of two nights.

"Two nights is too damn long," he said against her ear before sealing his lips over hers.

He lifted her in his arms, and she wrapped her legs around his waist. This was becoming a natural position for them— and he knew just where it would lead. The staircase was just a few feet away. The couch was even closer, but as he enjoyed the feel of her sweet body against his, the taste of her mouth as they devoured each other, and the warm slide of her tongue, he knew that landing in bed was the wrong thing to do. Paul's comment had whirred through his mind like a tornado, and his conversation with Trish hadn't helped. When he'd asked her about Fiona's job, Trish had raved about how good she was at it, how much her colleagues respected her, and how she thrived on discoveries—hands-on or academic.

He and Fiona needed to talk, and the sooner they did, the better.

They drove toward Los Angeles holding hands and talking about Jake's filming. He was procrastinating, but hell, why shouldn't he? Being unselfish wasn't always fun, and he was about to be as unselfish as a man could get.

"The research the guys are planning could mean major funding for future projects. They're going to try to bring in a world-renowned scientist who wrote a previous article. They're disputing his findings, which is going to majorly piss the guy off, I'm sure, but that's why they want to bring him in. He wrote his article two years ago, and they think if they can get him on board for the project, it will hold even more weight. It's brilliant, really."

Jake squeezed her hand. "That's great, Fi."

"Yeah, and Paul is so excited about it all. He feels like the attention the group will get from my article will drive their research forward." Fiona pulled out her cell phone and began texting. "I just remembered something. Sorry. I'm just texting Clark. They're taking our notes from this weekend and putting them into an outline, and I agreed to be listed on the article, so I want to be sure they use my home email as well as my work email so I don't miss anything."

Her excitement was palpable as she concentrated on the text with her lip trapped between her teeth and a smile pulling the edges of her lips up. A long-distance relationship wouldn't be that bad, would it? They'd still find time for each other. He could always sell his place and buy another that was closer to Fresno.

Commuting would be hell. But he could do it. He couldn't let Fiona pass up this promotion. Even if it meant risking what they had, he wasn't about to stand in her way.

He watched Fiona put her phone back into her purse, then pull it out again.

"I forgot to call Trish last night. I want to fill her in."

"Take your time." *I'm in no hurry to ruin what we have.*

A few minutes later she called Trish, and Fiona spent the rest of the ride filling her in on her upcoming publication as well as the project the other guys were planning. Her hands flew through the air as she described the project.

"I know!" She laughed and agreed with whatever Trish was saying.

She was still on the phone when they pulled up in front of his house. He used that time to try to figure out how he was going to tell her the very thing he didn't want to. The longer he stewed, the tighter his muscles corded. He felt like a caged tiger as he paced the front yard, waiting for her to get off the phone—and not wanting her to in equal measure.

He was standing at the edge of the driveway with his back to Fiona when he felt her arms circle his waist from behind and her cheek press against his back.

"I'm sorry, Jake. You drove all the way out to get me in Fresno, and then I spend the whole time either jabbering at you or on the phone."

He turned in her arms, and the trusting look in her beautiful eyes chipped away at his resolve. He needed to get this over with before he lost his nerve to do the right thing.

"It's okay." The gruffness of his tone surprised him. "Fi, I think you should take the promotion." There. He said it loud, clear, and without any room for misinterpretation. Why, then, was Fiona blinking up at him as if she had no idea what he was talking about and stumbling backward as if she'd been pushed?

"What?" The word came out incredulously.

These were the hardest words he'd ever had to say. Everything he'd never understood about himself, he understood when he was with Fiona. She righted his chaotic world and showed him how to feel again. He wanted her more than he wanted anything else in the world, but he'd spent the last sixteen years taking what he wanted. It was time for him to step back and make sure that Fiona got what *she* wanted. What she deserved.

"I want you to take the promotion. You've worked hard for it. You deserve it, and you can't tell me that you don't want it." He clenched his hands into fists by his sides, repressing the urge to tell her he was lying. "We'll figure out how to navigate a long-distance relationship."

"A long-distance relationship? Is that what you really want? You don't mean that." Her chest rose and fell as her breathing hitched.

"I do, Fiona. I want you to take the promotion." *Goddamn it.* He was dying a slow and painful death as the lie bored into his chest and sucked the blood from his heart. This must be payback for his years of living selfishly. And it sucked.

Fiona shook her head. "No. No, Jake." She closed the distance between them, tears welling in her eyes.

Jake looked away, biting back his own devastation.

"No, Jake! I know you, and you don't mean this. You don't want to be apart for a week or more at a time. I know you don't. You don't want to go on location and know that I'm a thousand miles away for five or six or twelve weeks."

He clenched his teeth so tight he feared they'd crack. It was either that or ruin the career she'd worked so hard for by telling her he was lying, that he wanted nothing more than to be with her every second of every goddamn day. He managed to shake his head, or at least he hoped he did.

"Why?" she snapped, her beautiful eyes full of hurt.

He swallowed against the lump in his throat.

She grabbed his T-shirt in her shaking fists. Her face went red, and her eyes narrowed. "Tell me why. Was this all a game to you? Because I don't fucking believe that for one second."

He met her gaze. His gut plummeted as her tears sprang free.

"Is this payback for my leaving you all those years ago?"

He reached up to wipe her tears, and she swatted at his hand.

"No. You don't get to touch me. You owe me an explanation." She stormed across the driveway, then turned around and stomped back again, standing so close he could see red streaks in the whites of her eyes.

Her eyes softened from anger to hurt, and her voice softened again. "I know you love me, Jake. Unless...unless I don't know you at all." She nodded, as if understanding was dawning on her. She stumbled backward.

His heart was shattering into smithereens inside him. If this was what it felt like to be unselfish, he was ready to kick the hell out of it. He was afraid to answer her. Afraid of the truth tumbling out like rocks.

"You love me, Jake. I know you do."

He couldn't stand to see her so unhappy. "I do love you, Fiona." *More than you could ever know.*

"Then why do you want to be apart?" When he didn't answer, she shook her head and backed away again. "This is messed up. I don't know what I did wrong, but long distance doesn't work for *me*, Jake."

Anger and sadness swirled inside him and bound together, pushing him forward with the force of a hurricane.

"What were you thinking, Fiona?" He stalked over to her, all the anger of the years spewing forward, and he had no chance of reining it in. "We're right back where we were sixteen years ago. Your fucking future is on the line, and I won't be the one holding you back. You wanted your freedom all those years ago and you got it. I didn't chase you, when that was all I thought about day in and day out. All I ever wanted was for you to be happy, and when that didn't include me, I thought, well, fuck me. It sucked, and it hurt, and I moved on."

"You hid from it," she spat.

"So fucking what? You got to live your life the way you wanted. I wouldn't stand in your way then, and in all those years we were apart, I became the most selfish bastard I've ever known. I didn't fucking care about anyone but my family. No one got close to me, Fiona. Not one damn person."

She blinked up at him, tears streaming down her cheeks, and she whispered, "Jake."

"No. It was what it was, and I was ready to let all that go. You made me a better person, Fi. In one goddamn month you made me realize what a self-centered prick I'd become, and it was the best thing you could do for me—and the worst. Because now here we stand. You're on the precipice of the pinnacle of your career, and here I am. Stuck." His arms shook with frustration. "I see you in everything I do. When I was jumping out of the damn building yesterday, all I thought about was being extra safe so I would be able to see you again. And when I picked you up at your house, it felt like coming home. But none of that matters, because if I tell you to stay, then I'm the same selfish bastard I'm trying my damnedest not to be."

"Jake—" She reached for him, and he backed out of her reach.

"No. Let me finish. I want nothing more than to marry you, Fiona. To keep you by my side every second of my life. I want to come home to you, to wake up to you, and you're the only woman I ever want to make love to again. I want to have a goddamn family with you—but none of that matters."

He spun away and scrubbed his hand down his face, trying to regain control of his anger. He sank his hands onto his hips, rounded his shoulders forward, trying desperately to ward off the desire to back down. After sucking in one deep breath after another, steeling himself again for the tears he knew he'd see, he turned around.

Her hand covered her mouth, leaving only her damp, wide eyes staring at him like he had three heads.

"Marry me?" she whispered.

He reached for her trembling hand. "Yes. Marry you. I'm sorry, Fiona."

"You're an idiot."

He nodded. "An asshole is more like it, but I'm trying so

hard to fix that. Not being selfish sucks, just so you know, but it doesn't change how much I love you."

She swallowed hard, then stepped closer. Their thighs brushed. She pressed her soft, warm palm to his cheek, and Jake closed his eyes, relishing in the comfort of her loving touch.

"I'm so sorry, Fi. I want this to work, but more important, I don't want to take you away from something that makes you so happy." He looked down at her, feeling his resolve slipping away. "You own me, Fi. You always have."

Her lips curved up in a smile.

"Be selfish, Jake. This is the one time you *can* be selfish."

"You're not making this easy. I'm really trying to do the right thing."

"This is the right thing," she said softly.

And it fucking sucks.

"*This* is the right thing." She circled her arms around his neck and lifted herself into his arms, then fastened her mouth to his.

Salty tears seeped into their mouths, and their hearts slammed a frantic beat against their chests. His strong arms cocooned her. She felt too damn good, too damn right. Maybe it wasn't the right thing to do, and maybe he really was a selfish man at heart, but with Fiona's approval, he couldn't lie anymore. He tore his lips from hers and stared into her loving eyes.

"The hell with the promotion. Marry me, Fiona. Get a job

here, or work remotely, or don't work at all. I'll support anything you want to do, except I'm not unselfish enough to let you go again. It's selfish, and I'm a goddamn asshole for asking you to give up what you love, but I want you, Fiona, and I let you go once. I'm not letting you go again."

She pressed her palms to his cheeks and gazed into his eyes with a serious look. "I already turned down the promotion and submitted my resignation earlier this morning."

"You…"

She nodded. "I knew you loved me. I don't want to love you from afar or wish I was with you on location. I want to be with you every second."

"You quit." He couldn't wrap his mind around it.

"I left you to find myself once, and I accomplished what I wanted to accomplish. I made my mark in my field, and I'll still publish as I'm able, but what I found when I went searching was that it's not the discoveries or publications that make me whole. I found myself, but a piece was missing all along. The most important piece. I'm not whole without you, Jake. You're my missing piece."

He touched his forehead to hers and breathed her in. "Marry me, Fi. Raise raucous boys and smart girls with me. Be my wife. Be mine. God knows I'm already yours."

"Don't you feel it, silly? I've been yours all along."

Chapter Twenty-Six

JAKE AND FIONA held hands and smiled like they'd just eaten an entire birthday cake meant for someone else, only it wasn't cake that had put interminable smiles on their faces. Monday's filming had been canceled at the last minute, and Jake and Fiona had taken full advantage of the day. They'd spent the day in each other's arms, making love more times than they'd ever fess up to, and had left their love nest only long enough to use the bathroom. They'd finally showered and dressed an hour ago. It was seven o'clock Monday evening and they were sitting on Jake's bed, dressed for the actors' dinner and staring at the monitor of his laptop.

"Ready?" Jake asked, hovering the cursor over the Skype icon.

"Click it already. Your driver's supposed to be here in ten minutes."

Jake pressed his leg to hers, causing the slit in Fiona's silky white dress to fall open. He placed his hand on her thigh and nuzzled against her neck.

"Are you sure? We can skip the Skype call with my family and skip dinner." He glanced over her shoulder at the bed and arched a brow.

Her cheeks flushed pink. "You're insatiable. Make the call."

They'd called each of Fiona's brothers last night to give them the news. Reggie, Jesse, and Brent all gave Jake applause-worthy big-brother threats about taking care of their sister. Finn had a gentler message for Jake. *Fiona likes people to think she's thick-skinned and strong as an ox, but really, she's a lovely, strong woman with a big, sensitive heart. Protect her heart, Jake, and we'll be good friends forever. Damage her heart, and you'll never know what hit you.* Jake respected her brothers' threats, because he had done the same thing to Dae with regard to Emily. It's what brothers who loved their sisters did. Family was everything to Jake, and he knew her brothers would never have to carry through a single threat. He planned on making Fiona the happiest woman on the planet every day of her life.

He fell more in love with her with every passing second. He looked at her now, then at the laptop, and finally back to her with a serious gaze.

"Okay, but remember, you're with me. Don't fall for my cousin Sam."

Fiona rolled her eyes with the tease. "Okay, I'll try to re-frain, but only if you can promise me that when the too-sexy-for-her-own-good Megan Flexx wraps her arms around you in a hug, you won't enjoy the feel of it."

"Shit. That woman's got nothing on you."

"Exactly. Neither does Sam on you." She pointed to the laptop.

Jake clicked the icon, and a few seconds later Emily's big brown eyes were staring back at them. She squealed and jumped up and down.

"Emily!" her mother called from behind her.

"Hi, you guys!" Emily waved like she hadn't seen them in years. Jake's mother peered over her shoulder.

"Hi, guys. Love you," his mother said.

"Hi," Jake and Fiona said at the same time.

Wes peeked in from the side.

"Hey, bro," Wes said. "Hey, Fiona."

"Hi," they repeated.

"You guys look…happy." Wes winked at Fiona.

Jake's eyes went serious as they swept from Wes to Fiona.

"We are, but we only have a few minutes." Jake laced his fingers with Fiona's.

"That's not what I heard. I hear you have a lifetime." Emily pushed Wes to the side and grinned. "Shea texted and said Fiona was staying in LA."

"I was hoping to give you guys the news myself." Jake looked at Fiona.

Fiona crinkled her nose. "Sorry. I sent her a text last night."

"That's okay." He kissed her softly.

Emily *aww*ed, Wes whispered, *Christ*, as if he were annoyed, but Jake knew he was just mocking the way Jake had recently made fun of all of his siblings' relationships. Then a deep voice Jake hadn't heard in ages boomed, "Dude. Are we in your bedroom?"

Sam's handsome face filled the screen. He had thick black hair, a sparse beard, and eyes full of mischief. He was Jake's second cousin, and owned a river rafting company on the East Coast near the rest of his cousins.

"Sam, it's been forever! This is Fiona, and yeah, we're in the bedroom," Jake answered.

"Cool. Hey, Fiona. I've heard a lot about you." Sam reached an arm out to the side, and Sam's sister, Shannon, appeared beside him. Shannon was in her early twenties, with long brown hair and warm hazel eyes.

"Hey, Shannon," Jake said. "This is my fiancée, Fiona." *My fiancée.* He had no idea what universal powers had blessed him with Fiona, but he wasn't going to mess it up this time. No way. No how.

"It's so good to see you guys. Emily said you would have only a few minutes, but we really wanted to say hi." Shannon lived in Peaceful Harbor, Maryland, and it had been almost three years since Jake had seen her.

"You look great, Shannon. How long are you two in town?" Jake asked.

Shannon pressed her palm to her chest. "I'm here for a couple months for an environmental project. Doing a study in the mountains. Maybe we can catch up next time you're in town. After visiting with everyone here, I'm going to stay with Uncle Hal for a while. And Sam..." She leaned to the side so Sam could look into the camera again.

"I don't know how long I'll be here, man. My team's putting things together for our next trip." Sam's company hosted rafting trips in different areas of the country.

Jake's mother peered into the camera again. "Jake, maybe after you wrap up filming, we can get together and celebrate your and Fiona's engagement."

"That would be great, Mom. Thank you." Jake pulled Fiona into a hug.

"Thank you so much. I'd really like that," she said to his mother.

"It's great to see you guys. Shannon, Sam, we'll catch up soon, I promise, but we have to get off the line in a minute and I need to talk to Wes. Can you pull him into the mix real quick?"

"Yo, bro." Wes appeared between Shannon and Sam. "What's up?"

"I just wanted to tell you that when we get together again, I'm going to pound the shit out of you." Jake smirked.

"Seems to me you should be thanking me for taking you to the bar that night." Wes lifted his chin in challenge.

"Yeah, you're right about that. For that, I'm not going to kill you, but for deceiving me, I'm going to hurt you pretty bad."

"Jake!" Fiona nudged his shoulder. "I won't let him do that," she said to Wes.

"It's okay, Fiona. I can take him," Wes answered.

"But we won't let him." Callie peered into the camera from over Wes's shoulder and lifted Wes's casted arm. "Your brother and his buddy Chip decided to go bull riding. The bull got the best of them. How about we call it a draw?"

Jake pulled Fiona in close. "I think I'm the clear winner."

ON THE WAY to the actors' dinner, they listened to the playlist Fiona had made for Jake and snuggled in the backseat of the limousine. They didn't talk about what the songs meant or why Fiona had picked them. They didn't need to. As with most things, now that Jake learned to follow his heart, they were both on the same page.

Fiona couldn't get over the way Jake had tried so hard to push away his feelings and be the most unselfish man he could by telling her to take the promotion. She teared up nearly every time she thought of it. She'd never met a man who tried so hard and dug so deep to change who he was.

But she knew Jake didn't really have to *change*. He had

only to find the part of himself he'd repressed, and she knew she'd made the right choice—the *only* choice she could live with. Paul had taken the news well, although he was sorry to lose her. He offered to let her consult as often as they could work out their schedules. For now Fiona was happy to be involved with Joe and Clark's new research paper. Jake had expressed an interest in spending more time at the cabin and in starting a family after they were married. But he was in no rush to fill up their time alone, and that suited her just fine.

"Babe, I spoke to my cousin Savannah's husband, Jack Remington, and got in touch with his mother, Joanie, and his brother Sage. They're both willing to give you art lessons. Joanie is a painter, and Sage is a sculptor and painter."

"Jake…" She didn't know what to say. She knew his cousin Savannah, Hal Braden's daughter, had gotten married, but she had no idea she'd married into an artistic family, and she was floored that Jake had thought of this. "When did you have time to do that?"

"When you were in the shower."

She smiled and shook her head. "Will you ever stop surprising me?"

"Probably not, but I want your dreams to come true. I figured since I have a break after filming this movie, before we go to Sweetwater for Zane's next film, we could fly to New York City, spend some time with the Remingtons so you can get to know them, and figure out a way to make a schedule for your art lessons." He shrugged. "Maybe we'll spend one week a month there while you learn to paint, or take a month when we have time off and knock around the city. Whatever you want."

"Oh, Jake." Fiona blinked several times, trying to stave off the tears in her eyes. "Thank you." She pressed her lips to his.

"We'll look for an engagement ring while we're there."

She felt her eyes open wide. "We don't have to—"

He pressed his finger to her lips. "I'm taking my girl to Greece for the most romantic honeymoon. You stole my romantic *I-love-you* moment; let me have this. Please."

The limousine pulled up in front of the restaurant, and before Fiona could say a word, Jake was out of the car and reaching for her hand.

Cameras flashed and paparazzi shouted questions, each one louder than the next. Jake tucked her beneath his arm and held her so tightly she thought he might leave fingerprints—and that would suit her just fine.

At the entrance to the restaurant, two fans pulled at Jake's arm. He tightened his grip around Fiona's shoulder, and when the young fans tried to push their way in on either side of him, he held them at bay.

"You can take a picture, but my left side belongs to my fiancée."

After the fans took their picture, Jake gazed into Fiona's eyes and pulled her into an embrace. He took her in a deep kiss that should have embarrassed her, given that about fifty cameras were aimed at them. Instead, it weakened her knees. Jake might have had to get accustomed to feeling again, but Fiona had a big adjustment of her own. Every passionate kiss and every warm embrace set her body on fire. She had to become a master at disguising the desire Jake stirred in her— and it was an adjustment she was looking forward to practicing.

He braced her against his body, wrapped in his powerful arms, and pressed his cheek to hers. "I've got you, Fi, and I'll never let you go."

Ready for more fiercely loyal, wickedly naughty Bradens?

Fall in love with Nate and Jewel in HEALED BY LOVE

The Bradens at Peaceful Harbor

Chapter One

"ARE YOU SURE you don't want me to come back after they leave?" Jewel Fisher grabbed her purse from beneath the cash register and checked the posted work schedule one more time, confirming that she wasn't due back until Monday.

"Yes. Positive. Go have fun. You haven't had a weekend off for months." Chelsea Helms, Jewel's boss and the owner of Chelsea's Boutique, gently nudged her away from the register. Jewel had worked for Chelsea for two years, although she'd known her much longer. Chelsea had gone to high school with Rick, Jewel's older brother, who had died two years earlier while serving in Afghanistan.

"I had a weekend off in February." Jewel walked toward the front of the store, straightening the display tables along the way.

Chelsea rolled her eyes. "That was two months ago, and you know I don't mean from here. Retail hours are always crazy. I mean from your family *and* work. Go do something crazy like lose that V-card of yours."

Jewel had about as much interest in losing her virginity as she did in taking time off from helping her family. It wasn't that she thought her virginity was something special or worth hanging on to. It wasn't something she thought about one way or another. Between helping her mother with her younger siblings for the past several years while going to school and now working full-time, she rarely had free time. Even though sex wasn't something Jewel thought about often, she could feel it all around her. When she was in college, Jewel had lived at home so she could help with the kids, avoiding the nightly peer pressure of living in the dorms, where sex hovered in the eyes of every guy and in the seductive smiles of the girls. Since college, the few dates she had gone on—all set up by Chelsea—had been duds. At least in Jewel's eyes. Guys her age were too immature, and she didn't exactly have the time or the desire to go out and meet older guys.

And then there was the kiss…

The kiss that kept her up at night and *did* make her think about lying beneath a certain man, feeling his hands touch her body in ways that made it hum.

"Earth to Jewel." Chelsea's furrowed brow told Jewel she'd been waiting for a response.

"Sorry. I, um…" *Have one thing on my mind, and he's six foot two and a million miles away, fighting the war that stole my brother's life.* "I want to go for a long hike and clear my head. I feel like I've been running on full speed forever."

"You have, Jewel. Go. Take a hike. Read a book. Do whatever will help you relax." Chelsea raised her brows. "But I still think sex is the greatest stress reliever around."

Chelsea waved her off to answer the phone, and Jewel headed out the door. She climbed into her Jeep and drove across town to her mother's house, trying *not* to think about Nate Braden, because thinking of Nate only confused her. The kiss they'd shared had been at a New Year's Eve party at his parents' microbrewery, Mr. B's. He could have easily turned at the stroke of midnight and grabbed any other woman in the room. She'd just been the one in arm's reach—and it was a good thing he'd put his strong arms around her and held her tight, because the kiss had turned her entire body to melted butter.

She pushed thoughts of Nate away as she parked in front of her mother's house and found her younger sister Krissy pouting on the front stoop. Her chin rested in her palm, and her eyes were trained on the ground. Their mother was taking Krissy and their other siblings to their aunt's in the next town over for the weekend.

Jewel sat beside her on the stoop. "What's wrong, Krissy?" At twelve, Krissy was almost as moody as fifteen-year-old Patrick.

"I didn't get the part I wanted in the recital." Their father had died when Krissy was four. When their eldest brother, Rick, had joined the military two years later, Krissy was so distraught over his leaving, their mother had thought she needed something fun to focus on besides the gaping hole their father and brother had left behind. It was a good call. Krissy was a natural dancer, and when Rick was killed, Krissy had clung to dance like a lifeline.

Jewel stroked Krissy's straight blond hair. With ten years between them, Jewel often felt like a favorite aunt rather than an older sister. As sad as it made her to know that Krissy had lost a coveted part in the recital, she was immensely glad that the issues her siblings faced were normal problems for kids their ages. She'd worked hard to make sure they didn't grow up with the same sense of responsibility for their family as she and Rick had. She didn't rue her family for her complicated lifestyle, but she wouldn't wish the responsibility of three younger siblings at sixteen on anyone else. She'd missed out on a lot over the last six years.

"I'm sorry, but you'll get the next one," Jewel reassured her sister.

"I hope so. Selina got the part this time. She's really good, and she deserves it, but I really wanted it. It's dancing opposite Tray Martino, and he's the cutest boy in dance class."

How could a twelve-year-old have more interest in boys than Jewel did at twenty-two?

She turned at the sound of the door opening behind her. Their mother, Anita, whipped past them carrying a suitcase in one hand and a grocery bag in the other, a messy ponytail perched high on her head.

"Jewel, honey, you didn't have to come by. I told you we were all set." Her mother looked closer to thirty-seven than forty-seven in her faded jeans and T-shirt. She'd had Rick when she was just twenty, and despite losing both her husband and her son in the span of six years, she'd somehow not only kept her sanity, but she was an amazing mother—even if tight on time. She'd worked from home as a part-time bookkeeper before their father died and had taken a full-time office job a month afterward. She'd recently been promoted to senior bookkeeper, and now she was taking classes to finish the accounting degree she hadn't had a chance to complete before they'd started their family.

Jewel patted Krissy's shoulder. "Keep dancing your heart out. You'll get the next part." She rose and grabbed two bags from just inside the door. "I wanted to make sure Patrick remembered his science project and Taylor had the lines she needs to study for her play."

Anita helped her put the bags in the car and wrinkled her brow. "Science project? He said he finished that earlier this week."

"Did you check?" Jewel asked.

Patrick lumbered out the front door. He was tall and lanky, like Rick had been as a teenager, with a mop of blond hair and the same almond-shaped blue eyes their father'd had. Patrick had sported a perpetual brooding attitude these past few months, and it worried Jewel.

"I'm his mother. Of course I checked."

"I don't need either of you checking after me." Patrick threw open the car door and sank into the passenger seat.

"Did you pack the book you have to read for English?" Jewel asked.

He sighed, ignoring her question.

Jewel shot a look to her mother, who pulled the book out of the side pocket of his suitcase.

"Jewel, we've got this," her mother insisted. Her mother always worked hard to make ends meet, but how was a mother with young kids at home and living on a limited income supposed to be in an office *and* taking kids where they needed to be at the same time? Not to mention grocery shopping, doctor appointments, and simply trying to survive after losing the man she'd loved since high school. Rick had quit college after their father died and had come home to help with whatever their mother couldn't manage without jeopardizing her new job. When Rick joined the military two years later, Jewel took over all of those responsibilities, and she'd been handling them ever since.

"I know, Mom, but an extra set of eyes never hurts."

The front door flung open and Taylor stepped outside. She put her hands on her hips and hollered across the yard, "Jewel? Where are my red Converse?"

Jewel shaded her eyes from the sun. Taylor's long blond hair hung in loose waves almost to her waist. She wore a pair of cute red shorts and a white scoop-neck T-shirt, and looked thirteen instead of ten.

"Front hall closet. You wore them to Katie's the other night, remember?"

"Oh, right." She ran back into the house.

"Honey, what are your plans for the next two days?" her mother asked.

"I'm going for a hike this afternoon, and tomorrow I'm cooking dinners for the week. I'll put them in the freezer, and I'll probably start that book you lent me."

Her mother pressed her lips together. "Why don't you call a girlfriend and go out? Have a drink, get some dinner. Do something fun. You know you don't need to keep cooking for us, Jewel. I *am* the mother. I can handle it."

"I know, and you're the best mother around. I don't mind

helping. Besides, between classes and work, you barely have time to breathe." Her mother was too proud to ask for help. In fact, she'd fought both Rick's and Jewel's efforts at first, until she'd realized that they were going to help no matter what. Their mother worked just as hard during her off hours as she did the hours she was paid for, and that made Jewel want to try even harder to help in the ways she could.

"Speaking of barely having time to breathe…" Her mother hugged her. "I love you, and I appreciate all you do for us, but please go do something fun. For me? I was married with children by the time I was your age, and you have yet to have a serious boyfriend. Go out dancing or something. Do all the things Dad and I took for granted."

"I'll have fun. I promise, Mom." Jewel's plan for a hike was fun, even if it wasn't the kind of fun her mother or Chelsea hoped she'd have. She helped them finish loading up the car and watched them drive away. Then she let out a long sigh, though the tightening in her chest told of the secret fears that kept her in her family's reach at all times.

Nothing good happened when family was separated. She'd learned that the hard way.

"I THINK I'M going to just stay away from Jewel." Nate Braden filled a beer stein, slid it across the bar to his older brother Sam, and lifted his chin to their sister Tempest. "Tempe? You up for one, too?"

Sure." Tempe didn't look up from the notebook she was writing in. She was working on a new song for her music-therapy business. Her blond hair covered half her face, but he knew she was listening to every word they said. She was the best listener. Someone who didn't know Tempe might think she was meek, because she was slim and delicate in appearance and she had a sweet nature, but Nate knew better. She was pretty straightforward and took no guff, which Nate *usually* appreciated. "No, you're not."

"Not what?" Nate asked as he set the beer in front of her. It was Saturday night, and Nate had just closed down Mr. B's, one of the microbreweries his family owned. He'd returned to civilian life a week ago, after six years in the military, and he was helping his parents out while he figured out his next move.

"Not going to stay away from Jewel Fisher," Tempe said.

"Yes, I am." Nate filled a beer for himself and took a long swig. He'd never talked to his family, or anyone else for that matter, about his feelings for Jewel. Unfortunately, his family had always been able to read him like an open book, and for whatever reason, Sam and Tempe had decided it was a good time to give him shit about Jewel.

Sam scoffed and sipped his beer. He ran his hand through his short dark hair and leaned one elbow on the bar. Sam owned Rough Riders, a rafting and adventure company, and he spent most of his days on the water, taking clients out on rafting or other wilderness trips, as evident from his year-round tan and muscular physique.

"You can't." Tempe shook her head. "You don't have it in you to stay away."

"Maybe not, but I can damn well try." Nate clenched his jaw at the truth of Tempe's insistence. Six years ago, after finishing college and ROTC, he'd joined the military with his best friend, Rick. Two years ago Nate had been trying to figure out how to tell Rick that he cared deeply about Jewel and wanted to ask her out. He'd decided not to spring *I love your sister* on him all at once. It was crazy, because Nate and Jewel had never even dated. Between their five-year age difference and out of respect for Rick, Nate had always kept his feelings for Jewel to himself. But six years was a long time to fight his affections for a girl he'd seen nearly every day for most of his life. Being apart helped. If he'd remained in Peaceful Harbor, Maryland, he wouldn't have been able to deny his feelings for her. Every time he returned home on leave over the years, it had been torture for him to watch Jewel blossom into a gorgeous woman and refrain from acting on his mounting desires.

Nate trusted his gut, and he trusted his heart. Two years ago he'd decided that one way or another, he was going to finally come clean to his best friend and see if he could earn

Rick's blessing to tell Jewel how he felt. But the month before the end of their tour, Rick was killed by a sniper while out on a routine supply run. Because Nate had completed ROTC during college, he'd been an officer, while Rick was enlisted. They'd celebrated landing in the same company, but Nate had never imagined that giving the order for Rick to go on that supply run would be the last order he ever gave him.

Rick had gone home in a pine box, and Nate had been unable to face the town in which he and Rick had grown up together—much less his feelings for Jewel. Nate had reenlisted for two years, but two years hadn't even scratched the surface of the guilt that consumed him.

It was hard enough being back home in Peaceful Harbor and facing all the places he and Rick had spent their youth. Add in the fact that Rick's dying words were for him to protect and take care of his family, and Nate's plans for a future with Jewel were shot. He was a war hero, a decorated officer, and so mired in survivor's guilt that he wasn't sure he'd be able to endure the memories of Rick without losing his mind, much less be able to ignore his love for Jewel.

"She's right, Nate." Sam held his brother's gaze. Sam was the second oldest of Nate's five siblings. He'd always been a straight shooter, but tonight it was tweaking Nate's nerves.

Nate had already fucked up when he'd been home over New Year's and had given in to his feelings for Jewel. They'd shared one mind-blowing kiss, despite his knowing he had no business seeking her out when he was the one who had put Rick in the fucking sniper's crosshairs.

"You've had a thing for Jewel forever, whether you want to have it or not," Sam added. "That's not going to suddenly change."

Nate swallowed his retort as his mother came out of the kitchen, humming a tune and smiling at three of her six children. She'd always worn her thick, curly blond hair loose and wild, which was in stark contrast to Nate's father's polished image. His father was right behind her, tall and broad shouldered—traits his four sons shared—and walking with a slightly stilted gait that most people probably never noticed. He was as dark as Maisy was fair and as clean cut as she was bohemian. Thomas "Ace" Braden had been in the military only a few years before a jumping accident had claimed his left leg from the knee down.

Maisy set her hand on Nate's forearm. "I missed you so much, Natey. I'm glad you're back."

He was glad for the subject change. "I missed you, too, Mom, but don't get too used to me being around. You know my plans are still up in the air."

She smiled, and it reached her sea-blue eyes. He'd missed her. He'd missed this—being with family, talking about things other than missions and how many men were lost, despite Tempe and Sam pushing him about Jewel. After two years, he'd finally given up hiding behind the war and had come home to face his past. He missed his family—and even though he was terribly conflicted about her, he missed Jewel.

"I know, sweetheart," his mother said. "But you're here now, and that's good enough for me."

"Besides, it's great to see one of my boys behind the bar again." His father wore his dark hair parted on the side and brushed away from his face. With his angular nose, cleft chin, and chiseled features, he was a dead ringer for Cary Grant. Even when serious, there was a softness to his eyes that Nate saw only when he addressed his children. Nate had seen him at his angriest and at his most protective, but when directed at his family, there was an underlying unconditional love that came through loud and clear.

"Have you taken a ride over to the old train station yet? I think Rick would want you to fulfill that dream, Nate." His father held his chin high, challenging him in a way that made it difficult for Nate to look away. His father knew how Rick's death had affected him, but that didn't stop him from trying to push him through it.

Nate took another drink to distract himself from the way his heart was telling him Peaceful Harbor was where he was supposed to be. He and Rick had shared a passion for cooking and had planned to open a restaurant—Tap It—when they were out of the military. Another dream shot to hell.

"Not yet," Nate answered. He'd not only avoided visiting the old train station he and Rick had had their eye on as the perfect venue for their restaurant, but he'd also been putting off visiting Rick's family and had yet to see Jewel since he'd been home.

Sometimes where a person was supposed to be wasn't the best place for them.

"We'll leave you kids alone to catch up. Don't forget, the annual Christmas-tree bonfire is next Thursday. I'm sad Shannon won't be here, but Ty said he'd get great pictures to send her. If you can make it, great, and if not"—Maisy shrugged as she walked around the bar and patted Sam's shoulder—"that's okay, too. And, Sammy, don't give your brother too hard of a time. He has a lot to deal with and he just got back." Every year after Christmas their parents stowed their Christmas tree in the shed to dry out. And in April the family got together for their annual Christmas-tree-burning bonfire, when they lit it up and enjoyed the visual feast of crackles, pops, and sizzling sparks.

Sam rolled his eyes. "See you Thursday, Ma."

"I love you, too, Sammy." Raising four rambunctious boys and two mischievous girls, Maisy had long ago learned to ignore eye rolls and attitudes.

"Nate, think about the restaurant. There are many ways to honor our fallen heroes." His father smiled, easing the pressure a little. "It's good to have you back, son." He took Maisy's hand, and she waved over her shoulder as they went out the front door.

"Seriously, dude," Sam said. "You need to deal with this shit. Rick's gone. There's nothing you can do about that. But Jewel's still here."

Tempe set down her notebook with a sigh. "Way to listen to Mom, Sam."

"Hey, I'm just telling the truth," Sam said. "What do you want from me?"

"A little compassion?" Tempe pleaded. "Nate, have you thought about talking to a therapist about all this stuff?"

"Don't you think I've done that? Three of the military's finest. I could write a book on survivor's guilt, plus you're always giving me advice—even when I don't ask. Tempe, it's not like I *want* to live with this shit hanging over my head." If only he hadn't been so damn ambitious and had skipped ROTC. He could have gone in as an enlisted man, like Rick had, and then he wouldn't have that deathly decision hanging around his neck. Nate had shared the details surrounding Rick's death with his family, but he hadn't had the courage to share them with Rick's family yet. Losing Rick six years after their father died was enough for them to deal with. They didn't need to know that the man they'd accepted into their family for as long as he could remember had been the one to send Rick on the mission that had killed him.

Nate would give anything to have been the one who had been killed. Rick's family needed him in a way that Nate's didn't. Rick had been a good man. When his father died two years after Rick had started college, he'd put his own life on hold to come home and help his mother with his younger siblings. While Nate had joined the military to fulfill a lifelong dream of following in his father's footsteps and having the career his father had missed out on, Rick had seen the military as a means to a better life for his family. He'd joined to make a career for himself and to give his mother one less mouth to feed, while sending money home every month to help. He'd been too good of a man, and too good of a friend, to die. Nate had missed him every day since.

Tempe reached across the bar and patted Nate's hand. "All I'm saying is that maybe if you continue to talk to someone, it would help. You can't carry the guilt around forever, Nate, and you can't let it rule your entire life."

Nate had had all he could take for one night. He knew his family meant well, but there was only so much pushing a guy could take.

"Know what the great thing about the military was?" Nate came around the bar and dug his keys from his pocket. "No one gave a shit about my personal life. Lock up when you leave, okay? I'm heading home."

Ten minutes later Nate was sitting in his truck at the stop sign on the corner of Main Street and Whippoorwill Avenue, thinking about Jewel. *Could* he keep his feelings to himself? He had no clue if he could or not, but he sure as hell could try. What he couldn't do was stay away from the Fishers altogether. He owed it to Rick to keep his promise and take care of them. He turned onto Whippoorwill and navigated through the maze of side streets to the Fishers' modest four-bedroom home. The driveway was empty, and the house was dark. Relief swept through him, followed by a whole hell of a lot of guilt. Now that he was twenty-seven and she twenty-two, his feelings for Jewel were finally acceptable, but his ties to Rick's death felt more ominous than their age difference ever had.

Nate's cell rang as he drove toward the river. He smiled at his youngest sister Shannon's image on the screen and answered the call.

"Hey, sis. How's it going?"

"Hi, Nate. Things are pretty good out here. I forgot how different Colorado was from the harbor, but Uncle Hal and everyone are great. Oh my gosh, you should see Treat and Max's kids. They're freaking adorable." Shannon was staying with their uncle Hal in Weston, Colorado, while she carried out a project monitoring red foxes in the mountains. Treat was the oldest of Hal Braden's six children, their second cousins. He and his wife, Max, had a daughter, Adriana, named for Treat's deceased mother, and a young son named Dylan.

"First I need to figure out my life." Nate silently considered Weston as an option if he decided it was too painful to remain in Peaceful Harbor. "When do you come back?"

"I'm not sure yet. It depends how quickly I can gather the data I need for my research. I'm sorry I'm not there to see you."

He pictured Shannon tucking her long dark hair behind her ear and wishing she were home. They'd always been close, and Nate missed seeing her. She was a little nosy, poking around in their private lives, but he and his brothers were just as protective of her and Tempe.

"So, you haven't seen anyone *else* yet?" she asked tentatively.

Nate knew she was asking if he'd seen the Fishers. It was on the forefront of his family's mind because they knew how much angst coming home was causing him. Shannon kept pretty close tabs on their family, and chances were she'd already spoken to Tempe or Sam and knew that Nate had just left the brewery—and that he'd been avoiding visiting the Fishers.

Would the guilt ever lessen? He turned down Mountain Road toward his cabin and ground out his response. "No. The Fishers weren't home."

"Oh."

Silence stretched between them, carrying the worry in her cryptic response. Nate flicked on his high beams to combat the darkness and to give himself something to do other than think about the Fishers.

"Nate?"

"Yeah?"

"It's all going to be okay. You'll know when the time is right. I have faith in you."

If only I had that same faith.

"Thanks, Shan." The road narrowed and curved near the hiking trails. The hair on the back of his neck stood up at the sight of Rick's red Jeep parked at the entrance to one of the hiking trails. The US Army bumper sticker was like a knife to Nate's gut.

"Hey, does Jewel still drive Rick's old Jeep?"

"I think so. Why?"

Nate parked next to the Jeep and cut the engine. "It's parked at a hiking trail, but it's after ten. It's pitch-black out here, and Jewel hates the dark."

"Maybe she's out with friends or something."

"You think?" Ever since Rick died, Jewel had lived her life in a safe little bubble, rarely veering from work or family. Anyone who knew Jewel knew that much. He doubted she'd be on a hiking trail after dark.

"No, not really. Try calling her."

"Cell coverage out here sucks, but I will. I'm going to look for her. I'll touch base with you when I know something." Nate grabbed his hunting knife and headlamp from the glove compartment, along with the backpack full of medical supplies he kept behind the seat. He hooked the knife to his fatigues and shouldered the backpack, then checked out her Jeep.

There were no personal belongings in sight, and the doors were locked. He was glad to see that Jewel had heeded his warnings about safety. After Rick died, he'd tried to step in and help their family when he was on leave, despite how difficult it was to keep his feelings for Jewel to himself. He'd brought gifts for the kids over the holidays and sent birthday presents, but the advice he'd given Jewel wasn't out of guilt or the desire to step in as a pseudo older brother. He cared deeply for her. So much so that as he made his way down the trail, his thoughts turned possessive.

What kind of friends would take her out in the wilderness at night when she was afraid of being out in open spaces in the dark? Luckily, Nate and Rick used to blaze their own paths through these woods. He could practically navigate them with his eyes closed. The summer before Rick was killed, Nate had thought about taking Jewel out here when he returned for the holidays, to show her all the secret spots he'd come to love. He'd even toyed with it being the place where he finally opened up to her about his feelings. But he'd still had a year left on his military commitment, and he'd thought it wouldn't be fair to ask her to wait for him. Then, when Rick died, all hopes of being with Jewel went out the window.

Guilt had a way of smothering a man's hopes and dreams.

The light from the headlamp illuminated a narrow strip of the dirt trail. The deeper Nate went into the forest, the thicker the umbrella of leaves and the darker it became. He pulled out his phone and called Jewel. The call went to voicemail.

Damn it, Jewel, where are you?

He cupped his hands around his mouth and shouted into the darkness. "Jewel?"

Met with silence, save for his own heavy breathing, he jogged down the path. Guided by the headlamp and instinct, he scanned the forest and repeatedly called out her name. He knew the trail branched off into two other trails, each stretching from four to ten miles. It was anyone's guess which trail Jewel might have taken, assuming she was there at all. Nate stopped at the entrance to the first trail and inspected the dirt for any signs of passersby. There were no fresh footprints, which wasn't surprising. It was April, and the trails didn't get busy until closer to summer. He hoped to hell he was on the right track—actually, he hoped to hell that Jewel wasn't in the forest at all. He'd rather she was safely hanging out with friends or in her mother's house.

He continued on to the next trail a mile farther out. He took off his shirt and used it to wipe the sweat from his brow, then stuffed it in his backpack as he checked the trailhead for fresh footprints.

Bingo. He followed the footprints deeper into the forest.

The thought of Jewel out here in the dark, alone and afraid, had his adrenaline pumping. He picked up speed and sprinted down the trail, hollering her name. He tried to think of other reasons her Jeep might be parked at the start of the trail. She could have had engine trouble and had gotten a friend to drive her home, but he knew Jewel needed her vehicle for work and to help her mother. She would have had it towed, or she'd have been back there with the Jeep and someone who could help her.

"Jewel!" he called into the darkness. "Jewel!"

"Here! Over here!" Jewel's trembling voice sent his heart to his throat.

He bolted over the crest of the hill and nearly tripped over her, lying beside a tree. He crouched next to her and did a quick visual assessment. Her eyes were wide and damp, as if she'd been crying. Her hair was tangled, and she had a streak of dirt across her cheek. She wore a pair of cutoffs, and her knees were also smeared with dirt. All of the emotions he'd been tamping down rushed forward.

"Nate? How did you find me?" Her eyes filled with tears. "*Why* are you here? I twisted my ankle. I thought I'd be here forever."

He gathered her in his arms, careful not to jostle her ankle, and tucked her safely against his chest, wanting to keep her there forever. Her tears wet his chest as he tried to soothe her.

"Shh. You're okay. I've got you. I saw your Jeep and was worried."

"I'm so glad you're here. I was so scared, Nate."

The way she said his name, full of gratitude and something deeper, threw him back to the kiss they'd shared. The heat that had enveloped them the moment their mouths had come together. He knew it was wrong, but he wanted to kiss her now, until the fear in her eyes subsided. And that made him an asshole, given the way her body was trembling against him.

"Thank you for looking for me," she said with a shaky inhalation.

Her voice pulled him from his thoughts, and he shoved those emotions down deep again. As if he'd flicked a switch, Nate pulled on his military training and reluctantly detached from his emotions and focused on evaluating Jewel's injury and getting her to a safe place.

"How long ago did you get hurt?"

"I don't know. It was still light out."

She'd been out there, injured and alone, for hours. If only he hadn't hung out with his family, or driven by her house, he could have found her earlier.

"I'm sorry, Jewel. I wish I had gotten here sooner. Why are you out here alone? How did you fall?"

"I needed to get away. Mom took the kids to Aunt Giselle's for the weekend, so I thought I'd come out here and..." She shrugged. "I pulled out my phone and it slipped out of my hands and over the ledge, and when I stepped down the hill, my foot caught on that stupid root." She pointed to a root sticking out of the ground.

"There's nothing wrong with you hiking. I know you're strong and capable, but it's best to hike with a friend."

"Yeah, I know that now." She smiled, and his eyes landed on her full lips.

He reluctantly tore them away. "I need to check your ankle."

Nate focused on her injury instead of on how warm and soft her skin was. He moved her foot to one side, then the other.

She winced and pushed his hands away. "Don't move it."

"I'm sorry, but at least it doesn't feel broken—just a little swollen. Let me get you fixed up and then I'll get your phone." He reached for his backpack.

"No. Can you get my phone first?" Her baby blues pleaded with him, and even though he would rather see to her first, he did as she asked.

He looked down the steep incline for her phone, but even with the headlamp, it was difficult to see clearly. He was glad she hadn't tried to navigate the slope on her injured ankle.

He didn't realize she'd been holding on to his boot until he tried to take a step away. He crouched beside her again and handed her the headlamp. "Here. You hold this. I'll only be a minute or two, and you can watch me every step of the way."

She clutched the light to her chest.

He didn't want to leave her for a second, but he had no choice. "I'll need you to aim it down the hill so I can see where I'm going."

"Oh, right."

She aimed the headlamp at him, and he felt her eyes on him as he climbed down the side of the mountain, searching for her phone.

"It fell over toward your left, I think. Be careful. Don't trip. Be careful." Her voice was filled with worry. She was always worrying about her family. The last thing he wanted was for her to worry about him, too.

"I'm fine, Jewel. I could cross this mountain blindfolded." His eyes adjusted to the dark, and after a few minutes of searching, he found her phone.

"I've got it." He held it up so she could see that both he and the phone were safe. Then he scaled the steep incline and handed her the phone.

"Thanks," she said, clutching her phone and the light. "The cell service out here sucks. I was trying to check in with my mom to make sure they made it to my aunt's safely, and I couldn't get a single bar. Now the darn thing is dead."

"We'll charge it, and I'm sure your mom made it fine. It's only an hour away." He dug through his backpack and pulled out an Ace bandage. "I'm just going to wrap your ankle. Then I'll carry you out of here."

"Wrap it? That's going to hurt." Her eyes widened. "And you can't carry me. We're probably three miles from my Jeep."

She had no idea what it was like carrying military gear across the desert. She was about five-three to Nate's six-two. He could handle her buck fifteen with one arm—even if he'd rather handle her with his hands, his mouth, and—

Shit. Really, Braden? Get a fucking grip.

He forced himself to focus again. "If I don't wrap it, your ankle will move around while I carry you, and it'll hurt worse."

Her eyes widened again. "You can't carry—"

He pressed his fingers to her lips and softened his tone. "Jewel, I'm carrying you."

She blinked up at him through thick blond lashes, looking innocent in a way she rarely did. She was usually so in control of everything around her, and it reflected in her serious, competent gaze. How could he have forgotten how one look from Jewel undid him?

"Wait," she said softly as she touched his arm. She slammed her eyes shut and tightened her grip. "Okay. Wrap it."

He'd helped dozens of guys in the field with all types of gruesome injuries and never once had he been nervous, but the sight of Jewel's scrunched-up face and the death grip she had on his arm made him acutely aware of her vulnerabilities—and his.

To continue reading, buy **HEALED BY LOVE**

Have you read Tru Blue and the Whiskeys?

If you enjoy badass heroes with hearts of gold, strong family ties, and real-life, complex and relatable issues, this series is for you! Loaded with heat, humor, and heart, these sexy stories will draw you in and keep you riveted until the very last page. All Whiskey novels may be enjoyed as stand-alone romances. Start the series with **TRU BLUE**.

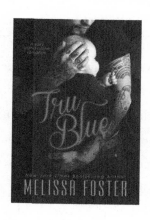

There's nothing Truman Gritt won't do to protect his family—Including spending years in jail for a crime he didn't commit. When he's finally released, the life he knew is turned upside down by his mother's overdose, and Truman steps in to raise the children she's left behind. Truman's hard, he's secretive, and he's trying to save a brother who's even more broken than he is. He's never needed help in his life, and when beautiful Gemma Wright tries to step in, he's less than accepting. But Gemma has a way of slithering into people's lives and eventually she pierces through his ironclad heart. When Truman's dark past collides with his future, his loyalties will be tested, and he'll be faced with his toughest decision yet.

Chapter One

TRUMAN GRITT LOCKED the door to Whiskey Automotive and stepped into the stormy September night. Sheets of rain blurred his vision, instantly drenching his jeans and T-shirt. A slow smile crept across his face as he tipped his chin up, soaking in the shower of *freedom*. He made his way around the dark building and climbed the wooden stairs to the deck outside his apartment. He could have used the interior door, but after being behind bars for six long years, Truman took advantage of the small pleasures he'd missed out on, like determining his own schedule, deciding when to eat and drink, and standing in the fucking rain if he wanted to. He leaned on the rough wooden railing, ignoring the splinters piercing his tattooed forearms, squinted against the wetness, and scanned the cars in the junkyard they used for parts—and he used to rid himself of frustrations. He rested his leather boot on the metal box where he kept his painting supplies. Truman didn't have much—his old extended-cab truck, which his friend Bear Whiskey had held on to for him while he was in prison, this apartment, and a solid job, both of which were compliments of the Whiskey family. The only family he had anymore.

Emotions he didn't want to deal with burned in his gut, causing his chest to constrict. He turned to go inside, hoping to outrun thoughts of his own fucked-up family, whom he'd tried—*and failed*—to save. His cell phone rang with his brother's ringtone, "A Beautiful Lie" by 30 Seconds to Mars.

"Fuck," he muttered, debating letting the call go to voicemail, but six months of silence from his brother was a long time. Rain pelleted his back as he pressed his palm to the door to steady himself. The ringing stopped, and he blew out a breath he hadn't realized he'd trapped inside. The phone rang again, and he froze.

He'd just freed himself from the dredges of hell that he'd been thrown into in an effort to *save* his brother. He didn't need to get wrapped up in whatever mess the drug-addicted fool had gotten himself into. The call went to voicemail, and Truman eyed the metal box containing his painting supplies. Breathing like he'd been in a fight, he wished he could paint the frustration out of his head. When the phone rang for the third time in as many minutes, the third time since he was released from prison six months ago, he reluctantly answered.

"Quincy." He hated the way his brother's name came out sounding like the enemy. Quincy had been just a kid when Truman went to prison. Heavy breathing filled the airwaves. The hairs on Truman's forearms and neck stood on end. He knew fear when he heard it. He could practically taste it as he ground his teeth together.

"I need you," his brother's tortured voice implored.

Need me? Truman had hunted down his brother after he was released from prison, and when he'd finally found him, Quincy was so high on crack he was nearly incoherent—but it didn't take much for *fuck off* to come through loud and clear. What Quincy needed was rehab, but Truman knew from his tone that wasn't the point of the call.

Before he could respond, his brother croaked out, "It's Mom. She's really bad."

Fuck. He hadn't had a mother since she turned her back on him more than six years ago, and he wasn't about to throw away the stability he'd finally found for the woman who'd sent him to prison and never looked back.

He scrubbed a hand down his rain-soaked face. "Take her to the hospital."

"No cops. No hospitals. *Please*, man."

A painful, high-pitched wail sounded through the phone.

"What have you done?" Truman growled, the pit of his stomach plummeting as memories of another dark night years earlier came rushing in. He paced the deck as thunder rumbled overhead like a warning. "Where are you?"

Quincy rattled off the address of a seedy area about thirty minutes outside of Peaceful Harbor, and then the line went dead.

Truman's thumb hovered over the cell phone screen.

Three little numbers—*9-1-1*—would extricate him from whatever mess Quincy and their mother had gotten into. Images of his mother spewing lies that would send him away and of Quincy, a frightened boy of thirteen, looking devastated and childlike despite his near six-foot stature, assailed him.

Push the buttons.

Push the fucking buttons.

He remembered Quincy's wide blue eyes screaming silent apologies as Truman's sentence was revealed. It was those pleading eyes he saw now, fucked up or not, that had him trudging through the rain to his truck and driving over the bridge, leaving Peaceful Harbor and his safe, stable world behind.

THE STENCH OF urine and human waste filled the dark alley—not only *waste* as in feces, but *waste* as in drug dealers, whores, and other deviants. Mud and graffiti streaked cracked and mangled concrete. Somewhere above, shouts rang out. Truman had tunnel vision as he moved swiftly between the tall buildings in the downpour. A dog barked in the distance, followed by the unmistakable yelp of a wounded animal. Truman rolled his broad shoulders forward, his hands fisted by his sides as memories hammered him, but it was the incessant torturous wailing coming from behind the concrete walls that had him breathing harder, readying for a fight. It sounded like someone—or something—was suffering inside the building, and despite his loathing for the woman who had brought him into the world, he wouldn't wish that on her—or wish the wrath he'd bring down on whoever was doing it on anyone else.

The rusty green metal door brought the sounds of prison bars locking to the forefront of his mind, stopping him cold. He drew in a few deep breaths, pushing them out fast and hard as memories assailed him. The wailing intensified, and he forced himself to plow through the door. The rancid, pungent scents of garbage and drugs filled the smoky room, competing with the terrified cries. In the space of a few heart-pounding seconds, Truman took in the scene. He barely recognized the nearly toothless, rail-thin woman lying lifeless on the concrete floor, staring blankly up at the ceiling. Angry track marks like viper bites covered pin-thin arms. In the corner, a toddler sat on a dirty, torn mattress, wearing filthy clothes and sobbing. Her dark hair was tangled and matted, her skin covered in grit and dirt. Her cheeks were bright red, eyes swollen from crying. Beside her a baby lay on its back, its frail arms extended toward the ceiling, shaking as it cried so hard it went silent between wails. His eyes landed on Quincy, huddled beside the woman on the floor. Tears streaked his unshaven, sunken cheeks. Those big blue eyes Truman remembered were haunted and scared, their once vibrant color now deadened, bloodshot with the sheen of a soul-stealing high. His tattooed arms revealed the demons that had swooped in after Truman was incarcerated for the crime his brother had committed, preying on the one person he had wanted to protect. He hadn't been able to protect anyone from behind bars.

"She's…" Quincy's voice was nearly indiscernible. "Dead," he choked out.

Truman's heart slammed against his ribs. His mind reeled back to another stormy night, when he'd walked into his mother's house and found his brother with a bloody knife in his hands—and a dead man sprawled across their mother's half-naked body. He swallowed the bile rising in his throat, pain and anger warring for dominance. He crouched and checked for a pulse, first on her wrist, then on her neck. The pit of his stomach lurched. His mind reeled as he looked past his brother to the children on the mattress.

"Those your kids?" he ground out.

Quincy shook his head. "Mom's."

Truman stumbled backward, feeling cut open, flayed, and left to bleed. His siblings? Living like this?

"What the hell, Quincy?" He crossed the room and picked up the baby, holding its trembling body as it screamed. With his heart in his throat, he crouched beside the toddler and reached for her, too. She wrapped shaky arms around his neck and clung with all her tiny might. They were both featherlight. He hadn't held a baby since Quincy was born, when Truman was nine.

"I've been out for six months," he seethed. "You didn't think to tell me that Mom had more kids? That she was fucking up their lives, too? I could have helped."

Quincy scoffed. "You told me..." He coughed, wheezing like he was on his last lung. "To fuck off."

Truman glared at his brother, sure he was breathing fire. "I pulled you out of a fucking crack house the week I got out of prison and tried to get you help. I *destroyed* my life trying to protect you, you idiot. *You* told *me* to fuck off and then went underground. You never mentioned that I have a sister and—" He looked at the baby, having no idea if it was a boy or a girl. A thin spray of reddish hair covered its tiny head.

"Brother. Kennedy and Lincoln. Kennedy's, I don't know, two, three maybe? And Lincoln's...Lincoln's the boy."

Their fucking mother and her presidential names. She once told him that it was important to have an unforgettable name, since they'd have forgettable lives. Talk about self-fulfilling prophecies.

Rising to his feet, teeth gritted, his rain-drenched clothes now covered in urine from their saturated diapers, Truman didn't even try to mask his repulsion. "These are *babies*, you asshole. You couldn't clean up your act to take care of them?"

Quincy turned sullenly back to their mother, shoving Truman's disgust for his brother's pathetic life deeper. The baby's shrieks quieted as the toddler patted him. Kennedy blinked big, wet, brown eyes up at Truman, and in that instant, he knew what he had to do.

"Where's their stuff?" Truman looked around the filthy room. He spotted a few diapers peeking out from beneath a ratty blanket and picked them up.

"They were born on the streets. They don't even have birth certificates."

"Are you shitting me?" *How the fuck did they survive?* Truman grabbed the tattered blanket that smelled like death and wrapped it around the babies, heading for the door.

Quincy unfolded his thin body and rose to his feet, meeting his six-three brother eye to eye. "You can't leave me here with *her.*"

"You made your choice long ago, little brother," Truman said in a lethal tone. "I begged you to get clean." He shifted his gaze to the woman on the floor, unable to think of her as his mother. "She fucked up my life, and she clearly fucked up yours, but I'll be damned if I'll let her fuck up *theirs.* The Gritt nightmare stops here and now."

He pulled the blanket over the children's heads to shield them from the rain and opened the door. Cold, wet air crashed over his arms.

"What am I supposed to do?" Quincy pleaded.

Truman took one last look around the room, guilt and anger consuming him. On some level, he'd always known it would come to this, though he'd hoped he was wrong. "Your mother's lying dead on the floor. You let your sister and brother live in squalor, and you're wondering what you should do? *Get. Clean.*"

Quincy turned away.

"And have her cremated." He juggled the babies and dug out his wallet, throwing a wad of cash on the floor, then took a step out the door. Hesitating, he turned back again, pissed with himself for not being strong enough to simply walk away and never look back. "When you're ready to get clean, you know where to find me. Until then, I don't want you anywhere near these kids."

To continue reading, buy **TRU BLUE**

More Books By Melissa Foster

LOVE IN BLOOM SERIES

SNOW SISTERS
Sisters in Love
Sisters in Bloom
Sisters in White

THE BRADENS at Weston
Lovers at Heart, Reimagined
Destined for Love
Friendship on Fire
Sea of Love
Bursting with Love
Hearts at Play

THE BRADENS at Trusty
Taken by Love
Fated for Love
Romancing My Love
Flirting with Love
Dreaming of Love
Crashing into Love

THE BRADENS at Peaceful Harbor
Healed by Love
Surrender My Love
River of Love
Crushing on Love
Whisper of Love
Thrill of Love

THE BRADENS & MONTGOMERYS at Pleasant Hill – Oak Falls

Embracing Her Heart

Anything For Love

Trails of Love

Wild, Crazy Hearts

Making You Mine

Searching For Love

THE BRADEN NOVELLAS

Promise My Love

Our New Love

Daring Her Love

Story of Love

Love at Last

A Very Braden Christmas

THE REMINGTONS

Game of Love

Stroke of Love

Flames of Love

Slope of Love

Read, Write, Love

Touched by Love

SEASIDE SUMMERS

Seaside Dreams

Seaside Hearts

Seaside Sunsets

Seaside Secrets

Seaside Nights

Seaside Embrace

Seaside Lovers

Seaside Whispers

Seaside Serenade

BAYSIDE SUMMERS
Bayside Desires
Bayside Passions
Bayside Heat
Bayside Escape
Bayside Romance
Bayside Fantasies

THE RYDERS
Seized by Love
Claimed by Love
Chased by Love
Rescued by Love
Swept Into Love

THE WHISKEYS: DARK KNIGHTS AT PEACEFUL HARBOR
Tru Blue
Truly, Madly, Whiskey
Driving Whiskey Wild
Wicked Whiskey Love
Mad About Moon
Taming My Whiskey
The Gritty Truth

SUGAR LAKE
The Real Thing
Only for You
Love Like Ours
Finding My Girl

HARMONY POINTE
Call Her Mine
This is Love
She Loves Me

THE WICKEDS: DARK KNIGHTS AT BAYSIDE

A Little Bit Wicked

Wicked Aftermath

WILD BOYS AFTER DARK (Billionaires After Dark)

Logan

Heath

Jackson

Cooper

BAD BOYS AFTER DARK (Billionaires After Dark)

Mick

Dylan

Carson

Brett

<u>HARBORSIDE NIGHTS SERIES</u>

Includes characters from the Love in Bloom series

Catching Cassidy

Discovering Delilah

Tempting Tristan

More Books by Melissa

Chasing Amanda (mystery/suspense)

Come Back to Me (mystery/suspense)

Have No Shame (historical fiction/romance)

Love, Lies & Mystery (3-book bundle)

Megan's Way (literary fiction)

Traces of Kara (psychological thriller)

Where Petals Fall (suspense)

Acknowledgments

Writing about Jake Braden was a challenge and a joy. Bradens are known for being gracious gentlemen, and Jake was so broken that he sort of lost that part of himself for a very long time. When I first met Fiona, I knew that the love she had for Jake would pull him back in to the man he really was, and I'm so glad I didn't let his bad-boy side sway me from bringing Fiona to him. I hope you've fallen in love with each of the Bradens and their significant others, and thank you, dear readers, for reaching out and demanding that I bring you *more* Bradens. In addition to our new Harborside Nights friends and the Ryders, Steeles, and Stones, you can look forward to two more hot, wealthy, and wickedly naughty Braden families: The Bradens at Peaceful Harbor and the Bradens & Montgomerys at Pleasant Hill and Oak Falls.

If you don't yet follow me on Facebook, please do! We have such fun chatting about our lovable heroes and sassy heroines, and I always try to keep fans abreast of what's going on in our fictional boyfriends' worlds. www.Facebook.com/MelissaFosterAuthor. Remember to sign up for my newsletter to keep up to date with new releases and

special promotions and events:
www.MelissaFoster.com/Newsletter

I am indebted to my amazing team of editors and proofreaders, whose meticulous efforts help bring you the cleanest books possible. Thank you: Kristen Weber, Penina Lopez, Jenna Bagnini, Juliette Hill, Marlene Engel, and Lynn Mullan.

And, of course, thank you to my family for your ongoing support.

Meet Melissa

www.MelissaFoster.com

Melissa Foster is a *New York Times* and *USA Today* bestselling and award-winning author. Her books have been recommended by *USA Today's* book blog, *Hagerstown* magazine, *The Patriot*, and several other print venues. Melissa has painted and donated several murals to the Hospital for Sick Children in Washington, DC.

Visit Melissa on her website or chat with her on social media. Melissa enjoys discussing her books with book clubs and reader groups and welcomes an invitation to your event. Melissa's books are available through most online retailers in paperback, digital, and audio formats.

Melissa also writes sweet romance under the pen name, Addison Cole.

Made in the USA
Coppell, TX
24 April 2023

15967228R00236